"As a serial killer sweeps across Spain towards Edinburgh, driven by a perverted sense of revenge, is the saviour destined to be a pastor with an eye for justice and a belief in the good in people? In David Hidalgo, Les Cowan has a unique take on the crime-busting religious protagonist and in Sins of the Fathers he has crafted a clever, twisted game of cat and mouse – where you're never quite sure who is the cat and who is the mouse."

Gordon Brown, author of *Darkest Thoughts*

"A dark insight into a dangerous and wounded soul. This is crime fiction with a spiritual twist."

Fiona Veitch Smith, author of the *Poppy Denby Investigates* series

Praise for Les Cowan:

"This is suspense at its best. There's a real freshness in the writing, that doesn't just stimulate the mind, but manages to captivate and harness the soul."

***Living Orkney* magazine**

"The second, just-as-good-as-the-first novel involving pastor David Hidalgo."

The Scots Magazine

"This is a series to treasure, I can't wait for the next book, but I'll have to! I can't recommend All That Glitters enough!"

"Topical subject, believable characters, exciting plot. Couldn't put it down, can't ask for more. Les Cowan has done it... king

Extracts from reviews

D1341363

Books by Les Cowan

The David Hidalgo series:
Book 1: *Benefit of the Doubt*
Book 2: *All that Glitters*
Book 3: *Sins of the Fathers*
Book 4: *Blood Brothers* (coming soon)

Non-fiction titles:
Loose Talk Collected
Orkney by Bike

SINS
OF THE
FATHERS

LES COWAN

A DAVID HIDALGO NOVEL

LION FICTION

Published by
Lion Hudson Limited
Wilkinson House, Jordan Hill Business Park
Banbury Road, Oxford OX2 8DR, England
www.lionhudson.com

ISBN 978 1 78264 273 2
e-ISBN 978 1 78264 274 9

First edition 2019

Acknowledgments

Unless otherwise noted all Scripture quotations taken from the Holy
Bible, New International Version Anglicised. Copyright © 1979, 1984,
2011 Biblica, formerly International Bible Society. Used by permission
of Hodder & Stoughton Ltd, an Hachette UK company. All rights
reserved. "NIV" is a registered trademark of Biblica. UK trademark
number 1448790.

Extracts marked KJV are from The Authorized (King James) Version.
Rights in the Authorized Version are vested in the Crown. Reproduced
by permission of the Crown's patentee, Cambridge University Press.

Cover image: Man © AlexSava & AaronAmat/iStock; Scott
monument © James Kurrle/Shutterstock

A catalogue record for this book is available from the British Library

Printed and bound the UK, July 2019, LH26

For Mija

ACKNOWLEDGMENTS

Once again grateful thanks are due to those who have helped this story on its way in any shape or form.

Firstly, thanks to Fiona, Angus, and Mija for reading early drafts and commenting. Thanks to Pako and others for sadly confirming some of the behaviours and cultural context this story recounts. It should be stressed, however, that all characters are fictional and I have no specific model in mind for Father Ramon.

Thanks to all reviewers of previous Hidalgo adventures – whether commenting in print, in cyberspace, or in person. Your encouragement helps a lot!

Grateful thanks also to Jessica Gladwell, Joy Tibbs, and the team at Lion Hudson for allowing David Hidalgo another outing. Finally, thanks to you who are reading. I hope you enjoy this story and will let me know at www.worldofdavidhidalgo.com.

And the Lord passed by before him, and proclaimed, The Lord, The Lord God, merciful and gracious, long suffering, and abundant in goodness and truth. Keeping mercy for thousands, forgiving iniquity and transgression and sin, and that will by no means clear the guilty; visiting the iniquity of the fathers upon the children, and upon the children's children, unto the third and to the fourth generation.

EXODUS 34:6–7, KJV

MORÓN DE LA FRONTERA – LATE SUMMER

Nothing about the outermost security door had changed in the last seven years. Maybe a dribble of oil or a lick of paint, but nothing you'd notice. The mechanism was as robust and secure as it had ever been. Yet as it slammed shut the metallic clang was totally different. The sound of a door locking you in is different from one opening to let you through.

The preliminaries had been completed right after breakfast. His few personal possessions were returned and signed for, then a shower, a change of clothing, and on to the governor's office.

Governor Daniel Lopez was not a brutal man. He tried to make encouraging remarks to all the men about rejoining a world they might have left five, ten, or even twenty years before. And he forced himself to be scrupulously fair. Whoever the criminal, whatever the crime – murder, rape, fraud, armed robbery, or even ETA terror attacks – they all got their full ten minutes in a comfortable chair with a reasonable cup of coffee. But this morning he just couldn't bring himself to do it. The file of reports in front of him seemed to describe a model prisoner who had paid his debt and was ready to rejoin society. Excellent conduct. Polite to officers and professionals. No big fuss about guilt, innocence, or wrongful conviction. Fully engaged in the prison's eduction programme, particularly given that he wouldn't be going back to his former profession. In fact, he had shown a remarkable aptitude for the computer skills course and had not only passed all the modules but had repaired the education department's computers several times, and improved internet access and record-keeping.

It all looked perfect, but Lopez simply couldn't get past the uppermost conviction sheet in the file. He was used to shocking details but had never been able to get his head around this one. How was it possible? How could a man betray a trust so grievously and show not even the slightest sign of remorse? The prisoner was left standing as Lopez scanned the salient points yet again for some sign of progress; some acknowledgment of the wrong and harm done; some sign of a change of heart that would bode well for the future. After all, that was the key. New skills, improved self-confidence, and supportive outside contacts were important, but without the desire to be different they had little impact. Did the man in front of him convey any desire to be different? Lopez accepted there was no shred of evidence of it. So the prisoner was left standing. There was no friendly chat, no *café con leche* and no avuncular advice. Lopez abandoned the normal pep talk and said exactly what was on his mind. Then he regretting being so unprofessional. In any case, it seemed to make no more impression now than the many counsellors and psychologists before him had, according to the file. The prisoner simply kept looking ahead, showed no sign of emotion and refusing to respond in any way.

The man standing on the worn patch of parquet in front of the desk had more or less expected this reaction and let it wash over him. He had heard it all before. Let them think what they wanted. The only thing that mattered was that the metallic clang was behind him now instead of in front. It had been a long time coming. Of course, he'd used the time as much to his advantage as he could while studiously ignoring all the counsellors, psychologists, and social workers they had thrown at him. He had turned to the library first but was disappointed to get through all the worthwhile reading in less than a month. Then there had been a desperate time of nothingness when life had been reduced to eating, sleeping, staring at the walls, and counting days.

In desperation one Monday morning, Sandra, the cheerful, optimistic, well-intentioned education officer, had suggested an IT course after finally accepting that woodwork and pottery were achieving nothing. He'd started with little expectation just to fill a few more daylight hours but had been surprised to find that it fitted his type of brain exactly. It was cold, precise, and logical. Emotions were irrelevant and there was no need for psychobabble about how it made you feel. But that didn't make it mechanical. It was a science but also an art. The science was getting the right answer; the art was doing it in the most elegant, economical, and graceful way. He found it natural and raced through the modules before branching off into much more interesting investigations of his own.

Standing patient and silent in the face of Lopez's tirade he wondered what the governor would say if extracts from his last steamy email to Rosa from the admin office were to be quoted back to him. Or better still if it was shared with Señora Lopez. She was enjoying a comfortable life in the suburbs while her husband pretended to be heading off to yet another conference. In reality he was between the sheets with a girl half his age in a cosy little *piso* – paid for with the half of his salary she didn't even know existed. He smiled slightly at the thought and got another rollicking for it. It was a nest egg he was keeping for a rainy day but maybe he'd cash it in a bit earlier after this. When Lopez finally ran out of energy he told the prisoner to pick up his case and get out of his sight. That suited both parties just fine.

Five minutes later the now ex-prisoner was standing in front of an open door. He walked forward a few paces and stood silently under the deep blue dome of Andalusian sky. A dry scrubby hillside rose to his left and endless lines of olive trees stretched away for miles in front. The southern sun was relentlessness. Just like the so-called justice of the country. Politicians with fat bundles of Euro notes in plain brown packets went free, while the judge thought justice demanded fourteen years – seven with good behaviour – in his case. Relentless and unforgiving.

The time had passed painfully slowly without a shred of the normal camaraderie among prisoners when everyone feels they have suffered an injustice. The *Centro Penitenciario Sevilla II*, better known as *Morón de la Frontera* after the nearest small town, even had its own semi-formal system of prisoner support after a spate of suicides. The *Internos de Apoyo* – the "Support Inmates" – watched out for those about to slip over the edge and tried to respond with encouragement and care. No one cared about a man like him. Being in closed conditions – the *régimen cerrado* – meant he very rarely had anything to do with the so-called "normal" prisoners, but there were times when he did. Like when the trusted ones serving meals would spit in his soup as it was passed through the hatch. Or when the hospital orderly had fed him a massive laxative instead of the cough medicine he had gone in for. He had seen the grins and sniggers when he was brought straight back in doubled up in pain. Still, it was over at last. This time the slamming door behind him was neither a fantasy nor a daydream.

It took almost a full minute to calm his thoughts under the still ferocious late summer sun. He gradually gathered his senses, then finally noticed the tiny, peeling, red Seat Ibiza parked as far from the main entrance as possible. So she'd come. He hadn't thought she would, but she couldn't deny her own flesh and blood. He picked up his cheap cardboard case and walked over to the car. She didn't get out, or open the door, but continued staring straight ahead as he got in.

"You're here," she finally said.

"I am here, Mamá."

"I've dusted your room and put clean sheets on. There's empanada and cheese."

The car's interior probably could have cooked the pastry or melted the cheese. He wound his window down but it made no difference. The air outside was heavy and dead, like the atmosphere inside it.

"You can't stay," she said. "You know that, don't you?"

He wasn't surprised.

"It's ok, Mamá, I'm not going to. I'm leaving."

"Where will you go?"

"It's best you don't know. I've got plans."

She grunted an acknowledgement, turned the key, and the engine coughed and started.

Plans. What a beautiful word. Big, beautiful plans. Plans he'd spent seven long years building, refining, honing, perfecting, dreaming. Beautiful, perfect plans. They would see what relentless and unforgiving really meant.

She pulled her black shawl tighter and kept staring rigidly ahead.

"Don't worry about me, Mamá," he said. "I'll be ok."

"I'm not," she said, revving the engine. "I'm just glad your father's already dead. Please God I soon will be too."

Chapter 1

CAFÉ CÓRDOBA –
THE FOLLOWING SPRING

Andrea Suaréz Morán did not like the way the guy at the corner table was looking at her. She carefully set down the tapas he had ordered – *sardinas a la plancha, pinchos morunos, albóndigas, chorizo en vino* – and a bottle of San Miguel and headed back to the safety of the bar.

"¿Piensas que ese tío parece un poco raro o es solo mi imaginación?" she asked José as she wiped the tray and slipped it back with the others.

"Hey, speak English, *chica*," he said. "That's what we're here for."

She rolled her eyes but knew he was right. Her English had improved enormously in the six weeks she'd been in Edinburgh, but it still needed more mental effort, particularly if she was worried or tired.

"Ok," she tried again. "Do you think that guy is a bit weird or is it just my imagination?"

"It's not your imagination," José confirmed, stealing a glance from under thick black brows as he dried a glass. "He comes in twice a week, orders exactly the same, always on his own, never smiles, no tip. Definitely weird."

"And he only ever speaks Spanish. There's something familiar about him but I don't know where from."

"I'll mention it to Martin so we can keep an eye on him. When do you finish tonight?"

"Ten."

"Ok. I'm on till eleven. Just wait in the kitchen till I'm done and I'll see you home."

"Would you?"

"Sin duda. ¡No hay problema, guapa!"

"Hey, speak English, dude – that's what we're here for!"

She gave him a playful punch on the shoulder and glanced around, laughing. The guy in the corner was watching, not laughing, and that took the smile off her face.

In the kitchen, while she waited for José to finish his shift, Andrea pulled out a second-hand copy of *Sons and Lovers* she was trying to plough her way through. The language was a struggle; she'd expected that. What she couldn't work out was why the British seemed to get so worked up – *was that the right expression?* – why they got so worked up about sex. Well, maybe that was just the mystery and also the fun about other cultures. People just see things differently, that's all. *Es lo que hay* – that's just how it is. She'd read that in Britain it was polite to keep your hands off the table at meals. In Spain it was just the opposite. If your hands weren't in view, maybe you had a dagger under the tablecloth you were just about to stab your host with. Total opposites for random reasons. Attitudes to sex, religion, politics, humour, physical contact, even greeting friends and strangers – all different. Why? Because that's just how it is.

She couldn't concentrate with all the orders being shouted through, pots and dishes clattering, and onions sizzling, so she put her book down, leaned back against the slightly sticky wall, and dropped her mind into neutral. Having a real job, earning real money, and being independent again had all come in a bit of a rush, but she was loving the sensation. It made her mind spin that so much could change in such a short time. It seemed incredible that it had only been six weeks ago she'd kissed and hugged Mamá and Papá at security at Madrid–Barajas Airport and got on the easyJet to Edimburgo – "Edinburgh", as she now had to call it.

Less than a year before had been the monumental three-day end-of-degree party which, looking back, now felt like an official farewell to youth and a welcome to the real world. That had been as long-drawn-out a group goodbye as they had been able to manage.

Four years together at the Complutense University of Madrid in the leafy suburbs to the north-west of the city had made them more than friends and closer than family – a few had even become lovers. Now they were simultaneously ecstatic at the thought of no more lectures and exams, terrified at landing directly on the unemployment scrapheap in the midst of the crisis, and heartbroken at the thought of losing each other. So they drank for three days straight and swore the current fate of 52 per cent of Spanish youth would not be theirs. They toasted their successful futures to come, cursed Prime Minister Rajoy and his infernal *Partido Popular*, blessed the new *indignados* protest movement, and prayed to San Isidro, La Macarena or any other god, saint, or virgin open for business for good results and a real job. On the final evening, after many *riojas* too many, she and Jorge had slept together one last time for old times' sake even though they'd broken up more than a year before. It seemed the generous thing to do. They kissed and swore they'd keep in touch, all the time knowing they wouldn't. The morning after, she had packed the last of her stuff, took her Beatles, Dylan, and Lorca posters down, gathered up bits of discarded clothing from around the flat, left the pot plants for the new tenants, and took the Metro from Moncloa to Atocha, changing at Sol. Finally, easing into her seat on the AVE train to Sevilla, she exhaled slowly, looked out the window, and dabbed away a tear.

Then the real battle began, compared to which essays and exams were frankly a stroll in the *Parque del Retiro*. With her father, older brother, various uncles and neighbours all out of work and her mum only doing part-time seasonal work at the bullring, she thought she knew what she was up against. But it's different when it's you. Very quickly she found she was fighting on two fronts, not one. Number one: get a job. Number two: keep positive and don't slide into self-pity and misery while dealing with number one. So she waitressed at the *Rincón de Pepe* (again), tried a cold-calling sales thing from home (phone bill more than the commission), and even tried her hand as a miracle cleaning products home demonstrator, soon to find her mother's prediction was true:

Spanish women thought soap and water was cheaper and bleach more effective. The day came when she actually thought about offering her services at Kiss Club just off the *autovía* south to Cádiz and finally decided enough was enough. She had to get out while she still believed she was better than a hostess in a brothel. So instead of poring over her job applications database on her laptop that morning as she always did, she opened Facebook and sent a personal message:

> Hey José.
>
> You were right. This country is in such a mess there isn't any chance any more. I'm getting out. Anything going in your direction?
>
> Un besito. Andrea.

Then she met a friend for coffee and tried not to keep checking her mobile under the table. It beeped after only twenty minutes.

> Hey guapa.
>
> What took you so long????? Edinburgh is beautiful. The boss is always looking for real (gorgeous) Spanish waitresses. You qualify. He says come. You can stay in my piso till you get a place. Let me know when to collect you.
>
> Besos. José.

Wow, she thought, *that's incredible. It wasn't that hard. Escocia, here I come!*

Good as his word, José met her at the airport, paid for her tram ticket, and welcomed her to the second most beautiful capital in Europe (he said). After a coffee with a view of the castle he took her to his flat halfway down Leith Walk where they dropped her stuff, then went straight to Café Córdoba to meet Martin, the owner. She started the following day. Bingo!

denly the smell of burning meat caught her attention as
or, the Catalan cook, grabbed a pot off the stove and threw it
bodily into a sink already full of dirty dishes while bawling at his
beleaguered assistant. She tried to stifle a smile just as José appeared
around the corner with a jacket and a beanie hat on.

"Ready?" he asked. "Your mystery admirer's gone."

"*Gracias a Dios*," she muttered, getting up and giving him a
grateful peck on the cheek.

The following morning – Saturday – David Hidalgo stepped out
into the clear northern light of a late spring Edinburgh day and
let the heavy door of the common entrance slam and lock behind
him. Left towards Tollcross, straight ahead across Bruntsfield
Links, or the long way around by the Grange? He wasn't in a
hurry; for once there didn't seem to be any threat of rain and he
could surely do with the exercise. He turned right onto Bruntsfield
Place, heading for Holy Corner. Like so much he remembered
from the Edinburgh of his youth, Holy Corner had changed a
lot since the seventies. It was so called for having four churches,
one on each junction, several of which had changed hands and
one had even been become the Eric Liddell Centre, celebrating
Scotland's best known Olympian. Seeing as Liddell was a devout
believer and had won his medal against all odds after refusing
to run on a Sunday, if anyone thought losing a church to him
made the corner any less holy, then too bad in David's opinion.
So, past the coffee shops, delicatessens, florists, and convenience
stores, smartly sidestepping dithering shoppers and sweaty
Saturday morning joggers. When things were going well David
acknowledged he had a definite weakness for whistling. Some
might call it an ailment but he was unrepentant. He maintained
it was a perfectly natural expression of feeling relaxed and happy.
Why not? Free the inner whistler. Depending on his mood, it
might be "Zip-a-Dee-Doo-Dah" (in praise of wonderful days),
Nina Simone's slow, bluesy "Feeling Good" (even the birds are
feeling good today) or something else that fitted the occasion.

This morning, maybe on account of the weather, "Blue Skies" came to mind. The sun was so bright and things were indeed so right. He smiled at the strangers he passed and breathed in the slightly hop-filled air.

Today was the once-a-month Saturday morning clean-up at Southside Fellowship's South Clerk Street premises. For some of them, such as Secretary, Treasurer, and general factotum Irene MacInnes, he knew it was all about "proper standards". *What would the world be like*, he could almost hear her say, *if we just let everything go to the dogs?* Morningside ladies like Mrs MacInnes knew that cleanliness wasn't just *next* to godliness; you'd be hard pressed to get an old-fashioned King James Bible page between them. While David had no objection to a bit of light sweeping and dusting, the way he saw it, that was more an excuse for the main event. Want to get to know your congregation? Forget the worship when everyone's in holy mode. And the post-service chat where people want to be encouraging despite that morning's sermon slipping out of mind quicker than the shipping forecast. To really find out what's going on there's no substitute for a football match, a new colour scheme, changing the order of service, or cleaning the hall. Then people said what was really on their minds. Christian theology might be profound and ethereal, but when it comes to the practicalities people can be alarmingly tangible.

Anyway, to more pressing matters: his contribution to lunch. Clean-up Saturday always involved a nice bring-and-share lunch and he liked to produce something unusual to spice things up. Mrs Buchanan's lentil soup was legendary, and Juan and Alicia would usually bring anything left over but still good from their Hacienda restaurant, often meaning half a pan of paella, tasty tortilla chunks, or plenty of fresh salads. But something out of the ordinary made it more interesting. So what to lob into the mix this week? Walking past the A&A MiniMart gave David an idea. Some of Ayeesha's fantastic marzipan and almond cakes and sweets would be perfect.

"Señor David, how are you? What can we do you for today?" The dapper little man behind the counter beamed at him. Sometimes

David thought Ali was more British than *he* was. He always wore a collar and tie to work, had a flawless accent, enjoyed the Scottish Fiddle Orchestra, and read Conan Doyle and Stevenson. On the other hand, he was also enormously knowledgeable about his South Asian heritage and kept a wide range of hard-to-find spices and authentic ingredients.

"Good morning, Ali. We've got a clean-up group at church this morning and I'd like to take them something sweet to finish off after lunch. What have you got?"

"You're in luck, my friend. Ayeesha was baking all last week. We had a big order for a wedding at the mosque. Then the bride's family took cold feet so it's all needing eaten. There's *gulab jamun*, *bonde*, *cham cham*, *malapua*, and a few things that don't really have a name, just her own invention. What would you like?"

Ali led the way around shelves piled high with gram flour, basmati rice, poppadoms, fresh ginger, and spices in kilo bags to a chiller cabinet full of pastries, desserts, sweets, and drinks.

"I've no idea, Ali. I trust you. Give me a mixture. What can I get for twenty pounds?"

"Plenty. Let me see."

Ali went back to the counter for some cardboard cake boxes and started filling them up.

"You'll have to be careful how you carry this," he said, delicately fitting in as many as he could.

"Business booming, then?" David asked as the process continued.

"Sure thing. We can't complain. You know it's forty years since Amin kicked us all out." It didn't take much to click Ali onto his favourite theme. "Our family had been in Uganda for generations. Then, just like that," he settled a bright green marzipan into the corner of the box and snapped his fingers, "out on our ear. If Britain hadn't taken us in I don't know what would have happened. So we lost everything there and had to start again here. I don't care if I never see Kampala again. Edinburgh's my home. I'm more Scottish than you. I've been here since I was seven. And I stayed put. Not off to Spain whenever I felt like it. Anyway, Edinburgh's been good to us and the business is doing well. Now, how about that? Enough?"

David took the pile of three boxes, one on top of the other tied up with string, over to the counter and put down his twenty pounds.

Suddenly a thought struck him.

"Ali, does this mean that you're moving into catering for outside events, not just the shop?"

"Indeed it does. Ayeesha's been planning this for years but it was tricky when the kids were young. Now Rasheed's twenty-six and Karim's nineteen. They're not interested in the business but at least they're out of our hair. Mahala graduates this summer in hospitality and business so we're hoping she'll get involved. She's a good girl."

"And the boys. Haven't seen much of them for a bit."

"Well, Karim works with his cousin in a carpet business in Glasgow. Rasheed's in IT out at South Queensferry. But to be honest we don't see much of them. There's been a new preacher at the mosque filling their heads with crazy ideas. They think we've sold out to the Great Satan because I pay my taxes, vote in elections, and have Christian friends – like you, for example. I tell them it was Britain that gave us a home when nobody else wanted us but they don't listen. We are not a radical family. We go to the mosque and observe Ramadan. I even did the hajj once. But we're British. I support England in the cricket and Scotland in the rugby. But that's not how many of the younger ones see it now. You know. I don't need to tell you. Ah well. Young people. What can you do?"

"Indeed. I sympathize, Ali, but I've no bright ideas. You know Rocío always wanted kids but it didn't happen so I'm no expert. Now everything's going to be changing though. You never know. I might be coming to you for advice."

Ali closed the chiller cabinet and looked up at David expectantly. "So, the outside catering. What did you have in mind?"

"Oh yes – sorry, I got sidetracked. Well, you know there's a certain wedding coming up in a few months' time?"

"Yes, I heard. Congratulations, of course." He reached out to shake David's hand.

"So, Hacienda are doing the main catering, but I wondered if you might be interested in the cake? If you do that sort of thing. I suppose it's not really very Asian."

"You'd be surprised. There's a fashion now for huge wedding cakes even for Muslim couples. I think Ayeesha would like the challenge. I'll ask her."

David glanced at his watch and gulped. Informal is ok – half an hour late would be far too Spanish.

"Look, I've got to get going," he said. "Why don't you and Ayeesha come up for dinner some time? I promise not to try a curry. We can talk the whole thing over."

Rushing down the Grange and arriving late – as his mother used to put it, "down to a greasy spot" – didn't seem such a good idea now, so instead he turned right and took the direct route across the Links. Careful not to bump the cakes now.

Edinburgh was relaxed and sunny and he was happy. It struck him it would be hard to imagine things being more different now than eighteen months ago when he'd first arrived back from Spain. Then it had been winter, with a bitter, biting wind off the Forth driving up over the city until everyone was shivering and bad tempered. Perhaps that's where Edinburgh got its chilly reputation from. It seemed like the winds came direct from Siberia without so much as a coal shed in the way and blew deep into the Scottish psyche. "Come in, come in – you'll have had your tea" was the traditional cold comfort greeting. Not as true in reality as the stereotype but it's hard to change a bad rap. But now it was practically summer. Young families, grandparents and grandkids, and groups of students in the latest Bethany Trust charity shop specials were out on the Links putting, tossing a frisbee, walking dogs, jogging, taking photographs, or just sitting on benches soaking up the mid-morning sun.

That winter he had fled back to Edinburgh for a refuge, abandoning most of a lifetime in Madrid. All these years he had done "the right thing", followed his calling, used his gifts and talents such as they were, and faced up to the challenges with faith, then watched it all come crashing down with a phone call and a bullet. He wondered if that was what it was like when an earthquake struck. Everything that had seemed so solid and secure suddenly starts swaying and shuddering before collapsing in utter ruin. In his case the whole process took about thirty seconds. Then, no sooner back in his childhood home, slowly trying to put the building blocks back together again, he had ended up looking for the missing granddaughter of a church member. In finding her, he had found himself. And, the greater miracle, found Dr Gillian Lockhart. There was no adequate name for what that finding had come to mean.

Seeing a bunch of girls doing taekwondo on the Meadows reminded him of another turn of events he couldn't have predicted and was at a loss to explain. Tatiana Garmash and Elvira Antonov had come to Scotland from Belarus hoping for work, freedom, and the chance to make something of their lives. Just like David before them, they didn't get what they were expecting. Behind a convincing facade, a local church was running a people-trafficking and prostitution racket. When a friend who was digging into the church's dubious finances was found hanging in his garage, David got dragged into that as well. But that had worked out too, despite his minimal contribution, and now he stood in awe of how, despite what these girls had come through, they still managed to remain intact – more than that, optimistic.

But that was all over now. Surely it was time to get on with "normal" life, if such a thing existed. Dodging through traffic on Melville Drive and striding up Jawbone Walk, he took a deep breath of the extra oxygen pumped out by the Meadows greenery and let the inner whistler out again with a blast of Ella Fitzgerald's "Blue Skies". You couldn't measure faith and optimism like numbers from a political opinion poll, but somehow he felt he was back in the saddle and willing to believe there was a bigger plan. Besides, there was a wedding to organize, a honeymoon to book, a life to live.

Southside Christian Fellowship's modest meeting space, above a DVD rental shop and a Chinese restaurant, was already largely taken to bits by the time he arrived and was in the process of being cleaned and put back together again. David climbed the stairs, looking forward to catching up with some of his congregation over a bit of light dusting, then a nice relaxed lunch ending up with some of Ali and Ayeesha's beautiful sweets. Gillian had said she'd some marking to do so hadn't been sure when she'd arrive. Without it quite becoming a conscious thought, he hoped she'd be there.

"Ah. The very man. Glad you could make it," a familiar voice called out as he pushed through the double doors. To David's eye, Gillian looked perfect even in overalls and marigold gloves.

"I thought you were going to be late."

"Well, I managed to get through the first years' accounts of the Great Vowel Shift quicker than I'd expected. And the second years have all asked for extensions so I'll leave them for a bit. So here I am. And on time too."

"Good morning, Señor David!" an altogether more brisk and business-like voice called out through the kitchen hatch. "I've just the job for you. We need the pelmets and cornices done. Stepladder in the storeroom, dusters under the sink, and hot water in the tap!"

David smiled. Commentators have claimed that Stevie Wonder is more a force of nature than a musician. They needed to spend a few minutes with Irene MacInnes to fully understand the concept.

"Ok. Just my line."

"And just before you start…" Gillian was smiling as sweetly as she could, which was very sweetly indeed.

He paused en route to the kitchen. "Do you want me to shine up the buttons with Brasso?"

"No. Easier than that. But also in your line, I think. Edinburgh University's Rationalist Society have their monthly debate on Tuesday night. They've had a dropout. I said you'd be delighted to help. You need to oppose the motion 'This house believes that God has outstayed his welcome'. Here's the feather duster."

Chapter 2

NEWINGTON

While the Plan had undoubtedly been the one thing that kept him sane through all the bitter weeks, months, and years inside, it did have one basic flaw, which he'd glossed over before but now had to face. It wasn't actually a *plan* at all. It was an intention, a goal, an objective. Nothing more. Turning it into reality would need research he simply couldn't do from inside Morón de la Frontera – even with the access to the internet they didn't know he had. And there wasn't anyone outside who would help. For most former colleagues he had simply become a poisonous pariah. In some cases that may have been for reasons of genuine disgust, but for the most part he was sure it was from an overwhelming desire to stop any of the mud landing anywhere near their own front doors. So he'd found himself dropped faster than the hot *castañas* they sell from little ovens on the streets in winter. Even the fact that one or two had returned his letters still didn't mean he could enlist outside help to get all the information he needed. For one thing letters were censored, and for another the location of certain people who had said certain things at his trial that he now might want to discuss with them might be hard to trace. Children have a habit of growing up, looking quite different, even moving to other cities and countries. So even if there was someone to help it would have been a full-time job to keep on top of it all. And it would have needed a very good explanation. He could hardly tell the truth, but an explanation was something he would never give. The Plan was his and his alone – not for sharing, explaining, justifying, or defending. It was his one and only comfort through the freezing winters and stifling summers, the tormented nights when he couldn't sleep, and the relentless days of boredom and emptiness with no one his intellectual equal to speak to and nothing he thought worthy of his time and talents to distract him. Just the Plan.

Only once the ride back to his mother's tiny *piso* in Triana in old Sevilla was over and he'd had his fill of home cooking, slept between clean, white, pressed sheets, packed a flimsy suitcase, and left without a word was he able to take stock of how things were. The Plan would need a lot of work to make it a reality. But he had time, some funds he'd managed to divert from the parish before everything fell apart, some skills, and above all, determination. He allowed himself a bitter smile getting onto the bus to the cheap tourist hostel he had selected as an initial base. They say revenge is a dish best served cold. On the contrary; he felt it gave a warm, satisfying glow. It was going to be very sweet.

"You volunteered me for what?" David asked, looking incredulous in response to Gillian's last comment.

"Calm down *caballero*. And keep your voice down," Gillian said soothingly, one hand on his arm and the other about to pop in the last mouthful of a perfectly light, yellow *cham cham*, coated in coconut flakes. The Saturday morning work party were sitting around a couple of trestle tables put together in the middle of the hall, which was by now pretty clean but still needed reassembling. Mrs MacInnes had assigned them to different tasks, Gillian on her knees cleaning the oven and David on a stepladder dusting plasterwork. So he'd never had a chance to follow up her parting shot of two hours previously. Now they were perched at the end of the table surrounded by the rest of the team, being well fed and watered. David was trying not to make a scene but he still couldn't believe it. In fact, he'd almost forgotten as he went whizzing around the cornices trying not to topple off his perch; but sitting down across from Gillian it came right back to mind.

"What on earth's the Rationalist Society?"

"You remember Stephen Baranski," Gillian pressed on, trying

to make it all sound very relaxed and pally. "He came to our engagement party."

"I do. The one that wanted to take you to the Springsteen concert."

"Yes, but don't hold that against him. Anyway, he's on the committee of the University Rationalist Society. Every year they have a big set piece they call their 'God Slot'. It's the 'Does God Exist?' debate."

"The result of which, I take it, is a forgone conclusion?"

"Interrupt you folks? More soup?" Mrs Buchanan was hovering behind David's chair with a soup tureen and ladle.

"Of course." David turned around, managed a beaming smile, and offered up his plate. "Delicious as usual."

"Well – just good food and plenty of it as my granny used to say. The secret is to soak the lentils overnight. There you are. And there's plenty bread on the table."

More soup and a fat heel end in front of him, David was finding it harder to maintain his outrage. He had another go.

"So because you turned him down for Springsteen, you're feeling obliged. He's one speaker down for lambs to the slaughter and you suggested me?"

"No, that's not it at all. Well… maybe. A bit. Anyway, wouldn't it be a great opportunity to explain exactly what you do believe to the sort of people who've maybe never heard that sort of thing? And you're just the supporting speaker. Each side has a leader and a seconder. You'd be the seconder opposing the motion."

"This house believes that God has outstayed his welcome."

"Exactly – which you don't believe. So all you need to do is say why."

David paused and sampled the soup. It really was delicious. Now he wasn't sure of the best continuing strategy. Speaking honestly, he should just have said, "Sorry, that's not my kind of thing." Debates and arguments don't change anyone's mind. *A man convinced against his will is of the same opinion still.* And everybody starts bickering about "evidence" when the issue is really relationship. Anyhow, if he just said "no" he knew it would look like a point-blank refusal without fully understanding what he was objecting to. But trying to clarify too much would be tantamount to agreement and just looking for a bit more information. He sighed heavily, looked at Gillian still smiling ever so sweetly, and knew he'd been nailed.

"Ok," he said. "Fill me in."

She would have given him a peck on the cheek if they'd been alone but in public she just mouthed a quick *love you* and said, "I knew you'd rise to the challenge." Then, looking at her watch, "Just time for a coffee before chat group then I'll tell you. Finished your soup? Caffè Paradiso?"

"Go on, then. Twist my arm."

But instead of twisting it she just took his hand, pulled him out of his chair, and headed for the door without letting go.

"Awww. Will you look at that?" Mrs Buchanan whispered to no one in particular. "Romance isn't dead after all."

Andrea stretched and yawned, turned over, and pulled the covers a bit tighter. Then she thought she'd better check the time. It was her turn for a Saturday morning off but still, she shouldn't waste the entire day. Ten thirty. Ok, time to get going. Her mother would be scandalized. Even when everyone in the house was unemployed she insisted that people kept proper working hours and didn't end up watching junk TV all night then sleeping all day. There was probably more of her mum in her than she cared to acknowledge. And there was still so much to see and do in Edimburgo – sorry – Edinburgh. She threw the covers off, checked that nobody else was around, then nipped into the bathroom and turned the shower on full blast. Hot water and lashings of body gel felt wonderful. She tipped her head back and stood luxuriating under needles of spray just on the verge of being too hot.

What was the right word? In Spanish she would have said *fantástico*, *estupendo*, or *increíble* but she wasn't sure if fantastic, stupendous, or incredible were right in English. She'd noticed that people here seemed to say "awesome" a lot. Maybe that was it. Life in Edinburgh was awesome. The castle, museums and galleries, the gardens, Princes Street shopping, hundreds of ethnic restaurants and cafés, traditional Scottish pubs, a piper blowing for all he was worth outside Waverley Station, old cobbled streets and classical New Town Georgian facades, a bewildering array of nationalities and fashions, and even a surprising number of Spaniards forming a little family far from home. Maybe that was even one of the best bits – lapping up the adventure while being able to share it with fellow nationals on the same journey. It was almost like being part of a Basque *cuadrilla* – that close-knit society of friends often formed at school then there for you throughout the rest of your life. She loved Andalucía with all its traditions and customs, but if there was one thing she'd have added it would be the *cuadrilla*. Now she had that as well. José had introduced her to his friends and she had one or two of her own contacts from around Sevilla now living in Edinburgh. These friends connected with other friends and new contacts through Facebook. Before long she'd found herself with probably more connections here than even at home. Everyone was fleeing the crisis, everyone had left home and family for a new start, and everyone was open, optimistic, and energized to make the best of it. None of them was employed at a level appropriate to their degrees, masters, MBAs, and doctorates but that didn't seem to matter. It was work – more than they could expect in Spain – and an opportunity to improve their English, all set in a beautiful, vibrant, multicultural city. It was almost too good to be true. *Awesome*. She gave a little shiver of pleasure, then decided she'd probably used up a week's showering time already and reluctantly turned off the flow.

Just as she was dabbing her face she heard the front door bang and a shout from the hall.

"Hey *chica*! Time to get going! English chat group – remember?"

Aargh! She'd completely forgotten. José had mentioned something to her just last night. She started rubbing furiously and shouted back.

"Coming!"

"Don't worry. I'll make a coffee."

By the time she managed to throw some jeans and a T-shirt on and hop through to the living room, one shoe half on and the other in her hand, José was sitting on the sofa in the bay window alcove with a copy of the *Diario de Sevilla* open on his lap.

"Look at this," he said. "There's a shop on the Royal Mile that has international papers. Two days old but better than nothing. I got it for you to catch up on your home news. Want a look?"

She made a face while still fighting with her sandal straps.

"*¡Qué va!* No way. I'm trying *not* to think about the crisis. It's just going to be the same old stuff."

"No – look at this. Serial killings in Sevilla! I'll read it in English:

Seville has been rocked by a series of brutal killings of both ecclesiastical figures and teenagers. Police are struggling to see what might connect the two. Inspector Diago Sánchez of the Criminal Investigations Dept. exclusively told Diario de Sevilla *there were no robberies, no sexual assaults, and no apparent pattern in four recent deaths. "Each of the victims died in different circumstances," he said. "We're baffled. The only thing they have in common is that they're dead!"*

"There you are. News that's not about corrupt politicians for a change! Had you heard?"

"My mum mentioned something the last time I called her. But it's still bad news. Everything from Spain is bad news. And politicians are criminals too – just a different sort. So it *is* just the same old stuff!" Andrea finally got the sandal on and flopped down exhausted on the beaten-up brown corduroy sofa.

José laughed then smiled at her from under thick black bushy brows, an unruly mop of hair the texture of Brillo Pads, a swarthy almost gypsy complexion, and a gleaming smile in the midst of a chinful of jet-black stubble. The original idea had been that she would couch surf for a couple of weeks at José's place till she got her bearings, had enough cash for a deposit, and found someone with a spare room. Then one of his flatmates had announced he'd got a job teaching Spanish to kids in California and was leaving. It seemed natural that she should move into the vacant room. Carmen and Rodrigo were easy company but she had to admit sharing with José was not, in itself, an uninviting prospect. He had been on the fringes of her set at Complutense and not particularly outstanding either way but here he was the soul of kindness, hospitality, and decorum and she'd felt only welcomed and never pressurized or uncomfortable. So she signed up, paid a deposit, threw out the remaining rubbish in her new room, stuck up her posters, and put twenty pounds in the Ovaltine tin that had served as a kitty through about twenty generations of occupants. *Who knows*, she thought, *maybe something'll happen that never happened in Madrid. Don't mind if it does.*

"'… Same old stuff…'" he repeated. "That's a great expression. You'll be speaking like a native by Christmas. Anyway, we need to get going."

"Sorry. I completely forgot. Where are we going?"

José folded the paper and dropped it on the coffee table.

"English chat group," he repeated. "I mentioned it last night. Too many vermouths maybe? Don't worry. It's very informal. About a dozen of us. Agustin who works at La Tasca invited me. I've been going for about six months. It's fun."

"How much?" Andrea asked, ever conscious that any positive spending decision meant some others that would have to be negative.

"Free."

"Free? Really? Who runs it? Why do they teach English for free?"

"Well, it's not exactly teaching. It's just chatting. The idea is to get everyone talking; then, if you get something wrong or somebody says something you don't understand, you can ask. So you just get to practise what you know and learn a bit more. No grammar and no homework!" He grinned again.

"Is it from the *ayuntamiento* then – I mean the council – or the university or what?"

"No, it's entirely voluntary. A guy called David Hidalgo. He's some sort of a priest but in the *iglesia evangélica*. He was brought up in Edinburgh but his dad was Spanish. I think he spent most of his adult life in Spain. Then something went wrong – not entirely sure what – so he came back to Edinburgh. His girlfriend, Gillian, helps too. I suppose he misses speaking Spanish."

"So it's religious then?" she asked, frowning slightly.

"No, not really. It comes up of course but everybody just says what they think and we talk about it. There's no pressure at all. He's quite an interesting guy. And the coffee's good."

"Where is it?"

"Newington. A restaurant called Hacienda. David knows the owners. So we meet on Saturdays if we're not working, have a drink and a tapa, and chat. That's it. So are you coming?"

"English language and Spanish coffee – are you joking?" She tried to put on her best Edinburgh accent. "Hold me back, boys!"

"Wow, you know more expressions than me. Awesome. Ok. *Venga. ¡Vamos!*"

David and Gillian walked the half mile from Southside to Caffè Paradiso holding hands in the warm spring sunshine. South Clerk Street was busy with taxis, delivery lorries, private cars, and the usual swarms of cyclists. A busker was singing "Knocking on Heaven's Door" very badly in a doorway, but despite that, God did seem to be more or less in his heaven and all was well with the world. Showing up for a couple of hours to defend the "God Proposition" was not in any way David's idea of a pleasant evening out but Gillian had a way of making it seem not so bad. All told, life with Dr Gillian Lockhart was definitely not so bad and the debate wasn't a high price to pay. What was the worst that could happen? He could go along, say his piece, and be savaged by a bunch of "rationalists" who had long made up their minds and brooked no dissent from the party line. So what? He very much doubted there would be minds open to change, but it's always good to see things from the opposite point of view. Actually, it might be quite interesting. He had heard all the arguments a hundred times. The question was why people got so angry about it. Of course, true believers in general could be the worst sort of zealots and bigots, but most of his experiences in the Christian community had been of the other sort – everyone unique, generally all too aware of their own deficiencies, and just trying to walk the walk as best they could. So it was neither fair nor accurate that the opposition tended to see them all as either stupid or wicked with nothing in between. Maybe there was an army of Christian extremists lurking in the backstreets of Bruntsfield or Burdiehouse, but if so he had yet to meet them. And as far as hypocrisy was concerned, they didn't seem any more hypocritical than folks who could stand to lose a pound or two going to the gym. You go not because you're already slim and toned but to pummel these pounds and make an improvement. He would have to give the matter some thought and maybe come up with something a bit different from what they were expecting. But not right now.

He took a deep breath, forgave Gillian for the ambush, smiled at no one in particular, gave her hand a squeeze, and started whistling "Zip-a-Dee-Doo-Dah" till she gave him a look. This warm, witty, wonderful woman had been the answer to prayers he hadn't been able to make. She could be as delicate as snowdrops when they were curled up watching a movie or needle sharp when he said something lazy or not thought through. She still teased him about his hopeless dress sense. "If you don't dump that overcoat and fedora I'll give them to some kids for Guy Fawkes," she'd once threatened. But still she was sensitive enough to try to improve things around the margins without seeming to take over. He didn't mind any of it. She had her own advancing career, her own tasteful flat, her own friends, and her own life experience so different from his. Yet she wasn't ashamed to move into his world, including being nice to all the oddballs, wing nuts, and weirdos that church sometimes attracts, as well as the salt-of-the-earth Mrs MacInneses of the world. Of course she asked questions and made comments; but she was well aware of how David himself sometimes only held on by his fingertips, so she didn't try to make him personally responsible for everything that seemed to make no sense or felt uncomfortable. He knew he could rely on her in a crisis – of which they had had a few already. What could be better? And how weird that she should propose him to defend a faith that she still didn't formally own herself. It did look suspiciously like she wanted to give him a platform, as if she really believed that what he had to say was worth hearing. Maybe she wanted to hear it herself…

He gave the hand he was attached to an extra squeeze as they arrived at the door, which he then held open for her.

"Giancarlo. *Buongiorno*," he shouted to the middle-aged man with the perfectly clipped moustache behind the counter. "Two of the usual, please."

The owner looked up from where he was polishing glasses.

"Señor David. Gillian. Nice to see you, as always. All the important people today." He nodded towards a window table behind them.

"Sandy and Sonia beat you to it. Two of the usual coming up."

David turned towards the window. A youngish couple, maybe mid-thirties – she in a pink jogging top and he in a cream linen jacket, a white shirt, and a smart tie – were sitting with two large coffees in front of them and a plate of pastries.

"I suppose I shouldn't be surprised to see the Benedettis in an Italian coffee shop, even when they should have been helping clean the church…" David said in a tone of mock reprimand.

"We've got an alibi." The woman held up her hands in defence. "Just got rid of the kids. Honest. Sometimes you just need a break and some of Uncle Giancarlo's coffee to recover."

"Absolutely. Just ignore him," Gillian put in. "You're looking very smart, Sandy."

"I know. It's a habit. I can't get used to not working."

"So even on Saturday he still gets up at 7.30 and puts a tie on." Sonia gave it a playful tug.

"Well, it could have been worse," Sandy countered, looking into his latte. "I could have been wearing a prison uniform, I suppose."

"So, anything on the horizon?" David asked, trying to move things along in a more positive way as Giancarlo arrived with the two large cappuccinos and they pulled a couple of extra chairs over.

"Not really. I keep sending off my CV and I do get a few interviews. It all goes well enough right up to where they say, 'Can you tell us why you left Salamanca Bank, Mr Benedetti?' Then they have to think of a polite way of throwing me out."

"I can imagine," Gillian nodded, though she knew she couldn't.

"Taking on an employee recently convicted of driving a truck and trailer through the money-laundering regs isn't something many banks are very keen on," he admitted, shrugging.

"But we keep on praying and keep on going." Sonia reached across and squeezed her husband's hand. "Something'll turn up."

"I'm sure," David agreed, trying to sound positive.

"So what's next?" Gillian asked brightly.

"I don't know," Sandy conceded, taking another sip. "Maybe I need to forget about banking and open another Italian coffee shop – like this one."

David actually thought that was the most sensible thing he'd heard Sandy say for months. He was an intelligent, professional man who could make his own decisions so he'd had never felt it right to butt in and give advice, but seeing him in church every week, well turned out but looking like he was at a family funeral, did not bode well for a career recovery. Maybe a change of direction was what was needed. Not necessarily a coffee shop but something different. In reality he probably *was* unemployable in conventional banking. He'd been taken in and manipulated by the crooks in charge of Power and Glory Church; then, for reasons that seemed for the greater good at the time, he'd fiddled the banking regulations to conceal the millions they should never have had. Although he couldn't have predicted the consequence it was a reckless and illegal act. So while he maybe wasn't ultimately responsible for the people trafficking and prostitution ring behind the so called "church", nor the death of a colleague who was investigating their accounts, that had only been a very limited mitigation to the authorities. That colleague,

Mike Hunter, a good friend of David's as it happened, was now dead and Sam Hunter was a widow while still in her thirties. A dozen police officers and a fair number of the great and the good were in jail and a senior civil servant had committed suicide. The ring was broken up and the girls liberated but that doesn't bring back the dead. Sandy Benedetti would have to carry that for life.

On the other hand, once he did understand what was going on, he had helped as much as he could in both the investigation and the prosecution, for which he got off with a suspended sentence and 250 hours of unpaid work. Having immediately lost his job, he had plenty of spare time for tidying old folks' gardens and painting fences. Unfortunately, six months later there was still no prospect of work. So the smart town house in the Grange – one of the most exclusive and expensive parts of Edinburgh – had had to go and now he, Sonia, and the kids were in a tiny flat in Sighthill. But at least they were alive, together, and somehow had managed to recover their faith and had moved into David's care at Southside. Sometimes David reflected that despite the gulf in circumstances he and Sandy weren't that different – just at different points of the trajectory. They had both found themselves in critical situations not entirely of their choosing. They had both unwittingly exposed parties close to them to very real dangers. The fact that Gillian was alive and Mike Hunter was dead made David a hero and Sandy a villain but what was the real difference? They were both damaged goods doing the best they could in an uncertain world. So, like Sonia had said, you keep on praying and keep on going. What's the alternative?

"So what have you got on today then now the hall's spick and span?" Sonia asked, sensibly breaking the silence. David looked at his watch.

"Chat group in about… twenty minutes," he replied. "In fact, we'll probably have to drink up and get going."

"How's that coming along?" Sandy asked, also keen to change the subject. "Happy to help if you consider a second-generation Italian Scot a native speaker."

"Actually that would be great, Sandy," Gillian answered, instinctively spotting something that would be good for him as well as the group. "We seem to be growing. People come and go but we have around a dozen regulars. I think they like it. Moving cities and cultures isn't easy so it's surprising how much you get drawn into their lives. One minute you're trying to explain phrasal verbs then the next someone's asking about assured tenancies and rent rises. But there's no agenda – just chat – so you end up chatting about absolutely everything. – politics, culture, movies, holidays, family, and faith stuff too. It's amazing how open people can be. I think somehow speaking in a foreign language seems to make it easier to say quite personal things. Don't know why."

"Hmm, interesting," Sandy replied. "Maybe I will come along some week. I think we could do with some advice on fair rents! And how are the girls doing? I haven't seen much of them for a while."

Over past months "the girls" had come to mean only one thing – Tati and Elvira – two young women trapped in the forced prostitution racket Sandy had been unwittingly protecting. It was to his credit that he was interested in how they were getting on rather than embarrassed to talk about it.

"Good," David said. "They've been very canny with the cash they got back from Power and Glory. It looks like the dream is still on track. I think they've had the first group of legal arrivals from Minsk and they're doing intensive language and secretarial training with them now. As far as I know the aim is to start placing them as temps sometime in the autumn. Then another group is coming before Christmas to get placed before summer. That's the plan anyway. I suggested Eastern Promise for the company name but I think they've settled on Supertempo."

"Much better," Gillian whispered.

David continued: "They've got a tiny office in Hanover Street and we let them use the hall for training."

"These girls are amazing," Sonia remarked meditatively. "After all they've been through. It's incredible."

"I know," Gillian added. "I very much doubt I'd have the resilience – or the energy. Tati is just like an ideas machine and Elvira works like crazy to keep on top of it all. They're fantastic, but what they really need is a good administrator and financial manager before it all gets out of hand."

David interrupted her, thumping his forehead in a Homer Simpson gesture.

"I've had an idea," he said. "Why didn't I think of this before?"

Ten minutes later David and Gillian were retracing their steps back along South Clerk Street.

"Nice move, Señor Hidalgo," Gillian remarked, hugging his arm. "Two birds with the one stone and all that. And I don't mean Tati and Elvira."

"I know – one of these things that seems so obvious once you've thought of it. What do you think they'll make of the idea?"

"I think they'll jump at it. As far as I know no one has ever held Sandy the least bit responsible for what was really going on. He was just as fooled as anyone. And it would be fantastic for him and helpful for them. He's not doing anything else, so why not? Especially when he said he'd look after all the admin and finance for nothing until he got another job or they decided to take him on properly. 'Win win' as they say. Did you see Sonia light up at the idea?"

"I did. It's been hard on her. Losing the house and having the kids change schools and all that. She's known a lot of insecurity. Then the thought of her husband in court and almost going to prison. It could have wrecked everything. But she's made of sterner stuff. I'll mention it to the girls the next time I see them and see what they think. How come it's all the women who're the tough guys around here, eh?"

"Just the way the cookie crumbles, sunshine. Get used to it!"

Before David could think of a witty reply that wouldn't get him into more trouble, they had to take emergency avoiding action when a couple jumped off the number 7 bus almost right on top of them. It took a quick round of sorries before anyone realized they knew each other.

"David! *¡Hombre!*" the guy shouted, then stood back to be recognized.

"José. Where did you spring from?" David gave him a friendly cuff on the shoulder.

"On our way to meet you, of course." He stepped forward and gave Gillian the customary *dos besos* – always left side first – then stood back again.

"*David y Gillian. Os presento una amiga muy especial. Desde Sevilla hace solo tres semanas. Trabajando conmigo y disfrutando de Edimburgo. Andrea. Andrea – David y Gillian.*"

Andrea smiled, stepped forward, and gave more kisses all round. The bare facts were brief and accurate: arrived three weeks ago from Seville, working in the same café as José, enjoying Edinburgh. But the bit she particularly liked was being "a very special friend". That sounded nice and held a variety of possibilities. She felt strangely inclined to include José in the kissing too then gave herself a mental note: *Calm down, chica. All in good time.*

Chapter 3

TRIANA

Triana is not tourist Sevilla. In fact, "*in* Sevilla but not *of* it" might be a good description. It's not entirely a joke that the locals call it the Independent Republic of Triana. It doesn't have the massive lump of a cathedral with its flying buttresses and tomb of Columbus or the neighbouring Giralda tower ramped all the way to the top so the muezzin could ride up to issue the call to prayer without ever getting off his horse. Likewise it lacks the draw of the Moorish Alcázar palace with its stunning geometric artwork, the Torre del Oro watchtower with its centuries of trading history, the Real Maestranza de Caballería bullring, and the gracious Plaza de España esplanade. In fact, although the streets are narrow, cobbled, and thoroughly authentic, it even lacks the tourist cuteness of Santa Cruz so doesn't appear on many walking tours either. Outside the city walls, it's almost an island jammed in with no elbow room between two arms of the Guadalquivir river. So instead of expanding into new territory, Triana simply had to cram more and more people into narrower and narrower spaces or pile the residents on top of each other like an urban dormitory full of bunk beds. Even some of what had made Triana prosperous in the past, like the tiny backstreet tile workshops that had turned out beautiful and distinctive ceramics since Roman times, has gone now. What it does still have, however, sprinkled like spicy paprika over the entire maze of narrow streets, is a lively gypsy flamenco culture and the intense local identity and loyalty of those that call themselves *Trianeros*. Intense devotion to the Virgin of Hope and a fervent faith among her devotees has remained the consistent stamp of Triana.

Ramon didn't care one whit either for what Triana had to offer or was thought to be lacking for locals or visitors alike. After one brief, uncomfortable night's stay at his mother's, he got himself installed in the Backpackers Utopia Hotel (ten Euros a night and free Wi-Fi) and set off on his first foray into the old town. The hostel seemed so utterly removed from real Sevilla with its staff of twenty-somethings from Austria or France or Madrid that he didn't have any worries about being recognized there; however, the heart of Triana was a different ball game and he would have to be careful. The beard was coming on well and the dark glasses wouldn't attract a second glance in the blazing Andalusian sunshine. Now that he was no longer a priest and had to look respectable, he'd also decided to let his hair grow. A trendy bun at the back looked quite cool. It all felt like a cliché but precautions had to be taken. Seven years had been interminable for him but it wasn't much more than a turn of the page for the old crones in their black dresses and shawls who'd once been his parishioners.

Hanging around anywhere near the Iglesia de Santa Ana, where so many years of spiritual anguish and struggle had been played out ,might have been thought needlessly reckless but he couldn't avoid it. It was a symbolic starting point, almost like settling himself into the blocks for the race ahead. The building was still as beautiful as he remembered it: towering walls the colour of marzipan, with darker bands of rich ochre red topped by an ornate ornamented tower with a hundred or so decorative spikes and pinnacles. He would like to have gone inside but couldn't risk it. No doubt the massive brick pillars, soaring Gothic-Mujedar roof, grey-brown high altar with its huge rococo altarpiece depicting the Blessed Virgin presenting the infant Jesus to Santa Ana would all be much as he'd last seen them nearly eight years before, but the meaning had changed. Seven years spent dwelling on the events that had taken place here or in the tiny cloakrooms, storerooms, and robing rooms and what had driven him to it had robbed the space of any beauty, grandeur, or sense of holiness it should have had. It was merely the scene of his disaster. Like Lucifer, son of the morning, he had gone from respected and honoured son to an object of horror in what felt like an instant. It was where he had been betrayed, first by his own body and mind then by the church that was supposed to have supported him. He would like to have gone in and committed some despicable act of desecration but didn't dare. Instead he contented himself with a table at the Taverna La Plazuela opposite and a cold beer.

A young, ambitious priest is surely not much different from anyone else at the gateway to their career, hoping to distinguish themselves and emulate their role models – or at the very least not screw up so badly as to distinguish himself in another way. He had done well at his seminary in Mondoñedo, a small market town in Galicia, but was not unhappy to eventually be placed in his home town of Sevilla at the opposite end of the country. He wouldn't miss the rain, for one thing. Andalusians had a reputation for being relaxed and happy, not gloomy and pessimistic like the Galicians. *Mañana* or even the day after would normally do so there was little pressure and here the church was still held in reasonably high esteem. No doubt a lot of it was nothing more than cultural Catholicism, village fiestas, and brotherhoods of the Virgin being a good excuse for male bonding and cold beer, not to mention the annual pageant of *Semana Santa* with its torchlit processions, hordes of visitors, and TV coverage. But while all of that might not be the meticulous theology he had spent his three years at seminary honing, at least it wasn't the curse of agnosticism that slid all too quickly into cynicism, then outright rejection. Elsewhere in the country radicals and hotheads were even agitating for the right to renounce their parents' baptismal vows and have their names struck from the parish register – unbaptized, if you like – but thankfully, so far not here. Andalucía was still an island of faith in a swirling sea of doubt and decay. He would be diligent, dutiful, and happy here, he'd had no doubt. What a joke that turned out to be.

He sipped his beer in the sunshine and watched the residents of the *barrio* passing by, augmented by one or two tourists looking a bit lost and confused. A man, maybe in his late fifties, in a threadbare jacket and filthy trousers, was kneeling on a cushion at the entrance to the church. From where Ramon was sitting he could just make out the wording on the rough cardboard placard hung around his neck. *I am a Spaniard*, it began, *without a roof, job, or money. Four children to support. Please help.* A dirty piece of cloth was laid out on the pavement by him with a few coins scattered on it. His hands were held out cupped in front of him and his eyes were cast down either at the coins or the feet of the passers-by. Ramon did a quick calculation. Let's give him the benefit of the doubt and say fifty-five. Maybe married at twenty-five and children every two years. That still meant that the youngest would have to be more than twenty – not exactly babies in the crib. So that part was no doubt a con. And while he probably didn't have very salubrious accommodation, nobody with family in Triana actually slept in the street. So he did have a roof over his head, even if that just meant sleeping on some relative's filthy sofa. On the other hand, "no job" was almost certainly true. As for "no money", while he might be getting fed at his brother's or nephew's or sister's table, he certainly wouldn't have any income from the crooks currently in charge and only concerned in fleecing the country against the day they got heaved out in favour of the next set of crooks. So, while half of the story was probably fiction – and of course dressed up to evoke the maximum sympathy from passers-by and tourists – there was enough truth to add up to a man who should have been cruising to a comfortable retirement surrounded by an appreciative family but now found himself begging on his knees in the street. Kneeling in the street must do something fatal to the spirit. He was struck by the fact that the first line of the beggar's explanation of himself was to make it clear that above all he was Spanish, not Romanian, Moroccan or Latin American. It's as if he was saying, *Look. I'm from this country. I'm not an immigrant fleeing poverty somewhere else. It's not supposed to be like this. A country is supposed to support its own citizens, not leave us like dung beetles trying to prise a living out of the detritus other people throw our way.*

Then there was the irony in his choice of begging spot. The doorway of a church is certainly going to be a more likely place than the doorway to a bank. It's meant to be a place of generosity and compassion, not exploitation and greed. But Ramon knew differently. Maybe the faithful passing by might drop a few *céntimos* onto the cloth, but the massive hierarchy of the church that provided the backdrop wouldn't be getting involved, that's for sure. Nobody knew just how rich the church was but that didn't stop the speculation. Every beggar in front of every church door in Spain could probably be set up in quite tidy accommodation and given a pension for life without it having any significant impact on the balance sheet. Maybe a few properties might have to be sold or some shares liquidated – nothing that would be more than a blip on the lifestyle of the princes of the church. Ramon hadn't risen very high in the hierarchy but high enough to know the colour of money. First the church had to maintain its status, reputation, and place in society. Then it wanted to preserve its hidden wealth. Only after that came what some might have thought of as its primary mission: to save souls and represent its heavenly chief and head. Ramon knew that his misdemeanours were a threat to all three and so had had to be aggressively disavowed. Paedophile priests on the front page of *El País* brought the church's reputation into the gutter. Lawsuits and compensation claims would certainly make a dent on the accounts, and fewer souls would look to the church for guidance and succour if they knew how their children were being treated on youth weekends to Santiago. So that was the motivation behind the machine that had dealt with his case. Just as relentlessly as the handles on the rack that wrenched confessions out of the victims of the Inquisition, the ecclesiastical machine had worked his case to prove above all else that no one in authority had had any idea what was going on, that not for one second did the church condone such behaviour, and that the strongest possible sanctions would be applied. And they were. As soon as matters were proved "beyond reasonable doubt", he was stripped of all the rights, privileges, and titles that go with the priesthood and cast before the secular authorities without so much as a character reference for all the good work he had done in the preceding fifteen years. Ramon's thoughts flipped back to the beggar at the door 50 metres away. He got up, left a few Euros on the table in front of him, walked over to the man, and dropped a fifty Euro note onto the cloth, then set off back to the hostel. After all, the money had come from the Parish of Santa Ana so it was fitting enough. By the time he'd caught the bus his mind was on other things. He had some appointments to arrange.

David Hidalgo pushed open the door of Hacienda restaurant and ushered Gillian, José, and Andrea inside. Juan, the owner, had obviously been decorating over the past week and the simple white walls had now been transformed with a rusty earthenware stucco effect. Some pictures had been changed to chime in with the new colour scheme and the doors and window frames were now a delicate rose tint.

"Nice," Gillian said as Juan saw them and advanced from behind the bar.

"Do you think so? Alicia is so much better on colours than me. It was her idea. I'm just – how do you say – unskilled labour. But she's eight months now and not allowed to do much. So I try to remember what she said and buy the right paint."

"I like it," Andrea ventured. "Very Andalusian. I'm from Sevilla."

Juan beamed at her.

"*Hola*. Welcome to chat," he said, and kissed her lightly on each cheek.

"Andrea – Juan, the owner," José explained. "Juan – Andrea. She's just arrived in Edinburgh. She's with me at Café Córdoba."

"How do you like our beautiful city?" Juan asked, leading them to a large table near the bar. "*Preciosa, no?*"

"*Sin duda*," Andrea replied, grateful for a little bit of Spanish. "*Me encanta.*"

David looked at his watch.

"Ok," he said. "English chat starts... now. Any use of Spanish will result in a fine of one round of *cerveza*."

"Well, that's you buying the first round, if I'm not mistaken!" Gillian put in pointedly. David groaned and rolled his eyes.

"Nailed again."

Juan grinned at him.

"How long have I told you, *hermano*, you have to watch this woman, *no*?"

"And that means you get the next round..." Gillian smiled sweetly, then winked at Andrea. "Don't worry," she murmured reassuringly. "There are no fines, no penalties, and no hassle. We like to tease the guys, that's all."

Just then the door opened and a crowd of six or eight young Spaniards came bustling in, laughing and joking.

"Let me introduce you, Andrea," David suggested, "but first of all, what would you like to drink?"

More Spaniards trickled in over the next few minutes, increasing the total to well over a dozen. David and Gillian had pushed Juan's two biggest tables together and a variety of *riojas*, *albariños*, *cervezas*, and a few coffees were in front of them.

"Ok," David began. "Welcome, everybody. We have a couple of new members this week so maybe we should do a quick introduction: your name, where you are from, why you are in Edinburgh, and an interesting fact. And if there's anything anyone says that you don't understand, please ask. I'm David, born in Edinburgh but spent thirty years or so in Madrid. I came back to wash dishes for Juan and a couple of other things. And one interesting fact... eh... I once played saxophone in Café Central in Madrid when the main act got lost. They paid me in tortilla. How's that? Ok? Next." David looked to his left.

"Gillian Lockhart. From Edinburgh, more or less. I work at the university. And I once met Bruce Springsteen in Tesco when he was on tour. He was buying milk and he was gorgeous!" That got both rolling eyes and mock swooning around the table, depending largely on gender. From then on, first José introduced himself, then Andrea, followed by Ricardo, Conchi, Cruz, Isabel, Mariangeles, César, Sergio, Juan Carlos, Antía, Iria, Maria Luisa, Miguel, and

Enrique. Although they came from all over mainland Spain as well as Las Islas Canarias and one from Minorca, the stories were remarkably similar. After a few introductions people even began looking around at those who had already spoken and saying, "Same as him." They loved Edinburgh and Scotland in general, hated leaving Spain but simply needed to find a job of any sort. Around the table were a psychologist, several engineers, a gynaecologist, a software developer, a concert pianist, a vet, two teachers, a film maker, and a few who couldn't list any profession as they hadn't worked since finishing university. They mostly said where they were working now, which was overwhelmingly in hotels, restaurants, cafés, or shops. One had managed to land a job in a multinational advertising agency on account of being fluent in Spanish, with a degree in German and French, passable English, and a bit of Mandarin. One was tour-guiding Spaniards on holiday, one worked in a Spanish specialist grocers and delicatessen, and one was in a call centre supporting Telefónica customers. It took fully twenty minutes to get round the table. Finally David summed up.

"Thanks, everyone. And a special welcome to José's friend Andrea from Sevilla – right? – and Cruz from Galicia. Great. Well, anyone who's been here a while, do you want to explain how it works? José, you brought Andrea – how about 'the authorized guide to English chat'?"

José did that wide grin again that was beginning to turn Andrea's knees to jelly.

"Sure," he said. "What can I say? I think we started with English but then we got to be friends and English is the excuse. That make sense?" Nods and smiles around the table. "So you can ask anything, say anything, bring anybody, and nobody mind. That's it. And David and Gillian looking after us and trying to explain English expressions. Even though is impossible." More laughs and exclamations of agreement.

"Well, we do our best. So, Gillian has an activity for this week."

Gillian reached down into her bag and pulled out a tub with about twenty slips of paper in it.

"Easy peasy this week," she started. "Sorry, that means 'very easy'. You're all Spanish, which of course means you specialize in parties. This is a selection of things you might say at a party. You pull out a slip, then you have to say whatever's on it to anyone you choose around the circle. Then they answer any way they want and you have a conversation. That sound ok? So, for example. I'll ask David."

She pulled the first slip out, read it, and had to stifle a laugh.

"Right," she said composing herself and turning towards him. "I'm going home now. Would you like a lift on my motorbike?"

Without batting an eyelid David smiled, put on an impression of Leslie Phillips at his most salacious, and oozed an oily reply.

"Certainly, my dear," he drawled. "Unless you would like a run in my Jag." Whoops and guffaws broke out around the table from those in the know. Andrea looked confused until José whispered in her ear.

"So that's the idea," Gillian concluded. "I might then tell my partner that I do not wish to have a ride in his Jaguar since I happen to know he's already married to a girl in Buenos Aires, has a second family in Barcelona, and that he and his Jag have a terrible reputation for taking advantage of young single girls."

"Take advantage of?" Ricardo whispered.

"*Aprovecharse*," Conchi replied.

"And I might protest," David continued, "that she must be thinking of someone else, that I've only had the Jag since this morning, and that I am a single man trying to make sure she is safe in a city of notorious scoundrels. *Sinvergüenzas*. So you get the idea. Just say whatever comes to mind."

So off they went. César had to ask Antía if she came here often, Maria Luisa told Enrique he had lovely lips, Sergio invited Cruz to a movie then fish and chips afterwards, and Ricardo asked Conchi how old she was as she only looked sixteen, at which she thanked him very much and told him to mind his own business. With lots of in-between banter and suggestions of suitable replies and offers, the activity took the remainder of the hour and a half till David, finally (after being asked by Andrea what he did for a living, how much he earned, and did he have a villa in the south of France) called a halt.

"Ok everyone – time just about up, I think. Better equipped for parties? I should add of course that Scottish young people would never ask such appalling questions – *preguntas horribles* – but just in case. You're welcome to stay and have another drink or whatever but that's it. And I've got a couple of Spanish newspapers here if anyone wants."

Nobody seemed in a rush, but eventually about half the group made it to the bar and paid then headed for the door. Amidst the general hubbub Andrea came up to David as he was gathering up his things.

"I just wanted to thank you," she began shyly. "I've really enjoyed the group…" She held up a napkin with scribbles all over it, "… and I've learned some new expressions too. It's great. I'd like to come back."

"Glad you liked it." David smiled in response. "We try to make it fun."

"Well, you have done your goal. Is that right?"

"We would say 'achieved your goal'. But I'm happy you liked it."

"And all for free. It's amazing. If you lived in Madrid you'll know Spaniards don't do anything for nothing."

"Well, to be honest we get a lot more out of it than we put in. It's a tragedy so many of you have to leave Spain but we've met so many fantastic folk. It's a pleasure to help. Look, why don't you and José stay for another drink if you're not going anywhere? Then we could get to know you a bit better."

"Ok, I don't think we have to go. I'll ask him. Any Andalusian papers?"

"Em, not sure. Let me see. *El País, Voz de Galicia, El Mundo*. Oh, here you are – *ABC de Sevilla*."

Andrea smiled and took it from him before looking around for José. He was deep in conversation with Sergio. Probably about football. That might take some time. So instead she sat down at the table, took another sip of her beer that wasn't quite finished, and looked at the headline. Gillian sat down beside her and was just about to ask how she'd enjoyed the group when she noticed her expression change.

"Is everything all right?" she asked. "What is it?"

"It… it's the paper," she stammered. "There's been another murder in Sevilla – my city."

"I heard," Gillian replied. "It was on the BBC news website last week. Young people and priests, isn't it? The police say they have no idea what the connection could be."

Andrea laid the paper flat and looked up at her. She had gone white as a sheet. She spoke almost in a whisper.

"But this is different. It's someone I know – Maite. I was at school with her. She was *estrangulada* – I don't know the word in English."

"Strangled," David translated almost inaudibly.

Andrea paused almost as if she couldn't believe what was forming in her mind.

"I've just realized," she said. "I think I know what the connection might be…"

Chapter 4

LA PARROQUIA DE SANTA ANA

There had been a time when an interview with the bishop would have had Ramon quivering in his boots. Would His Eminence approve of his progress? Was he conducting the mass with the appropriate degree of reverence and dignity, while still making the mystery sufficiently accessible for simple people? And his choice of homily, was it too long or too short, too intellectual or too narrowly biblical, did it take the text of the week and apply it sufficiently to the new Spain of the late 1970s – the post-Franco era – or was he being too contemporary and not sufficiently stressing the timeless truths of the gospel? With the death of the old dictator the church had entered into a new, uncertain world. No one was quite sure how the new democratic governments would treat the institution, which everyone knew had been more or less hand in glove with the Caudillo for more than thirty years. It was a nervous time in the cloisters of power and there was a lot of pressure on a young priest not to alienate the masses but rather to reinforce the bonds that bound them to the Mother Church. What would the bishop think of his progress? Maybe there had been complaints from the confessional. What did a young unmarried man like him know about the realities of the marriage bed and the tensions that could simmer in an unhappy union until they erupted into violence or infidelity? Well, as it happened, he knew more than enough about sexual tensions, without having to hear about it all day from frustrated spinsters and testosterone-filled young men. But that was another story. No doubt the bishop would have advice on that score as well, but it probably wouldn't be top of the agenda. So every appointment reduced him to a bag of nerves beforehand and a quivering jelly afterwards.

But, he had to admit, once he was sitting in the big red armchair in the bishop's study it never turned out as badly as he was expecting. In fact, more than once His Eminence had proved remarkably insightful in relation to some problem that he couldn't see a way through or a dilemma he faced. In these early years Bishop Ignacio had almost come to assume the role of a kindly uncle who occasionally had some stern words but always with the aim of building up, not breaking down. Gradually, his monthly meetings changed from feeling like he was appearing before an *auto-da-fé* – the feared religious courts of the Inquisition – to something more like a consultation of colleagues. Not of equals of course – that could never be – but of men of experience involved in the same profession, swapping war stories and sometimes having a laugh at other people or more commonly at themselves and their mistakes. All the more shocking, then, to see how quickly things changed once the press got involved.

To begin with he didn't dare say a word about his inner battles, despite the fact that they seemed to increasingly dominate his day. From his first waking moment these thoughts would be in his mind – sometimes even in his dreams before the day began – until the last flicker of consciousness as he curled up alone and put out the light. He was still able to function and fulfil his duties and even yearned for more activity to distract him so he threw himself into anything that presented itself – youth camps, Lent retreats, a pilgrimage to Lourdes, *cursillo* Bible study groups, preparation for First Communion, anything that took up his mind and his attention. But the movie director in his head was always ready with another showing in any moment of inattention. So instead of the relaxation and calm reflection he craved, he seemed to increasingly find his mind once again taken over by stories and fantasies that seemed to erupt from nowhere. Whatever he should have been thinking about vanished like smoke and the film began. Himself with some of the youth after lights out. Himself with the young widow he had been counselling that day. Himself and a group of teens he was taking on a picnic. Even himself as an eastern potentate with a willing harem or as a powerful businessman with adoring secretaries. And always with a predictable conclusion. The struggle to contain and channel his thoughts in the proper direction seemed both interminable and unwinnable – there was no point when the battle might be said to have been won as the next moment of inattention brought the enemy back stronger than ever. It was like battling demons that couldn't die and grew stronger with every encounter.

Maybe they *were* demons. Maybe he was possessed, going mad, sick – or just evil. Maybe he was beyond the help of God, cursed for some sin of his youth he'd forgotten or even for the sins of his forefathers. Didn't it say that the sins of the fathers would be visited upon the children? Regardless of how unfair that sounded it was in the Scriptures so it must be true. Maybe his father, who had fought for Franco had committed some ghastly sexual atrocity before Ramon was born and the punishment for that was now being visited on him. Or maybe it was just inexplicable. Just bad luck. He had ended up with bad genes or too much of some hormone or other and that's what made him as he was, in which case there was no solution. There could be no victory. This was the way things were, and like Paul's "thorn in the flesh" he would simply have to make the best of a bad job and limp through life trying to keep the fantasies from ever becoming reality and keep the dreadful secret to himself. Christ had said to Paul, "My grace is sufficient for you, for my power is made perfect in weakness." Maybe St Paul had laboured under the same burden all his life and that was why in his final letters he described himself as the chief of sinners? If Paul himself had suffered from some insoluble problem that Christ had never chosen to remove, then what hope was there for Ramon? Maybe, on the other hand, there was some special spiritual discipline that could make the difference and that would finally set him free. But if that was the case, then what might it be? More Scripture study? Prayer and fasting maybe? Spiritual retreat? Denying the flesh?

By the time he was on the point of choosing between suicide and surgery, he realized that outside help was needed. *This is ridiculous*, he thought. *Older and wiser heads than yours must have wrestled with this, both on their own account and for those who came to them.* It says, "confess your sins to each other and pray for each other so that you may be healed", doesn't it? So maybe he would have to think the unthinkable and confess until it was all out on the table. Then he might finally get the help he needed before he either went totally mad or committed some unpardonable sin. He phoned the bishop's office and asked if he could bring forward his regular monthly meeting. Crossing the threshold that morning had maybe been the hardest thing he'd ever done but he was determined. He would tell his story whatever the outcome. Perhaps Bishop Ignacio would rant and rave, ban him from religious service, strip him of his office, and send him back to the *pueblo*. He would accept it and go. Or maybe he would just shake his wise old head, look more sorry than angry, and tell him to pack his bags for Africa. Or maybe send him to a monastery in the hills for six months of spiritual formation. Whatever it was, he had no reserves left to argue. He would accept and embrace it and go. Any hope was better than this constant craving that was unfulfilled and could never be fulfilled while maintaining his calling.

The one reaction he wasn't expecting was what he got. His Eminence simply smiled and said nothing, then began to chuckle softly. Of course his face must have betrayed his reaction when Ignacio finally spoke.

"Don't be offended," he said. "I do apologize. I should keep a straight face and give you wise counsel. It's just that you remind me so much of myself. This could be forty years ago and I would be sitting in that chair and my bishop opposite me. Ramon, Ramon. You think you are unique. Well you are, I suppose, we all are. But your ailment is not unique. I'd even go so far as to say it's almost universal. The priest who doesn't experience tensions like these isn't human. And God did not call us to be robots. Christ entered into the sufferings of the world and we share in the sufferings of our parishioners. Our tensions may be somewhat different from theirs but each of us suffers in our own way. You must know by now that marriage isn't the solution to every problem. You think that a wedding ceremony means no more pressures or tensions for either party, in the marriage bed or out of it? Why do you think so many have affairs? Why do the clubs outside of town do such good trade? Why we are now seeing the American disease of immorality coming into Spain? Magazines and videos men look at in private or in the back room of the local bar and keep hidden from their wives? Sexual desire is simply a wild beast that cannot be tamed. Not by you nor me nor the men and women who come to mass every week or those that don't. Why God made us this way is not for me to say but that's the truth. You are not unique or cursed or unduly weak. You are normal, my brother Ramon. It's the nature of being human and male. Being a priest doesn't make it better or worse, just different. You have to somehow come to terms with that, as do I. But it can be done. Here I am. More than forty years in the priesthood and somehow still struggling on. Christ was a man of sorrows acquainted with bitterest grief. Should we be better than our master? My advice is simple, Ramon: don't take yourself so seriously. Don't bottle it up. Don't make it a drama that dominates your life. And if you need to find a friend to help you share the burden, then do it. As long as I don't know officially, I'll take no action. You won't be the first. And enjoy your life and your calling. God is good and life is wonderful. Enjoy it and go in peace."

It was funny how he could still recreate that interview in his mind almost word for word years later. The film director had his uses. And he had played the movie so many times. So that was it – no secret weapon, no silver bullet, no deeper spiritual journey. Just come to an accommodation with reality and if you have to compromise then do so. Just don't let anyone know. Authorized hypocrisy. He could hardly believe it. He walked home in a daze. When the bishop had said "find a friend", he had actually said "*amigo o amiga*" – a friend of either gender. The context was one of talking about "sins of the flesh", "carnal thoughts", "impure imagination" – or to put it in plainer language, what the rest of the world would call "sexual frustration". And Ignacio had said to find a friend – of either gender. So sex in any context outside of marriage was a sin for the laity, including adultery, fornication, homosexuality, and even "private vices". But for the clergy apparently not. "Life is good," Ignacio had said. "Enjoy it." It was almost as if he was saying sex was a gift from God, not a burden to be borne or a thorn in the flesh. Enjoy it any way you please but don't let me find out. Walking through the door that morning he hadn't been sure what reception he would get but he certainly hadn't expected that one.

In one way it was an incredible relief but in another incredibly confusing. How was he supposed to "find a friend"? An ordained, consecrated priest could hardly go to the discotheque or hang around the Sevilla nightlife. He couldn't put an advert in the paper or call up a girl he used to know in school. He felt like turning around, going back to His Eminence, and saying, *Hang on a minute; I don't think I entirely understood what you were saying. Do you think you could spell it out a bit more clearly?* Of course the bishop had chosen his words very carefully. Spelling it out was definitely a bridge too far. He was supposed to get the drift and work it out himself. Ignacio would probably have said, *You're an intelligent man, Ramon, work it out for yourself and don't come bothering me with your pent-up problems.* Wow. Incredible. He made it the rest of the way home without touching the pavement. His housekeeper, who was certainly not the best cook in town, had made an appalling apology for fried fish but he didn't care. He complimented her on her fine home cooking, which confused her as well, then he went for a walk down by the river, fed the ducks, had a late supper in Alfredo's bar, wandered home slightly squiffy, fell sound asleep, and dreamed he was five years old and lost in a sweet shop. Hallelujah. Amen.

Next morning he began to wonder just exactly how he should go about putting the bishop's advice – or was it an instruction? – into practice. Public places were surely ruled out, even he knew that. What about a club, that peculiarly Spanish euphemism for a brothel? No way. As a seminarian he and a classmate had actually been sent by their professor to order a beer and spend at least fifteen minutes drinking it in Latin Lover, a club near Mondoñedo. The object was to show how uncomfortable non-practising or non-

Catholics feel in church. Although they were in "off duty" attire the experience almost killed him. The girls seemed to go on the premise that more make-up and tighter jeans were always better – poured into their clothes and "no one said stop", as his mother would have put it. They seemed to all be Brazilian, Cuban, or Dominican (the Republic not the Order) but smiling, laughing, and hanging on like robots, not real human beings. Never again.

Just when he was beginning to think it was impossible, Isabel, his housekeeper, came into the room with a second cup of breakfast coffee and a little light dawned.

"Isabel. Can I ask you something a little... a little delicate?" he blurted out before he had time to stop himself.

Isabel was maybe in her late fifties but had worked in the parish house for forty of these years and served countless priests, probationers, students, visitors, and a few future bishops. While the Catechism of the Roman Catholic Church and its commentary might contain the Curia's guidance on almost any matter of debate, Isabel knew how things really worked. She might not be a learned woman but she was a walking encyclopaedia who had never yet failed to answer Ramon's questions or doubts in a manner at once entirely truthful and explicit but yet utterly discreet. Maybe this was a question she had never been asked before but Ramon was sure she would be both helpful and unshockable. And if she thought the worse of him for asking she wouldn't show it.

"Certainly, Father. Anything."

"Well, I've been having a discussion with a fellow priest, a brother I was at seminary with. I say that for a priest to have a... what can I say... a liaison with someone in the parish while serving is both a sin and impossible in practical terms. I say they would always be found out and have to leave in disgrace. He says God would forgive and that it happens all the time and nobody knows. You've been here a long time. What do you think?"

Isabel kept hold of the coffee cup she had brought to the table and gave him a long look. *That's it*, he thought. *The game's up. She knows exactly what I'm asking and she'll go straight to the bishop.*

"Well, as to it being a sin, I'll leave that to you, Father," she replied matter-of-factly. "As to whether it happens, you are wrong and your friend is right."

"Really?" Ramon answered, trying not to sound too excited. "So how does it happen? I mean, how would a parish priest have a relationship with someone without people finding out?"

"Well, sometimes they do find out and nobody cares. That's one thing."

"I'm surprised by that. Don't the people value the celibacy of the clergy?"

"No doubt they do," she replied equally deadpan, "but sometimes they prefer their clergy to get their hands a little dirty in the real world. I mean, how can you tell a priest your husband is no use in bed if he's never been in bed with anyone but his teddy bear?"

Her plain speaking shocked him. He was seeing his housekeeper in an entirely new light. It was a revelation.

"So how does it happen? I mean, just to prove it's possible?"

He had a feeling she was on to him but if so she didn't show it.

"Oh, a thousand different ways. Sometimes it's the housekeeper. Sometimes a Sunday School teacher. Sometimes a cleaner, a youth worker, the local organizer for Caritas. I've known the secretary in the Catholic bookshop – not the present one of course – a teacher in the religious school, a frustrated housewife who confesses a little too much, even a nun from the convent. You wouldn't believe it."

"No, I do, Isabel, I do. That's incredible. Thank you very much."

"No problem, Father. I hope you win the argument." She went to finally lay the cup on the table but Ramon took a deep breath and interrupted her. This was the moment. It would be much harder to broach the subject a second time.

"One more thing, Isabel. If you don't mind…"

"Certainly Father, though your coffee's getting cold."

Ramon studied the ceiling for a few seconds and knew he would never get a better chance. It had to be now.

"Isabel, I am a parish priest and you are my housekeeper." She said nothing. "I wonder if I can ask you something that a parish priest should never ask and his housekeeper should never have to answer." He took her silence for assent.

"If I felt I needed to 'dirty my hands a bit with the real world', as you put it, would you be able to help me – I mean, to make some inquiries? Discreetly, of course. Find some way it could be done? I know what I'm saying to you could be the end of my career. It's just that… well, I don't suppose you've noticed. Being a priest is a lonely job. Actually I'm at my wits' end. It might be this or jumping from the Giralda." He hoped a bit of humour might help soften his words but it wasn't that far from the truth. "I don't suppose a priest has ever asked you anything like that before. I know it's totally unreasonable. If you have the slightest hesitation just say no and we'll never mention it again. I promise."

Ramon looked up from the coffee cup in front of him, expecting to see a look of outraged hostility on Isabel's normally impassive features. She was looking as if he had just asked for another cup of coffee.

"Wrong again, Father Ramon," she said. "I've been asked that more often than Paco on the corner is asked for the bill. Forgive me for my hesitation. I thought you might be asking for my services. There was a time once but not any more. Let me ask *you* something. How long have you been here?"

"Em… about twenty months, isn't it? Not two years yet."

"That's probably about average. I've known one priest who asked that question – and not in such a delicate way I might add – in the first week. He didn't last. Forgive me again for plain speaking. My husband says it'll be the death of me but it saves time. You are young and you are new. You know your Catechism but you have no idea about your flock. You know how to say the mass and hear confession, but you know nothing about what's going through the minds of the men and women sitting in front of you – I suppose. Two things you need to learn. First, the people hold their priest in very high regard. They know something – not everything, but something – of what you've given up and they're grateful. They know you are a good man trying to live a good life and help them to do the same. And secondly, they also know you are not superhuman. And because they respect you they are willing to help you. I don't know if you're aware, Father, but you're actually quite popular. You keep the sermons short and smile a lot. When Father Jacob is on, every week's like a requiem. You make some jokes, you tell the children stories, you play the guitar and get us singing. They like you. I've already had several offers from women of the parish who would be quite keen to help you. But I've turned them all down. I was waiting until you were ready yourself. Now I have someone in mind who would be perfect. Someone who likes you, who isn't a neighbourhood whore, who's a good Catholic girl, and whose discretion will be absolute. I can guarantee it."

"Who?" Ramon asked, dumbfounded by every word.

"Maria. My youngest. She's only fifteen so don't expect experience. But she's a good girl and I know she'd be happy to help. You'll like her."

Isabel had brought Maria to the parish house a few times before and Ramon had not been blind to the charms of the carefree, playful girl who seemed to bring a spirit of effortless fun wherever she went. Yet again he couldn't believe his ears. First the bishop, now his housekeeper. For all his years in seminary and probationary posts he felt he had been absolutely clueless about the realities of the church. So there was a solution to his problem after all – and it wasn't in any sense unique to him. In fact, everyone seemed to think it was both normal and natural that he should break his consecration vows and jump into bed with one or more willing parishioners if the need arose. And the need had certainly arisen.

"I... I don't know what to say, Isabel," he stammered. "That's... that's incredibly kind of you."

"Don't thank me too soon, Father," Isabel responded, still utterly down to earth. "Let's try it out and see how it goes. If you're not happy there's no need to continue. I have some other ideas too. But Maria will do what she can to please you. I'll see to that. Saturday evening all right?" And with that he finally took a sip of the coffee. It was stone cold but he didn't care.

The following week passed in a blur. Day succeeded day, each with its requirements, obligations, and a certain amount of free time. He much preferred his busy times to the off-duty hours. At least while he was saying mass a certain amount of concentration was required. At home in the evening he could think of nothing else. Maria's face and figure danced in front of his eyes. As far as he remembered she was quite a well-developed girl for her age, maybe even a little overgenerous, but she seemed happy, even joyful, full of fun and utterly spontaneous – everything he was not. She almost reminded him of a girl he had once liked in the pueblo, but then he had been sixteen and she fourteen. Now Maria was fifteen and he was twenty-seven, something of a difference. Finally, feeling like he had passed through all eternity in the course of a week, Saturday arrived. He did some visiting in the morning and took a funeral in the afternoon. Then he went home, had a bath, and made himself a *bocadillo*. At about half past seven he heard the door and his heart almost burst out of his chest. He felt his throat as dry as sandpaper and his palms sweating. Isabel came bustling into the living room as if she were bringing him his morning paper. Maria came behind, smiling anxiously. She was wearing an orange polka dot *sevillanas* dress with a white shawl and bright red leather flamenco dance shoes. She looked utterly divine.

"Do you like it?" she asked nervously.

"Of course," Ramon replied. "You look very beautiful."

She blushed and smiled, dropping her eyes.

"Well then," Isabel interrupted. "That's fine then. I'll leave you two young people together. I'll be back at 8.30. Sharp." With that she turned on her heel and closed the door firmly behind her.

Ramon didn't know what to do or say next. They stood facing each other for ten or fifteen seconds. Finally he stepped forward and took her hand.

"God forgive me," he muttered and led her to the stairs.

Chapter 5

HACIENDA

"It all came out in the trial," Andrea said quietly.

She had sat, stone-faced, looking at the newspaper in front of her until only David, Gillian, and José were left around the table. She had made an attempt to begin explaining but only got a few words out before the dam broke. José held her hand, Gillian put an arm around her, and David got Juan to make more coffee. Explaining in English was beyond her so she switched to Spanish, which everyone but Gillian understood easily and even she got the gist of it.

"I think it had started with his housekeeper's daughter – pimped by her own mother, they said. That went on for a bit till the girl got pregnant and was sent away. Then kids in the youth group, boys and girls. He seemed to have got a taste for it and realized a priest can be really very powerful, especially in the south. Apparently it went on for years without anyone really paying attention. The prosecution case was not only that Ramon was guilty but that the bishop knew exactly what was happening and did nothing. Whenever anyone went to him to complain they were either fobbed off, threatened, or bribed. It was claimed that he told Ramon to stop but the prosecutors said he was only told to be more careful. The church claimed he was sent away for some sort of counselling or correction but personally I don't believe it. The judge found that Ramon was guilty of all sorts of child abuse and underage sexual activity and that the church was complicit more or less from the start. There was compensation for the victims, punitive damages against the church, the bishop was forced to retire, and Ramon got… I think it was twelve or thirteen years. So with good behaviour he must be out by now, I suppose.

"My mum told me about the killings. José said it was in the *Diario* a few days ago but I didn't really connect it. Then I saw Maite's name this morning. She was a victim too and we supported one another through the trial. When I saw her name it suddenly all fell into place. I counted back. It was about eight years ago the investigation started. The court invited witnesses to come forward. We went to the police station together. We were there for six hours. And that was just the first time. In the court the church lawyers tried to say we were lying but it was a bit half-hearted, as if they knew the game was up and they weren't really trying too hard. The only thing they really wanted was to show that Ramon was a maverick, an exception – one paedophile priest that was now a shock and a disgrace to the whole church. 'If only they'd known,' they kept on saying. Measures would now be put in place. But it was all rubbish. They knew and everyone knew they knew. Ramon went to prison but the church got away with it. Again. Now this. I'm sure he's back out. It looks like everyone who spoke against him is disappearing – one by one."

She flopped back in her chair, twisting a napkin in her hands.

"This is one of the reasons I left Spain. I just wanted to forget all about it and start again somewhere else where the church doesn't have such a grip. But it follows you wherever you go."

No one spoke for some time. José just sat squeezing Andrea's hand.

"I didn't know," he said finally. "I'm so sorry. I would never have mentioned it in the paper this morning if I'd thought."

Andrea shook her head.

"It's not your fault," she whispered. "It's not exactly something I tell everyone."

"I think you were incredibly brave to speak up in the first place," Gillian said in her best Spanish after taking some time to prepare what she wanted to say. "You helped stop the abuse for others and put him away. Whatever's going on now just shows what a dangerous man he was – and is. At least you're out of it."

David took a sip of coffee then cleared his throat.

"I'm actually not sure about that," he said. "I entirely understand that you wanted to get away, but somehow you've made a connection the local police don't seem to have made, or maybe didn't want to make…"

Gillian looked incredulous.

"Are you actually suggesting they would cover up a series of murders to protect the church?"

David shrugged.

"Stranger things have happened," he said, "especially given the history of Spain. What does it say?" He picked up the paper and scanned the report. "The former Bishop of Sevilla, a lawyer who used to work for the church, two other young people from Sevilla, one being your friend Maite. I think there are two issues now. Firstly, whether you want to speak up about the connection. There may be some other explanation and it's just a coincidence but maybe not. I know that would involve going back into something you'd much rather leave behind. That would be entirely your choice. The second thing I hesitate to mention… but if he's systematically going around everybody responsible for his conviction, then we have to think about your safety as well."

That brought the conversation to an abrupt halt. Andrea could be seen wilting where she sat. She dried her tears but didn't make eye contact with anyone. Juan, who had been tidying behind the bar but listening in to the conversation, gestured towards the coffee machine and David nodded.

"Whatever you decide, *chica*," José said quietly, "you know I'm here for you."

Andrea nodded. The coffee arrived and Juan whispered something in David's ear. He nodded again.

"Well, everyone," he said with some reluctance. "Juan lets us use the restaurant for chat but he'll have to open up for paying customers soon. We can continue at a corner table or go somewhere else. I'm afraid I can't stay much longer though. I've got something on this evening I need to prepare for. What do you think?"

Andrea knew it really depended on her and she only hesitated for a second before responding.

"There isn't really a lot of choice, is there?" she said. "There were more witnesses than the ones he's got to already. And everyone in the family and our neighbours know I'm here. I don't want to spend the next three years looking over my shoulder all the time. For all I know he could already be in Edinburgh…"

José squeezed her hand again and fired a glance at David. A thought had just struck him that he wasn't sure he should share.

"I need some time to think," she said. "Thanks for listening."

Ramon had little difficulty tracking down His Eminence Ignacio de Silva Fernández, former Bishop of Sevilla. Ignacio had had to leave the Bishop's Palace of course when he retired from official duties after the trial, but he had always found that the church looks after its own – with certain obvious exceptions. So he had taken up residence in a spare wing of a retreat centre on the outskirts of the city. Very pleasant really – away from the noise, traffic, and endless administration of a busy diocese. And also away from that horrible man who had tried to drag the whole church through the gutter just to protect his already sullied reputation. So the former bishop had settled down to a quiet life of reading, writing, helping out in some of the youth retreats, and generally reflecting on a life well lived and a ministry carried out with humility and discretion… except for its tawdry and wholly unjustified conclusion. Some days he almost thought he might like to come face to face with Ramon one last time to tell him exactly what he thought of him. Of course his sexual proclivities were entirely beyond the pale, but the bigger issue was the long-term damage done not only to one generation of young people associated with the Parish of Santa Ana but with tens of thousands – maybe even millions – across Spain who had followed the trial in the papers and on TV. Those who already had nothing to do with the church would be confirmed in their opinion and tell their drinking buddies and neighbours why. Those who might be occasional visitors at special masses and confession once a year would be less likely to do their duty. Those who were regulars might become more infrequent, and everyone would view the church in a less positive light. This was not just a matter of a couple of dozen youngsters, though he was willing to concede that it probably hadn't been a very pleasant experience for them either. This was a matter of the eternal security of millions of baptized Catholics who would be living their lives with less of the guidance and succour of the church and might indeed be passing beyond its grace without the necessary rites and rituals that would secure their eternal rest. Damn that man and all his doings.

It was a sunny evening. Ignacio – still known as "Little Nacho" to his aged aunts and uncles – was reclining in his garden rereading something of St Teresa for the hundredth time. His housekeeper brought him a plain envelope she said a boy had handed in at the gate but hadn't waited for a reply. He ripped it open and read. His housekeeper – an experienced woman in the service of the church who did not speculate on matters beyond her understanding – couldn't help but notice a cloud pass over the bishop's face. He evidently read the short note several times before making up his mind, then put it back in the envelope and dropped it by the side of his chair.

"Just some unfinished business from the parish, Loli. Nothing to worry about. Would you mind bringing me a glass of something? *Pacharán*, perhaps? Plenty of ice, please."

Next morning, he got up before dawn, dressed in his warmest overcoat, and headed out without disturbing any of the household. He started up the new Mercedes saloon the diocese had recently been so generous as to provide him with and headed north towards the foothills of the Sierra Morena. He knew exactly where he was going. The country park of El Gergal had been a favourite outing for prayer days and times of contemplation among the religious of the parish for as long as he could remember and he had been there many times both as a trainee, consecrated priest, and bishop. He even knew the spot the note referred to overlooking the reservoir.

His new Mercedes had satnav and lots of other gadgets the bishop had no need for. He turned them off and put on some beautiful choir music from the Carmelite convent in Ávila. He didn't know exactly what he would say but he had gone over matters so often in his mind he had no doubt the right words would come when required. No need to be harsh, but this was a time for straight talking.

North of Sevilla the ground began to rise up towards the Sierra and about an hour's drive brought him to the foothills and into the park. He left his car by the roadside, then walked a few hundred metres in the still relative cool of the morning and sat on a convenient rock to wait. He spent the time quietly, looking out over the water and humming one of the beautiful Carmelite chants.

"Bishop Ignacio. So good of you to come," he heard a familiar-sounding voice behind him say.

"Ramon," he replied, turning. "I'm here. I can hear your confession if you wish."

Ramon snorted.

"And what of yours, Little Nacho? Do you feel you have anything to confess?"

The former bishop stiffened at the insult.

"The church didn't do this to you, Ramon," he said. "You did it to yourself. You have no one else to blame. And you have done incalculable damage. More than you know. When any priest's calling becomes too much for them they have a duty to seek advice and if necessary move to another setting. Or retire. Or seek another profession. Or marry. Allowances can be made. There are dispensations. What you did has damaged the church in our region and in the whole of Spain. The words 'paedophile' and 'priest' seem to go together everywhere nowadays. That's what we are in the public mind – not ministers of God, not servants of the people, not even teachers and guides. We are depraved child abusers and parasites, and you are to blame. You and others like you. If you had pleaded guilty the whole thing could have been dealt with in a week and the damage and publicity limited. But dragging it out for three months and calling dozens of witnesses, calling us all liars and perverts... even me, Ramon. You left us with no choice. We had to respond. What did you expect – kid gloves? You did it to yourself. You shouldn't complain now."

Ramon had sat down on another rock nearby and listened with a half smile on his face. He had waited seven years for this moment and there was no need to rush. All in good time.

"Well, Nacho. What an interesting point of view. A pity it's wrong in every respect. The church is the architect of its own downfall, not me. It's a hangover from the medieval world trying to survive in the wrong century. You haven't even come to terms with the Reformation, never mind the modern world. You lure young people into your service with the promise that they'll be serving God, then it turns out they're only there to keep the wheels going round; to keep the populace compliant and the money rolling in; to keep the ear of the state and all the privilege that goes with it – though you've lost that as well nowadays. And you refuse to allow young men to have normal and appropriate relationships, so what do you expect? If you believe we are as God made us, then why deny the fundamental drives he placed inside? It's like telling a teenager to stop breathing or eating or sleeping because they're just distractions from homework. So you force us to bottle everything up till the dam bursts. Just like the lake down there. The rain falls and the wind hammers away, making the water deeper and the walls weaker. What do you suppose is going to happen?"

Ignacio sighed and looked around him. If he had had any hope of helping Ramon see sense that had dissipated in the tirade.

"And what of you, Ramon?" he asked. "Are you a happier, more contented man with all these ugly thoughts? Are you closer to God now that you hate his Holy Church?"

"We're not here to talk about me, Little Nacho," Ramon replied quietly.

"So what are we here for then? Did you ask me here just to insult everything I've given my life for?"

"Not at all," Ramon smiled. "These are just preliminaries. I want you to understand what I'm going to do before I do it. You see, it's not just about the church – though that's bad enough. The people are complicit too. After all these centuries of programming they expect the priest to be their servant and ask nothing in return. They want their confessions heard, their miseries comforted, their sons and daughters welcomed – and all from the ever present, ever helpful, priest. They might drop a few *céntimos* in the plate if they remember but that's it. They pay with their devotion to the church and the Virgin but they simply have no idea – or don't want to know – what it costs the priest. 'What an easy job,' they say. 'The one-day week. He just stands up there and goes through the script then goes home for lunch.' No unemployment, no poverty, no hunger, no night shifts, no crisis for the priest. Well they don't know, do they? Remember that time I came to you and asked for guidance? I was on the point of killing myself. I couldn't see a way forward to go on meeting the needs of the people while I was being torn apart. And you laughed at me, Nacho. Yes you did. I remember it like yesterday. You told me not to take myself so seriously and to 'find a friend'. So I took your advice. I found lots of friends. It was the only way to carry on. So the people got what they thought the priest should give them. And I got something too. I think of it as a bit like taxation. Remember the myths about when the villagers had to sacrifice a virgin or two to keep the monster satisfied and stop the village being destroyed? Well it's not that different. Triana kept its priest. I did the baptisms, the first communions, the confessions, the marriages, births, and deaths. I listened to all their pathetic tales and kept them happy. But there was a price to pay. Then the church saw its interests in jeopardy, so the first whiff of scandal and the drawbridge came up. Poor Ramon was left outside. No one spoke up for me, Nacho. Nobody. None of the years of hard work mattered any more. It was protect the church; protect its reputation. Now I was the one who had to be sacrificed. And you have a happy retirement in your garden reading the classics. Yes, I was watching you, Nacho. Very nice."

The former bishop was silent for a time. When he finally spoke his voice was old and tired.

"I had hoped we could have some reconciliation, Ramon," he said. "I can see now that was a foolish hope of an old man. You are my one failure, the one big mistake I made. I should have kicked you out right away that day you came to me. I should never have tried to help you. You weren't worth it then and you're not worth it now. So, I ask you once again, Ramon. What are we here for if there's nothing positive to be said? Bitter words are sometimes better left unsaid. You will never find peace with God or with your own conscience when you have so much anger in your heart. You must find a way of freeing your spirit, of healing the hurt."

"Oh, but I have a way, Nacho, I really do," Ramon replied with a smile, getting up from the rock he was sitting on. "I have exactly the right way to deal with my feelings, the church, the people, and you."

Ignacio looked worried for the first time.

"Good God, man. What are you going to do?"

"This," Ramon replied, and before Ignacio could move or respond he bent down, picked up a rock the size of a melon, and brought it down with all the force he could on the old man's head. The former bishop's face was twisted into a grimace of horror and surprise as he fell forward. Ramon dealt him a second blow behind the ear as he went down and a third as he lay prone on his face. The dry soil quickly darkened with blood.

"Bless me, Father, for I have sinned," Ramon whispered before throwing the rock aside. He glanced quickly around, then dragged the now lifeless body to the edge overlooking the dam. Quickly he pulled a canvas sack from the small haversack at his feet and began loading it with stones. When it felt heavy enough he pulled the drawcord tight, then tied it round the old man's feet. Finally, satisfied, he stood back to admire his work and gave the body a push.

"Goodbye, Little Nacho," he whispered. "May you have all the peace you deserve."

With a slither and rattle of loose stones the body slid down the steep rocks, into the water, and disappeared with a splash and a few bubbles.

"Number one," said Ramon, smiling as he headed back towards the path. The Plan was taking shape very nicely.

Chapter 6

WEST NICOLSON STREET

The Blind Poet pub on West Nicolson Street ("Beer is my religion, the Blind Poet is my church") was the Rationalist Society's favoured watering hole after meetings and was always busy on a Saturday night even before the rationalists arrived. The famous Stevie Agnew Band played on a Wednesday night – so, wonderful as it was, at least they didn't have to compete with an eclectic set ranging from "Shine On You Crazy Diamond" to "I Wanna be Like You (Ooh, Ooh)". Despite the crush, Dr Stephen Baranski managed to make it from the bar to the corner table balancing a tray of drinks with only minor spillage.

"Ok, gin and tonic for the lady," he began, putting a tall glass in front of Gillian. "Cuba Libre for another lady. Red wine for the Italian. Pint of lager for the Spaniard – bit out of character I would have thought – and a real ale for the American. Everybody happy? Cheers."

Glasses were chinked and the brew sampled, followed by a communal sigh of contentment. David Hidalgo and Gillian sat side by side. Next to them was Sandy Benedetti, then Stephen Baranski, and finally his latest female companion, the very long-legged, very blonde, but also brain-the-size-of-a-planet Fran McGoldrick, originally from Waikato University in New Zealand but currently jobbing in Edinburgh University's Linguistics Department. She was always up for a good-looking, bright enough bloke to hang out with and Dr Stephen Baranski was currently fitting the bill.

"Well, I have to say, David," Stephen began, wiping his lips, "full marks for showing up in the first place. And for your performance. That's the weirdest defence of the Christian faith I have ever heard, but maybe the most effective too. I think it got lots of people thinking in ways we're not used to."

"Glad to oblige," David responded, unwinding over another sip of the amber nectar while also feeling his usual vague sense of something missing in a Scottish bar without a tapa in sight. Well, at least the beer was cold.

"Told you so," Gillian put in with a slightly smug look as if to say, *That shook you all up a bit, didn't it?*

"Very interesting," Fran commented. "I wouldn't call myself either a believer or an unbeliever, though I hope I'm at least rational about it. But what you said made a lot of sense. I'll be thinking about it a bit more."

"What I liked," Stephen continued, "was the complete absence of appeals to bogus 'proofs' – philosophical or scientific – unlike your leader in the debate. That gets us precisely nowhere. You say 'fine tuning' and I say 'multiverse'. You say 'moral law' and I say 'the evolution of altruism'. You say 'intelligent design' and I say 'bollocks'. For every watertight proof there's some bloke with a sharper penknife who's going to cut it open. And anyway, even if the proof seems to work right now it's all God of the Gaps anyway. Next week the Large Hadron Collider comes up with some new theory of physics that blows it all out of the water – to mix my metaphors somewhat. You were talking about human nature, which I think is a lot less changeable. What was it – 'Eternity in the heart of man'? Very nice."

"And very poetic," Fran put in.

"*De nada*," David murmured, though he was somewhat surprised and certainly gratified by the response. Stephen's earlier interest in Gillian was long past and forgotten as an honest and indeed very understandable mistake.

"No, I'm serious," Stephen pressed on. "I think you made a very good point that when we talk about the need for 'evidence'," he did the mid-air inverted commas gesture, "that needn't only be interpreted in a scientific sense. There's also the concept of courtroom evidence. We use exactly the same word – as you pointed out. It isn't the same sort of evidence but it's still valid. In any case absolute proof is only possible in mathematics, which a few of my colleagues seem to forget. So an individual's testimony in the legal sense does mean something if God is primarily relational – as you claim – and not just a philosophical idea to be batted about.

"And you're saying that you can only know if there is a God by being willing to enter into a relationship with another mind, another personality. Until you get to that personal place of engaging you're not really in the game at all."

"I think so," David replied, taking another sip. "I liken it to playing poker for matchsticks. Nobody really cares who wins; it's artificial. It's only when there's real money on the table that it actually matters what cards turn up."

"Nicely put. And where do you fit into this, Dr Lockhart?" Stephen gestured with his drink in Gillian's direction. "Playing your cards close to your chest?"

"Maybe," she smiled and took another sip of the G and T. "On a journey, I think I'd say."

"And any encounter with this other 'mind' yet?"

"Stephen, that's too personal," Fran complained. "Just ignore him."

"No. It's ok," Gillian answered. "It's a fair question. I was sort of the red corner opposing the motion even though I didn't speak. I think I'd say 'yes'. I've had some encounters. It's sometimes not so easy to pull apart what you want, what you're hoping for, what's your imagination, and what's real, but I'd say 'yes'. It feels real. Jury's out but I think the evidence is looking quite strong."

"Very interesting. And what about the Italian gentleman? Keeping very quiet. Just enjoying his Lambrusco?"

"Just glad it's not Lambrusco for starters," Sandy replied. "No, just listening and learning. Remember I'm more of a numbers man. I like things you can count. It all gets a bit philosophical for me."

"But I think David's pushing us to be less philosophical, isn't he? Or less theoretical anyway. I think you're on 'team Hidalgo', aren't you? At Southside Church? So you must have a view."

"I do," Sandy replied quietly.

"And…?"

"All I can say is that faith changed my family. There were things we needed to see work out and we prayed and had a strong feeling it was in higher hands. Things didn't necessarily go the way we wanted but we would definitely say there's been a higher power – a personality, if that's what you want to call it."

"Fair enough," Stephen acceded. Sandy Benedetti's financial misdeeds and appearance in court had been well reported in both the local and national press. There wasn't any need to press him on what sorts of things they might have needed to see "work out".

"So what do you think the rationalists all made of it then?" Gillian asked. "I mean, we lost the vote by about a million."

"Well, that doesn't mean very much." Stephen shook his head. "That was always going to happen. The point is to make people think. For my sins I'm president of the society but even I think they need shaken up a bit. Lots of lazy thinking. Lots of 'what everyone knows' – you know, received opinion that never gets challenged among a like-minded peer group. Oh, and by the way, I need to apologize for the personal attack. That's never justified. We'll have a word."

"You mean the little Spanish guy?" David half laughed.

"I think Italian. But yes, you know who I mean."

"Definitely not Italian," Sandy put in quite firmly.

"Well, he says he's Italian," Fran said.

"He may say that but he's not. I can hear it in the accent. Mediterranean but definitely not Italian."

"What's his name anyway?" Gillian asked.

"Andretti. Nicolas Antonio, I think. He hasn't actually been around that long – though maybe that's not his name at all if he's not even Italian. Anyway, whatever. There's no excuse for that tirade. It seemed to be personally directed at you. All religion as diabolical but you seemed to be particularly in the firing line. It was definitely a little weird. We do not allow *ad hominem* abuse. The committee with be chatting with Signore Andretti or whoever he is."

"It doesn't bother me," David assured them. "I've been called a lot worse. But he was a very angry man. I wonder what's at the back of it?"

"Indeed. Anyway, a stimulating evening. So thanks again for your contribution. Cheers."

"See, it wasn't as bad as all that," Gillian murmured as they walked back across the Meadows towards her flat in Marchmont and his in Bruntsfield. The evening light had almost failed but the air was still warm and fragrant. Some cherry blossom was on the trees and the rest was under their feet like a long oriental rug. "If you ignore that little agitator everyone was at least civil, and you clearly made them think a bit."

"Yes, I dare say. Who'd have thought it? Still way out of my comfort zone though."

"Well, Stephen was positively glowing. For a man out of his comfort zone you seemed remarkably relaxed."

"Prozac is a wonderful thing. Anyway, I don't consider it my job to try to convince anyone. That's far too mysterious a process. So I suppose I don't need to get hung up on a 'performance'."

"Well, for a non-performance it seemed to go remarkably well."

They walked on for a bit in silence breathing in the Edinburgh air, a unique mixture of hops from the local breweries, the scent of the blossom, the grassy smell of the first cut of the year over the Meadows, and a certain whiff of traffic fumes. Gillian gripped David's arm a little more tightly and spoke again.

"On another subject, what do you make of today's other bit of drama?"

"You mean Andrea? Horrific," David said without hesitation. "It makes me embarrassed to go out and defend anything that might be called 'religion'."

"What do you make of the story?"

"Incredible. But what she said seems entirely plausible. I've read about some of the stuff coming out of Spain. There seem to be more revelations every month. Apparently Granada and the south was a particular hotspot so it seems to have been going on there or thereabouts. The bit I still can't get my head around though is how she's been able to put it all together when the local police either can't or won't. It should be so much more obvious on the scene."

"Agreed. I think we smell a rat, don't we?"

"We certainly do."

"But the big question, if she's right, is – has he got to the end of his list yet and is Andrea on it? And what the implications might be if he hasn't and she is."

Gillian gripped David's arm a little tighter still.

"The question that always strikes me," she added, "is how such a thing is possible in the first place. I mean, we don't hear about a plague of paedophile plumbers, do we? Priests are supposed to be the ones their congregations look up to, not have to guard themselves against."

"True," David sighed, "all too true. I'm quite relieved no one mentioned it tonight. It's indefensible – and inexplicable. Do these men choose a calling that somehow suits their weaknesses or does a celibate life with that amount of opportunity and power just prove too much?"

"Maybe it's a kind of rage against their circumstances. Lashing out at the restrictions?"

"Could be. It's a mystery. There but for the grace of God…"

"But remember," she said gently, "it was the very work you were doing that caused your tragedy. Did you never feel like lashing out against God or against someone else?"

David was silent for a moment, reflecting. "No, I don't think I did," he said finally. "I was disillusioned. Flattened, in fact. Hopeless and getting quite cynical. But I never felt like taking it out on anyone else. I guess I wasn't a very nice guy to be around for a while but it was more turned in than out. No one around me had done me any harm. How did it seem to you? You were there through some of it."

"You had a habit of just going quiet," she said, looking into the distance over the Meadows. "Just zoning out. That used to worry me. I felt you were going somewhere I couldn't reach. But you always seemed to come back, eventually. I simply couldn't imagine you deliberately hurting someone else to relieve your own anxiety. It's just not you."

"Well, that's a relief. But since we're speaking candidly, you know it was you that brought me back. Whether God sent you or you came of your own accord, you were the one that changed everything."

Gillian squeezed his arm again.

"You know what Juan would say to that, don't you?"

"Yes," David laughed. "I do. 'And where do you think Gillian appeared from?'" He put on a passing resemblance of Juan's English with a heavy Castilian accent. "'Out of a magic box? She's a gift from God, my friend. *Seguro.*' That part I definitely agree with."

"I love you, Señor David."

"I'm glad. Maybe if the priest had had someone who loved him things might have been different."

"Well, it definitely doesn't hurt."

"I'm glad nothing like that came up in the debate tonight. You end up trying to defend something that seems completely corrupted by the behaviour of its main exponents. In a way, at least the thugs in charge of Power and Glory Church last year had a bit more honesty about them. They were in it simply for the money and didn't care who was brutalized along the way. That was crime, plain and simple, if you like. This is hypocrisy of the highest order. It just makes my blood boil."

"Well, calm down, honey. I wasn't asking to get you worked up. I was just wondering whether you think there's anything we can do to help Andrea now it's all come back to haunt her."

"I don't know… listening, I suppose. Maybe she won't want to share it all that widely."

"José seems like a solid friend."

"Looks like it. That's lucky for her. Far from home and nobody to support her isn't good."

They had reached the end of Jawbone Walk and paused at the lights on Melville Drive. By this time on a Saturday night it seemed that every second car was a black cab. Maybe half the others were doing pick ups on the fly but you could never tell. The lights changed, the traffic eased to a stop, the green man lit up, and they hurried across.

"What do you think she'll decide?" Gillian asked as they made their way up the hill into Marchmont.

"I don't know. She seems quite a robust individual. She's certainly had a lot to cope with. It must be like the final reel of a horror film – you know, when things look like they've settled down, then the nutcase with the axe pops up again."

"But you've got contacts in the Spanish police. Couldn't we ask Andrea if she would want us to get in touch and tell them what we think?"

David grimaced.

"I could," he said, "but that would feel like going over Andrea's head, like forcing her hand. Whatever connection there might be, it's her evidence…"

"And you've got some other things on your mind right now, I suppose. Well, I hope so anyway!"

"True. We seem to have found ourselves sucked into all sorts of weird stuff in the last year and a bit. Bad planning or recklessness, I'm not sure. Maybe if I book the hall and the honeymoon that'll keep us out of trouble. Which reminds me – I was speaking to Ali the other morning and he says Ayeesha is getting into outside catering and cakes. Have we got anyone lined up for the cake?"

"Not exactly. I was thinking of putting it out to tender on *The Great British Bake Off* but they might have difficulty modelling Calatrava La Nueva Castle."

"Oh – anything but that. I don't like even thinking about it. But seriously, what do you think?"

"We can certainly talk about it. She could show me what she's done in the past. Just so long as it's a normal fruit cake and not the South Asian variation. Delicious I'm sure, but just not my style."

"I think we can specify that – though it might cost more. But I'll insist, because you're worth it."

"You are a smoothie, you know. Why not invite them for dinner some evening and we can talk about it?"

"I had the same idea. I said to Ali I'd discuss it with you."

"But anyway, just before we get lost in wedding cakes and holidays, I'm happy that we support Andrea and you can even speak to the police but no more than that, please. No running off to Spain to corner a killer. Promise you'll stay in Edinburgh at least. If he comes here looking for her that's another matter, but low profile is the key. Ok?"

"Of course." David turned and gave her a promissory kiss.

"So are you planning to pass this on?"

"I don't see how we can avoid it – if Andrea agrees. It's her evidence and she has to explain it herself. I can't say it for her. She's seems like a brave girl though. I have a feeling she'll speak up when the time comes."

"So an informal word? What about Stuart McIntosh. Is he still detecting?"

"As far as I know. I'm actually seeing him tomorrow for lunch. We still get together from time to time. I think he considers me partly responsible for his career advancement. I'll mention it and see what he says. It's a serious issue even if the guy never sets foot outside of Spain."

They walked on for a bit in companionable silence up towards Gillian's flat on Marchmont Road.

"So. Señor Hidalgo," Gillian finally announced, fumbling for her keys. "Thank you for graciously getting me out of trouble. Another successful foray into the lion's den. Care to come up for a coffee?"

"You wouldn't be the spider inviting me into her web, would you?"

"Absolutely. But it's a very nice web. And no rival spiders or flies about."

"I'm sold. Just for a coffee, you understand. Lead me to my doom."

She deftly turned the key in the lock and ushered him in.

Andrea had left the Saturday chat group with more to think about than she'd expected. She set off home on foot to try to clear her mind. Was it better to know or not know? Probably the pieces would have fallen into place sometime, and while being a long way from home meant she didn't have friends and family around her, surely that distance would make her safer. If – and it was the big if – if she was right, if it was Ramon out of prison and bent on some sort of killing spree for all those involved in his downfall, if he remembered her evidence, which had been quite brief, if he considered her part of the whole affair, and if he was prepared to even travel outside of Spain to take his twisted revenge: if all these ifs lined up then she should be worried. But it was a lot of ifs. *Don't panic yet*, she thought. Why let an uncertain future blight a perfect present? Apart from the shadowy figure of Ramon, the present was very good. Whenever she had told friends in Sevilla that she was moving to Edinburgh the answer was almost always the same. *Wow. ¡Escocia! Qué bonito. ¡Buena suerte!* (How lovely. Good luck!) Perhaps there had always been something in the back of her mind about living in a foreign city, but now the crisis had made a virtue of necessity and she'd been here almost three months. Edinburgh was "awesome" but there was still the rest of the country to explore. She was determined to get to *Los Highlands* whenever she had a few days off. Maybe catch a glimpse of the monster – they were sure to ask back home. But if not, at least climb some mountains, fish in some "lochs", swim from some beaches (the lack of a beach was one of the few failings of Sevilla), see wild deer, listen to the pipe band, go to a folk concert, maybe even find out once and for all what's under the kilt – another question she was endlessly asked. She'd already tried haggis and liked it – it was not too unlike something similar they make in Burgos. Fish and chips was of course a great tradition and she loved the way people were so relaxed and could eat an entire meal in the street, something Spaniards would never dare to do. The weather was pretty criminal of course but so was Sevilla at the opposite extreme. Something strange in Spanish could be referred to as "*una maravilla, como la lluvia en Sevilla*" – a marvel, like rain in Sevilla! So even the frequently overcast skies and rain showers weren't an excessive price to pay. You didn't need aircon and you didn't need to dodge from shade to shade to move about the city.

The word "criminal" jerked her thoughts back to Ramon. His actions had been criminal in the past; now here he was – if she was right – compounding it. She couldn't imagine a state of mind so bitter and vengeful and didn't want to try. What would she do if the worse came to the worst, if somehow he were traced to Edinburgh – if he had come hunting for her? Should she just move back to Valencia? Or lose herself in Madrid? Or move on somewhere else? Anxious and nervous as she was, she was determined that wasn't the way. Why should she let a man who had already stolen so much of her childhood keep on taking what was rightfully hers? She was here: working, living, making friends, maybe with the prospect of some romance around the corner. Ramon would not be allowed to steal these dreams too. She would stay where she was and fight for what was hers. Let him come; she wasn't so innocent and compliant now. Whatever happened, he would have a fight on his hands. And if it was really nothing, then so much the better. Prior to Maite, the press reports said the last killing had been months ago and the police said they still didn't have a single lead to go on. Maybe whatever had been going on had already run its course and now she was worrying about nothing. Perhaps it would be like a lump you find that turns out to be benign and has already disappeared by the time you get to the doctor. Maybe it was all just worrying about something that had already come and gone. That was a more positive thought.

While Andrea had been walking in half a dream down South Clark Street and the Bridges then easing through the Saturday bustle at the East End before heading down Leith Walk, José had made an excuse outside Hacienda about having to do some shopping. He headed in the other direction, then turned as soon as he was sure Andrea was out of sight and went back to the restaurant. He managed to catch David and Gillian just leaving. They had a brief conversation on the doorstep that left him grim-faced but at least satisfied. He set off after Andrea, hoping to catch her before she got home.

David arrived early for church on Sunday morning as he always did but was rarely early enough to steal a march on the redoubtable Irene MacInnes, who always seemed to be up with whatever birds woke up the larks.

"There we are," she announced as he came in the swing doors. "All ready for the onslaught."

They had recently decided to swap the order so that rather than tea and coffee afterwards, people were encouraged to come early, grab a latte or Earl Grey, and catch up with friends – or get to know someone new – before things really got going. It was an experiment but seemed to be working well.

"Teaspoons at the ready as ever, Mrs MacInnes," David replied, hanging up his coat and sticking his grey felt fedora on the hook above. Mrs MacInnes adjusted the angle of the trolley slightly, shoogled the biscuit tin a fraction, and wiped her hands on her pinny.

"It's getting hard to know how many cups to put out. So many people seem to be coming early these days. Still, it's a good problem to have I suppose."

"Indeed it is. But I understand it can make things awkward."

"Well, you wouldn't want people turning up and nothing to wet their digestive biscuit on, would you?"

"Sure."

She made a few more minor adjustments before speaking again.

"And how is, I mean how are... em... you know... all the preparations?" Mrs MacInnes had a rare note of hesitation in her voice. Normally, she was a woman who could call a spade a spade as if she had a lifetime of navvying behind her, but she instinctively recognized that asking a potential groom about plans for the wedding was a bit like asking roller coaster riders to do hard sums midway through the ride. They just didn't have it in them. And men, in Mrs MacInnes's long and conclusive experience, simply could not do flowers, invitations, booking of premises, catering, decorating the hall, shows of presents, or choosing the menu. Getting them to choose a best man and show up on time to say "I do" was the limit, which she'd managed once and once was enough.

"Good, I think," David replied, trying to sound in control and optimistic.

"Hmm," Mrs MacInnes replied, shorthand for *I thought as much*.

"You know," she continued, "we just love Gillian. She has been so good for us all, not just you. A breath of fresh air, in fact. Keeps us fuddy-duddies going. I think new points of view are good for us."

She seemed to be in a chatty mood this morning and with no one else in the building David thought he would try his luck.

"Mrs MacInnes, can I ask you something?" he began. "You know Gillian isn't really from a church background. She does see things differently, as you say. She's on a journey but I don't think it's likely she's going to be on the platform giving her testimony any time soon. Do you think people see that as a problem?"

Mrs MacInnes paused only for an instant.

"Only if people think it's preferable to have our minister in the Royal Ed.," she replied, referring to the city's psychiatric hospital.

"Is that how bad it looked?"

"Worse. When you first came here I was on the point of bringing you a cup of cocoa last thing at night just to check you hadn't put your head in the oven. The change has been, well, remarkable. We believe God is in control and he works things out in his own way, but Gillian Lockhart was without a doubt the means. So, I think I'd say nobody gives a hoot. Well, nobody that matters anyway. So you just get on with the planning and don't worry. I'll look after any grumblers there might be. You can be sure of that."

David was certain of that and felt reassured. It was just something he had to check from time to time.

Just then the door swung open behind him and the first coffee hunters came in, leading up to the usual logjam about fifteen minutes before starting time. Teas, coffees, and conversations were in full swing when a face appeared at the door David recognized but would not have expected.

"Fran?" he asked, trying to sound welcoming rather than dumbfounded. "Nice to see you. Come in. There's tea and coffee on the go."

"I know," she replied brightly. "Gillian told me to get here early so as not to miss the buzz."

David queue jumped without a conscience and grabbed her a coffee.

"I have to ask," he began once they were both sorted, "what brings you here? Stephen would be scandalized."

"Well, that as may be; however, atheism won't be the only thing we differ on. For example, he likes sushi, which I find even more inexplicable. No, I think I'd call myself a seeker still. I'm not dogmatic on God or no God. I think you've got to be willing to expose yourself to the other point of view and see what's changed when the dust settles. Know what I mean?"

"I do. I had to go through that myself some years ago – as I explained at the debate."

"I remember. I thought that was actually quite brave. A formal debate can be quite a pressured environment. People claim to be passionate about whatever they're pushing but it can be all about scoring points and showing off. To actually talk about something that changed your life in a personal way and expose yourself to however people might react is pretty unusual. And I think it went down well, at least among the open minded."

"Like you?"

"Like me. I had a word with Gillian just as you were leaving the bar the other night and thought I'd come along and hear a bit more, from the horse's mouth, so to speak. We agreed to meet here just before eleven."

"And here comes the lady now," David remarked as Gillian came in the door.

"Hi Fran," she said. "Wasn't sure if you'd make it."

"I managed to get off the leash for a bit. Left Stephen reading the Sundays."

"Well, I think I have to leave you intellectuals together while I cobble together a few disjointed thoughts."

With that David headed down the aisle, had a quick word with Juan on the PA, smiled at the beatific but enormous Alicia, and stepped up onto the platform. Fran and Gillian sat together. Fran was leaning slightly forward. *This might be interesting*, she thought.

David did his customary introduction and welcome then stepped down to hand over to the worship team. He didn't notice a stocky man of average height with a beard and black beret slip into the back row.

Chapter 7

SEVILLA

Luis Castillo Herrero gave a grunt of disgust and snapped the file in front of him shut. He took his glasses off and rubbed first the bridge of his nose then his temples. It was ridiculous. The law was expected to be somewhat arcane or else how could it be preserved as "a conspiracy against the laity", as George Bernard Shaw had so neatly put it. It was essential to maintain some boundaries; otherwise every Tom, Dick, and Harry would be submitting affidavits and appearing in court. Instead Spain remained one of the most lawyer-heavy countries in Europe. He'd read there were more lawyers in Madrid than in the whole of Germany and he wouldn't have been surprised. In any case, as good fences make good neighbours, so good law and good lawyers make for an ordered and rigourous society. That was fair enough but the contents of the file in front of him still made him fume. His client was not a poor man – breeding top quality fighting bulls was still a profitable business, though for how long was open to question. Anyway, Señor Gonzalez had lots of cash and had recently found another potential Señora Gonzales to share it with. In any civilized country that was not going to be much of an issue, but bull breeders are notoriously traditional in their views, which in Spain meant devoutly Catholic. The hitch was that the Catholic Church still maintained its traditional attitude to divorce, a matter Señor Castillo also had personal reason to regret. It was said by critics that from the church's point of view it was preferable to be a mass murderer than divorced and remarried because then at least you could confess, be forgiven, and get on with life. Those who had remarried outside the church were considered to be committing the sin of adultery against a previous partner or partners continually. Or maybe, in reality, twice a week plus extra in the holidays. What was the point of being forgiven when you just go straight back home and do it all again? So ways had to be found for the faithful – and generous donors – to slip the bonds of matrimony in ways acceptable to the church. It cost money and it needed lawyers. Castillo was happy about the money, but after almost forty years practising on behalf of the church and in religious affairs, he didn't really need more. What he needed was less hassle running down rabbit holes in search of legal fictions that got those the church considered worthy off the hook.

So grounds for annulment had to be found related to the state of the parties *before* vows were exchanged. Were they free to marry? Did they freely exchange consent? Did they intend to marry for life, be faithful to one another, and have children if the Lord so provided? Finally, did they intend "good for each other" and exchange vows before witnesses in a ceremony overseen by a church official? Obviously, as in all matters of motivation, this made for exceedingly muddy waters. What people had intended twenty or thirty years ago was not often easily provable and inevitably meant for lots of mud-slinging if one party didn't want to go quietly. "Medieval" was a high tariff insult in Castillo's book, reserved for things that deeply offended or frustrated him: everything from hospital waiting times to the ban on smoking in bars. This whole business he considered "*positively* medieval". But the client was paying and the church wanted it to go through so here he was labouring over the file for hours at a time when all his colleagues, secretaries, and even the cleaner had gone home on a Friday night. Anyway, enough was definitely enough. Having managed to swing his own divorce and remarriage last year, he was now heading home to little Conchita for a delicious supper and a relaxing weekend.

He stood up and stretched the stiffness out of his back. Maybe a bath and a massage too. Nice. He picked up the file, locked it in a drawer, turned off his desk lamp, and wandered through to the back office to check all the lights were off. It was then he heard something he didn't expect – a knock at the front door. No one should have been able to get into the main entrance lobby without being buzzed in from one of the offices that shared the building, and he was pretty sure everyone else had shut up shop long ago. Even if someone else had let a caller in they would surely be visiting their offices, not his. Well, this was one late night consultation that would take about thirty seconds. He clicked the main light on again and went out to the entrance foyer. A peek through the spy hole showed a middle-aged man he didn't recognize with a bushy black beard and a black beret. He seemed to be standing somewhat awkwardly as if holding something heavy out of sight. Well, he'd be sent packing in a moment, and then the new Audi A7 would be purring out of the underground garage and off into the suburbs. He pulled back the catch and opened the door. He hardly had time to draw a breath for what he was about to say when the blow hit him squarely on the temple. He went down like a chainsawed tree, heavily banging the opposite side of his head against the door jamb.

By the time Señor Castillo came to, he found himself tightly bound to his own office chair, some sort of adhesive patch over his mouth and a pain in his head such as he had never experienced before. It made him feel so sick he could hardly take in where he was or what was happening. The office lights were mainly still off as he had left them, though his desk light was back on shining directly into his face. What was outside its arc of light he couldn't tell. He sat silent and numb for several minutes, blinking and trying to calm his breathing. Behind the patch he could taste blood. The urge to panic was almost overwhelming but he tried to master it given that he could hardly breathe as it was. *What had happened? Who had been at the door? Was the visitor still here or was he alone?* He could hardly form the questions in the face of a profound confusion and disorientation. Then he dimly noticed movement behind the light.

"Señor Castillo. Nice of you to join us. How are you feeling?"

The short man with the beard but no longer wearing the beret leaned forward and angled the desk lamp upwards. The beam bounced off the ornate plaster ceiling, reflecting a soft glow back over the entire room. Castillo could make no reply and didn't try.

"Oh, sorry. You seem somewhat incapacitated. Let me help."

The man leaned further forward and pulled the adhesive patch roughly off his mouth. Castillo gasped and retched. Blood, saliva, and vomit dribbled down his chin.

"Who are you?" he managed to get out.

"Don't remember?" the man asked in a tone of mock politeness. "Dear me. So many cases. So many clients. So many problems to solve. Let me remind you. The Parish of Santa Ana, eight years ago. A renegade priest in danger of damaging the spotless reputation of the Holy Church. The press sniffing about. Something had to be done. And it was. Safely quarantined. Then the firm of Castillo *Abogados* could quietly move on to other matters."

"Ramon?" the lawyer whispered. "Ramon from Santa Ana?"

"The same." The man smiled at him. "Back from the dead, more or less. D'you know being in prison is a lot like being dead? Except your friends don't remember you with affection. They try not to remember you at all, in fact. Dead and buried, while still continuing to breathe and eat and such like. But the big difference of course is that sooner or later – in most cases – you come back from the dead to haunt the living. So here I am. Consider yourself officially haunted."

Ramon gave a short bitter laugh at his joke, leaned forward again, and slapped Castillo sharply across the face.

"Don't fade away on me now," he said. "I need you to pay attention. Now, where was I?"

"But what do you want with me?" the lawyer slurred through the blood and loose teeth. "You were prosecuted by the state, not by me. Not by the church."

"True-*ish*. That may be the official position for the benefit of the readers of the *Diario*. But we know the truth, don't we? We have that in common. You with your nice house in the suburbs and a nice new wife too I believe. Conchita isn't it? We had a lovely chat earlier today."

"What have you done? Have you harmed her?"

"Not much. I think we got on splendidly. She'll recover – which is more than I can say for you, my friend. Still, we're getting ahead of ourselves. I was guilty, prosecuted by the state, and sentenced to rot in Morón de la Frontera for fourteen years. Out with good behaviour in seven. Do you know they don't even have air conditioning in prison yet? It's inhuman. 'Medieval' I think you used to say, didn't you? So I wasn't able to eat in Casa Pepé, drive a nice new Audi, make lots of money from the many and various ways the church still fleeces the flock, and at the end of every day go home to the lovely Conchita. And she is lovely, I'll grant you that."

"You beast," Castillo spat out. "They should never have let you out."

"But they did. And here I am."

"What do you want? If it's money, I can tell you the safe combination. There's 80,000 Euros on the premises. I can get more."

"Oh, I dare say you can. Money's not of interest. Well, not of primary interest. But you can tell me the number anyway. It wouldn't hurt."

Castillo did so, told Ramon where the safe was, and watched helplessly as funds held in safekeeping for an important client were unceremoniously dropped into a canvas shoulder bag and dumped at the door.

"So, back to the main event. Why am I here? I am here, Señor Castillo, because you, in your role as primary counsel to the diocese of Sevilla, advise the church on legal matters. That includes matters where the church is involved, though may not be either plaintiff or defendant – as in my case, for example. And, like all lawyers, you tell your client what they want to hear. I believe in this case you told the authorities you work for – and in particular Bishop Ignacio – that great damage had already been done to the church's reputation by my inhuman actions but that some damage limitation might be possible if I were to be repudiated by the church in the strongest possible terms. Apparently I had been given several warnings, counselling had been offered then insisted on, professional help and support was given, my activities were limited, and when none of that seemed to work moves were afoot to transfer me to a closed order where I would be supervised twenty-four hours a day – much like Morón de la Frontera in fact but without the possibility of parole. And throughout this time, so the story goes, I gave every impression of acknowledging my sins and shortcomings, spoke warmly of the great benefit I was experiencing from all the help I was offered, and gave cast-iron assurances that the matter was no longer a problem – all the while secretly pursuing a reign of terror and exploitation among the vulnerable poor of the parish, which was only uncovered by the bravery of these innocent youngsters and the encouragement of the church that they should speak up. At the same time, the 'church' – that's to say *you*, Luis – were taking statements from everyone you could lay hands on, from the altar boys to my housekeeper, and feeding them to the prosecuting authorities. Needless to say, my request for character witnesses was turned down flat. More or less right, Luis, isn't it? You needn't deny it; I read all the emails while I was supposed to be picking up useful IT skills in jail."

The lawyer sat slumped to one side against the tape that bound him to the chair. His face had begun to take on a grey pallor and beads of sweat stood out on his brow and ran down his cheeks.

"No, no – it wasn't like that. I had no choice. The bishops, even the cardinals, were involved. It was decided. I just did what I was told. I don't decide the policy. I just carry it out."

Ramon let out an oath that even Luis found shocking.

"You filthy liar," he said quietly. "You advised. You counselled. You corrected. You suggested. You led them through the whole process. The church never gave me support of any sort. Celibacy is some sort of sacred cow but the church never gives any help to cope with what that means for individuals on the front line."

"Well that's not my fault," the older man mumbled. "You did what you did. The court found you guilty."

"Well Luis, we're not here to conduct a debate," Ramon said, more briskly now. "Another court has sat, the evidence has been heard, and the sentence passed, in a manner of speaking. Now my job is the final act. To carry it out."

Castillo summoned what little strength he had left and tried to sit up.

"What are you going to do?" he whispered.

"Put an end to all the words," Ramon replied. "Lawyers are all about words, aren't they? Too many words. So I'm here to turn off the flow. It won't make much of a difference to the big picture, I grant you, but everything helps. So…"

Ramon stood up, went over to the door, picked up his canvas bag, and pulled out a roll of silver tape.

"You can't!" Castillo screamed, seeing what was coming. "How can you? You used to be a man of God!"

"God? God?" Ramon stopped in his tracks and spat out the word as if it were bitter on his tongue. "Let me tell you, Luis, God has been a grave disappointment. Do you have any idea how many hours I spent on my knees, begging, pleading for some relief? God, we are told, works miracles. That's what I needed. It never came. So human nature – the nature God had made – took over. Much more satisfying than being a man of God, I can assure you. Anyway, where were we?"

Castillo sat aghast and silent now, watching as Ramon carefully peeled back about a fifteen-centimetre length, ripped it off, and laid the rest on the desk. Going round the desk, he taped it carefully over the lawyer's mouth against the older man's squirming and struggling. Then he peeled off another length. This time the lawyer knew without a doubt what was coming and was jerking and kicking for all he was worth. Ramon had to circle around behind the chair and pin both his arms onto the older man's shoulders to keep him still. Even with all the struggling, it took less than ten seconds. The second strip went over his nose and was pushed tight onto his upper lip, sealing off any airway. The lawyer continued to jerk and struggle.

"That's it, Luis," Ramon soothed. "The more you struggle, the quicker it comes. And as a last favour, though you don't deserve it, I think I'll pop back and update Conchita on her new status as a pretty young widow and heiress. I'm sure she'll want to show her gratitude."

The lawyer's eyes were wild and pleading above the line of silver tape.

"Number two," Ramon whispered, and turned out the light.

"José! Over here!" David called from a table for four at 1.15 the Monday after Saturday's chat. He had been first to arrive and was making himself comfortable and having a quick scan through the lunchtime menu with a large lemonade and lime in front of him. José had just arrived and seemed a bit lost, searching the tables for a familiar face. He spotted David, looked relieved, and headed over.

"Welcome to the wonderful world of Indian cuisine, José. I hope you're going to like it," David said, pulling out a chair.

"I don't know. I hope so," José responded, sitting down somewhat nervously. "What's *cuisine*?"

"Sorry, a French word. We use it to describe high-class cooking."

"So a French word in English to describe Indian food? No wonder I'm confused."

"It's just that we use lots of French words to describe things we think are refined or classical. *Couture* is fashion. *Coiffeur* is a hairdresser. *Ballet* is dance. *Patisserie* is pastry. You get the idea. Anyway, I think Navadhanya restaurant deserves to be *cuisine*, not just cooking. If it's your first taste of Indian food I think you'll like it."

"I hope so." José was still looking nervous. "Anyway, thanks for letting me join in."

"No problem. I think it'll make more sense coming from you. Have you spoken much to Andrea since Saturday?"

"Not really. We were both working yesterday so there wasn't time. Then you're too exhausted after work. And I didn't want to bring it all up again. I think we know what happened and what she says seems to make sense in connecting the murders. I know she phoned Maite's aunt. I heard her trying not to cry."

"Do you think she'd want me to start asking questions?"

"We'd need to ask her but I wouldn't be surprised. She's a strong girl really. She wants to do what she can to stop any more killings. I think she's less worried about herself."

"Well, let's hope that's justified. Oh, here's Stuart. Let me introduce you."

DI Stuart McIntosh headed over to their table and pulled out a chair.

"Hi Stuart. Did you get my text? Let me introduce you to José, one of our chat group members. He shares a flat with Andrea, the girl I mentioned in the text."

"Pleased to meet you."

McIntosh settled himself and took the menu card David handed him.

"Haven't been here before. Hear it's quite good though."

"Well, TripAdvisor says so, and so does *The Scotsman* – whichever you prefer to believe."

The waiter came over and took their drinks orders, ushering in a time of quiet reflection over the sacred text of the lunch menu.

"How are we doing?" David asked. "Remember, it's my shout today. I'm sure you did last time."

"Shout?" asked José again confused.

"Sorry again. *Os invito*. I'm inviting." Then to the detective, "That means I'm paying. In Spanish you invite, you pay. So much more straightforward."

"Is that right? Interesting," the detective commented. "I can see that would avoid all that getting our knickers in a twist when the bill arrives."

"Don't even ask," David advised José with a grin. "I'll tell you later."

By mutual consent they satisfied themselves with small talk until their orders had been placed and the food arrived. McIntosh updated David on his promotion hopes. His PhD had been accepted and he'd recently finished a special project on improving European liaison in the light of open borders.

"It's a bit of a challenge," he explained. "There's just so much variation. Some forces are pretty on the ball, others half-hearted to say the least – what you'd expect I suppose. In political terms, the big issue is tracking down villains living on the Costa del Crime. Nice little jolly for our guys going over there but if you keep drawing blanks then you start wondering if it's worth the candle. Know what I mean?"

David nodded but José was now completely lost. He contented himself with nibbling at his starter of grilled cheese with figs and seemed to be granting it grudging approval.

"Nice?" David asked over his own scallops in a light fragrant sauce.

"Yeah. Not bad. Not too *picante* so far at least. Do you say 'the jury's out'?"

"We do indeed. Nice expression."

"Yours ok?" McIntosh asked David.

"Lovely. I'm just reflecting that the last time I had an Indian meal with the polis it was with your former colleague DI Charlie Thompson – and also discussing murder if I remember rightly."

"Oh yes – Oor Wullie. Not a colleague any more of course. Five years in Saughton Prison and dishonourable discharge, as you'd expect. I'd have happily kicked him all the way there from the High Court given the chance."

"Oor Wullie?" David asked.

"His nickname. He got it when he was DC Thompson. You know, the newspaper people. They do *The Sunday Post...*"

"In which appears Oor Wullie. I get it. Neat. Anyway, I can imagine how it must have made the straight cops feel. Protecting prostitution and keeping all these girls in that situation when he was supposed to be the very one appointed to protect them. Not a glorious day in the force's history I suppose."

"Absolutely. Anyway. Maybe that brings us to the paedophile priest. What's the story?"

"I think I should let José take over here. He's Andrea's best friend in Edinburgh."

"Ok. Fire away then," McIntosh offered, scraping up the last fragments of sauce from around his garlic prawns.

Guessing that meant to get started, José rapidly summarized the story while the starter plates were cleared away, the mains arrived, and DI McIntosh continued to listen attentively. When it came to an end he sat back, slowly breathed out, and studied the ceiling for a moment.

"So," he began reflectively. "We've got four issues as I see it. A killer the Spanish police are looking for. They assume that it's a serial case as they've never had so many murders so close together before – in time or locality. Second, is there a connection? Your Andrea thinks so – and I assume you do too – but, at least according to the papers, the Spanish police are at a loss, or so they say. So number two is whether there is a connection, and number three is why they haven't spotted it or at least aren't saying anything if they have. Number four is whether a potential victim now living in Edinburgh might be at risk if numbers one, two, and three all line up. That about it?"

"Summarized very succinctly," David said.

José nodded.

"And your involvement, David, just to be clear...?"

"Only the bearer of bad tidings, I think. I'm hoping not to be suspect, victim, target, accomplice, accessory, or rescuer. Not like last time anyway."

"Last *two* times, from what I hear."

"Well it's not by design – that's all I can say."

"Ok, so my role then. What are you expecting of me?"

"Advice, I suppose, first of all. What do we do with what we've got? I don't think it would be responsible to just sit on it."

José frowned in confusion again. David noticed but pressed on anyway.

"I've just met Andrea and I'm certainly not her pastor, nor of José. So not as a pastor but just as a citizen. We have to speak up don't we? Evil triumphs where good men do nothing and all that."

"Ok," McIntosh replied at length. "I can put it into the system. As far as I would guess Police Scotland would have no interest in the case, but we do liaise with foreign counterparts. As it happens I have some contacts now in Spain through my special project. I can contact a Captain Rodriguez, who was my main link in Madrid, and see what he advises."

"Esteban Rodriguez?"

"I'm not sure of his first name."

"Used to be involved in the national drug squad?"

"Could be. He's just short of retirement now so I suppose they gave him a desk job."

"Sounds like it might be the same man. He was very helpful to me in the past, when I was still with Warehouse 66 in Madrid."

"So we contact Rodriguez and relay our suspicions and they probably take it from there."

"Unless Ramon is in Edinburgh already," José chipped in. "Andrea is my main worry. If he keeps on killing people in Spain that's bad enough, but if he comes here then he'll have to come through me."

"Very commendable, José," McIntosh remarked, not altogether encouragingly. "Despite what David may have told you we try to encourage private citizens to give us as much information as they have, then leave it to us."

José shrugged. He wasn't going to argue but David had the sense that whatever McIntosh said, if there was a risk he wouldn't be deterred by matters of protocol.

"There is one other thing I haven't mentioned but I think we need to think about," José continued. "We have an occasional visitor at Café Córdoba – that's where Andrea and I work. Neither of us recognize him but he comes in quite regularly, on his own. Just eats a meal then leaves. No – how do you say it? – small talk. And he keeps watching Andrea. She finds it really uncomfortable but it's not something you can actually ask him to leave for. Quite a stocky guy. Heavy beard. Wears a black beret. I didn't want to worry Andrea but I just wondered… you know…"

David looked thoughtful.

"Sounds a bit like the guy that had a go at me at the debate on Saturday night. I suppose that description could fit a whole load of folk though."

"Ok José. Thanks for that," McIntosh summed up. "I'll keep it in mind. If there's any chance you could try to grab a photo on your phone the next time he's in that might be a help."

The meal was almost over and they were chasing stray puddles of sauce and clumps of rice around their plates with the not-very-efficient means of the last chunks of naan bread.

"So, José – your verdict on Indian food. Has the jury come back in yet?" David asked, trying to change the subject.

José took a last slurp of lager, now sadly at room temperature, popped in the final fragment of butter chicken, and reflected.

"If I was in Spain I'd be saying *qué rico*," he announced. "When I get tired of *jamón* and tortilla – which might be never – this would definitely be second best. But I have to get going now. I got Miguel to cover for me and I think I'm over time already. Nice to meet you, Mr McIntosh. I hope you can help us."

McIntosh inclined his head and smiled as José shook hands around the table.

"See you at the next chat," he said in David's direction, "and thanks for the lunch." He headed for the door.

"What d'you reckon then?" David asked as soon as José was out of hearing.

"Well, I didn't want to alarm him but I think you're on to something. It wouldn't be the first time we've had a nutter get off the plane at Edinburgh Airport and think they can go stomping around Edinburgh like they did in Bogotá or Kuala Lumpur or wherever. I'll be rattling cages and have a look at immigration records. See if there's any sign. How would you feel if I asked permission to get involved officially? It fits in very well with my project and it would be good to test out the protocols in a real-world case."

"That would be fantastic. I hate to think what would have happened if you hadn't been involved last time."

McIntosh smiled grimly in assent.

"So, thanks again for lunch. I'll be in touch. By the way, I've never asked how things are with you and Gillian."

"Good," David smiled. "Wedding preparations aren't my forte but it seems to be all rolling ahead. Gillian remains lovely as ever and I'm trying to be a bit lovelier myself – despite all the things they keep asking me to have an opinion on."

"How would that be possible?" McIntosh asked all innocence. "And church?"

"Plodding along. Just trying to keep a low profile…"

"But somehow that doesn't seem to be working, does it?"

"You may be right. We'll see."

Chapter 8

MADRID: A-2

Spain is a country long plagued by poor communications. Few navigable rivers and too many mountain ranges have for centuries made it a nightmare to get from anywhere to almost anywhere else. More recently, thanks to EU funding, it now has one of the most logical and practical networks anywhere in Europe. Madrid is surrounded by three circles of ring roads and from these radiate the six major national routes reaching the entire country. Ramon had driven up from Sevilla that fresh spring morning, skirted Madrid on the M-40, then caught the A-2 and was now cruising smoothly north-east through the "corredor" towards Alcalá de Henares. Soon he would be leaving the city behind. In fact, he would soon be leaving Spain itself and Morón de la Frontera in particular far behind. The last few months had seen quite a change in his fortunes. The prison yard now seemed like a nightmare he'd finally woken up from. That felt good. Also, after years of unreliable rust buckets provided by the parish, he had decided that the time had definitely come for a change in his mode of transportation thanks to the contents of Luis Castillo Herrero's safe. Audis, Mercedes, and BMWs were all two a penny so he went into a dealership in Granada and paid cash for the exquisite comfort of a V6 three-litre Jaguar XF. Nice. Who said crime didn't pay?

With the Plan well on its way Ramon should have been very content, but it had not been proving quite as satisfying as he had expected. Nagging doubts, misgivings, and flashbacks were plaguing his thoughts however much he tried to suppress them. The bishop had been the first to go and he felt not a tinge of remorse about that. Then the lawyer – likewise. After that things had begun to get a bit messy. Camila, he discovered, still lived in Sevilla but worked in her uncle's hardware shop in Brenes, a small market town of around 12,000 people half an hour to the north-east. He acquired a small white workman's van and stopped to ask directions at the bus stop Camila waited at every morning.

"Brenes?" she said. "Just follow the A-8004. It's a straight road. You can't miss it."

"I'm hopeless with directions," Ramon replied, his black beret well down and dark glasses on. "Are there any landmarks?"

"Well," she replied, "you skirt along the Guadalquivir a bit of the way but really it's completely straight. Look, I'm waiting for the bus for Brenes myself. If you want to give me a lift I'll direct you."

It was as simple as that.

Halfway there he turned off on a country road. "It's not this way," she said, sounding slightly confused.

"I know," he replied. "I just need to take a piss. We'll not be more than two minutes."

But he had driven on for at least five minutes as Camila beside him was clearly getting more and more uncomfortable. Finally he pulled to a halt next to a stand of bushes and turned to her.

"Sorry," he said, "I don't even know your name."

"Camila," she replied quietly.

"Do you know my name?" he asked.

"No," she replied. "I don't even know you."

"Do you not? I'm Ramon." He took his hat and glasses off. There was a moment of blank lack of recognition, then the penny dropped. She tried to grab the door handle but he was too quick. She was acting on impulse, not knowing what to do – he had been planning this for years, going over it carefully in his mind, imagining and savouring every second as he lay on his bunk in Morón de la Frontera.

After that it didn't take long. A length of rope. A youngster barely out of her teens and a reasonably robust man in his forties. She did fight like a wildcat though. Part of the movie he had built in his head involved hauling her into the back of the van before the coup de grace. When it came to that bit it was all he could do to hold on tight while she bucked and twisted, gurgling sickeningly, her eyes standing out and her lips turning blue. The deed done, he was disappointed in himself when he had to get out of the van and throw up spectacularly at the roadside. A man on a bicycle in the distance might have seen him but he was cycling across a field and not past the van, so no panic. Quickly he cleaned himself up and took a swig of water and spat it out, then waited until the cyclist was well out of sight. He went around to the passenger side and dragged the body out. The face was hideously distorted as he dragged her deep into the bushes, covered her with some sacking and twigs, and set off back the way he had come. The taste of vomit was still in his mouth by the time he got back to Sevilla. Number three.

After that he needed a break. He was surprised to feel cheated and hollow, not buoyed up and elated as he had expected. A corrupt church official and a grey-faced paper shuffler – that was one thing. A young woman, full of life and potential, kicking and struggling, desperate to live – that was quite another. He worried that all the gouging and scratching might have captured his DNA under her fingernails, which could maybe prove unhelpful in future. Still, at this stage he really wasn't thinking of consequences or the aftermath. The Plan was the thing. Everything for the Plan. It had given him purpose and hope for years. Now he owed it to himself – he owed it to the Plan – to keep going. He swallowed down the discomfort and got on with it.

With more of Luis's money, he finally managed to leave the noisy, good-natured, infuriating youth of the Backpackers Utopia and rented a modest chalet-style house in the northern suburbs where the ground begins to rise and it gets slightly cooler. To begin with there had been something effervescent and life-affirming about having so many young people about in the hostel, constantly with a bottle in their hand and laughing over some vapid joke. Ultimately, however, he had come to resent it. They were youngsters full of life and love with their futures ahead of them. They had yet to taste the bitter disappointment of the middle-aged or the one-way ticket to nowhere of the old. From mild irritation he found himself drifting to open hostility. He knew they talked about him – the grumpy old git that looks like he wouldn't recognize a good time if it jumped up in front of him with a Bacardi Breezer in its hand. Well, sod him. We're having a laugh.

They didn't exactly ask him to leave – his money was as good as anyone else's – but you can tell when you're not welcome. So he'd gone shopping, found a fully furnished property in an out-of-the-way street with a weekly cleaning service, and paid three months in advance. Besides, police and public interest was beginning to build around the mystery murders and it was time for a lower profile. Sevilla is not downtown Miami and three murders in quick succession – two being very prominent citizens – were definitely out of the ordinary. However, the police couldn't seem to find any connection between them, or so they said. The lawyer's safe had been emptied so that was a motive, but who would want to kill the bishop? The girl, while a shocking find for the farm labourer whose dog had turned her up, hadn't been molested and had nothing of value to steal, so why kill her? She didn't have an enemy in the world. He could almost hear the scratching of heads even in the suburbs and he enjoyed the sensation very much. On the other hand, it could only be a matter of time before some bright spark connected these three dead bodies with the Parish of Santa Ana; then the *mierda* would hit the fan, so he had to press on with the Plan and get it all done and dusted one step ahead of the woodentop detectives.

Maite, was no longer living in town, that much the neighbours were sure of, but they couldn't say exactly where she was. They knew she was a singer so maybe she'd gone off with the group of flamenco performers she'd been friendly with. She certainly seemed pretty friendly with one of the guitarists anyway. Her mother had died the year before and her father seemed to live in the park with a couple of boxes of cheap Don Simon *vino tinto* for company. When Ramon approached him he surfaced sufficiently only to swear that he had always paid the proper maintenance and didn't know where Maite was now. However, thank heavens for social media. Initially, in prison, Ramon had not the faintest clue what social media was, but there was a module on it in the IT course and he quickly cottoned on not only to its power to change society but to how he could use it to further his research. Sandra, the education officer, barely knew how to switch the computers on of course and there was no firewall or other limitations to speak of, so he had more or less a free hand while pretending to be developing a stock locator for an imaginary shoe shop. Now all that practice came in very useful.

He already knew Maite's full name and her former place of residence so it wasn't that hard. He did a search and found her quite quickly. She still had a little bit of the childlike look about her but now it was wild child. Her hair was orange and green in equal proportions, and a tattoo of a flower with blue petals around a yellow heart curled across her forehead. *I'd give it five years tops before you regret that*, Ramon thought. He quickly invented a persona called Pablo – someone who claimed to have seen her performing and wanted to follow the band. He added a generic young, good-looking Spanish face grabbed from Google to round off the picture. She "friended" him within forty-eight hours. *If only she knew*, he had thought. "Friend" wasn't really the word, but he pressed on anyway, sending her a barrage of adoring posts. It turned out the band was "touring" village halls in La Mancha but had also played an open air show in the impressive shadow of El Escorial. The big breakthrough was only a contract away and they would soon be heading back to Sevilla to practise and regroup. *"Refund"* more *likely*, Ramon thought, but never mind. So long as she was within striking distance. Much better to sit tight like the spider waiting for his fly than go crawling around the country where he could control neither time, place, nor action. Three weeks later and they were home. "Pablo" was desperate to meet Maite and hear her sing again. She would be in a bar in Triana the following Friday night. She was clearly flattered and was looking forward to seeing him again. She didn't admit she had no idea where they had met.

Friday came and Ramon sat in his car opposite the bar. He watched her arrive with a few friends and saw the piles of amps, speakers, mike stands, and leads being carried in. Around ten o'clock the music started – the rhythmic, hand-clapping, wailing, uncompromising assault on the senses that is flamenco. Whether in love or hate the singer seemed to be saying, "No prisoners taken here." As a parish priest he had known Maite and her family quite well. Before her mother died, her dad had made a reasonable fist of keeping the drink in its place and the family had been, if not entirely respectable, at least mostly on the right side of the law and clear of the various *bandidos* who also lived nearby. Also as a priest, Ramon knew how often the cards were stacked against the gypsy people both in terms of prejudice from without and low expectations from within. Maite's mother had wanted her daughter to become a proper citizen, get an education, and break out of the ghetto, so that was one of the reasons she had encouraged her to go to church and get involved. What a bad idea that had turned out to be.

Ramon waited an hour for the bar to get busier, the music louder, and the drink to flow a bit more before heading across the road. He pulled his beret down, made sure the large, heavy-framed glasses were well up, and walked in. Maite's band had yet to come on and a local flamenco trio were going at it full tilt. The singer was a woman who looked at least in her sixties but was twirling, stamping, and wailing like someone still in her prime; maybe she was. She had on a red and black polka dot dress with a huge swirling hem. Ramon didn't speak Caló so couldn't exactly follow what she was singing but from the anguished tone it didn't take much working out. Some no good man had done her wrong and now she was out for blood. It was like the American blues on steroids. She wasn't just going to give him a piece of her mind when she caught up with him; she was going to teach him never to mess with a gypsy woman. Ever. Ramon enjoyed the performance, feeling a certain solidarity with the wronged party out to take revenge. In the meantime the second of the trio was clapping for all he was worth in the background, and the third – a young but obviously very talented guitarist – was working hard to keep up. Ramon wondered if they were her two sons. He ordered a beer and sat at the back. Eventually the clapping and wailing came to a crescendo to loud cheers and applause all around the room. The singer finished with a triumphant swirl and stamp and held the pose to a gale of clapping and more stamping. She looked proud but exhausted, held her hands up high, and acknowledged the crowd. A force to be reckoned with. *Maybe there was something to be said for celibacy after all*, Ramon thought.

After a twenty-minute break for new equipment to be wrestled onto the tiny platform and mike stands set up, Maite's band took up their places. A mop-haired drummer in a collarless shirt, a red velvet waistcoat, and a spotted bandana sat at the back with a tall, skinny bass player on his left and a guitarist with fashionable three-day stubble seated on the other side with his foot up on a stool and the guitar cradled in his arms, Spanish style. Maite came to the mike to roars of approval. She was obviously local hero made good. She clipped a huge white bloom of the *Lliri de Sant Bru* – the Andalusian St Bernard's lily – to her mike stand and smiled round at her fans. The room went quiet; then, after a single drum beat and a sustained strum from the acoustic guitar, she began. It was low and gentle to start with but with an eerie hint of menace like a Ferrari ticking over before a foot steps on the gas. She sang in Spanish but with lots of Triana slang, which Ramon could follow perfectly well. Gradually, the volume and intensity rose. The general import seemed to be "you think by leaving me for her you can start all over again – have another think my friend – I know where you live". She was stunning. Her deep natural contralto could sooth and coax the notes or spit them out in a rasping scream. It was pretty impressive stuff and the crowd loved it. Ramon listened spellbound for around forty minutes till, dripping with sweat and exhausted, Maite took a final bow and a huge gulp of beer and collapsed back into the crowd, promising more later.

Now the moment of decision. Should he act now or leave it for a while? If he spoke too soon she might get suspicious or be put off by someone else. Better to catch her unawares and flattered. Ramon got another beer and a tapa and bided his time. The second set was, if anything, even more dramatic. By now her flimsy T-shirt and skinny jeans were an entirely different, darker colour. The range of songs covered some love but mostly loss. No-good losers who were good riddance, those she had thought were good men but turned out to be as bad as the others, lecherous bosses and rich smoochers who tried to take advantage, hoodlums who thought they owned the neighbourhood and everyone in it, and a range of other, similar, cruel injustices. She saved for last a touching, haunting tribute to the love she had lost in a Triana gunfight. "He was the only good man I ever knew," she sang, "and you took him from me for the fifty Euros he couldn't pay." It was heart-rending and the crowd went wild. They wouldn't let her sit down till she'd sung the chorus three times more. Ramon let the heat die down a bit, then approached the stage quietly and shyly as they were beginning to unplug things and wind up cables.

"Excuse me," he ventured quietly. "Maite?"

"Yes. Did you enjoy the show?"

"Amazing," he replied, in all honesty. She was a unique talent and it would indeed be a shame to snuff out this flower just beginning to bloom. "We haven't met," he continued, "but I believe you have been in contact with my son, Pablo?"

"Yes," she replied, brightening, "Pablo. I thought he was going to be here tonight. Couldn't make it then?"

"Well, that's why I'm here actually. He was so looking forward to hearing you sing but I'm afraid he just isn't strong enough."

"No? What's wrong. Is he not well?"

"I'm afraid that would be something of an understatement," Ramon replied gravely. "He was really looking forward to tonight but the doctors said no. He's had something of a relapse recently and it just isn't safe."

"What's the matter then?" Maite asked, now genuinely concerned.

"Advanced leukaemia," Ramon answered in his best concerned priest's voice but being careful to keep the pitch and tone different from his normal speech. "Yes. He's had it for five years now and we keep thinking he's recovering, then it creeps back again. You didn't know?"

"No, not at all. We've been in touch on Facebook and WhatsApp but he never said. We met at a concert last year in Cáceres, I think. I suppose he must have been able to travel then?"

"Yes. He's had his good spells, then it all goes wrong. He asked if I'd come along in his place this evening and see if there was a CD he could buy or something. Maybe you're all digital downloads nowadays…"

"No, we have a CD. I'll get you one. Lucas," she shouted, "get one of the CDs, would you? Here you are. No charge. I can sign it if you like."

"Could you? That would be fantastic. I'll give it to him myself tonight if he's still awake when I get home." Ramon grabbed a quick glimpse at his watch. "I think I should make it. We live just over the bridge. He'll be so disappointed he didn't see you but this'll make up a lot for it. Actually, the news isn't very good just now. He'll probably never make it to a concert again."

Maite looked troubled. She seemed to be in a moment of indecision then made up her mind.

"Where do you live?" she asked.

"Las Castañas. About twelve kilometres. Just over the river then out the Huelva road."

"Twelve kilometres," she repeated. "So about twenty minutes." She quickly glanced at her watch, then round at her bandmates. "I'll tell you the truth," she whispered. "I *hate* packing up after a gig. If you like I'll come with you. I can give Pablo the CD myself. How about that?"

Ramon made as if he simply couldn't believe his luck.

"Really? Would you mind? It would mean so much to him."

"Just give me two minutes to let people know then I'll be ready."

Ramon smiled again as modestly and gratefully as he could and waited quietly by the door. This was going better than he had imagined. The idea had always been to entice her to drop in on "Pablo" but he was prepared for it to be another day when it suited her better. He saw the guitarist look in his direction then shrug. He didn't look too happy but turned back to what he was doing and Maite grabbed her denim jacket and came to the door.

"Don't worry about him," she whispered conspiratorially. "Permanently grumpy these days. I don't know. Ok. *Venga. Vamos.*"

They got into an old banger Ramon had picked up and drove on for a while in silence as he navigated through the narrow streets leading to the bridge on the west side of Triana, away from Sevilla and towards Huelva.

"D'you know," Maite remarked, "I'm sure I've met Pablo but I just can't remember it very clearly. His picture on Facebook seems familiar."

"Oh, never mind," Ramon replied soothingly. "People change, don't they? Youngsters grow up and men grow older. I'm sure you'll click when you see him."

By this time they had left the river behind and were climbing up on the main road. The *urbanización* of Las Castañas was only ten kilometres or so away now. But something odd seemed to be happening to the motor of Ramon's old and clearly unreliable car. The engine would start racing, then it would shudder as if the gear were too high, then clunk and shudder again. Maite couldn't see what he was doing with the throttle, brakes, and clutch so she assumed it was a mechanical problem. It didn't sound healthy.

"Sorry," Ramon muttered. "It does this sometimes. It should clear in a bit."

But it didn't clear and seemed to get worse, losing power on every rise or corner. Finally it seemed to drop out altogether. Ramon managed to coast to a halt off the main road in a rest area shielded from the road by trees and bushes.

"Sorry again," he muttered. "I'll have a look. I think I know what's going on. Shouldn't be a minute."

He reached down, popped the lid, jumped out of the car, and flipped it up. Maite could see the flashes of a torch beam under the hinge of the bonnet. He came around to the passenger window and she wound it down.

"I'm really sorry about this. I can fix it but I need to reach into the distributor. Would you mind just holding the torch for me?"

Maite shrugged, a little concerned but not yet alarmed. She knew how to handle herself and had had to do so on more than one occasion. She jumped out and followed Ramon to the front of the car. He handed her the torch and told her to lean in and shine it down to the side of the block. Just as she leaned forward he slipped a cord over her neck and flipped the catch, bringing the heavy engine hood crashing down on her head and shoulders. She gave a cry and dropped the torch. Now he put his knee into her back and pulled. If Camila had fought like a wildcat, Maite was a tiger. First she clawed behind her and tried lashing back into his groin. Then she pulled her arms in to get the bonnet slightly raised to get her head free. Then, twisting wildly, she managed to get half turned. This was not going according to the Plan. Ramon pulled all the harder but now he was pulling partly against the side of her neck, not just the windpipe. In the struggle the beret and his glasses had come off. The headlight of a passing car briefly illuminated his face.

"I know who you are," she screamed, cracking her elbow into his ribs. Ramon did not answer, as he wrapped one leg around hers and dropped all his weight onto her shoulders. She held on for a bit, then they were in the dirt. He tried again to get all his weight onto her back and she scrabbled for anything to hit out with. It wasn't supposed to be like this. It took fully twenty minutes, but eventually the body that so wanted to live was overcome, and its last breath came with a gurgle and a rattle. Number four.

Ramon lay in the dirt, exhausted. *What made them fight so hard?* he thought. The little vixen. She should have gone as quietly as in his fantasies. Once again there was no fun at all – just a cat fight to the finish. By the time he'd got back to his *chalet* in the suburbs he was filthy, sweaty, and his hands and arms were torn to pieces partly by Maite's screaming and scratching and partly by the briars and thorns he'd had to drag her through to dump the body. He felt awful and headed first for the bathroom and threw up in the sink. Then he slumped in the edge of the bath, head in his hands, breathing heavily and unable to get the sight or sounds out of his mind. It was as if Maite lived on but was now inside his brain, still twisting and screaming – a memory is harder to kill than a mere human being.

That was very messy, he thought. His heart was thumping and not with exhilaration as it should have been. It had been touch and go. And if he'd let go or she'd squirmed out, the game would have been up and he would be the hunted one. He decided that would never happen again. A gun was what he needed and he had an idea where to get one.

Ramon leaned forward and turned the air conditioning up a bit. The kilometres were sliding by very nicely. He put on a CD of Mendelssohn's *Italian Symphony* and relaxed. Leaving Spain behind was a good feeling. It was his home country but he didn't feel patriotic. Spain had not been the motherland it should have been to him. It had been more like a brutal, vengeful, implacable father – the one who tells you what to do but gives you no help whatever in doing it – and, like God in Catholic theology, not hesitating to punish the guilty. *Breath in*, he told himself. In and out, in and out. Calm down. We've been through this a million times. He focused on the delicate dancing music until he felt better. Whatever Spain was or was not and whatever had happened, he was on his way out. The Plan was going very well and this would be the final step. One more death, then the Plan would be complete and he would be free from the burden of revenge. And after that? *Maybe Norway*, he thought. *Or Denmark*. A country as different from Spain as he could imagine. Leaving it all behind. A nagging doubt sometimes made him wonder if it would be finally possible to leave behind the four living flames he had snuffed out so completely, but he shrugged and tried to stifle the voices in his brain. A man who was sufficiently determined could accomplish almost anything – and he was determined. The cold, heavy weapon in the glove compartment was further evidence of that.

Ramon often reflected that one aspect of the priestly function that's rarely thought about is what you do with all that information you are uniquely party to in the confessional. People pour out their sins and sorrows, get a word of wisdom and a minor penance, and head off contented. The priest has a quick sip of water before the next one comes in with more of the same. Some of Ramon's colleagues went to great lengths to try to forget what they had heard. For some reason he always remembered. And now it had come in useful. Pancho was essentially a minor crook but tried to run what looked like a legitimate operation. He used muscle when he needed to but as time went on increasingly preferred to avoid the hassle. He was gravitating to easier pickings, building his mainstream business, and was even thinking of running for office. Ramon fell into step with him one evening as he was walking from his office to the car. He reminded him of some indiscretions of his youth, which would not do his hopes of election any good at all. The price for silence was very modest: a modern, working firearm and ammunition and a replacement set of number plates. Pancho shrugged. Whatever a defrocked priest would want with all of that was none of his business. His second wife, Maricarmen, was already looking forward to the functions and receptions he would take her to as a successful politician and would tear him limb from limb if something as stupid as a protection racket from thirty years ago got in the way. He shrugged his shoulders and agreed to meet Ramon in two nights' time.

A police car with its lights flashing and siren blaring pulled past Ramon's Jag halfway to Guadalajara and jarred him back to reality. Luckily it kept on going. He thanked his foresight for the new number plates, then leaned over and opened the glove compartment just to look. Pancho said the Beretta was a good gun. Ramon had no idea but liked the sense of comfort having a quick and efficient killer always in reach brought him. On the downside, it meant there was no possibility of going through airport security so he had to drive. He sat back and tried to let the adrenaline surge that the siren had produced ease away. He attempted to push the images of the final moments of Camila and Maite out of his mind though they didn't want to go. His arms and face still bore the scratches.

But it was all in the Plan – maybe not exactly as he had envisaged but the Plan nonetheless. The Plan would be fulfilled. It had to be. It had become his destiny – and that of those on the list. Now only one remained. He let out a long, weary sign and tried to relax. The aircon and cooled seats were wonderful. They would need to be. He had a long road ahead of him. He was heading for Edinburgh.

Chapter 9

BRUNTSFIELD

José had once had a job as a night security guard and had perfected the art of sleeping soundly but jerking awake at the slightest disturbance. Now he was instantly fully aware. There it was again. A gentle tapping at his door.

"Who is it?" he called quietly.

The door slowly opened. Andrea's face appeared in the gloom lit only by the orange sodium street lights outside.

"Can I come in?" she asked timidly.

"Of course. What's the matter?"

She came and sat on the edge of his bed.

"Nightmares," she said simply.

José pushed himself up on his elbow, wriggled up the bed till he was sitting, then wrapped his arms around her. She started to shudder and shake. He smoothed her hair and rubbed her back. After some minutes he managed to get one hand free enough to reach a box of tissues.

"Want this?" he asked.

"Thanks." She sniffed, wiped her eyes, and blew her nose.

"Want to talk about it?" he asked quietly.

She shook her head but told him anyway.

"I'm back home in Triana. It's dark. Dad has been drinking and throwing bottles around the house. Mum isn't there. I can only find one boot but I put it on and get out of the house anyway. Then a man without a face is chasing me in the street. I know it's Ramon. Everywhere I run he's ahead of me. I turn around and try a different direction but he's there too. Just when he's about to grab me I wake up."

"Is this the first time you've had that dream?" José asked.

Andrea gave a bitter laugh and shook her head.

"No. Dozens of times I suppose. I was hoping leaving Sevilla would end it all but it hasn't worked. Now all this news about the murders and Ramon has brought it back even stronger. I'm getting afraid to go to bed. And there's another thing. That guy that's been coming to the café – you know the one that keeps watching me. I've been thinking – that could easily be Ramon. Older, heavier, a beard, glasses, and that hat but it could be him."

"I know," José admitted. "I've had that thought too. I hope you don't mind. I spoke to David Hidalgo again after chat on Saturday. We met for lunch on Monday. I told him I was worried. I'm sorry for doing that without telling you but…"

Andrea sat back a bit and interrupted him.

"No, don't be sorry. I know you didn't want to worry me. Thanks. I think he's a nice guy. I don't know if there's anything he can do, but it's always good to have a friend. I suppose he has some connections we don't have. He sounds like he wants to help."

"I think that's right," José agreed. "He really does want to help if he can. He has a friend who is a detective in the Edinburgh police. He came for lunch as well. We talked a lot about it. He's going to try to connect with Spanish police and pass on what you were saying."

"Wow!" Andrea said, brightening for the first time. "You have been busy. What happens now?"

"I don't entirely know. I suppose we keep in touch with David and see if he hears anything. Maybe we should tell him who you think the guy in the bar might be."

"I suppose so. It just makes me shiver. The thought that he could actually be right here in Edinburgh. You know. Watching."

They were quiet for a few moments, letting the implications sink in.

"José," Andrea said at length.

"Mmm."

"Can I stay with you tonight? I don't mean doing anything – you know – just to be with someone else, not on my own."

He drew her close and again began smoothing her hair and stroking her cheek.

"I didn't want to suggest it," he said. "But since you mention it…"

They were quiet for some moments, then he took her shoulders, lifted her slightly away from him, and lightly kissed her forehead.

"We will do only what you want to do, when you want and how you want. I want to make a safe place for you. I'll never force you to do anything. Believe me?"

She nodded and got up as he threw the covers aside. She pulled her Mickey Mouse baggy T-shirt down to be sure it was respectable and slid in beside him. He put an arm about her and drew her to him as she placed her head on his chest. They lay like that without moving till morning.

In the business it's called "doorstepping". A reporter who wants a story doesn't phone up and make an appointment but instead just turns up unannounced and knocks on the door. The reasons for no advance warning are many. First of all, the interviewee might just give a flat "no" to an appointment but even if they don't it gives them time to get an army of friends and family round to protect and support them and ultimately throw said reporter out if things get too uncomfortable. They also have the chance to get their story together – which may or may not accord with reality – and be ready to say what they want to say and no more. And they'll be more emotionally composed, which is another thing the doorstep reporter doesn't want. The reporter does not want a calm, measured, prepared statement. They want unguarded remarks and raw emotion. David Hidalgo had apparently become a "story". He opened the door to a not untidy young man in his late twenties dressed in a dark jacket, good-quality pressed jeans, and fashionable boots. His hair was combed back in a thick wave and he had the customary hipster beard and earring.

"Reverend David Hidalgo?" he began pleasantly enough.

David didn't naturally take to unannounced visitors and often sent canvassers and marketeers on their way with what Mrs MacInnes would call "a flea in their ear".

"No," he said.

The man at the door was slightly taken aback.

"You're not David Hidalgo?" he asked

"And who might be asking?" David fired back.

The hipster pulled out an ID and showed him it.

"Charlie Ferguson," he said. "Crime writer. *Edinburgh Evening News*. You're not Reverend David Hidalgo?"

"No I'm not," David replied. "I am David Hidalgo, plain and simple. How can I help you?"

"Oh, ok – sorry. Would it be possible to come in? I could explain better. Do you mind?"

David sighed. He could see the task he'd left to answer the door being considerably delayed. Ali and Ayeesha were coming for dinner in three hours' time and feeding such food experts needed careful preparation.

"I'm really in the middle of something but I can give you ten minutes. No more."

Charlie Ferguson stepped into the hall, took his coat off, and looked around for somewhere to hang it. This was already beginning to look like more than ten minutes. David escorted him into the living room, firmly closing the kitchen door as he passed.

"Nice place, David," Ferguson commented, sitting down in the bay window.

Whether it was or it wasn't, Charlie Ferguson's opinion was neither sought nor welcomed.

"What can I do for you?" David said.

Ferguson tried an amiable smile but got no response.

"Ok," he said. "Two things really. I write about crime in Edinburgh. I'm aware that you've been involved in a couple of major investigations over the past few years. We think the idea of a minister of religion who's a crime fighter would be of interest to our readers. We'd like to do a profile. 'Man of the Cloth is a real Crime Fighter.' Something like that. We'd interview members of Southside Church – that's it isn't it? – and some of the girls who escaped the prostitution ring last year. The girl you helped rescue from being kidnapped to

Spain. It's an amazing story. We'd like to make it really positive. Could be good for your congregation…"

At that point David stood up, went for the reporter's coat, and handed it to him.

"Sorry," he said, "I really don't think I can help you with that. I honestly had very little to do with the events you might have heard about. And I don't think the congregation would thank me for that sort of publicity."

Charlie Ferguson didn't stand up or make a move to take his coat.

"Ok, well there is another angle," he said. "I understand you help young Spaniards who have moved to Edinburgh to find work."

"I help with a Saturday morning chat group. That's all."

"So we could do 'Spanish scroungers steal Scottish jobs'. We'll be writing something. I just think it would come over so much better if you were willing to participate, that's all."

David stood looking at the reporter for a few seconds.

"Are you threatening me?" he asked.

"No, not at all," Ferguson laughed. "Just something to think about, that's all. Anyway, thanks for your time. I'll see myself out. Here's a card. Give me a call if you think again."

"You're sounding cheerful," Gillian remarked as she came into the kitchen. David had grumbled something unintelligible when she said "hi", gave her a perfunctory peck on the cheek, and turned back to the risotto he was working on.

"I'm sorry," he said, dropping a wooden spoon into an already overcrowded sink. "It's just one thing after another. Was there not a time you could get on with sermon prep and visiting the sick without having to be a crime-fighter and fend off the press as well?"

"Sit down. Tell me what happened."

David recounted the conversation of an hour ago in the gloomiest of terms.

"So," he concluded, "you either play ball and give them what they want or they write something ridiculous that misrepresents you anyway. That seems to be it."

"Is that all?" Gillian asked, eyebrows raised.

"Well, that's it. I happen to think it could be really unhelpful, either way."

"It could be, or it could be helpful. Of course if you're determined not to speak to them, don't. If they say something that isn't true, then you can sue or complain to the editor. I'm friendly with a couple of the law lecturers in Old College that I'm sure wouldn't mind advising. Anyway, I certainly wouldn't worry till you have to. Don't let it spoil the evening. What are you cooking?"

David sighed and gave some onions and mushrooms a stir.

"I hope you're right. Anyway, I thought I'd better avoid anything curry-ish so we're going Italian. But I had the idea of doing Italian meets Indian for fun."

"Not curry carbonara, I hope!"

David laughed and Gillian felt some satisfaction in turning his mood around.

"Indeed not. One of the things I love about an Indian restaurant is all the different bits and pieces you get. So poppadoms and dips, rice, naan, pakora, bhajis, three or four mains you can share. That kind of thing. So I thought I'd have a go at doing that with Italian food."

"Sort of like Italian tapas then?"

"Yeah. Or a Greek meze. There's lots of cultures that do it, just not the Scottish normally."

"So what's on the menu then?

"The usual garlic bread, olives, provolone cheese, and so on to start, but also melon wrapped in parma ham. Then mushroom and pea risotto with a rocket salad, ravioli stuffed with spinach, prawn linguine, and mini anchovy pizza slices."

"Wow. Sounds like a lot of work."

"Yeah, it is a bit. Probably why I was so rattled by the newspaper guy. Maybe I should call him up. By the way, I hope you're still doing dessert…"

Gillian carefully lifted a large cut glass bowl out of a woven Tesco's Bag for Life and laid it on the worktop.

"And here it is. Eton mess a la Nigella: strawberries, meringue, cream, and pomegranate juice. Simple but effective."

"Is that the pudding or Nigella?"

"Ha ha. Nigella and I haven't met so I couldn't comment. Anyway, no idea if that counts as Italian but I think it should go down ok."

"Guaranteed to."

"What time do they arrive?"

David looked at his watch.

"Less than an hour," he said.

"Ok then. Better stick this in the fridge. And I think you maybe should call the guy. Tell him what happened. Say it was nothing to do with you, if you like. Then see what happens. No sense in antagonizing a potential ally."

The doorbell rang right on time, exactly as David had expected, and Ali stepped into the hall, dapper as ever wearing a tartan tie, a dark blazer, and white flannels. He had a cardboard cake box in one hand and a carrier of alcohol-free beer in the other. Ayeesha right behind him had on a sari printed with black and red flowers and enormous gold earrings.

"Ali – on time as usual and immaculate. Ayeesha, you look fantastic. Come in."

"*Muy puntual como los británicos, no?*" Ali announced. "That's from Google Translate. I hope it's right."

"Spot on," David smiled. "Anyway, come through. Gillian's in charge of light refreshments."

Ali and Ayeesha had learned the customary two-kiss Spanish greeting over the years and insisted on using it whenever possible, so once all kisses had been exchanged Gillian got drinks and they sat down.

Gillian complimented Ayeesha's vibrant sari style and the two women immediately launched into a discussion of colours and designs.

"Oh, almost forgot, David," Ali said, reaching into an inside pocket. "Here's something I bet you've never heard before. Indian jazz!" He handed over a CD. David read the title.

"*Fabulous Notes and Beats of the Indian Carnatic.* T. K. Ramamoorthy. You're right. I didn't know Indian jazz existed. Let's have a listen while I stir the sauce."

"Anything I can help with?" Ayeesha asked in David's direction as he popped the CD in.

"Take my advice," Gillian whispered. "Safer not to. I've learned the hard way. Too many cooks. You know?"

Ayeesha nodded sagely.

"I do. Exactly."

David worked between the kitchen and living room, popping back and forth to catch a fragment of conversation or turn down a gas. Gillian and Ayeesha were animatedly talking cakes and it looked like it had already been decided that A&A Catering would take on the commission at a cut-price rate as a trial. Ali found himself a bit out on a limb and decided to risk wandering into the kitchen to see how things were going.

"Smells fantastic," he announced, popping his head around the door.

"Good. I'm glad you think so. Nobody does fragrant sauces like the South Asians so that's a compliment. We're having a go at Italian tonight. I hope that's ok."

"Absolutely. When we go out to eat on our own we often try Dario's or the Bar Italia. Sometimes you need something that doesn't have garam masala in."

David smiled and kept stirring.

"So, everything going ok? Church, Spanish classes, wedding preparation?" Ali continued, propping himself up on a kitchen chair.

"Yes, I think so," David replied, opening a tin of anchovies. "You'd better ask Gillian about wedding preparation though. My contribution is trying to sound interested and nod at the right moment."

Ali paused for a moment then added: "I just wondered, as you were sounding a little bit stressed when we came in. I hope it's not the cooking. I'm sure we'll love whatever you come up with."

"Well, I hope so. There is something else going on though, since you ask. You know we do an English chat group at Hacienda on Saturday mornings? Well, a new girl turned up last week and was reading one of the Spanish newspapers I'd brought. There was a story about a series of murders in Seville – where she's from. The police say they can't work out what the connection might be – if there is one. Anyway, the long and the short of it is that she thinks she knows what it might be about and she thinks it actually might connect to her as well."

"You mean she thinks she knows who it might be?"

"Yes, but worse than that: she thinks it's all to do with a paedophile priest who was convicted almost eight years ago. The deaths have all been of people connected with the case. And she gave evidence at the trial as well. She was one of the victims. So she thinks she might even be in danger herself if he's coming after everyone that helped put him in prison."

Ali let out a low whistle.

"You do pick them up, don't you?" he said. "This is like walking into 221b Baker Street. Do you know Conan Doyle modelled Holmes on Dr Bell from Edinburgh? He could have chosen Pastor David from Edinburgh."

David gave a grunt while popping the anchovy pizza into the oven.

"Hardly. Anyway, we're doing our best to support the girl in the meantime while I try to pass it on to a CID contact. I want to see her get the help she needs, but to be honest I'd just as soon see someone else – a proper professional – taking over."

Ali couldn't resist a dish of toasted almonds waiting to go through and had unconsciously helped himself to a handful.

"Hey!" David interrupted him mid-chomp. "That's the starters you're eating!"

"Oh, sorry," Ali managed to get out through a half-chewed mouthful. He held out his offending right hand and slapped it.

"My problem is I take your Christian teaching too literally. I don't let my left hand know what my right hand is doing!"

"Ha, ha," David rejoined. "But anyway, church is fine. Teaching is mostly good fun and Gillian is… well, as you see, happily planning the nuptials. But I'm worried about this girl. We're beginning to think the assailant might actually be in Edinburgh already. Then, if so, we have to think about how we can keep her safe. And how you could possibly track someone down just on the basis of what they *might* do."

"Complicated."

"It is. And the other troubling thing – although I'm probably the only one bothered by it – is I take exception to this being a former priest. In my line of work everyone gets tarred with the same brush. So every paedophile priest makes it that much harder to be a pastor. People are getting to the point that anyone involved in what they think of as religion is a legitimate target for suspicion."

Ali grunted.

"Huh. Tell me about it. Try being Muslim. People come into the shop and I can see them hesitating. We sell gram flour and rice but it's the Twin Towers or the London bombing that seems to be more on their minds. We get on well with our neighbours and folk like you, for example. But people who don't know us seem to think that being Muslim means you hate the West and want to blow everything up. It's crazy."

"I know," David agreed. "So I'm a danger to children and you're about to plant a bomb in Waverley Station. But how do you counter it?"

"I think they could catch that priest for a start. And if you help them, then so much the better. You shouldn't avoid it if it comes your way. If you're a pastor catching criminals it might give someone a better impression. The *Daily Mail* isn't going to be our friend, but if you can give a more positive spin to the people who at least know you then that's a start. It's what I try to do. I want every customer to go out with a better impression of Muslim people than they came in with. Drip, drip, drip; it's the only way. And speak out when you get the opportunity."

"Hmm. Funny you should say that," David remarked thoughtfully. "I had a newspaper guy here this afternoon wanting to do a profile, would you believe. He's heard something about the pastor that helps the polis and thinks the Edinburgh public would be interested."

"Well, maybe they would be. To be honest anything that shows people of faith in a better light can't be bad. Is there a chance you might need a Muslim sidekick? Like Batman and Robin?"

David laughed.

"What a great idea. If I need to go undercover I'll call you."

Just then the girls appeared at the kitchen door.

"Come on, you men," Gillian said sternly. "Sounds like all fun and no food. We're starving."

"Anything I can do to help?" Ayeesha offered.

"Could you maybe take that lot through?" David said, nodding at a table covered in dishes as he drained the pasta and stirred the risotto.

They managed to more or less keep off politics, religion, Idi Amin, and crime-fighting as David produced dish after dish and they experimented with Italian tapas. Having a succession of different flavours succeeding one another seemed to fit the multicultural tone of the evening perfectly. Ayeesha explained her catering ideas, Ali talked about how proud they were of Mahala and their hopes for her taking the business to another level, and of course they talked weddings – Muslim, Christian, Pagan, and every flavour in between. Finally, Gillian produced her fruit and meringue masterpiece and they finished off with decaf coffee.

"Thank you for a lovely evening," Ayeesha said at length. "Unfortunately, tomorrow is another working day. Apparently I have a wedding cake commission so I'll have to start thinking up some designs. I suppose you just want a married couple on top, not fleeing criminals chased by Señor David Hidalgo?"

David groaned.

"That's the last thing," he said. "For once let's just be conventional and boring."

Just then the doorbell rang. David looked at his watch– eleven thirty. He shrugged, got up, and went into the hall. From the living room they heard the door open and a quick conversation in Spanish. A few seconds later David reappeared with José, who was looking embarrassed and holding his beanie hat in his hands.

"I'm really sorry," he began. "I didn't think you'd have visitors. I can come another time."

"Not at all," Gillian said, getting up. "It must be important or you wouldn't be here. Please. Have a seat."

"And it really is time we were going," Ali said, getting up just as José sat down. "Besides, I'm sure this is personal. We shouldn't intrude."

José held up his hands.

"It's ok," he said. "No problem. If you are David's friends…"

"What's happened?" David asked. "Is it Andrea? Is she ok?"

"Yes, yes. I think so anyway," José quickly reassured them. "I left her at the flat anyway."

"So what then?" David asked.

"It's the man that comes to the café," José said. "I've got his photograph. Andrea thinks it could be Ramon."

"Wow," Gillian murmured. "That's incredible. So we can pass the photo to the police and they can check with the Spanish police. Do you mind if I have a look?"

"Not at all." José held out his phone and together they peered at a man perhaps in his mid-forties with the dark beard and thick black-rimmed glasses José had mentioned. A black beret lay on the table next to him and he was leaning forward, a forkful of something on its way to his mouth. There was a moment of silence as they took in the implication that this might be the serial killer the Spanish papers had been full of, a man who by all accounts had already murdered four times and might be in Edinburgh for number five, calmly enjoying a plate of paella.

"That's him, I'm sure of it," David whispered.

"Who?" Ayeesha asked. "Have you seen him too?"

"There was a man at the debate I was taking part in last week. He claimed to be Italian but we thought he might be Spanish. He was pretty aggressive. He fitted the description José had of the man who'd been coming to Café Córdoba. I'm sure that's him."

"And he was in church last week," Gillian said, stopping the conversation dead.

"What?" David asked, incredulous.

"I didn't tell you. I'm sorry; it just slipped my mind. I was talking to Fran after the service, then we went home for lunch. I just forgot. This man came into church on Sunday morning during the worship time before you began to speak and left during the last song. So you probably never saw him. I'm 95 per cent sure it's the same man."

"Well," David said pensively, "it appears Señor Ramon may have been checking us all out. But at least if we all agree it's the same man, then all we need to do is inform the police and hope they track him down – though how you do that in a city of over a million I have no idea. Unless he keeps going out for lunch or coming to church."

"No need," José said closing his phone. "I followed him after he left. I know where he lives."

Chapter 10

STOCKBRIDGE

David Hidalgo sent a text message at nine o'clock the following morning and was pleased to get a reply by 10.30. It simply said, "I'm on the case. Meet me at St Leonard's at 12.00." At the set hour David presented himself at the desk of St Leonard's police station just one street behind South Clerk Street and Southside's premises and asked for DI McIntosh. The detective appeared almost immediately and took him into an interview room. Unlike their conversation over Indian food, he was all business this time.

"First of all, I've got permission to work the case," he began. "I'll be putting a team together. It seems to tick enough boxes in terms of European liaison and the fact that we've worked together before."

"Well, that's good," David replied, "but I really don't intend to be what you would call 'working' on this one. I'm strictly the conduit between the Spaniards in Edinburgh and the officers of the law. That's it."

"Fair enough," McIntosh responded, "but that's still an important role. Andrea trusts you and José clearly sees you as his first point of contact. And you speak Spanish if there's any question of misunderstandings. Even if you're just willing to be around to hold hands and translate that would be helpful."

David shrugged.

"Ok, but I've promised Gillian!"

"So you said José claims to know where this guy they think is Ramon is living?"

"That's what he says."

"Well, can you get the two of them – and yourself – back here this afternoon? I'll get a DC to take statements and we'll get a watch on the property. In the meantime I've been in touch with Madrid, who passed me on to the local guy. Turns out my Señor Rodriguez is indeed your Señor Rodriguez too but he's tied to a desk now. They're sending a young officer from Seville."

"Does that mean they do accept that Ramon might be the connection between the killings?"

"Rodriguez sounded a bit cagey. I'm not sure what's going on there, but they must be taking the possibility sufficiently seriously."

"So what then?"

"Let's take things one step at a time. We'll get everybody's statements this afternoon if you can manage it. Then we keep an eye on the address. Follow him if he goes out but wait till the Spanish cop turns up. It should be his arrest if he has a European warrant. Then we question the man and take it from there. If all the ducks line up then he's packed off back to Spain and you can get on with booking your honeymoon."

The mention of honeymoon jolted David out of his train of thought. He had faithfully assured Gillian that he wouldn't be getting involved and had just been telling McIntosh he was the middle man, nothing more. If it all went as they had just been discussing that was fine. But if not? *Well, like Stuart said*, he thought, *let's just take things one step at a time*. It's surely not going to get *that* much more complicated.

The statements were taken that afternoon and David returned home but just couldn't settle to the kingdom of God being like a narrow door through which only a few might enter, which was supposed to be the text for the upcoming Sunday. Sadly, European borders were quite the opposite. That was ok for young workers needing to make a new life in another European city but unfortunately also worked for middle-aged murderers intent on revenge wherever that might lead them. But there were still lots of "ifs": if Ramon was the common thread; if Andrea was at risk; if he knew where she was; if he was sufficiently determined to come to

Edinburgh; and if the man they had identified was indeed Ramon. It was quite a tribute to McIntosh's good will and professionalism that he had been willing to go out on a limb with the little they had. Obviously he had been furiously pulling strings behind the scenes to get things organized so quickly, not to mention getting on the blower to Spain, lining up a Spanish officer to come to Edinburgh, putting his own team together, and arranging for statements. David was impressed. If the whole thing could now be wrapped up in a day or two – at least as far as his involvement was concerned – then that would be a highly satisfactory outcome. Goodness knows the implications of the narrow gate were tricky enough to deal with without a crime detection sideline. So far he had been lucky, or fortunate, or blessed, or whatever epithet Juan would be comfortable with given his dogged assertion that "there's no such thing as luck". In two previous cases things had worked out incredibly well. The guilty had been caught, the innocent rescued, and he had come out of it more or less unscathed. Maybe this was the time their luck (or whatever) would finally run out. Still, you had to travel hopefully.

He glanced down at his notes and made another half-hearted attempt to marshal his thoughts. Thinking of unlikely projects, surely the incarnation really took the biscuit. If Jesus' words were true about the narrow door, then he must have accepted right from the start that faith was always going to be of limited take-up. At any given time, place, or circumstance, the majority would not even be trying to get in, at least in terms of the personal relationship he always tried to highlight rather than nominal religion. And Ramon was a case in point. Assuming he had at least started his journey "in good faith", at what stage had it all gone sour and he'd given in to the dark side of his nature? If that was a fair interpretation. So, even those who looked as if they had got through might end up outside. How incredibly depressing, and how many questions that raised not just for the incarnation project but the whole creation project itself. How could God bring humanity into existence already knowing that the great majority would end up in an eternity separated from all that was good? Was it all worth it just for those who would believe – and not abuse their beliefs, their power, and their influence? And how to communicate the positives of God's love and sacrifice on account of the few when questions about the fate of the many were so taxing – was it even something he dared preach on with so many unresolved questions? Thinking about Ramon somehow seemed to bring it into even sharper focus.

He was just about to flick open the *Lion Handbook to the Bible* for a list of "Kingdom of God analogies" to see if there was something a bit less troublesome to deal with on Sunday when the phone rang. What a relief; it was McIntosh. Could he be at Edinburgh Airport international arrivals in an hour and a half to meet the officer from Seville? Not a problem. He happily got up, leaving Bible, commentaries, handbooks, and coffee cup as they were, grabbed a coat and his fedora, and was out of the door in one fluid movement. He hoped Gillian would understand. He grabbed a number 23 through Tollcross and Lauriston Place then down George IV Bridge to Waverley, got the airport bus, and was there inside an hour.

"Teniente Marcos Campos Ibañez, apparently," McIntosh informed him, holding up an A4 clipboard with the name on it as they waited at international arrivals. "No idea what his English is like. I haven't spoken to him directly before."

The *teniente* when he arrived was a tall, lean, dark-skinned young man with neatly clipped jet black hair in a short-sleeved olive-green shirt and well-fitted black trousers. He had a businesslike manner that seemed to stand out from other Seville arrivals even before he recognized his name and headed across to the welcome party.

"Marcos," he announced, holding out a hand. "You are Mr McIntosh, no?"

"Yes," McIntosh replied. "This is David Hidalgo. Not a police officer but giving us some informal help in the case, and a fluent Spanish speaker if any translation is needed."

"Señor Hidalgo. *Encantado*. This is a privilege," Campos said with a smile. "I've heard of you from my colleague Captain Rodriguez. He speaks – how do you say – he speaks highly of you."

David nodded and shook the outstretched hand.

"Your English is very good, Señor Campos. That is exactly what we do say, though whether it's justified in this case is another matter."

Ten minutes later they were in McIntosh's car heading back into Edinburgh.

"One thing I just don't get," McIntosh commented, pulling past the Royal Bank of Scotland headquarters campus after the pleasantries were over. "You've obviously been given permission to come here and see if our suspect is Ramon, but according to the Spanish papers – David has shown me some of the reporting – local police are at a loss to see what the connection is between the various murders. That doesn't quite seem to add up."

"Yes, I think I know what you mean," Campos agreed. "What can I say? I don't know if you know Spain well…"

"I lived there for thirty years," David informed him.

"Holidays in Marbella," McIntosh offered with a shrug.

"Ok. So we are a culture in transition. The old traditional Catholic past has really gone. We are a modern secular society in many ways. But still, underneath it all, nobody really likes to see the church dragged through the mud – is that the expression? Senior officers tend to be quite conservative in any country, I suppose. Andalusia is probably the most conservative region in Spain. Add them together and you get – how can I put it – a deep reluctance to see the church further damaged. The child abuse revelations have hit very hard, all over the world, I suppose, but especially in Spain with all of our heritage. To find out that our priests have been systematically abusing those in their care… well, it's horrible. So Ramon was convicted and we hoped that was an end to the matter. But now we have a string of murders of people all connected with the case within fairly quick succession of him coming out of prison. It seemed obvious…"

"Unless you don't want to see it?" McIntosh finished the *teniente*'s sentence.

"Exactly. So there was a lot of time spent looking for any other explanation. Those of us with a more open mind were frustrated.

We thought we should have been looking for Ramon from the start. But every initiative was blocked. Officers were suspended. Others threatened to resign. It was chaos. Some of my colleagues were threatening to take matters into their own hands. And now we have four cases. If we'd gone after Ramon right away maybe we could have saved the two young people at least. Finally the 'higher powers' – is that right? – the higher powers intervened and a new chief was appointed. That wasted more time but now we are clearer that the cases must be linked and Ramon must be our man. When we got your information we thought it could be the lead we were looking for. So here I am."

"That's helpful," McIntosh replied. "We'll keep it off the record. So if our man is your man we can maybe at least prevent more deaths, and with a bit of luck you could be back on the plane by Friday."

"Ah, that would be a pity," Campos said regretfully. "I have always wanted to visit Edinburgh. Maybe we can make the paperwork 'spin out a bit', no?"

David wasn't sure how Gillian would take his trip to the airport and now semi-official advisory role when he told her that evening curled up on the sofa after lasagne and pavlova at her Marchmont flat. But the only question she asked was, "So what happens next?"

"Well, Campos has just arrived so there's to be a briefing tomorrow morning. I've been asked to attend. Then I suppose he'll want to speak to Andrea and José. Then I guess they send a couple of cops round and pick up our suspect and see what Ramon – or whoever it is – has to say for himself."

"And is there anything more they want from us?'

"I don't think so," David said slowly, thinking Gillian was now on her guard.

"Because if there's anything more we can do," she continued, "anything – to protect Andrea and anyone else that might be on his list – we should do it, shouldn't we?"

David felt relieved and somewhat surprised.

"Absolutely. But I thought you were totally fed up with 'helping the police with their inquiries'?"

"I am, but when something like this falls right at your feet, what can you do? If Andrea became another story in *The Scotsman* you'd never forgive yourself if you could have done something more and didn't."

David gave her a grateful kiss.

"Just how I feel about it," he said. "It's not as if we go out looking for trouble after all…"

"For sure. You know I was reading a verse the other evening. Paul talks about 'good works prepared in advance for us to do'. Maybe Andrea falls into that category. I think of them like little gems sitting on your path waiting to be picked up. And it's only on your path. Other people have others suited to them. You have the choice of bending over to pick it up or walking on by. But if you don't pick it up, then nobody can – which makes us the right people in the right place at the right time to help Andrea."

"That sounds like a big responsibility. What a nice idea though. You know I've been struggling with Sunday's sermon. You wouldn't like to talk about that instead, would you?"

Gillian laughed.

"Not just yet," she said. "I know you put absolutely no pressure on me. And nobody else does either – except for Dr Stephen Baranski sometimes as his idea of a joke. But I am feeling that sooner or later I have to get up and say something."

"Well, only when you're ready," David said softly, trying not to betray the leap inside.

"I knew you'd say that," Gillian answered, snuggling a bit closer. "But sometime soon I really need to get my act together. I've never used the term before but I think if I was challenged I'd have to say, 'Yes – I'm a believer too. I believe it. I try to live it.' So sometime I need to nail my colours to the mast. Getting up in front of the Southside folk might be the best way to do it."

David opened his mouth to say something then stopped – tried again and stopped again. Was this it? So simple, so conversationally

– in the middle of talking about something else, in the middle of just getting on with life and its challenges. No big theological debate, no moment of crisis, no "altar call". Was Gillian now saying she had come to her moment of decision? Was she confessing faith? Relationship with the creator and redeemer? Sometimes he thought we set the bar much higher than Scripture itself with confessions of faith, creeds, rites of passage, and all the rest of the paraphernalia. The Word says that if you confess with your mouth and believe in your heart that Christ rose from the dead then you will be saved. Pretty simple really. Was that what she was saying? He felt an overwhelming urge to say something like, "Sorry, do I understand you correctly? Are you saying...?" but resisted it. Instead he wrapped his arms around her, pulled her close, kissed her hair, and whispered something nice in her ear. She smiled. In the background Bob Dylan was singing about sheltering from the storm. That seemed to sum things up very nicely. He whispered something else in her ear and they changed positions to stretch out together holding each other close. Wonderful, surprising, peaceful shelter from the storm. He had thought he might call Campos and offer him some company on his first night in Edinburgh but that idea had just slipped off the agenda.

The briefing was appropriately brief. Campos gave the background in pretty competent English and McIntosh gave the up to date. David was asked to speak about his conversations with Andrea and José and did so in thirty seconds. McIntosh then outlined a plan of attack that had obviously been run past the Spaniard and got his approval. Other DCs and DSs around the table had their roles outlined and the hour was set for 10.00 the following morning as there didn't seem any pressing reason to go for the middle of the night. The address was being watched and its occupant never seemed to emerge before lunchtime. The property was about halfway along St Stephen Street in Stockbridge, quite a chic neighbourhood, not as upmarket as the New Town but equally handy for the city centre. Somewhere in among the bookshops, beauty parlours, boutiques, and bistros might be a serial killer.

And that was it. Next meeting 9 a.m. sharp at St Leonard's prior to two cars heading for Stockbridge. Campos would knock on the door along with a DC while the back was also watched. A ram for forced entry was available and firearms were issued to the specialists who would initially stay one step back. David was offered to sit in one of the cars but turned it down. Campos was a native speaker so what could he add to the proceedings?

As soon as the meeting was over he took a bus down Leith Walk, having been asked by McIntosh to meet Andrea and tell her what was going on. She might be called on to identify the suspect and had a right to know that her worries were being taken seriously. David sent her a WhatsApp from the street outside and took her to the nearest coffee shop as a neutral venue.

"José at work this morning?" he asked as they took two lattes to a corner table in the almost empty premises.

"*Sí* – I mean, yes. Martin's been really good. He's let me have a couple of days off until this is – can I say – 'sorted out'?"

"Yes, you can. Sorted out is perfect. I hope in a couple of days it will be. I'm sorry Edinburgh hasn't been a better experience for you."

"No, Edinburgh has been perfect. Really. This is a Spanish problem – a problem of the Spanish church, and of Spanish society that we've tolerated for too long. Anyway, once this is over I want to enjoy Edinburgh again. And the rest of Scotland too."

"It's been great that José has been there to support you."

"I know. He's been so sweet. *Cariñoso*, we say – well you know that. And the others. I couldn't have asked for better. And you and Gillian too of course."

"Glad to help. I needed a lot of help when I came back to Edinburgh myself about eighteen months ago. It's nice to be able to pass it on."

"Do you mind if I ask why you came back? José said something happened in Spain but he didn't know what. If it's too personal of course…"

"Not at all. It is personal but it's over now. I was a pastor working with drug addicts. That threatened the gangs that controlled supply.

136

My wife was killed as a consequence. I didn't have the heart to carry on. I'd been brought up in Edinburgh and had some Spanish friends here – Juan and Alicia from Hacienda. They looked after me till I could begin to function again. And I met Gillian. That's it 'in a nutshell', we say."

Andrea was watching him intently but looked down at the napkin she was twisting in her hands.

"I'm sorry," she said. "I shouldn't have asked."

"No, that's ok," David replied, taking another sip of his latte. "I'm in a much better place now. And I suppose at least it means I can empathize with the traumas other people are going through – like you, for example. I have no idea what your experiences have felt like and I'm not going to say I do. But I can understand something of how it leaves you."

"It leaves you empty," Andrea said flatly. "Really empty. Like everything good has been sucked out of you. And spoiled. So instead of being clean and complete for whoever you really love, you feel no one would want what's left. So sometimes you get involved with people who aren't really good for you just because they seem to accept you. It's horrible. I hope they get him but nothing they do can give you back what you've lost. *Entiendes?*"

"Yes I do, I think. Some of the addicts I've worked with used to say something similar. The drugs robbed them of their humanity and they ended up just a shell. You should talk to Juan though. He was an addict for about fifteen years. But he completely recovered and now he's one of the most positive guys you'll ever meet."

"Is he an *evangélico* like you?"

"Yes he is – in some ways he has a lot more faith than I do. By the way, we tend to just say 'Christian'."

"But there is a difference from the Catholic Church, isn't there? They all say they're Christians too."

"Yes, there are differences but also a lot in common. I mean between people with a serious personal commitment. I'm not talking about those we call 'churchgoers' who don't go any further than that. I have lots of friends from a Catholic background I regard as every bit as much believers as I am – and many much better people. There are differences but we get over them."

"Well, I can't believe the same word could be used to describe both you and Ramon. You've been really good to us. You and Gillian. Once this is over…"

"I know. We can get on with living."

"And chatting!"

"And chatting. So are you ok with what's happening next? I mean, do you understand the plan?"

"Yes, I think so. They are doing something tomorrow and I'll probably be contacted the next day – that's Friday isn't it? I'll have to say if the man they've got looks like the man that – you know, looks like Ramon."

"That's right. Nothing much more we can do now except wait. Would you like another coffee?"

Andrea actually didn't but nodded anyway. Better this than go back to an empty flat and too many thoughts.

"Actually, I've a better idea," David suddenly announced. "Have you been to the Botanical Gardens yet? No? Why don't we go there? It's not too far and it's too nice a day to sit inside. It's one of my favourite places in Edinburgh – peaceful and beautiful. Knocks spots off *El Retiro*. Sorry – that just means it's better. How does that sound?"

That sounded perfect. A couple of hours less to dwell on the past and a beautiful day to spend in the present. Andrea wanted to give David a *beso* of appreciation but didn't know if that was allowed. Instead she gathered up her things, put on her most positive smile, and followed him out into the sunshine.

David got the call mid-afternoon the following day. Having made zero progress on his sermon he'd turned to filing the million bits of paper scattered around what he laughingly called an office. That gave him sufficient activity to be somewhat distracted but could still be done more or less on autopilot when two-thirds of his brain was elsewhere. The phone managed one ring and half of the second before he had picked it up.

"Hi Stuart. Certainly. Half an hour."

For the second time that week David Hidalgo grabbed his coat and hat not entirely sure what was coming next.

"So he opened up like an oyster at the deli counter," DI Stuart McIntosh explained as they walked down the corridor of St Leonard's police station. "Then as soon as he cottoned on it was the police he made a dash for it into the living room. He almost got to a firearm before the heavies landed on top of him. That was totally unexpected. After that he came more or less quietly – and quiet has been the name of the game ever since. He has a Spanish passport in the name of Alfonso Bances Marroquin but refuses to confirm or deny anything Campos puts to him – with one exception. When he was asked why he had come to Edinburgh he said, and I quote, 'to kill someone'! In clear English. How about that?"

David gave a low whistle.

"Sounds like it fits the bill then but I'm surprised at any admission of guilt. So what can I add to the party?"

"Well, that's the other peculiarity. He's said almost nothing to any question or remark, but when someone in the interview room mentioned your name – I think in terms of bringing Andrea along tomorrow – he just about exploded. Campos tells me it was a colourful stream of Spanish swearing. I'll take his word for that."

David raised an eyebrow.

"But I've never met Ramon and I knew nothing about the case until Andrea opened up at the chat group. Strange. So what do you want me to do? Meet him?"

"Yes, if you're willing. It's about the only thing that's caused a reaction. I'd like to know why. Are you up for that?"

David nodded.

"By all means. I'm as mystified as you."

"Ok then. Once more unto the breach, dear friends."

DI McIntosh pushed open a door marked "Interview Room 1" and ushered David in. The suspect was sitting at a simple table with only an empty mug on it. The chair opposite him was vacant and a uniformed cop stood in the corner behind the door. At first the suspect looked up without interest and seemed to be taking some time to focus. Then he let out a roar and launched himself from behind the table as if catapulted across the room. His hands were around David's throat before anyone had time to react and it took the uniform, McIntosh, and another passing cop to prise him off. Handcuffs were rapidly applied and with his hands locked behind his back he was forcibly sat back down, breathing heavily. David meanwhile was slumped against the door jamb pulling his collar open and rubbing his neck. Campos burst into the room at that point.

"What's going on?" he asked.

"Your Spanish friend just had a go at David," McIntosh reported, also breathing heavily. Then, slowly and clearly to the suspect who was still red faced, panting, and glowering in David's direction: "I think you understand English. You are going to be charged with assault whatever else happens. Now would you like to explain why you feel the need to attack this gentleman?"

Whatever other effect David's arrival had had, at least it was no longer a question of who could hold out longest – Campos asking the questions or the suspect refusing to answer them.

"It's all his fault!" he spat out. "If it was not for him Ramon would never have even become a priest. He wouldn't have been in Triana and my little Camila would still be alive. Live with that if you can!"

Chapter 11

ST LEONARD'S

"My name is Alfonso Bances Marroquin, just like it says on the passport," the suspect began, hands still locked behind him but now breathing more easily and seemingly calmer. "Of course I'm not Ramon. I'm here to kill him."

Teniente Campos was sitting across the table with an A4 pad in front of him. David Hidalgo stood behind his shoulder with his tie loosened and his shirt collar opened. He was still red in the face and looking like he'd just finished fifteen rounds with the heavyweight champion. Stuart McIntosh sat in the second seat on the door side of the table. The tape recorder and cameras were running.

"We have fingerprints and photographs coming from Morón de la Frontera any time now so we'll soon know if that's the case, but suppose you start at the beginning and explain what just happened. You can speak in Spanish if you like. This officer will translate."

"No, I speak English," the man claiming not to be Ramon said in a voice still heavy with emotion. "I was an English teacher in Triana for thirty years. I am the uncle – I *was* the uncle – of Camila Bances Cardoso. Ramon Murillo Zapata was our parish priest at Santa Ana. I used to help him sometimes with his homilies. We met in a bar and chatted. He was a thoughtful man. But sometimes too intense. I kept telling him to relax. He used to say, 'I have problems you don't know anything about, Alfonso, and nobody can help me.' It seemed to gradually get worse, not better. He'd be sitting talking then all of a sudden he'd begin to shake and start breathing like he was running a marathon. I urged him to tell me what was troubling him but he refused. He said I wouldn't understand and that no one could help him. Then later, when the papers got involved, I understood. While I was sitting helping him and sympathizing he was abusing our children. Right under our noses."

More of what McIntosh guessed was Spanish invective followed till even Campos raised an eyebrow.

"... and it's all *his* fault," the suspect continued, scowling in David's direction. "His fault. If Ramon had never listened to him none of this would have happened!"

"What are you talking about?" McIntosh broke in. "David Hidalgo has nothing to do with this. He passed on some information, that's all. He has never met Ramon and had no knowledge of the case until it came up in the papers. What do you mean?"

The suspect breathed out and studied the ceiling.

"What I mean," he said slowly, as if spelling it out for not very bright students, "is that Ramon Zapata Murillo only decided to become a priest after meeting David Hidalgo, pastor of Warehouse 66 *Iglesia Evangelica* in Madrid. That decided his life's direction. If that hadn't happened, then everything would have been different. These children would have been happy now and my niece and her friend would still be alive. That's what I'm talking about."

For a moment nobody could think of what the next question should be. Finally David spoke.

"What happened?" he asked quietly. "What was it? What was the circumstance?"

"You were the principal speaker at an event for Catholic youth in Madrid in 1990. Ramon was fifteen. He went with his youth group from Triana. He told me about it many times. He said it was like a lightbulb in his mind. He went because of a girl he liked but he forgot all about her when you started to speak. You were talking about how you found your own faith, how the church got started, and about the work you were doing. Ramon said that he instantly felt that was what he should do with his life. He felt he couldn't leave the Catholic Church because of what his parents would think, but he wanted to be as like you as he could. He bought your books, listened to you on the radio, visited your church. There were interviews in the magazines. He said he met you once after church and asked you to sign his Bible. Apparently you refused and told him to speak to the author. He was young, impressionable. He thought he had a calling but he was mistaken. He said you gave him encouragement when he had doubts, so he went through seminary, came to Santa Ana, and we know what happened then.

"I was ashamed I'd spent so much time listening to him talking about the stresses of the priesthood and never guessed. When he was sentenced I felt it should have been longer and I was worried even then about what he would be like when he came out. You could see he was given to obsessions. He was obsessed with the great Pastor David Hidalgo. Then it was a sexual obsession with young people. I was worried that when he came out of prison it would be some other obsession even more dangerous, but I didn't guess right away what he would do. When the bishop was murdered I didn't immediately think of Ramon. Lots of people hate the church for different reasons. Then it was the lawyer. That made me think. Then when Camila died I knew. I went to the police and told them but they didn't want to listen. We were broken-hearted. She was a lovely girl. She seemed to have recovered well from what had happened to her. She had a job, a boyfriend, a future. Ramon took all of that away from her. So when the police didn't seem interested – or wanted to protect the church from even more damage," Campos looked down for a moment, "I decided there would be no justice unless I did something myself. So I came to Edinburgh. If I was right I knew Andrea could be next on Ramon's list. I found out where she worked and tried to keep an eye on her without worrying her.

"And I kept an eye on you too, Señor Hidalgo. I wanted to know who could have had such an influence to shape a young man's life in a direction he was wholly unsuited for. I found out about your church here. I wanted to hear what you had to say about your faith so when I saw the poster about the debate I decided to come. When I hear all that rubbish about 'a real relationship with God' it makes me want to throw up. It's all power, pretence, and manipulation. I knew how a young mind could be manipulated. I've been teaching children all my life. It's a sacred responsibility not to form them in your own image. You must let them make up their own minds. Then I came to hear you preach. More of the same *tonterías*. I think I saw Ramon in the street one day. If these 'gentlemen' hadn't interrupted me I would have found him and stopped him, stopped him damaging anyone else's life – permanently. Still, the police know best, don't you? A fair trial for Ramon and I'm to be charged with assault for trying to stop the problem at its source. All you priests and pastors; you're all the same. Promising us – how do you say – 'pie in the sky when you die', if we just behave ourselves and keep you in a job. And taking our young people who might have led a useful life and filling their heads with nonsense. It's disgusting. If I had a second bullet after Ramon I'd finish you off as well!"

"Well, that was nothing if not forthright," McIntosh remarked dryly over a coffee in the canteen later on while a formal statement was taken and signed. All the fight had gone out of the man they were now calling Bances and Campos was questioning him in Spanish to get the full story. The prints and photos had come through and confirmed that he was who he said he was. Photos of Ramon showed him to be considerably younger and clean shaven. Seville police further confirmed that a man with Bances' name had been an English teacher in Triana and was the uncle of Camila Bances, a teenage witness at Ramon's trial recently deceased. Apparently the black beret, beard, and heavy glasses were entirely his normal appearance and not an attempt at a disguise at all. Andrea would be contacted and told not to bother coming in. The suspect was not Ramon.

"How are you feeling, David?" McIntosh asked. "That was quite an onslaught."

David Hidalgo had been cradling his coffee mug in both hands and not saying much. He didn't reply right away.

"I'm trying to recall Ramon as a teenager speaking to me," he finally said. "It's impossible. There were so many. I think I can remember a talk to a youth group but as to someone who got specific inspiration from it – I just can't place it. And if he did develop some sort of fixation I was totally unaware of it."

"I don't think you need to beat yourself up over this one," McIntosh counselled. "One of those things, that's all. And talking of obsessions, I think Bances has a few of his own. From what you've told me and I've heard from other sources, what you did in Madrid was remarkable in how much it helped so many people. Our friend in the black beret seems to think that none of that counts for anything just for the sake of one nut job who didn't know when to quit. Ramon sounds like he was an extremist from the start, and if it hadn't been you it might have been some apologist for ETA or the Red Brigades, I don't know. Go home and take Gillian out for a drink and forget all about it."

David nodded.

"Good advice," he sighed. "But what happens now? Bances seems convinced Ramon is in Edinburgh and that Andrea is on his list. I'd like to know how he knows. But in any case we're back to square one, aren't we? Andrea needs protection even more now and it's even more urgent that we track down the real Ramon."

"Without a doubt. We'll be pushing Bances for how he's so sure, and speaking to Andrea about taking precautions. If Bances could track her down at work so easily I suppose Ramon can too. In fact, maybe it would be better if she got some time off and was able to find somewhere else to stay till we're sure she's safe. What do you think?"

"Well, I believe Martin, the boss at her work, has been pretty understanding. It might be easier if I speak to him for her. As for somewhere else to live, I'm sure that would be a good idea. She has lots of friends but then they're all in the ex-pat Spanish community. I don't know where… no… hang on. I do. I know where would be absolutely perfect if she agrees. I'll make a few phone calls. I think we can drop her out of sight for a bit. Though how we track down Ramon…"

"Well, that's our problem now. I wondered if having you around might provoke a reaction from the suspect and we certainly got one. I don't want to ask any more of you or Gillian will certainly never speak to me again. The thought of no more peach pavlova. Ahhh."

Gillian was sitting at home with a pile of student essays and a gin and tonic when David called. She didn't really believe in drinking alone but would make an exception when it came to reading torturous dissertation proposals. The things some people thought you could make a legitimate academic study out of. One wanted to research the changing representation of Scottish dialect in the Broons *Sunday Post* cartoon family over fifty years. And that was relatively sensible compared to "English, Scottish, Poppish – the language of Wet Wet Wet: A study in late-twentieth-century popular music vernacular". However, it was one thing to instinctively feel something was either undoable, undesirable, or trivial; another to critique the proposals, which, to be fair, usually had a reasonable amount of thought put into them. Then you had to try to find something positive to say to steer the student in a more productive direction. And every paper she picked up, when she tried to remember whom it belonged to, the only faces she could conjure up were of Andrea and her friend José. Were they gems placed on the path of life in front of her to be picked up and cared for, or just a nuisance that made you stumble and got in the way of real life? But what was real life anyway? Murders were pretty real. The most important things in life are called the matters of life and death, aren't they? Andrea was alive but might not be for much longer if they – that's to say mainly the police but maybe David and herself as well – if everyone around didn't do their bit. At least they were now forewarned. The two girls in Seville hadn't had a chance.

She tried to turn her mind back to the Broons but it seemed such a comical juxtaposition. Murders didn't happen in the comfortable world of *The Sunday Post*'s long-running cartoon family. Grandpa Broon lost his teeth or Joe got stood up by his latest girlfriend, but, as a family, they continued happily and dependably on generation after generation. The real world wasn't like that – which is probably why they remained so popular. People like predictability. She admitted she had a fondness for it herself. There was something comforting in the ancient rhythms of the academic year, with new enrolments, Freshers Week, lecture programmes, exams, graduations, holidays, then the cycle starting all over again. Her own life had been entirely less than predictable over recent years but now she felt on the cusp of getting things back on an even keel. There was a wedding coming up in only a few months: her own. What many girls did in their twenties she was now embarking on in her forties. But it was totally delicious. It made her feel like she was twenty-two again but doing it right this time – waiting till the wedding night, fussing over dresses, decorations, menus, invitations, the guest list, a million people to speak to, and a to-do list longer than the Manhattan Project. But she loved it all. David was in charge of the honeymoon and showing up in a suit. It wasn't that she was excluding him but they had realized early on it was simply a question of who did what best. She would no more ask him to choose the flowers than she would try to lead the Southside congregation. But that seemed fine all round. And she was enjoying herself so much it was getting very hard to think about anything else. Including the Broons or Wet Wet Wet. *Gillian*, she told herself sternly, *concentrate. Three more and you can have the night off*.

Just then the phone rang and the direction of her evening changed completely.

David Hidalgo very rarely took a taxi anywhere. Walking was first choice, buses second, trains for events outside of Edinburgh, and Gillian's silver MX5 for Sunday afternoon runs down the East Lothian coast. So Gillian was surprised when she was told to expect him in a taxi in ten minutes if she was free for an hour or so. Dissertation proposals were happily dropped, the gin and tonic gulped down but not refilled, and she put a warm evening coat on.

The offices of Supertempo were in Hanover Street off Princes Street and up the hill a bit. Tatiana Garmash and Elvira Antonov

– Tati and Elvira, together simply known as "the girls" – had managed to rent a tiny flat above the office for convenience and taking account of the huge amount of late-night working they did.

"Of course we'll look after her for sometimes," Tati had said when David rang her. "Is a sofa we can make in a bed in the flat. No problem. Come to the office though. We are still working. Then we can go to upstairs."

So the taxi pulled off Princes Street opposite the Scottish National Gallery and stopped across from a branch of Santander Bank just before the pedestrian lights for Rose Street. The Friday night centre of the town was buzzing with eaters and drinkers, tourists, students, and smart executives off duty and out on the randan. But the lights were still on in Supertempo and work was continuing. Andrea had been quiet all the way, preoccupied with her thoughts; neither David nor Gillian felt it right to intrude on them. She had a black carry-on case with her, a handbag, and a backpack with a Union Jack design. She was nervously biting her lip and fiddling with the straps of the backpack. As David leaned through to pay the driver, Gillian whispered in her ear.

"This is going to be fine. Honestly. The girls are lovely. They'll look after you."

Andrea muttered a thank you but didn't feel altogether grateful. Leaving José behind had left her bereft and adrift in a city she still didn't quite think of as home, sheltering from a murderer with former prostitutes she had never met. It didn't feel like what a twenty-four-year-old *chica* should have been doing on a Friday night. They crossed the road and David rang the bell for the Supertempo office. Elvira answered almost immediately and ushered them up the stairs into a cramped white office with three desks, each with a computer monitor taking up most of the space, a couple of filing cabinets, and walls covered in year planners, a magnetic whiteboard, and a massive card index. On top of one of the filing cabinets was a coffee maker and mugs and the other had a collection of pot plants. In short, it was a perfectly ordinary modern office like a thousand others in the city. Nothing suggested anything other than purposeful activity by busy entrepreneurs – which is exactly what they were. Tati was on the phone speaking in Belorussian or at least not in English. She looked up, smiled briefly, then returned to the conversation while jotting furiously on the notepad in front of her. The desk opposite must have been Elvira's as it was vacant and had a collection of just the sort of knitted toys David would have expected of her. The final desk in the bay window space and furthest from the door had an even bigger monitor partially obscuring the figure behind it, but, as they waited, the face of Sandy Benedetti appeared from behind with a nod of greeting. Elvira whispered a welcome, kissed Andrea, squeezed her hand, and as silently as possible filled up the coffee maker. They waited rather awkwardly until Tati had finished with only the gurgle of the coffee machine for company. Finally it sounded like she was rounding up and saying goodbye. She put the phone down with a sigh of relief and apologized profusely.

"So sorry!" she said. "That was the minibus firm that will bring our next group of girls. You have to check every single thing or they treat them like cattle. I want them to have a better experience than we had!" While that was a reference to how they and many like them had been trafficked across Europe, it was said with good humour and made David marvel once again at how balanced and healthy they seemed to be. It would have been so easy to become bitter and resentful. It was almost miraculous.

It struck him how different the outcome of their story was from Ramon's. To take the most sympathetic view possible of his history, he could be seen as a man struggling with the inner tensions of frustration and unfulfilled desire. But in his case a genuine problem had led to a wildly inappropriate "solution" where other innocent parties had been made to compensate for his problem. That descent into exploitation and horror now seemed to have led to a man who had entirely lost any sense of right and wrong, victim and victimizer. Tati and Elvira, on the other hand, along with so many others, had been real victims of real violence with no control whatsoever over what had happened to them and so much more reason for resentment and bitterness. But somehow they had risen above it and were now gainfully employed, happy, and balanced – even joking about what they had been through. What was the difference? Good genes? A happy disposition? A supportive environment? Was it the grace of God or a key decision of the will to choose the light? David didn't pretend to know but every time they met he had to pinch himself to believe it was real. They were maybe the realest people he knew.

"Coffee anyone?" asked Elvira. They sat down in a few spare chairs around the office or perched on the edge of a desk while David explained the situation in more detail than had been possible on the phone. Tati nodded at intervals while Andrea studied the floor. Sandy apparently just kept working on whatever he was doing, his keyboard rattling busily.

"So that's it," David summed up. "We need a safe place for however long it takes. No idea how we find this guy or how long it's going to be. But everybody seems to think it's a serious threat. I thought you 'Supertempos' would understand."

"Of course," Tati confirmed without hesitation. "No problems." Then to Andrea: "We have a bed sofa – or is it sofa bed – I never know. You can sleep there as long as you want. If you're bored in the days you can come and help us – or not – what you want. But one of us can always be around. We can do plans for that. Is ok? We go upstairs?" Andrea smiled weakly and let them lead the way. Gillian tagged on as Andrea's only known friend and left David and Sandy together.

"So midnight oil and all that, Sandy?" David prompted.

"'Fraid so. But I don't mind a bit. There was quite a lot of catching up to do but I think we're getting on top of it. They haven't done anything fatally wrong. They had all the information; they just didn't have an easy way of calling it all up. Same with the finances. But we've got it all into Sage Accounting now so that's a massive job we won't have to do again. And I think we'll be making quite an impact on the tax bill too. So it's really all going pretty well."

"And Sonia doesn't mind you spending all your working days locked up with two young single women?"

"Are you kidding? She would lease me out long term. The feeling of having a job again – even one that doesn't pay – it's been really good for us both. It feels sort of normal again. And the fact I can help the girls that… well you know… were part of Power and Glory. That's icing on the cake."

"It sounds like a firm of accountants the way you say it."

Sandy Benedetti smiled. I think that's what they wanted – to sound as legitimate as possible. And they were good at it. We were all taken in. If Sam hadn't refused to believe the police verdict on Mike and you hadn't kept on at them – well, it could all have been so different."

"But you might still be in a job…"

"Yes, but still having the wool pulled over my eyes. Thinking I was listening to the gospel and in fact it was all marketing for a racket. I much prefer this. It feels like I've got a life back again. And helping the girls just makes it so much more worthwhile. Maybe undoing a bit of the damage. I love it."

Just then Gillian came back through the door.

"I think that's them sorted," she said, "at least for now. Tati and Elvira are calling it a night. They'll be down in a minute to switch everything off then they're going to take Andrea to a tiny Italian place just a few doors up."

"I recommended it," Sandy whispered.

"Then it's off to bed. I think Andrea's frankly exhausted with the stress and anxiety. And you need to go home to your wife and family, Mr Benedetti."

Tati, Elvira, and Andrea finished their meal with decaf Italian coffee and Tati asked for the bill.

"Can I pay something?" Andrea asked.

"It's no problem," Tati replied. "If David asked us to run the Edinburgh Marathon with no shoes I think we would try. This is not so hard."

"I haven't really got to know him much. We just met at the chat group about a week ago. It's all happened so quickly."

"David is not a usual kind of man," Elvira said with an air of conviction. "He seems very ordinary but is not ordinary things go around him." She took another sip of coffee while choosing her words very carefully. "Do you know he save our lives? And the other girls. I'm sure we would not be live if he hadn't helped us. Is a long story but I have confidence in him."

As if by silent agreement they hadn't spoken about Andrea's situation or David's involvement with the girls over quite a noisy dinner but by now the restaurant was quietening down. A few glasses of Chianti had helped Andrea relax and she was beginning to trust the two young women – not much older than she was – who seemed to have had such an incredible story and were now running their own business. If they spoke well of David Hidalgo, then that should count for something. It would have been so much easier to express herself in Spanish but that wasn't available so she tried to compose her thoughts as carefully as possible and turn them into reasonable English.

"You're right," she said. "When José introduced me, first I thought he seemed a bit like a teacher I used to have. Friendly but a bit old-fashioned. You know? Nice but not someone you can imagine doing anything exciting. Now some of the stories I've heard seem incredible. And Gillian is lovely too. They seem to do a good team together."

"Make a good team?" Tati suggested.

"Of course – 'make a good team'. 'Do' and 'make' are hard for Spanish speakers."

"I can imagine. English is mystery sometimes but is very important. When you have good English you speak to half the world. But is not the only mystery. Sometimes I can't believe what happened to us even myself – and I'm in the story! I think David show what can happen if you are determine do the right thing. Whatever happen. You know? I'm sure he'll do the very best thing to help you."

"Thanks again," Andrea repeated. "It all feels very complicated right now. Like it's a game of chess and I don't even know the rules.

And the other player's pieces are invisible. You have to guess what they are going to do then do something to stop them!"

"I know is not easy, but don worry – things will work out. For sure," Elvira said. "You must be patient. Anyway, let's talk about something better. Tomorrow is Saturday. What you want to do?"

"I don't know. Am I allowed to go out? I thought I had to stay inside all the time?"

"I don think so," said Tati, frowning. "It's not a prison. I think we can go out. We are working late every night this week. We need a day off. Let's go shopping!"

Andrea brightened at the prospect and they made the short journey back to the office then upstairs to the flat in better spirits. To help her think of something else, Elvira asked her what her worst mistake in English had ever been and that started them off with more and more extreme mix-ups and misunderstandings until by half past midnight they were helpless with laughter. Many seemed to involve body parts. Elvira admitted to talking about how sport can make your logs ache instead of your legs. They were all aware of the alarming similarly between sex and socks, sacks, sax, six, sags, sucks, and seeks. That had them in fits for another five minutes.

"'Appiness," Elvira said suddenly with an entirely straight face. "Say it only a little bit wrong and it comes out a bit rude." It took a second or two for the penny to drop then there were more gales of laughter.

"I was in big trouble once," she added, totally deadpan, "when I said all my life I am searching for 'appiness." That cracked them up again.

"When you find 'appiness you have to hold onto it," Tati offered.

Then even Andrea managed to join in with: "Sometimes 'appiness is hard to find but you'll know it when you see it."

"There's a joke in Spanish," she added once they had managed to calm down a bit again. "It says, my pronunciation is so bad that when I order a beer I never know if they'll bring me a beer, a bear, a bird, a beard, a pear, or a peer!"

"I solve the problem," said Tati. "You must only ever order gin and tonic," which started them off again.

"Thanks goodness we don have any neighbours," Tati giggled once they had calmed down. Eventually Elvira recovered herself enough to go and make cocoa and then they had to seriously settle down to avoid getting chocolate all over the cushions. Finally Andrea started yawning and Tati took the hint. She went for sheets and a downie and together they folded down the sofa.

"Just before we go to bed," she said, "can I make you a suggestion? If you don mind. When we got out of the house first used to come nightmares, every night. Was horrible. So I ask David what to do. He came to our flat and he pray with us. He read a little book with some Bible verses. Then he pray. Never more nightmares. I don know why but never more. None of us is pastor but if you like I can pray. Is not hard. You just say what you want then say thank you. You like I should pray for you?"

Andrea felt tears coming and tried to blink them back.

"I would like that very much," she whispered. All the tension of the past week seemed to have evaporated, leaving her exhausted and calm. Ten minutes later she was drifting off to sleep on the sofa still feeling good and giving thanks for her new sisters though precisely to whom she wasn't entirely sure. *What a nice thing*, was her last thought of the night. *To be able to speak to God just like a friend.*

By unspoken mutual agreement David and Gillian had also felt they needed time to calm down and catch up but in quieter surroundings, so they turned the opposite way from the busy, clubby, trendy, watering holes on Queen Street for the quieter surroundings of the Caley Bar in what was now calling itself the Waldorf Astoria Hotel but for locals would always be the Caledonian. Despite the bar having the layout of a railway carriage they managed to find a quiet table for two.

Gillian thought she had probably had enough gin for one night so had settled on a soft rose-coloured Martini Rosato.

"Well done, *caballero*," she said.

David took a sip of his usual ten-year-old Laphroaig and acknowledged the compliment.

"Once it struck me, it seemed so natural. If anyone could understand what Andrea must be feeling it would surely be the girls. And listening to their story might help her believe she *can* leave it all behind. Sometimes things *do* work out."

"Indeed. It seems to be working out for us, *amante*. Or at least, so far so good."

David laughed with the release of tension and perhaps the first glow of the warm, peaty spirit in his veins.

"Don't say that. It makes it sound like the jury's still out. I just want to spend the rest of my life with you and not be distracted chasing criminals."

"Here's to that. But just before planning our retirement on a Polynesian island, do we have any idea why Bances is so sure Ramon is in Edinburgh if he doesn't know where he is?"

"Yes we do," David replied with half a grin. "It's actually quite cute. Stuart told me they were going to lean on him a bit and maybe use the possible assault as a bargaining chip – strictly forbidden, of course. I'd said I didn't want to press any charges but Bances wasn't to know that. So he eventually coughed up. Turns out he has a cousin who has a car dealership in Granada. One night they were having a drink in Triana and the cousin tells him about this bloke who came in and put 20,000 Euros on the counter for a second-hand Jag – no questions asked and no identity papers. Well, in the crisis, that was a bit of a windfall so no questions were asked. But in the rush to get the car out the door they forgot to reprogramme the anti-theft security tracker. So when the car was driven off it was still reporting to the dealership. The guy didn't leave any address or documents so they had no way of contacting him to change things over. Bances smelled a rat and wondered if it could have been Ramon since the papers had reported a substantial amount of cash missing from the lawyer's safe after they found him tied up and suffocated to death. The cousin let him look at the CCTV and despite the beard and glasses Bances was sure he was right. The cousin gave him an app on his phone that relays GPS data and tells him exactly where the car is. So – QED – he knew for certain that at least the car had come to Edinburgh. Which makes it almost certain that Ramon had too. Neat, isn't it?"

"Very cool," Gillian agreed. "And where is the vehicle now if we know that?"

"We do," David replied. "It's in a long-term leased parking place in the multistorey at Greenside Row at the top of Leith Walk. Stuart sent a DC there this evening and it's confirmed. They even took prints off the door handles and they match. They're going to put a watch on the car from later tonight and see if he turns up to use it."

"So Bances was just reluctant to tell all to protect his cousin who shouldn't have been selling a vehicle for that amount of cash without further inquiries?"

"Exactly. But I think Stuart has done a really good job. Apparently Bances' all on side now and wants to do anything he can to help find Ramon, even if shooting him is kind of off the agenda."

"And shooting you, I hope, too. Are they going to charge him with anything? I would have thought turning up with a gun and telling police you intend to kill someone isn't altogether legal."

"Don't know. Would it be conspiracy to commit murder or does that need somebody else to be conspiring with? As you know I'm strictly an amateur in matters of the law."

"Yes. And I'm trying to keep it that way. Against all the odds it seems."

"Well, you really can't blame me for Ramon coming to a meeting I spoke at twenty-five years ago and getting star struck."

"Ok, I'll give you that. Changing the subject, it's nice to see that Tati seems a bit less star struck herself and is getting on with things and making a go of it on her own account."

David took another sip of the amber spirit and glanced around the bar with an air of quiet satisfaction.

"That is so true," he agreed. "What these girls have been through and where they are now... it's incredible. And Elvira just seems to have such a naturally sunny nature. As far as she's concerned there's absolutely no question that the business is going to thrive. I think Tati is more reserved. She knows it takes working like crazy and getting some lucky breaks."

"Well, goodness knows they deserve them. And maybe Sandy deserves one too. I know Sam finds it hard to think positively of him, but he was fooled the same as the girls. And he clearly wants to do all he can to make up for it, which is turning out to be good for them and for him. But what about when the girls found your name on the list they stole from the office of the brothel – was that just a lucky break d'you think?"

"Who for – them or me? Don't let Juan hear you using the 'L' word. And was it a lucky or an unlucky break for Ramon that he heard me speak? I've been thinking about what Bances had to say about the way we influence our young people. I just can't decide if he has a point or not."

"Not," said Gillian flatly and put her drink down. "I've helped out at Sunday School and Kid's Club. And I've spoken to the youth group. These kids are not warped and twisted by some weird brainwashing. It's not perfect but we encourage exactly the sort of values we want in our young people: honesty, diligence, study, respect for one another – particularly the opposite sex – self-restraint, a sense of justice. I could go on, you know. And it's not as if parents, teachers, and youth leaders just sit in front of their kids and tell them to believe whatever they like; everybody has a set of values we want to instil in the next generation. Everybody. My dad has always been an atheist as far as I know but he brought us up not to tell lies. That's a value. Saughton prison isn't full of kids from Bible class. It's full of people who never had appropriate mentoring to give them the values they need in life. If I'd been there I'd have given Bances a slap. Ramon chose his own route in life. You are not to blame. Say after me: I am not to blame!"

David couldn't help laughing out loud and not just because of the relaxing effect of the dram.

"You are… well, what can I say? Can I say perfect?"

"No, not perfect. But maybe just right for you. That's enough. It's not rocket science, as they say. I just know you well enough by now. It's a good thing to be willing to see the other side of an argument but you need to know when to say, 'No, that's rubbish. I'm right. End of story.'"

"Care for another libation, Dr Lockhart? I like the way this conversation's going."

"Don't mind if I do, Señor Hidalgo. Another one of the same, *por favor.*"

But before David could get to the bar his phone rang. He spoke quietly for a few moments, looking increasingly concerned, then closed the phone and went back to the table.

"The car's gone," he said. "He's taken off before they had time to get a watch on it. He must know we're on to him."

Chapter 12

CRAMOND

"Careless, careless, careless!" DI Stuart McIntosh berated himself as he flicked through a series of photos of parking bays in Greenside Place multistorey carpark on his laptop and explained Friday evening's events the following Monday morning. Campos, David Hidalgo, and Alfonso Bances were with him around the table in a small committee room in St Leonard's. The question of whether Bances was to be charged with possession of a firearm with intent to endanger life was on the back burner for a bit, though McIntosh was clear that a report would be sent to the Procurator Fiscal. So while felons awaiting formal charges were not normally included in matters in which they had been criminally involved, Bances – as the only one who knew Ramon personally and had an idea of his mindset – was seen as an asset. On the way to the meeting he had come up to David and apologized for some of his comments the previous week.

"Just some of them?" David asked innocently.

"Ok, I apologize for my remarks," Bances conceded. "It's just that it's a subject I have strong feelings about and I am still very angry that Camila couldn't be protected. I accept that you are not personally responsible for what Ramon has done – or what he turned into. I am partly responsible too for not guessing sooner what was going on. I'd be grateful if we could put that conversation behind us. If you'll forgive me speaking freely, I don't like you and I don't like what you do but I will do anything I can to help stop Ramon – including working with you."

"Well, at least we know where we stand then," David shrugged. "I agree the point is to stop Ramon. Whether we like each other is a separate matter."

So they had gone into the meeting with the air somewhat cleared and were now listening to McIntosh's account of the weekend.

"The officer we deployed to the garage at 11 p.m. on Friday called in to ask exactly where the vehicle was. Said she couldn't find it. Then we checked CCTV and saw it had been taken out at 10.30. We missed him by half an hour. And the tracker has been disabled so we have no idea where he is now."

Bances swore first in English, then in Spanish, and David was tempted to join him.

"But you have the registration number at least, I suppose?" David asked.

"We do. There's an all-points alert out for it. We have number recognition on motorway cameras so there's a chance we may pick him up."

"And otherwise?" asked Bances.

"Old-fashioned police work: door to door, ports and airports, bobbies on the beat. Maybe even *Crimewatch*, you never know."

"That seems more than just a coincidence, doesn't it?" David remarked. "There's a conversation about knowing where the car is and it disappears just before the officer gets there to keep an eye on it. There's a conversation about the tracker and it gets turned off. To me that's more than just bad luck. It's almost as if Ramon is listening in, though I've no idea how."

"Well, a police station is generally thought to be a pretty secure environment. He wasn't hiding in a cupboard. And I can't imagine he's bribed a bent cop to keep him informed; he's only been in Edinburgh a matter of weeks. What else is there?"

"*La informática*," said Campos, without further explanation. David and Bances immediately understood what he meant but McIntosh looked confused.

"Information?" he asked.

"No," Campos explained. "I think you call it IT. Computers. The internet. Hacking. Everything like this. You have a database with all the information in the case?"

"Yes, of course," McIntosh countered, "but there was no time between the interrogation in the afternoon and when the car disappeared in the evening to update anything. I had my laptop open and I was taking some notes as we spoke but I didn't even have a browser open. And I wasn't connected to the Police Scotland system. I think we can rule that out."

"You may be right," David commented, "but I've been caught out that way before. I have a contact I think we should talk to. If he says no then I'm happy to let it lie."

"You mean Spade?" McIntosh asked.

"The same. We keep in touch. Gillian thinks his powers in the dark arts are the equivalent of witchcraft but he's not been wrong yet. I'd just like to ask his opinion – and have him look at your laptop if you don't mind."

McIntosh shrugged.

"We have our own IT guys who could give it a once over but I have no objection, so long as I'm there when it happens. And by the way, why did you immediately jump to '*informática*'?" He directed the question to officer Campos.

"Before I flew over I pulled his prison file. He did some courses in *informática*. The education officer thought it had all been a wonderful success and would help him find a job in something other than the church. But there was also a handwritten note saying that since he'd been released they've been having all sorts of problems with the computers at the prison. They brought a professional in and found the whole system riddled with stuff that should never have been there. Their opinion was that somebody had been using it as a personal gateway to dozens of other government sites – places that should have been absolutely secure. The thing that proved it was Ramon was that his entire criminal record had been deleted and replaced with passages from Cervantes. And someone had hacked his prison file and replaced the photo with one of the Pope. Who else could it have been? The teacher thought he was a star pupil but he was more than that."

"He was just playing with everybody," Bances said flatly. "That's the sort of man he is. He thinks he is so much more brilliant than anyone else that he would just do it for fun. Knowing it would be found but only once he was out would make it even more amusing."

"You didn't mention this before," McIntosh said with barely contained irritation.

Campos shrugged. "I didn't think it was relevant," he said. "He was good with computers, so what? He wasn't killing people online, was he? But now we want to know how he knows what we've been discussing. I'd bet my pension it's got something to do with *la informática*."

McIntosh managed to restrain himself. Taking it out on Campos wouldn't help anything now. And this did put a new spin on things. Maybe Spade should have a look at his laptop just to be sure.

"No doubt about it, boys," the man in black announced with happy confidence. "Nobbled. And nicely done too." Danny McGuire, aka Spade ("coz I dig for things") had once taken a bullet in the shoulder meant for David Hidalgo, but by a complicated sequence of events the two had become unlikely friends. Spade had played a crucial role in exposing the illegal side of Power and Glory Church so had already proved his unorthodox credentials beyond reasonable doubt.

"Absolutely," he confirmed, as if further confirmation was necessary.

Once the possibility of the leak being of the IT variety had come up, McIntosh, to his credit, had wasted no time. He asked David to call his contact and set up a meeting. Spade, having no regular job and no regular hours, was pretty flexible – at least once out of bed – and seemed to particularly enjoy showing up the polis as "a bunch of tumshies" as he put it. So they had trooped round to his coding nerve centre – a disastrously untidy tenement flat in Duff Street, Gorgie Dalry, since Spade, while happy to help, did consider it consorting with the enemy actually being summoned to a police station. In any case all his tech tools were located in the one scrupulously tidy space in the flat – what he called "the Bridge", from his other major obsession, the Starship Enterprise. So David, Alfonso, and DI McIntosh crowded into the tiny space while Spade went to work on the laptop.

"That's incredible," David commented once Spade had announced his results. "You're saying that someone – let's assume it's Ramon – is able to listen in to conversations using the laptop mike and even use the laptop camera at will?"

"No question," Spade confirmed. "It's not that difficult and it's something you have to protect against – either with software or the more conventional way."

"And what's the more conventional way?" McIntosh asked dryly.

Spade grinned at that.

"Just search for 'Zuckerberg camera covered' and you'll see. There's a bunch of photos of Mr Facebook sitting at his desk with his laptop. Some bright spark noticed that if you zoom in you can see he's got sticky tape over the microphone and the camera. If the boss of Facebook – with all the protection they're gonna have – doesn't trust hackers not to turn it all on and join the party... well, what can I say, gentlemen? According to what I've been able to unpick in here," he gave the laptop a friendly pat, "I think somebody – let's say your pal Ramon – has been up to something similar. If you had the laptop on and open at any time in the conversation he could certainly have been listening in. And from what you say about the car and the tracker... I think it's a cert. That what you gents wanted to know?"

Despite Bances bristling at the reference to "your pal Ramon", he nodded grimly. David assented with a shrug. McIntosh said nothing.

Spade closed the laptop and handed it back to him.

"And where do I send the bill?" he asked politely.

The remainder of that week passed without major incident but also without major developments. McIntosh kept David up to date by email, having got a completely new laptop out of stores set up with only the bare essentials and every security device known to humankind – supervised by Spade. He assured him they were busy with "routine inquiries", but for those not involved there was nothing to do but go back to normal life and hope for a breakthrough. Gillian taught her classes, marked work, and sat on endless curriculum development committees. David did his evening Spanish class and kept on working through the kingdom of God parables trying to get them into some sort of shape to preach through in an orderly manner. Tati and Elvira worked at building contacts in companies they thought might use temporary help and continued their intensive training with groups of girls not long arrived from Belarus. Andrea sat upstairs in the flat most of the time trying to lose herself in chick lit. She had given up on D. H. Lawrence and turned to what she would normally have considered frothy rubbish in Spanish. She forgave herself by accepting that she just couldn't concentrate on anything else right now. Having just found a new lifestyle that suited her – a job, new friends, a great new city, and maybe a boyfriend – it was immensely frustrating, particularly not knowing how long it was going to last. The weather was getting steadily warmer, the cherry blossom was out, the nightlife was hotting up, and she was more or less locked in a tiny flat isolated from it all. David and Gillian went round any free evening they could to keep her updated and she was grateful but it wasn't like mixing with her own age group and doing what she wanted to do.

However, the following Saturday morning Tati announced a trip. They had a late brunch of waffles and bacon then headed out to the bus stop. As they rolled and rattled down to Cramond on the banks of the Forth, Elvira explained they were going to visit "a very special friend". Dr James Dalrymple, former anaesthetist, walker, dog owner, and now – surprisingly, in his retirement – people-trafficking campaigner, welcomed the girls in his usual awkward Scottish style halfway between shaking hands and hugging. On the way Elvira had told Andrea how important he was in their story but didn't say why. All she would say was, "He also save my life. David and Dr James too. And Maxi."

This was all getting too confusing for Andrea, who thought it would be too much to ask who Maxi was, but she found out soon enough when a rather elderly golden retriever who should have known better came bounding out of the house threatening to knock everyone over, all arthritis forgotten for the moment.

"Get down, Maxi! Confounded dog!" Dalrymple ordered while being totally ignored.

"Maxi," his wife Sarah said quietly, coming out of the house with a tray of drinks and a stern look. Maxi stopped in her tracks, looked at James, at Sarah, and at the visitors then lay down.

"Magic touch," Dalrymple sighed. "Goodness knows how she does it. Anyway, welcome all. Any vegetarians here? No? Good! It's about time for our first attempt at a barbecue this year. Let's see how we get on."

"Not many vegetarians in Spain, I imagine?" he asked Andrea once everyone was sitting around on hastily wiped garden chairs and he had taken up station at the barbecue trying to coax some life into a stubborn pile of cold, black charcoal. There had been no reference to why Andrea was staying with Tati and Elvira, no mention of Ramon or police or priests gone wrong. To all intents and purposes it was just a group of friends of varying ages and nationalities getting together for a Saturday afternoon celebration.

"No, not many," Andrea agreed. "Salad is a starter and you might get a plate of chips with the meal but meat is the main thing. Except in the north, then it's fish and seafood."

"Well, I'm with the southerns then," Dalrymple announced. "Carnivores of the world unite."

Eventually the charcoal did light, the smoke billowed up then died down, and trays of sausages, burgers, steaks, and chops started emanating from the kitchen door.

"It's the only time he cooks!" Sarah whispered sotto voce to Andrea. "He likes to think he's mine host even though I've spent the last three hours getting everything ready. I find it works best to humour him."

Andrea grinned and sipped her ice-cold beer. Men and barbecues seemed to be the same the world over. However, she was surprised by the sheer quantity of everything that kept appearing. She counted at least two dozen burgers and the same in chicken legs, more than two pork chops each, and apparently innumerable sausages. *Well,* she thought, *they must know what they're doing here but there's more meat than an Argentinian gaucho feast.* Just then she heard the crunching of wheels coming to a halt in the drive at the front of the house and matters resolved when David, Gillian, Stuart McIntosh, Campos, and even Alfonso Bances appeared around the corner. Kisses, hugs, and handshakes were exchanged depending on nationality and temperament. While Andrea was pleased to see them all – at least partly got together for her benefit – she couldn't help feeling deflated that the one face she really wanted to see wasn't there.

"Oh, by the way, one other thing," David announced absentmindedly after everyone had sat down and had a drink. "I think we forgot the desserts." He turned towards the path to the front of the house and shouted: "Do we have any cheesecake?" Andrea didn't know what to say for several seconds when José appeared around the corner, grinning, with a couple of bags. He was almost knocked down as she threw herself at him, careless of any cheesecake that might be at risk. There were grins all round. Gillian squeezed David's hand, said "You are awful" and gave him a look. Once José had managed to peel Andrea off, the bags were whisked off to the kitchen and he found a folding chair next to hers. She gripped his hand like she was frightened he might disappear in a puff of smoke.

The afternoon progressed as Scottish barbecues normally do. There were threats of rain, a cold wind off the river, a few drops that eventually came to nothing, then the skies cleared for long enough to get through the mountain of meat, piles of baked potatoes and salads, and plenty of wine and Irn Bru – Dalrymple refused to have Coca Cola in the house. The puddings were left for round two as everyone seemed to need a breather. The girls, plus José, whom Andrea wouldn't let go of, decided to take Maxi for a walk by the river, which allowed Andrea to get alongside Sarah and discreetly ask just exactly how Maxi had saved Elvira's life. It was incredible. Elvira – bound hand and foot, half-drowned – had washed up on the shore one foggy morning when Maxi sniffed her out and James had resuscitated her and nursed her back to health. Andrea was beginning to feel like she was trapped in an episode of the *Miami Vice* reruns that play interminably on Spanish TV. And it transpired that it wasn't just her story that David and Gillian had been involved in. According to Sarah, there had been an Edinburgh girl kidnapped by a Colombian drugs gang and rescued from the south of Spain. And a people-trafficking and prostitution ring concealed behind the facade of a church. It made her feel weak at the knees when she thought of what that must have been like for these very girls walking alongside her right now on a sunny Scottish spring day. But in another way, it gave her a strange feeling that maybe things would work out. Maybe Ramon could be caught and life could begin again. Maybe there was hope. David and Gillian seemed to have a way of seeing things through to a good conclusion.

"It was just about here, I think," Elvira said, pausing by the water's edge. "If Maxi didn't have a good nose I'd be – what do they say in Scotland? – I'd be history…"

"Maybe you were wearing your best perfume," Tati suggested, trying to take the grim edge off the story. "Anyway. 'All's well' they say too." Then, suddenly remembering that Andrea's story wasn't over yet, she squeezed the hand José wasn't holding and added, "It will be good for you too. I know it."

"So do you have any plans after this is all over?" Sarah asked. "Will you go back to Spain?"

"Yes, for a visit but unless there's work… José and I have been talking. We'd love to open our own Spanish bar. And we wouldn't charge twelve pounds for a jug of sangria like some. Good authentic drinks and tapas. No sport or bullfighting on the TV and maybe live music too, no?"

José mumbled "sure" but didn't elaborate. It wasn't easy feeling an attraction come to life for a girl he'd known for years but with the simultaneous sense that events beyond his control might take her away from him at any moment. In some ways he wasn't a guy who thought much about the future. Coming to Edinburgh had been a spur-of-the-moment thing and it had worked out well. Lots of decisions seemed to go like that for him. "You can plan too much," he used to say in the endless discussions they had about their futures after Complutense. "Just get on with life. Take it easy. It'll come to you." But this suspense was killing him. How could you get on with life – or a relationship – when any moment the floor could open up under you? Maybe better just to be content in the moment.

Out on the Firth of Forth a dozen little dinghies were scuttling about like ducklings, with an inflatable safety boat keeping an eye on them like a mother duck. He wanted to protect Andrea but felt it was beyond him. He'd been happy when she'd sent him that email what seemed like ages ago asking if there was any chance of work and he'd wasted no time in speaking to the boss. He'd been careful not to take anything for granted and not to make it seem like he had some sort of proprietorship over her time and interests. Then, in the midst of this whole situation about Ramon, they had taken comfort in each other. It felt nice. He hadn't planned it and thought she hadn't either but it was happening anyway. That was how life was supposed to work. But not when life could be taken away at any time by some crazy guy's twisted idea of revenge. First you do evil, then you kill the people you've already hurt just because they stood up and told the truth. Crazy. It was frustrating but there seemed to be nothing he could do. It had been deeply disappointing when it turned out that the action he had taken to identify and track the man he was sure was Ramon turned out to be nothing of the kind. Now things had turned into a waiting game. The fact that exposing Bances had proved without any doubt that Ramon was in fact in Edinburgh was a mixed blessing. Good to know but not good that it confirmed what he had come for.

The safety boat was chasing all the little dinghies back to the shore. He wondered where he and Andrea might end up – safe in a harbour or grounded on the rocks. He picked up a stone and sent it skimming lightly over the water. It would be good to skip over all these problems and get to where they should be going. But not as easy as throwing a stone…

The conversation among the men back at the cottage had taken on a grimmer tone.

"So the car's gone missing, you, Alfonso, are not Ramon – who turns out to be an IT genius as well as a cold-blooded killer – and that girl is next on the list." Dalrymple summed up the situation.

"That's about it," McIntosh agreed. "And I imagine the black beret and glasses Alfonso saw in the CCTV at the garage will have gone too by now."

"He must have enjoyed the mistaken identity," Alfonso Bances added ruefully. "Something else I'll have to have a word with him about when we meet."

"So what do we do now?" Dalrymple pressed the detective. Doing nothing didn't suit his nature and that seemed to be all that was on the table.

McIntosh shrugged.

"There's only so much you can do when someone otherwise unknown to UK police starts operating here. They have no home address, no known associates, no accomplices, no bank, no utility companies, no lawyer to contact, no source of income, no family. It's a needle in a five-million-stalk haystack."

"Surely not that bad," Dalrymple countered. "If he's looking for Andrea then he's got to be in Edinburgh. That makes it around a million stalks for a kick off. Then he knows you're looking for him so there's nothing to be lost by circulating an image – there're good recent photos, I presume? Why not put some pressure on? He may have a fair amount of cash but it can't last forever. He must have some timescale in mind. He surely can't wait six months or a year to make his move. It's like when you want to attack a cancer but you need to get every single cell. There's no way you can take them all out by surgery; chemo is basically just killing everything in the hope that the cancer stays dead and everything else recovers. The newest techniques are to flood the system with antibodies that uniquely attach only to cancer cells and only kill the things you want dead. Ramon is a cancer. There has to be something we can directly target at him that'll force him to show himself, then you can act. This waiting – well, it might go on forever. We owe it to that girl to give her a life."

Nobody disagreed with the retired doctor's diagnosis but nobody had a bright idea as to how to accomplish what he suggested.

"So if there's nothing in Scotland that he's connected to, what about Spain?" David asked after some moments. "He must have some family, even if not very many friends nowadays. Is there anything there that can force him to show himself?"

"Maybe," Campos said thoughtfully. "He has a mother still living. She collected him when he came out of prison but he only spent one night there before he moved to a tourist hostel in Sevilla, then a rented house. That was after the lawyer was killed and he'd cleaned out the safe. She's been questioned and says she has absolutely no idea where he is. She had already disowned him after his prison sentence. Now the fact that he's killing for revenge – well, she doesn't want to have anything to do with him at all – even if she did know where he was."

"I've just had a thought," David said slowly. "Maybe she wouldn't have any influence on him alive. What about if she were dead?"

"What are you suggesting?" Campos replied. "That we kill the old woman then see if he comes back for the funeral?"

"More or less."

"I can see where you're going with this," Dalrymple said with a smile. "Not actually kill her of course, but let him believe she's deceased – something quick and unexpected, heart attack or the like – then a funeral and all the trimmings and see if that flushes him out. Capital!"

"Interesting," McIntosh said thoughtfully. "I'd have to check with my team, but it could be something that forces the issue."

"Chase him out," Dalrymple added, enjoying the idea. "Rattle his cage a bit."

"Or what about just 'dangerously ill'?" McIntosh suggested. "Then he has to get back to Spain pronto to try to catch her before she dies."

"Even better," David put in. "Certainly worth a try."

"What do you think?" McIntosh asked, turning to the Spanish officer. "Think you can set it up?"

Campos was grinning.

"I learned a new expression the other day," he said. "'Just watch me!'"

Chapter 13

TWO CITIES

At first Maria Zapata Lopez refused to let the two officers in. The door was double locked and all the blinds were down. Campos and his partner had been knocking for ten minutes when at last they heard shuffling from inside and the door opened a crack.

"Who are you? What do you want?" demanded a voice. A black shawl covered her hair and even in the crack of light from the hot afternoon she looked grey and shrunken. Town hall records showed she was only sixty-seven but she looked more than eighty.

"We're from the *Policía Nacional,* Señora. We want to talk to you about your son Ramon."

"I have no son Ramon."

"I understand how you feel, Señora. It must have been a terrible blow. But something has happened that concerns Ramon. We are trying to prevent further distress to everyone. It'll only take a minute. Can we please come in and talk to you?'

There was a very long pause, then the sound of a chain being unhooked. The door swung open. The whole house was in darkness. The Seville heat normally keeps everything bone dry, but despite that there was a musty smell and a hint of sour milk. The old woman shuffled back to let the officers pass.

"In there," she said.

They advanced into an almost pitch-black room. Dim lights were switched on, barely illuminating cobwebbed yellowing walls. The floor was tiled in deep red and heavy dark furniture was arranged around the walls. As his eyes grew accustomed to the gloom, Campos noticed a bureau covered in a plethora of photographs large and small, presumably of children, grandchildren, nieces, nephews, and all other variations. There were a number of empty frames. *How interesting,* he thought. *Instead of simply taking the photo down or putting another picture in its place she leaves the frame up with the photo removed.* It was making a statement – even if just to herself.

"Wait here," she said and disappeared. The clinking of glasses could be heard from the kitchen and she shuffled back in with a silver tray and three tiny glasses of *jerez* the colour of mahogany.

"So what do you want? I don't know where he is. He wouldn't contact me and I would have no use for it if he did. I told you, I no longer have a son called Ramon."

"I understand perfectly, Señora," Campos reassured her. "We know you don't know where he is and we're not here to pressurize you. However, the fact is we desperately need to find Ramon before he does something even worse. We have reason to believe he may be in Scotland. We think someone else connected with the trial may be in danger. We want to keep you from any further grief. If we can stop him we think we can maybe save a life. Would you be willing to help us?"

"What do you want me to do?" she barked.

Campos explained. All they wanted was that she should take a brief holiday. Perhaps her sister in Córdoba? While she was gone they had hopes that Ramon might be encouraged to come back to Spain where he could face charges and not be involved in any further bloodshed.

"And why would he come back just because I'm on holiday?" she demanded.

"Because we think Ramon still values his *mamá*. If the word got out that you weren't well – perhaps not likely to live – well, he might think it his duty to see you once more. Even if you didn't want to see him."

"Deathbed reconciliation?" the old woman asked astutely, immediately grasping the point. "Devious *cabrones*, aren't you?"

"In a manner of speaking," Campos admitted. "The point is to stop him doing more damage."

"Who is it then? Who is he after now?"

"A girl."

"Name?"

Campos' colleague shot him a quick glance but the senior officer didn't hesitate.

"Andrea Suaréz Morán."

The old woman grunted.

"Hmm. I remember her. Father was a good dancer in his time. Mother bit of a fishwife but that's not a crime. Nice girl. So he's trying to get to everyone who testified against him? Only one question then."

Campos nodded.

"If he comes back, if you get your hands on him – could I see him wherever you lock him up?"

Campos was surprised. He shrugged.

"Sure," he said. "Why not? But I thought you didn't want to see him."

"I don't. But in that situation I'd like to visit him. Just give me two minutes. You wouldn't need a trial."

It was easy enough to invent a terminal illness. The director of the local palliative care hospital suggested lung cancer since Maria had chain-smoked since her teens. It wouldn't be surprising. Sometimes in an advanced case where the patient has not sought treatment the end could come remarkably quickly. An ambulance at the door would attract attention. A too-talkative driver and orderly would spread the word among neighbours used to knowing everything about each other down to the contents of the Sunday soup pot. She seemed to live such a reclusive life that the sudden poor prognosis wouldn't attract much attention. Nobody would be saying, "Oh, I saw her last week at Alfredo's; she was the life and soul of the party." The harder point was how to get the word out in a way that Ramon would be likely to pick up on but that wouldn't seem overblown and unnatural. One of Campos' colleagues hit on getting the local priest – Ramon's replacement of about eight years now – to broadcast an appeal to the black sheep to come home one last time to see his mother before she received the final unction and passed beyond this world to the mercy of the Saviour. No one thought he would be stupid enough to make an appointment, but there was a chance that he might somehow try to linger on the fringes and catch a glimpse or even watch the interment from a distance. It was worth a try.

"We recognize that Ramon has not perhaps been everything a mother might have hoped for," Father Felix intoned mournfully. "But he has paid his debt to society. His mother would like the opportunity to see her own flesh and blood one last time and be reconciled to him. She does not wish to pass into the next life with unresolved matters on her conscience. She feels there may perhaps have been more she could have done and wishes to assure Ramon of her love and prayers and that she will continue to pray for him among the *ánimas benditas* until she takes her place with the blessed in paradise. If he would be willing to return even for one final moment that is all she would ask."

What a farce, thought Ramon, watching TV Sevilla online in his hotel bedroom. It's disgusting. They probably twisted her arm to say that so it would look good, or she said nothing of the sort. God is loving, forgiving, and merciful and the church is his body on earth. One last tender moment to set things right. Then the priest and the bishop take the credit for another rescued soul. The fact that she was ill and might not have long for the world didn't particularly surprise him. Lung cancer, they said. Well, the old crone had been kippered for years. The fingers on her right hand were the colour of cinnamon sticks and the strand of hair over her eyes was tinted by the constant plume of smoke. It wasn't at all surprising.

Of course the press were loving it and the priest was surrounded by cameras and microphones shoved in his face. What a story. Notorious child molester brought to repentance and peace by a mother's love. It fitted exactly the Spanish psyche. That's why the Blessed Virgin always seemed just that bit more accessible, understanding, and gracious than the godhead. In a sense the Son was bound to hold to the party line that sin was sin and had to be dealt with. Not as ferociously angry as God the Father of course but still grieved that the sins of the world had needed such a remedy. Maria, on the other hand, as a wife and mother, knew how hard it was to meet the demands of a demanding father – albeit a heavenly Father. She was everyone's ideal mother, the one you go to when you know your father will just say no in an angry tone and might take his belt to you for good measure. Maria would never do that. She would take your wants and needs – a boyfriend, a husband, a baby, a job, or simply a *better* boyfriend, husband, baby, or job and explain them in a way the Father couldn't refuse. He might not grant your direct request but could not refuse the mother of his Son. Ramon knew the psychology off by heart. He had preached it for fifteen years. Nothing but bogus blarney of course; but still, in the case of his own mother, he couldn't simply ignore the fact that such a highly unlikely event might still be possible. What if she did want to see him? What if age and pain and the thought of imminent departure had changed her mind? Perhaps she had come to see after all how the priesthood was an impossible task and that he had honestly tried his best, given it everything he had, and found it to be not enough. He was a weak and vulnerable man – which was only to say he was human.

He flicked the video slider back to the start and watched the whole thing again. Felix was certainly giving it his all, droning on as if sadness and grief were the lifeblood of the church – which they more or less were. *Semana Santa* proved it. Given a choice of death, darkness, and despair on Friday or joy, resurrection, and new life on Sunday morning most of the church worldwide chose the latter. But not in Spain. God died and it was your fault. You are the God killer. Theocide – a new crime specifically invented for Easter. No wonder the supermarkets were more and more full of chocolate bunnies. Who in their right mind would want to put that guilt on innocent children? So you are responsible for the death of God and – guess what? – the only possible way of expiating your sin lies in the hands of the church. Consider the power that would give over human souls, wallets, votes, whatever. It was a no-brainer. Hence the processions of tearful Virgins and tortured Christs carried about by the brotherhoods and followed by the mob every *Semana Santa* and the way that Sunday morning was more or less ignored. No doubt about it: Felix was bang on message, tugging the heartstrings and the media loving it.

But what about the real figure of his mother somewhere at the bottom of the rotten pile? The press had been remarkably quiet of late about the Sevilla murders. Both city and national police confessed themselves stumped. A bishop, a lawyer, and two teenagers; it didn't fit the normal profile of a serial killer targeting a string of prostitutes and junkies or even a backpacker or two. He couldn't believe that nobody had joined up the dots. He had started off so focused on the Plan that the thought of getting caught and sent back to Morón or somewhere worse hadn't really been high on the radar. Supposing he accomplished his Plan then died in a hail of gunfire, so what? Justice had been done. But as time had dragged on, as first the bishop, then the lawyer, then Camila, then Maite had died and he still remained at liberty, the thought of life began to again take root.

He arrived in Edinburgh and was astonished by how beautiful the city was, how vibrant and multicultural. It was living. He was here on a mission of death but in Edinburgh it was spring and the days were refreshing after the baking heat of Sevilla. The grass was green, not grey, and the flowerbeds in Princes Street Gardens were newly planted. Crowds of Japanese and Korean tourists were jostling for the best place for a selfie with the universal Victory "V" sign. Life. He was here only to kill. It would be a bittersweet kind of victory. For the first time he almost regretted it. But the Plan had to be fulfilled. Still, once that was over, if the Scottish police were as stupid as those in Sevilla... maybe he could make a new beginning. The long years he had spent rotting in a provincial jail had to be paid for, but then it might be a time to live again. Then maybe the howling, screaming voices in his head would be silenced. He had even found a speciality suited to his intellect and talents that did not involve having to endlessly sympathize with the poor and pathetic of a Catholic parish. *La informática*. It even had a nice sound rolling off the tongue. Using only *la informática*, he could roam the world, removing cash from accounts, buying and selling credit card details, trading in bank account details or changing his own. What fun. Yes, once Andrea had been dealt with, perhaps then there would be a time to live. It would require a last final burst of determination.

In the meantime, the girl seemed to have vanished off the face of the earth. She wasn't at work and didn't seem to be at José's flat any more – at least, if she was, she never came out and wasn't visible moving about inside, even with binoculars. The next step was following David Hidalgo, his sometime hero, the evangelical pastor who had no business meddling in affairs that didn't concern him – maybe there would need to be a settling of scores there as well. But his routine seemed unchanged. Church meetings, the Saturday chat group – minus certain key members – Spanish classes for bored housewives and failing students in the evening, dinner with his mistress or whatever she was, Friday nights at the Jazz Bar in Chambers Street. The only change seemed to be paying a bit more attention to the Belarusian girls who had set up in business. Maybe they were struggling and needed pastoral support, or perhaps he was planning a little fling with one of them. Or both. They were certainly cute enough.

Either way that was irrelevant. Andrea was not to be seen and he was growing impatient. This couldn't go on forever. Luis Castillo's money had all but gone, along with the funds he had siphoned off from the parish. He had had some luck early on in scamming gullible internet users who really shouldn't have been allowed out on their own, far less permitted a bank account, but that took time and concentration. The cheap hotel he was living in didn't have fast enough internet access and it was hard to devote himself both to fruitless searches in a bustling city full of wandering tourists and making money from the simple-minded at the same time. Maybe he needed a break. A trip back to Sevilla in the sleek, comfortable Jag he had still held onto – now with that stupid tracker disabled. See his mother one last time if it was possible – or maybe just a glimpse from a distance would be enough to close that chapter. Then one final push in Edinburgh to close the book and open something new. Then he would be free. Still he would have to be careful. Not everyone was completely stupid and blind to the obvious. The conversations of Hidalgo, McIntosh, Campos, and Bances proved that.

David Hidalgo also had some unfinished business. He had a guilty conscience for having been so short with a young man who was presumably only doing his job and had probably been sent by his editor. Gillian wasn't harassing him, but he knew she thought he should put things right. The newshound had been too familiar by half but he also recognized his own mixed feelings about the whole "crime-fighter" thing. Events had unfolded around him in wholly unexpected, unpredictable, and uncontrollable ways. It was not a comfortable fit. In Madrid he'd had reasonably frequent contact with the whole "law enforcement" machine, but that was routine, predictable. It might involve going to court along with a junkie trying to get clean, come to church, and wanting to change his address, or trying to persuade the local police to go easy on a girl shooting smack in a doorway, who couldn't go home because her boyfriend had just beaten her up for the umpteenth time. There were sympathetic cops and obstructive ones – those that could see what Warehouse 66 was up to and wanted to help and those that thought they might be due a bung for looking the other way. But in general they rubbed along ok. He did his job and they did theirs. But this was different.

When he butted up against Raúl and his mob just arrived in Madrid from Colombia and used to breaking heads if they felt the slightest resistance to their operations, everything changed. David's work – the work of the whole church in fact – was getting so many off chemical supports and into community, family, and faith that it was actually hitting local sales. Raúl felt it would set a bad example for that to go unpunished. So David was threatened. Street workers were roughed up. The church building was vandalized. But, as a team, they felt they had a commission from God. As Paul put it, "If God is for us, who can be against us?" But of course Paul himself understood that the final outcome of the war did not determine the result of every single battle. So Paul was taken to Rome after appealing to Caesar and probably died a martyr. One evening after work Rocío was bundled into the back of a black 4x4. David got the call in the middle of appearing on a radio phone-in. Maybe half a million people heard the gunshot that ended his marriage and his ministry. Many times in the difficult early days of their marriage and later on in tricky circumstances in church life, he and Rocío had sat together and wondered what would become of them. Now there was a final answer. Rocío was dead and he was finished. So he went running back home to Edinburgh and the strangest twist of all, the recovery he never expected – a new love in his life when he thought he was too old for another start. But, weirdest of all, finding himself at the centre of not one, not two, but now three criminal investigations. Who'd have thought it? "Charlie Ferguson: Crime writer. *Edinburgh Evening News*" might not have thought it, but now he wanted to write about it. Reluctantly, David picked up the phone.

They met in Henderson's vegetarian restaurant on Hanover Street not far from Supertempo. Neither were meat-phobic but David liked the huge selection of fresh ingredients and discreet booths deep in the back of the building. Ferguson piled up his tray with assorted veggies after first making the mistake of asking for a burger, then followed David into the bowels of the restaurant.

"If you don't mind me asking," he began, "why the secrecy? It's a good news story. You would come out of it very well. So would your church. Good publicity for the business the girls have set up. There are private investigation firms in the city that would give their eye teeth for what you've achieved. So why not let people know about it? I'm sorry, but I don't really get it."

"Because I am not a private investigator," David shot straight back, then took a deep breath and tried to keep his cool. "I am a pastor. That's all. Not a very good one, but that's what I try to do. And I could be a lot better at what I do if it wasn't for these sorts of things that seem to keep happening around me. Being a pastor inevitably means that people come to you with their problems. Sometimes these might involve issues with the law, but usually they're looking for help to get off with something: maybe a character reference, or spiritual help that impinges on criminal matters. Addiction is a case in point. Now, for example, I'm getting more and more young men wanting to talk about their pornography addiction. That's usually not against the law but it can become illegal if it gets out of control. These are the things I care about. I'd much rather the police dealt with crime and I work with the individuals that need the help of a pastor. It just doesn't seem to be working out that way. Does that make sense?"

Ferguson was in the middle of crunching his way through a bowl of celery salad with grapes but nodded and chewed a bit more so as not to spit half of it across the table.

"I get it," he said. "So you're not just playing hard to get or something. The crime thing really isn't the main event?"

David rolled his eyes.

"No, it's not," he said with a note of resignation in his voice as if to say *finally*! "And I have a private life. Which I'd prefer to keep private."

"Yes, I know," Ferguson immediately responded, glancing at the spiral notebook he had laid out on the table next to his spinach lasagne. "Dr Gillian Lockhart, isn't it?" he asked.

"How did you get that name?" David demanded. "You have no right…"

"Calm down, David," Ferguson soothed, holding his hands up. "We understand privacy and we respect it. One of your church members… eh, a Mrs Buchanan I think… mentioned her. That's all. That wouldn't be part of the story."

"We have not yet agreed there's going to be a story," David said, gazing upwards and trying to calm down a second time. This wasn't going well.

"Ok, ok. We're still talking about it. That's all. But if there was a story…"

"Were," David interrupted.

"What?"

"Were. If there *were* a story. It's subjunctive. I thought you were a writer."

Now Ferguson rolled his eyes.

"Ok. Were," he said patiently. "If there *were* a story, what we'd want to highlight, besides you as an individual, is the sort of problems that you've found yourself involved in – drugs, the sex trade, trafficking, whatever. We'd be highlighting the problems these cause in twenty-first-century Edinburgh and where people can go for help. Say you have a drug habit and it's becoming a problem. How do you get some help and not end up addicted or controlled by the dealers? And the girls that are brought in from Eastern Europe. They get their passports taken away and are threatened that if they try to complain to anyone they'll just be deported. The girls you helped get free prove the opposite I suppose. They were treated sympathetically and two of them even started a business. And the gang behind it are all in jail, including some of our fine constabulary and the great and the good. So the idea would be not just to focus on you but to reach out to the sort of problems you've found yourself involved in. That sound any more appealing?"

"It does," David said with a little hesitation. "That's the first thing you've said I can relate to. No – strictly no – mention of Gillian Lockhart. Passing reference only to the church and focus on those that might be victims of whatever it is. That's the deal. And copy control."

Now Ferguson looked a bit put out.

"That's pretty unusual," he said guardedly. "We wouldn't normally give anyone final say over the text of a piece, particularly an extended feature like this."

"Well, that's what's on the table," David replied. "Take it or leave it. And no reference to anything going on right now."

"Is there something going on right now then?" Ferguson asked.

Uh oh, David immediately thought. *I should not have said that.*

"There might be," he said. "But that's irrelevant. Whether there is or there isn't, it does not get a mention. Real lives are more important than readership. Are we clear?"

"As a bell," Ferguson said, smiling. "I'll have to run it by the editor but I can see where you're coming from. I think we can do something win–win. And not a word about the current investigation."

From feeling as if he was making progress David's spirits had immediately sunk again. *Idiot*, he thought. *Why can't you keep your big mouth shut?*

Chapter 14

CÓRDOBA

The sleek silver Jag ate up the miles first to the Channel Tunnel, then around the Paris ring road and south to Bordeaux, then over the border at Irun, around Madrid via the A-2, and finally south on the A-4. But then a choice arose: direct to Sevilla, or somewhere else – somewhere intermediate to gather information, get a sense of whether he was walking straight into a trap, his mother's health being as good as ever? Maybe somewhere to take soundings that were impossible in Scotland might be a good idea. The internet allowed many things that had previously been impossible but there was still no substitute for being physically present to ask questions, smell the air, get a feel. In any case, if he went directly to Sevilla he'd have to dump the car somewhere unobtrusive on the way and come in by public transport. If there was any chance they were waiting for him then the car would be a liability. Audis, Mercs, and BMWs were much more popular, making a Jag a rarity and noteworthy – even with the different number plates. So at the very least he'd need a temporary halt. He decided on Córdoba – not too far but not too near and not too much of a diversion. Anyway it was a city he loved. A night in the Parador de Córdoba would be just the thing. Although it was a modern hotel and lacked the Moorish heritage for which Córdoba was famous, it was slightly out of the city and higher up, which made it cooler. If they were looking at all they'd be looking in Sevilla. Perhaps he could have a couple of nights to recover from the miles and enjoy parador cuisine as well. He set the GPS and pushed a button to ease the seat back slightly.

But before the parador there was one other address to visit. His aunt lived in the old Jewish quarter, and prior to his prison sentence had been about the only family member he felt he could unburden himself to. She had led what could only be described as a colourful life. After training as a dancer she had worked in Madrid, then London, Paris, and even Moscow. When he was still in his teens she used to tell him shocking stories about the Party commissars who came to her dressing room after shows. "Better call it the undressing room," she used to say, laughing uproariously. Later, as a priest in training, he had kept in as close contact with her as he could. She always referred to his "calling" with one eyebrow raised and toned down the juicier stories but she was the only one whose advice he always took seriously even though she had no more use for organized religion than for chopsticks. While nominally Catholic, she never went to mass and had last confessed at the age of seventeen. "If I have something to tell God I'll say it directly," she used to say, even once Ramon had been consecrated. "What do I need a priest for? Do they think God doesn't understand my Andaluz accent?" After his conviction and prison sentence, she was the one family member who wrote to him. "You got caught," she had said. "That was your crime. The church has a monopoly on forgiveness but don't expect them to apply it to their own black sheep. I'm a black sheep too so I should know. When you're high enough up you can do as you like. The Kremlin or the Vatican – it's all the same. But you weren't high enough and now they'll squash you like a fly. Come and see me when you get out."

Now he had the opportunity and the time. He thought she'd be surprised. When Aunt Lucia opened the door she certainly was.

"Who is it?" another voice shouted from inside before his aunt had come to her senses and shouted a warning.

Ramon had expected to make an entrance but this was something else.

"Who is it?" the voice repeated. The door was pulled wide open from behind her and a familiar figure appeared as large as life and a good lot cheerier than the last time he had seen her, a cigarette as ever in her hand.

"*Madre mía*," was all his mother could say, appropriately enough.

"Well, you'd better come in then," Lucia finally managed, "and not stand there like a virgin on his wedding night."

"The bishop and the lawyer I don't blame you for – assuming it was you," said Lucia as they sat down over olives and almonds that had been prepared in silence. "But the girls. That's not fair. What have you become, *Ramonito*? And whatever you're involved in now, pack it in. Hold onto whatever remains of your soul."

"I thought you didn't believe in the soul, Aunt Lucia?" Ramon asked, ignoring her earlier comments.

"I don't but that's not the point. You know perfectly well what I mean, so stop acting the fool. You are a fool but there's no need to make a meal of it. Whatever's going on now they've got the knives out for you so give it up. Take that pimpmobile you have out there and disappear. I won't shop you, at least not for a week or two. Disappear. Let the world forget you – it'll happen soon enough. And whoever they're trying to protect from whatever you're planning, let them get on with their life and forget about you as well. What have you got to gain from more bloodshed?

I told you to abandon the priesthood but you wouldn't listen. Listen to me. I'm an old bird these days but I've been around the block a few times. You can start again. New beginnings aren't available in *El Corte Inglés* but that means you don't need to pay premium prices for them either. I've had a dozen new beginnings in my career. I could tell you stories that would make your hair stand on end. But I can't be bothered with all that stuff any more. There's a lot to be said for living a quiet life. Juan who used to own the hardware store takes me out to dinner once a week and I let him sleep with me once a month or so. It keeps him happy and it makes me happy too. All the wealthy suitors I've never told you about, the commissars and the counts, and the priests and bishops I might add – they don't mean anything now. You lose your passion but you need to find *com*passion to put in its place, for others and for yourself. Give it up. Find the man you could have been. Find

186

a friend and leave it behind. Confess if you have to. Then let the church go to hell. For God's sake salvage something of your life."

Ramon said nothing and neither did his mother, though the way Lucia's words echoed the advice he'd had from the bishop so long ago struck him. His mother had taken a packet of *jamón reserva* out of the fridge, put it on a plate, and was peeling off slices, pushing them into her mouth and chewing in a daze. She looked as if her dead husband had reappeared on the doorstep. Ramon stayed that night. He inquired after his mother's health but she told him to mind his own business. But Lucia was chirpy and chatted all evening. They listened to Tchaikovsky on an ancient gramophone "given to me by Stalin himself," she claimed, "a randy old goat if ever there was one." Ramon had no idea whether to believe her or not. They ate lamb chops, peppers, fried potatoes, and hunks of crusty bread. His mother disappeared as soon as the coffee and liqueurs had gone and didn't reappear the next morning.

"Don't mind her," Lucia counselled over a breakfast of strong coffee and slices of sweet cake. "She never could see the funny side. Not that I'm saying it's funny, but you need a sense of proportion. Whatever you're involved in now, it could be the end of you, and someone else I don't know about. Just knock it on the head. That's all. Now. Or I'll disown you too. She may never speak to you again, I don't know, but you can still give her some crumb of comfort. They wanted her to play dead to get their hands on you. Lung cancer I think. Well, between you and me, I wouldn't be surprised. She smokes like the factories of the Ruhr and coughs like trying to start a tank. It might well get her in the end. Then how would you feel if she snuffs it, believing her best boy was roaming the earth like the grim reaper? Whatever you're up to there's no need to make a career of it. You can make a decision to change. Think about it."

He kissed her on both cheeks, put his bag back in the boot, and glanced up at the first-floor window. The curtain gave the slightest quiver so he knew she was there. He got into the car, nodded to Lucia, and drove off, leaving his parador reservation unused.

He reached out automatically to set the GPS to Edinburgh, then stopped and wondered why. The Plan. The beautiful, perfect, accursed plan. Lucia was an old bat now but she had clearly been a society beauty in her time. She had lived life to the full and had seen and done more than all his professors and teachers put together. They should get her to do the pastoral theology in Mondoñedo, not some fusty Jesuit who had lived all his life with his nose stuck in Thomas Aquinas and Ignatius Loyola. *Think about it* was her parting shot, and he did. Advice he would have ignored from anyone other than Aunt Lucia somehow lodged in his brain. He thought about it all the way from Córdoba to Madrid. Then, for lack of anywhere else to go, all the way back to the Channel Tunnel then up the M6. He thought about it in the motorway travel lodges and cafés. He thought about it while pouring another 800 kilometres' worth of gas into the tank. And he thought about it when he couldn't get to sleep.

From years in Morón he understood that the fights that often broke out weren't always won by the biggest, heaviest, or toughest. He'd seen small guys emerge bloody but triumphant from scraps with apes who should have crushed them. The key factor was almost always confidence and the will to win. He'd never doubted either since the Plan had begun to unfold. But Aunt Lucia had knocked him back on his heels and now he was wondering, what if he just stopped now and changed direction? Who would be the poorer? It wasn't as if there was some supernatural examiner waiting to mark his work. *Did you finish what you set out to do? No? Why not? Failed!* It was strictly up to him. Do it or give it up, as Lucia had urged him. Leave the girl to live her life and try to find a new one of his own. Maybe he'd find a woman who knew nothing of his past and he could invent a more worthy history. Maybe in time he could even come to believe it himself. The constant voices in his head might fall silent. He could get up in the morning, eat breakfast with a sweet, caring woman, go to the offices of some IT company, come home at night, eat a nicely prepared chicken stew, watch a bit of TV, then make love to his wife and sleep contented knowing he'd done the right thing for once in his life. Or he could keep on with this bitter war against those who had wronged him. As the miles rolled by the alternatives went round and round like a mantra in his head. *What about this? What about that?*

Finally he realized he'd have to make up his mind and stick to it. Determination and the will to win were what mattered. To hell with them all. This wasn't the moment for scruples and dithering. He would take Lucia's advice but not just yet. He would find Andrea and he would pay back whoever came up with the idea of using his dying mother as bait. He put his foot down a bit harder and sped all the faster towards Edinburgh and whatever was waiting for him there. It would be what it would be. If only the dying sounds of Camila and Maite breathing their last would stop…

"Let's fall in love," Diana Krall was singing, suggesting after all the benefits might just be worth the gamble. For a special birthday treat Gillian had surprised David with two tickets for the Friday night gala concert at the Usher Hall on Lothian Road. A full jazz orchestra was piled up on rising stands behind a huge grand piano and a tiny figure that packed a big voice. It was really towards the easy listening side of jazz rather than full-on bebop but that was a compromise that worked for both of them. They had negotiated the art of meeting in the middle pretty early on. It wasn't about abandoning your own tastes and desires to accommodate the other, simply bringing them with you to meet halfway. Diana finished her second encore, took a bow, left the stage, and the lights came on. The hall was filled with a buzz of happy conversation as friends, couples, and families compared notes on their favourites. Clever, interesting melodies full of twists and turns, sizzling, witty lyrics, swinging arrangements, and a sure but delicate hand on the keyboard. What's not to like?

"Enjoy it?" Gillian asked needlessly as they filed slowly towards the exits. "Happy birthday."

They exchanged a kiss on the lips longer than strictly necessary.

"Lovely," he replied. "I'm floating!"

"On a sea of jazz," she said, completing his thought.

Eventually they spilled out along with the crowds onto the pavement halfway up Lothian Road and somehow found themselves washed into Dario's Italian restaurant a few hundred yards further up towards Bruntsfield. It was all perfect, tunes still playing in their heads, the warmth of shared experience with others of a similar taste, and an evening of companionship with the one you love. David particularly cherished the thought that the best was yet to come. With a bit of luck – or whatever – they might be doing something similar for thirty or more years to come. What a dream.

"What's it going to be like?" he asked over his usual simple but perfect carbonara.

"What do you mean? What's what going to be like?"

"Just a few months now. Then I won't see you home to Marchmont and trudge back up the hill."

"Nice," she replied.

"Just nice?"

"Yes. My English teacher always told us never to say something was nice if there was any other possible word. But there are some things that are just nice. It's an uncomplicated feeling. For once not mixed up with anything else. So, yes – nice."

David smiled an easy, satisfied, warm-glow smile.

"Touché," he said. "But lots to do between now and then. You maybe think I'm not that interested in the process, just the result, but I'm really very grateful that you're taking the lion's share of it."

"I don't mind. I enjoy it. I want to squeeze every drop out of it. So I'm enjoying the planning as well as the doing. Well, I expect to enjoy the doing as well!"

"*Claro que sí*. And the cake, which is about the one thing I've contributed to. How's that going?"

"Good. Turns out Ayeesha and I have pretty similar tastes, which seems surprising. We both prefer simple and elegant, not baroque."

"So just a jam sponge then?"

Gillian stuck her tongue out at him.

"Not that simple!"

"Do you think it's a sin to be so happy when others aren't?"

"Well, you should be the expert on sin. Who did you have in mind – the starving millions?"

"No. Just one girl knocked off her bike and in the ditch when she expected to be on the highway."

"Andrea?"

David nodded.

"Sorry," he said. "Didn't mean to put a dampener on things."

"Don't worry. I don't think one person's happiness diminishes another's. In fact the happier you are, the more you want to make other people a bit less miserable. At least that's how I think about it. This'll be the end of her second week now stuck in that tiny flat. How do you think she's doing?"

"More bored than frightened right now. She knows there's still a risk but I think she's getting cabin fever."

"And nothing more from Spain? No sign of Ramon?"

David banged the heel of his hand into his forehead.

"Idiot," he said with feeling. "Sorry, I completely forgot to tell you. Campos was in touch with Stuart McIntosh. It seems Ramon must have smelled a rat. Apparently he did pick up the scent and go home but decided to stop off at his aunt's on the way. That was exactly where they'd suggested his mother go to hole up during her 'last fatal illness'. They say he knocked on the door and came face to face with his mother not on her deathbed but drying dishes. According to his mother – who then went straight back home – he only stayed ten minutes and they phoned the police immediately he'd left. Believe that if you like. Anyway, nice try but no cigar, as they say."

"How long ago was that?"

"They think Tuesday this week. So, three days ago."

"Plenty of time for him to be back in Edinburgh then if he's still determined to see it through."

"I'm afraid so. I should go round to see Andrea tomorrow morning and update her."

Eventually pasta and pizza both disappeared, along with most of a bottle of 2007 San Angelo Toscana Pinot Grigio. A shared dish of ice cream finished things off. They wandered out into the still buzzing nightlife and wandered dreamily up towards Tollcross, over the lights, then out across the Meadows towards Marchmont. The evening wasn't cold, the skies were clear, and a smell of recently mown grass was in the air. The night seemed to be full of lovers. Gillian wrapped her arms around her man and they walked like something more than just a couple, almost as if they were melting into each other.

"Coming in?" she asked.

"I'd love to but better not," he answered, glancing at his watch. "Eleven fifteen already. Then it'll be twelve-thirty by the time I get home. And Sunday's instalment of the kingdom of God parables still isn't quite in the bag. Like you said, it would be nice. But it won't be long now."

They kissed. Slow, deep, satisfying.

"Mmmm," Gillian murmured, digging in her bag for keys. "See you Sunday then, Señor David."

As she was fiddling with the keyring and finding the right key David's phone went off. He held up his hand as if to say, *Don't go yet till I find out who this is.*

"Hi. Ok. Yes. Loved it. Sorry I had it switched off in the concert. What is it? When? That's three hours. Oh no. I'll be there in half an hour."

Gillian almost didn't need to ask. She felt her insides turn to lead and her legs to jelly.

"Andrea?" she asked in barely more than a whisper.

"Yes – she's missing. The girls were working late. When they got back she'd gone. No note, no packing. But no sign of a break-in either. Just gone. They've been trying to get me for the last two hours."

By the time they got to Supertempo Elvira was standing on the street outside looking like she'd lost a loved one, which in a way she had. The two weeks Andrea had been with them had been a strain but they had also laughed uproariously and talked about all their best and worst moments. The bond though short had grown deep. Now the new-found sister had vanished and they were thinking the worst.

"I'm so sorry, David," she began as they came up to the door. "Is all my fault. There is so much work we have to do. I leave her too much. I should have been there looking after her."

"Where's Tati then?" David asked.

"Looking. She is walking all around to see if anyone see something. See her leave or see anyone coming."

"Have you told the police?"

"Yes. I mentioned a policeman on Princes Street but didn't seem to do anything. So I say to another. He called on his radio but nobody come. Look. Tati is here."

Tati arrived almost at a run. Her face was pale but she looked determined rather than shocked.

"Thanks God," she said. "You have come. I don't know what to do."

"Until the police get here we do nothing, I think," David answered. "You've been asking around? Ok. That's good. DI McIntosh gave me a number to call if there was a problem. Not the usual 999 and not just a desk sergeant. He said whoever had the phone would have been briefed. I called in the taxi so there should be somebody here soon."

The relief of David arriving seemed to have given Elvira permission to break down entirely. She flopped down on the step of Supertempo and sobbed. Tati sat and put her arm around her. Gillian leaned against a railing looking very concerned and David kept a lookout for anyone he recognized. An unmarked car pulled up in less than five minutes and two DCs got out.

"David Hidalgo?" the first asked.

"Yes."

"Hi. I'm DC Fraser. This is DC Greig. This is about the girl Andrea. A possible abduction?"

David sighed heavily.

"I guess so," he said. "Your colleague DI McIntosh is leading a team looking for a Spanish guy called Ramon Murillo. He was a Spanish priest convicted of child abuse offences and did seven years for it. Now he's been going round after anyone he thinks contributed to his conviction. There have been four murders in Spain and we think this girl, Andrea, might be next on his list. So she's been living with some friends here." He nodded in the direction of the girls still sat on the step. "They were working late this evening. When they got home, I think about two and a half hours ago, Andrea had gone."

"Ok. I see, sir," Fraser responded. "We'll take it from here. We've got a scene-of-crime squad on the way to fingerprint the premises so we can't go back in till they arrive. Then we'll take some statements. So I think the best thing to do right now is maybe get some coffee and calm down a bit. That all right, sir?"

David looked to Gillian, who nodded.

"I'll take the girls," she said. "I think there's a Costa or Starbucks or something around here. Give me a call when there's news."

Gillian and the girls out of earshot, David briefed the two detectives in a bit more detail.

"This was exactly what we were afraid of," he explained. "It wasn't an ideal hideout but it seemed to be working. The girls got on very well but the reality is they're trying to run a complicated business. It was inevitable that Andrea got left on her own quite a lot. Now we've maybe seen the result."

"Well, let's not jump to conclusions," Fraser said in his best 'reassuring the public' tone. "She's maybe just gone for a wander and taken a bit longer than expected. We'll see if we've got some prints, then we'll try to get some witness statements if there are any. Then see what the morning brings. However, I'm afraid we may be at it for a while yet tonight."

Just then a marked car pulled to a stop behind the CID vehicle and two young women got out. They all obviously knew each other and with a minimum of fuss the premises were pointed out and the SOCOs got to work. Half an hour later it was done and David called to let Gillian know. Then it was inside and some basic statements taken that could be augmented later at St Leonard's. Finally by almost 2 a.m. as much seemed to be done and dusted as could be that evening. David had another quiet word with the detectives, who seemed to be nodding and reassuring him. With some hugging and more tears the girls finally went inside. David and Gillian were about to head down to Princes Street for a taxi when Fraser wound down the window.

"Where to?" he asked.

"Marchmont and Bruntsfield," Gillian replied.

"Ok. Hop in."

"What now?" Gillian asked as they headed up the Bridges.

"They're going to contact McIntosh first thing in the morning. He'll probably want to speak to everyone, whether in the flat or St Leonard's I don't know. Then he'll tell us what the options are from here."

"So bang goes my Saturday morning lie-in."

"And my sermon prep."

The mood was no more buoyant the following morning. McIntosh had phoned David early and suggested the Supertempo flat would be a less threatening place to convene. "Ten o'clock ok?" he'd asked. "Whatever – yes, that'll be fine" was the reply.

It was a sober affair by the time Stuart arrived. David and Gillian had beaten him only by minutes and the kettle was on but the girls looked like they needed more than tea. Elvira was pale and red-eyed and Tati grim-faced sitting on the edge of a chair. There had been no word overnight, no sign this morning, and no update from the detectives who had shown up the previous evening.

"We've got Ramon's prints from Spain," McIntosh began once the tea had been handed round. "I've asked for top priority from the labs to see if we have a match, though of course the girls here would have been coming in and out since Andrea disappeared so we may not get clean prints anyway. Still it's worthwhile. Of course we don't know for certain Ramon is back in Edinburgh but we do know he didn't take the bait in Seville. That was almost a week ago so if he was coming back he'd have had plenty time. How he would have tracked down the location remains to be seen. Difficult as it may be, we have to go on the working hypothesis that this is Ramon and that Andrea has been abducted – that somehow he did find out where she was and either had a bit of luck or waited till he was sure the girls were out. There's no sign of a forced entry though so that'll have to be explained. We'll just need to hope we'll get a break. He's in a foreign country and doesn't have a secure base, not like in Seville, so maybe somebody'll see something or he'll put a foot wrong. That may give us a window to work with."

David nodded but could see this was high-quality flannel. The fact was, they had failed. Failed in the man they first thought was Ramon. Failed in the ruse to get him back to Spain where there was a better chance of nailing him, and failed to keep Andrea's location sufficiently secret and secure to prevent her being got at. The possibility of the next definitive news being a dead body in the water of Leith was a strong possibility, maybe probability.

McIntosh went over the statements he had from the previous night on an iPad and asked Tati and Elvira some further questions to try to clear up things that either hadn't been addressed or needed clarification. Gillian and David sat quietly, feeling superfluous. Elvira didn't cry again but always seemed just on the edge, dabbing her eyes and sniffing. Tati was clear but tense. Finally, after another hour and a half – McIntosh was a thorough man – just as he was getting up to go, the doorbell rang. Tati apologized and ran downstairs. Upstairs they heard the door open, a few words, then a scream.

"David!" Tati shouted. "David! Come!"

Everybody came, jamming the stairs and spilling out onto the pavement. A smartly dressed middle-aged woman was standing just outside the office window. Next to her, looking very much the worse for wear, was Andrea.

Chapter 15

HANOVER STREET

"*Lo siento mucho, muchísimo, por toda la preocupación que he causado,*" Andrea whispered, sniffing, perched on the edge of the sofa.

"She's very sorry for all the worry she's caused," David translated dryly.

"So sorry, everybody." Andrea risked one look around the room then resumed her study of the floor.

"Jan McMaster," said the woman, holding out her hand to David. "Street Pastors."

"Street what?" Gillian asked.

"Street Pastors. It's a voluntary thing run by the City Centre Churches. We do Friday, Saturday, and Sunday nights. Nine to three. Mainly just helping people stay safe. We give out flip-flops for the girls that can't walk in heels and get them a taxi. We liaise with the police and the clubs but we don't have any authority. If there's trouble we can try to calm things down but then we call the cops like anyone else. We got a call last night – this morning to be precise – from Benji at El Barrio just up the road. He said they had a girl in who had had a good lot too much to drink and maybe needed a bit of chaperoning. 'Totally off her face' I think were his exact words." She smiled at Andrea but Andrea wasn't responding.

"So I went round and met Andrea. Diagnosis pretty accurate, I think it's fair to say. Apparently she'd spent the last hour annoying people by demanding to know if they knew Ramon and saying she would 'kick him in the *huevos*' when she found out where he was. No ID of any kind. Lost her phone, I think. All we could get out of her was 'Supertempo', which sounded like something Spanish. Nobody knew about the business here. So, since she was on her own and nobody had a clue who to pass her on to – and she was clearly unfit to be left alone – I took her home."

"Wow," said Gillian. "Thank you so much. We were so worried. Has Andrea explained the situation at all?"

"Yes. Briefly. We can talk about that later. I don't want to make this any harder. So anyway, after she'd thrown up a couple of times we got her into bed then I woke her at half past ten this morning, gave her some breakfast and strong coffee, and here we are. She didn't have any phone numbers or I'd have called earlier. Sorry for dragging it out."

There was a stunned silence for what felt like an age. The mood seemed a mixture of relief, disbelief, release of tension, and a certain amount of "what-on-earth-were-you-thinking?"

"Well, thank goodness you were around," David said at last. "I hate to think…" They all hated to think.

"No problem. Glad to be of help. I think Andrea maybe needs a bit more shut-eye now to catch up – and some paracetamol. I'll get going. Brownies trip to the zoo!"

"I'm really sorry," Andrea repeated as soon as the Street Pastor had left. "It's unforgivable."

"No it's not," David said firmly. "Reckless but not unforgivable. You need to be in bed. We'll speak about it later."

"No, I'd like to say now. Then I can sleep. Could I have a couple of tablets though, and a drink – of water?"

Tati went through to their tiny kitchen while Gillian mouthed "let her" to David, who nodded.

"I'm so sorry," Andrea started again but David interrupted her.

"I think we've got that, Andrea. No more sorry. Just tell us what happened."

"I was bored," she said simply. "No, not bored. I actually felt like I was going mad. You know. I hadn't been outside for a week, not since Dr James's barbecue. And going down to the office. The girls were *genial* but I felt I just couldn't – do you say 'stand'? – I couldn't stand being inside a moment more. I thought there couldn't be much risk just going out for a breath of air. So I walked up the road. Then I noticed this Latin bar, El Barrio. I thought I'd go in and speak a bit of Spanish. And just one drink. Actually I don't remember much more."

McIntosh had been sitting quietly during the entire exchange. He did not look happy.

"Andrea," he said slowly. "I understand your frustration but more than twenty officers have been out looking for you. We've involved police labs to check fingerprints and circulated a description throughout Police Scotland and to Spain. Do you realize…"

"Thank you, Mr McIntosh," David interrupted. "Yes, I think Andrea does realize. It was foolish, though I think, in the circumstances, not entirely unreasonable behaviour. I'm sure it will not happen again. Now, I think Andrea needs to go to bed. Gillian has marking to do and I have a sermon to prepare. Ok everyone? Show's over."

Outside McIntosh was even more unhappy.

"I've a good mind to charge her with wasting police time," he hissed at David. "'Andrea does realize' – what utter garbage!"

"Stuart. Calm down. You are entirely justified to feel upset and I'm sorry for interrupting. I just think there's a time and a place. She's been under a huge amount of pressure. We might have guessed that something had to give and it did. It could have been a lot worse. Let's let things cool off a bit over the weekend. Could we speak again Monday morning? I think we're going to need a change of strategy. This can't go on forever. It's neither fair nor realistic. Ok?"

"Ok," McIntosh answered reluctantly. "I'll try and pour oil on troubled waters. It's not just me, by the way. I'll call you on Monday."

Arriving back in Edinburgh presented Ramon with a dilemma. Cash was running dangerously short, not helped by hundreds of Euros for fuel, tolls, ferries, and accommodation. The limit of how long he could hold onto his Royal Mile address was growing dangerously close. At the same time, moving to something cheaper called a "guest house" in the suburbs would take him inconveniently further from the routes he needed to keep a watch on for the day Andrea reappeared. After visiting one where you had to ask for the bath plug and there was a five-pound deposit for the key for the front door, which was locked from the inside at 10.30 sharp, he decided he would stay where he was for an absolute maximum of four weeks more before the problem couldn't be put off any longer.

Another matter, even more fundamental, was also troubling him increasingly – Aunt Lucia's parting shots as he'd left Córdoba. Sometimes it felt as if he'd actually forgotten why he was doing this at all. It had started off as payback for all his lost time and reputation, but what was it now? Simply the need to keep on going and finish the job? There had been a satisfaction in ushering a hypocritical old imposter like the bishop into his eternal rest. Likewise a self-serving lawyer whose only commitment was to keeping his clients out of trouble instead of even occasionally telling the truth. Camila and Maite had stood up in court and painted him as a man devoid of feeling, only concerned about his own perverted pleasures. They knew nothing of how he had struggled over the years before coming to this. But Andrea? She had probably spoken for less than half an hour. Her evidence didn't add anything to the case. Aunt Lucia seemed to be asking, quite reasonably, "Why does she have to die as well?"

And the result of her death – what would that be? Some small satisfaction on the one hand but maybe his own total destruction on the other. If he was caught they would really throw away the key this time. From where he stood right now there was still a chance to get clean away and begin again. From being his one comfort and consolation, this wretched Plan was getting close to being simply a millstone around his neck. What to do? Drop the whole thing and live to regret not seeing the job through to the end? Or wield the knife one more time and live to regret a final act of meaningless vengeance?

And where was Andrea anyway? A few more weeks and there'd be no money left and he'd have to give it up. Quitting when he was ahead might only be accepting the inevitable just a bit sooner.

Why not? Morning, noon, and night the questions wouldn't go away, despite thinking he'd got things settled in the car during the drive from Spain. In bed trying to get to sleep or prowling around the streets by day – round and round and round. What he needed was some way of squaring the circle. Of reconciling opposites. Of finishing off the last witness against him without actually having to take responsibility for it. Some way of making it dependent on something outside of himself – a throw of the dice. Russian roulette. Even better if someone else he needed to deal with could be the party whose actions or inactions determined where the spinning chamber with one bullet in it stopped. An idea was beginning to form.

Then suddenly, from nowhere, he was stunned to see Andrea one morning getting on the bus to work. She popped out in her break to do some shopping, then back home to José's flat at finishing time. Then she was back to exactly her previous routine and didn't seem to be looking the least bit nervous. It was as if she had been on holiday, not in hiding. Very strange. What did it mean? After the dying mother that wasn't, he was suspicious. Was she surrounded by plain-clothes bodyguards ready to jump on him as soon as he moved? Had she been on a training course or something so she'd be turning a gun on him? Impossible to know. But he watched and watched and waited. If she was being followed they would have to be invisible. One morning she took a walk across Leith Links a quarter mile from any other human being. With a good enough rifle he could have hit her and been miles away before the alarm was raised. What was going on? And what to do now? In the meantime, the idea of coming at this from another angle was taking shape. Making someone else nominally culpable was very attractive. Plan B was firming up in his mind.

"I understand the risks. I'm grateful for everything everybody has done but I just can't go on like this," Andrea had said, sitting on the edge of the sofa in the Supertempo flat. David, Gillian, Tati, and Elvira were sitting with her. It was the Monday following the Friday night. There was no ready reply.

"It's not just being – how do you say – 'cooped up' all day. It's that I'm still afraid, even though I'm here. I'm afraid he'll break in during the night, or plant a bomb, or shoot through the window or something – I don't know. He's already taken too much of my life. Now he's taking even more. I have to live. I have to get out into the world and just take what comes. And I don't want a hundred policemen around every corner. I just want to live an ordinary life. My mother says you've only got a certain number of heartbeats. When that number's up it's time to go, wherever you are. So maybe I might not have many left. But I want to enjoy what I have. I didn't come to Edinburgh to hide in a bedroom. I'm sorry if that causes a problem."

David and Gillian exchanged glances, as did Tati and Elvira, but nobody tried to dissuade her. She wasn't a prisoner. She had made her mind up and expressed it very clearly. David could foresee the conversation with Stuart McIntosh and wasn't looking forward to it. But it was like the old democrat's motto – I hate what you say but I'll defend your right to say it. The truth was he didn't like what she was saying one bit but could understand entirely where it was coming from.

"So is there anything we could do to protect you that would still leave you feeling you were living as you want?" he asked.

She shook her head.

"I don't think so. No tracking devices, no bodyguards, no special measures. I'm going back to how things were before. I'm not living with fear any more."

"Plucky girl," Gillian remarked as they walked out onto the pavement moments later. "Is there anything you can think of that she didn't mention on the forbidden list? I feel dreadful letting her expose herself to that risk knowing what happened to the others."

"Yes, I think there is," David said matter-of-factly. "I'll be praying."

When it happened it was quick, clean, and unexpected. José saw the whole thing from the other side of the street. The Jag pulled alongside Andrea as she walked to the bus stop after a lunchtime shift. Why she didn't run immediately he didn't understand at first. She just stood there frozen. The driver's door opened and out got, not Ramon, but Silvia, one of the other waitresses from Càfé Córdoba. She just stood there too, hands cupping her face. Even at a distance he could see she was weeping and shaking. Then Andrea got in. No fuss, no hesitation. Then the car drove off. Just like that. When he got to Silvia she was close to hysterical. "A gun, a gun" was all she could say. "He had a gun." José phoned 999 immediately and tried to explain but it felt like every word of English he'd ever learned had deserted him. Then he phoned David and spoke in Spanish. "Don't worry," David told him. "I'll contact the police." They agreed to meet at Café Córdoba fifteen minutes later. When the story came out, what had happened on the pavement made more sense. A man in some sort of luxury limo had pulled up beside Silvia on her way to work to ask directions. When it turned out he was Spanish her initial fears were allayed. He was a *compadre*. Nice to be able to help. But as soon as she leaned towards the open window the gun came out. "Don't move a muscle," he said, keeping the weapon trained closely on her as he shuffled over to the passenger side. "Get in. Drive." She had never driven anything like that before and stalled several times. He was impatient and barked instructions. He knew exactly where to go. Only two hundred yards ahead Andrea was on the pavement heading for the bus stop. "Pull up here." The window slid down electronically. Andrea was instantly on her guard but she didn't expect to see Silvia in the driver's seat. A split second later she took in Ramon – and the gun he had jammed in Silvia's ribs. Had it just been Ramon she would have run and taken her chances but the implication was clear: somebody's going to die today. It could be you or it could be her. You choose. What could she do? The door swung open and Silvia stepped out, shaking. The gun never lost its aim till it switched to Andrea. "Get in. Now you drive." Then they were gone. It only took a minute. Gone.

David listened grimly to the story when he got to Café Córdoba. He phoned McIntosh, who was there in twenty minutes and heard the whole thing again. It had happened. No waiting and wondering like the last false alarm. This was a fact. Witnessed. Incontrovertible. What they had feared, tried to protect against, hoped might never happen was now in the catalogue of past events. Unchangeable. David looked at McIntosh and raised his eyebrows.

"Ideas?" he said.

"Not many. However, this is a crime on Scottish soil now, which does liberate more resources. We can do the full thing – press conference, news interviews, public appeals, we'll check CCTV on the street, recent photos, newspapers, the works. I'm afraid that may not influence Andrea's safety but I think we'll stand a good chance of nailing Ramon."

José listened, saying nothing. The euphemism of "Andrea's safety" didn't fool anyone. It meant whether she's alive or dead. They might even then be in a position of hoping against hope that something wouldn't happen when it already had. José had supported Andrea in her choice to go back to a relatively normal life despite his misgivings. Now he wondered how he could have been so stupid. Even if she didn't want it maybe he could have done something without her permission – spoken to the police, got some sort of covert protection, even paid for something private out of his meagre earnings. She would have gone ballistic if she'd found out of course but now he reflected that might have been something he could live with. Right now what he couldn't live with was the fact that she was gone and he had done nothing, just stood and watched, rooted to the spot. Less than an hour before she'd been popping back and forth between the hatch and tables with a tray of drinks or a section of tapas. Now that space was empty. There was a space inside him that was empty too. He tried to shift his thoughts back to what David and Stuart McIntosh were talking about. They seemed to be planning an information campaign to get Ramon's name and image out there on the assumption that somebody would have had something to do with a middle-aged Spaniard newly arrived in Edinburgh since, try as he might, even *he* had to interact with normal human beings.

The talk dragged on for about an hour, with José tuning in and out as his levels of energy and concentration rose and fell. They were sat in a corner booth in the café. It wasn't busy but customers were coming and going. Other waiters and waitresses were at work. The kitchen was turning out food. Martin was making up bills and wished people *buenos días* but it was all happening in a dream. Finally they seemed to be grinding to a conclusion. McIntosh stood up and gave José a grim sort of smile.

"It's not over yet," he said. "Let's do what we can and keep hoping."

José barely nodded.

"I better speak to Martin," he said. "I just can't do a normal day's work after that."

David texted Gillian the news but knew she was busy and didn't propose a meeting. He went back to Bruntsfield, flipped open his Bible, a commentary, his notebook – then ignored them all. He sat at his desk and simply stared into space. How had he allowed this to happen? It wasn't logical to blame himself but he was older, presumably wiser, and had been through a few situations akin to this before. He tried not to think about the day Rocío disappeared and how that had worked out, even though he hadn't known she was gone until it was too late. Why, knowing all of that, had he let it happen? Andrea had made up her own mind and was determined but there are ways and means.

Simply for diversion he flipped open his laptop and went to the BBC News page wondering, entirely unrealistically, if it might be showing up yet. More mayhem in the Middle East but nothing relevant from Scotland. He clicked the tab for his email on autopilot. The usual random clutter: cut-price shirts, printer supplies, fifteen local women who want to meet you. Then something caught his eye. In a second his attention was riveted. The subject line read "Ramon's Revenge: would you like to play a game?" He opened it. There was only a web link, nothing more, but it was something. He picked up the phone and selected McIntosh's number. *Pick up, pick up, pick up.*

"DI McIntosh. Hello."

"Stuart. David. There's something here I think you should see."
He explained then made a second call. Finally, to keep her in the
loop he let Gillian know by a brief text. Half an hour later he and
McIntosh met outside a tenement block in Duff Street.

"What d'you reckon?" David asked.

McIntosh shrugged.

"Let's go and have a look."

Just as they were about to go into the close Gillian's car came to
a sudden halt at the kerb. She jumped out and slammed the door,
looking pale but composed. David hugged her.

"Thanks for coming," he said. She squeezed his hand and
followed them in.

Spade opened the door while David was still knocking. He
knew what was going on and was intrigued. They went through to
the Bridge. David put his laptop on the desk.

"You're using a web-based email service I suppose?" Spade
asked.

David nodded.

"Ok, then we'll forget your laptop. We'll open it up on here. I've
got more protection on this machine than the Celtic goalmouth
playing Stenhousemuir at home." He opened a browser, typed in
the address of David's email server, then typed in the name and
password David gave him. Now was not the time for niceties.
A second or two of delay then more shirts, hotels, and money-
saving offers. And the one email they were interested in: "Ramon's
Revenge: would you like to play a game?"

Spade opened it up and clicked the link. The screen cleared
to a single image – strongly blurred. A human figure was sat in a
chair in front of an open window. The light behind made it almost
a silhouette. Despite the lack of clarity it was Andrea. No doubt
about it. "Click to continue" appeared near the foot of the screen.
Spade clicked. A video box opened up. It was the same scene
against the same open window but this time Ramon was sitting
in the chair.

"Greetings, Pastor David. It's been a long time. Would you like to play a game?" he said.

Spade let out a guffaw.

"What's funny?" David demanded.

"Wargames," Spade replied. "It's a joke. It's an eighties film where two teenagers have to win a computer game to save the world. He's got a certain style, I'll grant you that."

Under the video box the options "Y/N" appeared.

"What does that mean?" McIntosh demanded.

Spade explained slowly as if to a not very bright student.

"Ramon wants to be cute. Looks like he's inviting you to play – either against the computer, against him, or some other combination. I think we can guess what the stakes might be. Ha! Look at that!"

Under the "Y" option a tiny animation had appeared of a smiling girl with love hearts exploding from her head. Under the "N" option a tiny guillotine was repeatedly pulling up and dropping its blade.

"All this in the last few days? I'm impressed," Spade remarked. They played the video again several times in case of some nuance they'd missed. Ramon was sitting in what could have been a hotel room but there was nothing distinctive to show one way or the other. The window behind him was open and he was sitting against the light, which hid his features. Outside noises were just noticeable in the background: traffic, birdsong, some music.

"It's totally sick," said Gillian. "I vote we don't play. If we play and lose and Andrea dies then somewhere in his sick imagination it's our fault. We can't let him manipulate us."

"On the other hand," David said slowly, "maybe not agreeing to play would be tantamount to his winning and our losing in his mind. We say no and Andrea gets the chop." He nodded towards the image under the N.

"So what's it to be?" Spade asked.

"Yes," said McIntosh. "I agree with Gillian about being manipulated. But for me the point of the game is to keep him talking. He's feeling secure. He thinks he holds all the cards. He's showing off how clever he is. We play the game – obviously we want to win but the main thing is to keep the channel open. He might do or say something that gives us a lead. We say no and that immediately closes the connection. It might certainly make up his mind in some perverted way but it also means we have no way of communicating."

"I vote yes," David agreed. "Similar reasons. The problem is we have no idea what the game is or whether we have any chance of winning but at least we don't immediately lose. If we say no that's the risk."

Gillian shook her head.

"I'm not happy with that," she said, "but I'll go with the majority. I think he's decided what to do already and he's just playing us along in some sort of mind game. It's like we're giving him permission to mess with our heads."

"Spade?" David asked. "You're the computer games man. Any opinion?"

"Play," Spade said without hesitation. "You've got to be in it to win it. If it's any sort of computer game he's invented I've probably played something very similar. And if not I'm plugged into a network that would make Mr Ramon look like a toddler with a beachball in the Cup Winners' Cup. They'll wipe the floor with him. But we have to see what kind of game it is."

"Ok," David concluded. "With reservations we play. I don't think we've got time for a case conference on this. Stuart will continue with everything the police can do using conventional channels. But we have to take him on. Spade?"

Spade reached forward and tapped "Y". The screen burst into a cascade of colours accompanied by a trumpet fanfare. "Congratulations," it said. "You have chosen to play a game. Click for instructions." Spade tapped the spacebar. The screen cleared again to text.

CONGRATULATIONS.

You have chosen to play Ramon's Revenge, an exciting new entertainment for adults.

Three days, three levels, three prizes but only one life. Click to begin at level one.

"Click?" he asked.

David nodded.

The screen cleared again.

DAY ONE: LEVEL ONE.

Click for your first challenge. When you are ready you may upload your image.

To pass the level your upload must pass evaluation by our panel of experts. Only original images are permitted.

Spade clicked again. Now the screen was filled with a Nintendo-style fairy-tale castle with a princess trapped in the highest tower. The drawbridge of the castle had lines of text in a medieval font. David read aloud.

DÍA UNO: NIVEL UNO:

¿Quién está a la puerta? Es Juan el devastador. Está llamando. ¿Pero quién es y dónde vive?

Jueces 16:28–30

David translated aloud. "Day one: level one. Who is at the door? It's Juan the destroyer. He is calling. But who is he and where does he live? Judges 16:28–30."

"What on earth does that mean?" McIntosh asked, bewildered. "And what sort of photo are we supposed to upload?"

"I think you're on your own with this one, boys," Spade commented. "Not my kind of computer game I'm afraid."

Gillian looked at David. She'd seen him do this sort of thing before.

"Ok," he began slowly. "Maybe we start with what we know or can find out. Jueces 16:28–30. That's the book of Judges in the

Old Testament. If I'm not mistaken chapter 16 might be around the story of Samson. You have a Bible?" He looked at Spade, who looked back as if to say, *Are you mad?*

"Fair enough. I'll find it on my phone." It only took a couple of taps before he began reading:

> *Then Samson prayed to the Lord, "Sovereign Lord, remember me. Please, God, strengthen me just once more, and let me with one blow get revenge on the Philistines for my two eyes." Then Samson reached towards the two central pillars on which the temple stood. Bracing himself against them, his right hand on the one and his left hand on the other, Samson said, "Let me die with the Philistines!" Then he pushed with all his might, and down came the temple on the rulers and all the people in it. Thus he killed many more when he died than while he lived.*

"So we have Juan the destroyer and Samson who destroyed the temple of the Philistines. What else?"

"The word 'revenge'," Gillian put in. "Can you translate one more time?" He did.

"Do you think Ramon is making some sort of reference to his revenge and how many he's killed? And what about the name? You said Juan but it could be John, couldn't it?"

David nodded.

"Sure."

"So who is John the Destroyer? We're in the Bible with Samson, so is there any John who destroys things?"

"John wouldn't be Samson's middle name, no?" Spade put in but was ignored.

"Not the apostle John? He was the apostle of love, wasn't he, not the destroyer? Though John also wrote the Revelation, didn't he?"

"Plenty of destruction going on in there, isn't there?" McIntosh put in.

"John is at the door," Gillian repeated. "He's calling. *Llamar* is to call – yes? *Está llamando* – he is calling, at the door. But who is he? He is the destroyer. And what door is it? Is it the door of destruction, the door of his house, or the door of somewhere else? This is crazy. It's impossible."

"And if I read it rightly, we have to solve one level a day," David said. "I don't know if that means before midnight. Maybe it does. So that's," he looked at his watch, "seven hours. Any other ideas?"

"Seven hours," Gillian commented bleakly. "I don't think I could solve this in seven years. He's at the door. He's calling. Let's assume it's his house. If Ramon wants a photograph then the answer must be a place – something you can photograph. And a place we can get to before midnight because it says only original images are allowed. So a place in Edinburgh or very nearby. Think. Think."

They were all thinking. The soft whir of the computer fans was the only sound. Spade's impulse was to rule himself out as the game did not involve role-playing adventure or a first-person shooter but he had also played lots of adventures with clues and puzzles to solve, which gave him an idea.

"You're the expert in Spanish but could any of the words be translated differently? I'm just thinking. When the Fellowship of the Ring are stuck outside the Mines of Moria, Gandalf reads the inscription and translates from the Elvish, 'Speak friend and enter.' So he thinks you have to say some opening spell and the doors will open. He tries everything he can think of but nothing works. Then Frodo gets it. Gandalf translated 'Speak friend' but it should have been 'Say friend'. The password is simply the Elvish word for 'friend'. You say 'friend' and the doors open. Simple as that."

David drew a deep breath and looked at the text again.

"I don't think so. It's all very straightforward Spanish. *Llamar* can also be to phone and a few other things. But basically it's to call. Door, destroyer, the verb to live. It's all pretty basic stuff."

"So what do we do now?" Gillian asked. "While we have no idea."

"I haven't a clue," David said with a heavy sigh. "Keep worrying away at it till we get something more?"

"But it's not even the sort of thing you can guess at," McIntosh added. "We have to upload an original photograph so you have to know exactly where to go."

"And I'm afraid you'll have to go somewhere else to do your thinking," Spade put in. "Monthly meeting of the Warhammer Tribe. Gotta go in five minutes. Sorry."

"This is exactly what I was afraid of," Gillian remarked, going down the common stair. "An insoluble puzzle that somehow in Ramon's crazy mind makes it ok to do whatever he wants to do and it's our fault because we failed. We failed Andrea when we had her with us and we've failed her again. I just can't imagine what she must be going through right now. Poor thing."

They gathered for one last moment on the street outside Spade's flat.

"So what happens if an hour from now one of us gets inspiration?" Gillian asked. "I suppose we have to come back here since the whole thing is on Spade's computer. Which is his flat again, just in case I have to come back and ring on my own?"

"Fourth floor, left," David said. Gillian looked at the grid of entry phone buzzers. Not surprisingly, it didn't say Spade but she noted which it was just in case.

"And if he isn't back from his Warhammer thing – even if one of us does get it, we still won't be able to upload the photo. I can see myself standing here ringing at five to midnight."

"Ok, everybody," McIntosh summed up. "We'll keep in touch. Any inspiration, send it to the group WhatsApp. You're taking David home, I suppose, Gillian? Gillian?"

Gillian was standing looking heavenwards.

"Just a minute. Let me think," she said quietly. Then, "Got it, got it, got it! How could we be so stupid! Yeeessss!"

David shook his head.

"What? What is it?"

"It is *llamar* – Spade was exactly right! Call is a mistranslation. It isn't call at all."

David looked confused.

"Yes it is," he said. "*Llamar* means to call. It's Spanish 101. *¿Cómo te llamas?* – what do you call yourself, what's your name?"

"Yes – but not in this context." Gillian was bouncing up and down while the two men looked completely confused. "It does mean to call. But you don't call at a door. What do you do?"

"Ring? Knock?" McIntosh suggested.

"Ok. I'll give you that," David agreed reluctantly. "Juan knocks at the door. But so what? I don't see how that helps us."

"But it's not Juan, you idiot. It's John."

"So John knocks at the door. I still don't get it."

"You didn't specialize in Scottish history, did you? John knocks at the door. Who is he and where does he live? It's John Knox of course. John Knox's house, on the Royal Mile! And he was the destroyer of Catholic faith in Scotland. He opposed Mary Queen of Scots because she was Catholic. It's a riddle from a Catholic point of view. It's John Knox. Simple!"

It still took a minute for the penny to drop, then David was grinning, shaking his head in disbelief.

"You are a wonder," he said. "Quick. Back up the stairs before Spade goes out. He might let one of us stay here till we can take a photo and upload it."

They caught Spade just double locking his door and about to lug a bike down the stairs. Even he smiled at the solution.

"Cool," he said. "Course you can stay. Do you know how to upload a photo? No? Ok. I'll be back by 11.15, give or take a bit. If one of you can get the photo on your phone I'll upload it. Cheers. And well done the lady."

"I'll get the photo," Gillian offered. "I know exactly where I'm going. Back in a jiffy."

David and Stuart McIntosh went in and tried the living room and a spare bedroom but everything was such a tip they ended up back in the Bridge.

"Clever cookie," McIntosh commented.

"I can't disagree," said David. "I was thrown by the passage from Judges. I thought it must be something biblical."

"Excuses," McIntosh teased him. "She's just brighter than both of us put together."

Gillian was back in about forty minutes, not only carrying her phone triumphantly but also bearing three big boxes of pizza and a bottle of Irn Bru.

"Food and drink, gentlemen," she announced. "And the solution to level one!"

Spade kept them on the edges of their seats as he didn't get back till 11.40 but the image went up in seconds and the screen cleared. *Level one: processing...* it said next to an animated egg timer, which spun around for a few seconds before clearing to say *Congratulations. Level two awaits you...*

McIntosh heaved a sigh of relief. "Well, looks like we can call it a night – some of us have work to do tomorrow morning. Reconvene earlyish?"

"I think so," David agreed. "Spade, would you mind letting us know how it turns out by text first thing in the morning? And what turns up for level two?"

"You are the bee's knees, *chica*," David said in the car on the way home. "How did you get it?"

"Looking at the buzzers to get back in. I like to do bits of translation sometimes just to keep myself thinking in Spanish. I looked at Spade's buzzer and said to myself *tengo que llamar a la puerta de planta cuatro a la izquierda* – I have to knock on the door of floor four, left side. Then it struck me. Knock at the door. John knocks. John Knox. Voila. And sorry for calling you an idiot…"

"No, I agree with your assessment. Any chance of some Spanish lessons then, if you have a free night?"

"Well, come up and see me and I'll see what I can do!"

Chapter 16

SOMEPLACE IN SCOTLAND

David Hidalgo and DI Stuart McIntosh met the following morning at 9.30 in a small conference room in St Leonard's. Gillian was at work, Spade was probably still in bed, and José was trying to concentrate on setting tables at Café Córdoba. He had finally decided it was better to keep busy than sit at home and go mad with anxiety. Elvira and Tati were doing their morning routine of cold-calling companies that might want a temp but didn't want to pay premium prices. Bances had had to return to Spain for a family funeral.

"David, can I introduce Dr Alison Stokes?" McIntosh said. "She's a forensic psychologist who's worked on a number of serial killer cases. I thought her input might be helpful. I've explained your involvement in the case. She has some ideas that might help us in relation to Ramon's mental state. Alison?"

"Hi David. Pleased to meet you. I usually get involved when we have no idea who the killer is and are trying to put together a profile. That can give us some kind of head start on what sort of person we might be looking for. This case is a bit different – in fact, maybe unique, at least in my practice – in that we know exactly who we're dealing with, we have a mountain of information about him – career, past history, MO – but now things are in a new phase."

"So, if we can get some insight into what's going through his mind right now then that might help us predict what he'll do next?" David continued the train of thought. "Why do you think we're in this bizarre situation anyway? I mean, if he wanted to kill Andrea why not just do it? And if he didn't, then why kidnap her in the first place? We've opted to play the game but I've been struggling all night to think why on earth he would go to all that trouble."

"Responsibility," the psychologist replied. "In a word. There's a concept in psychology called cognitive dissonance. It's when you find yourself with two conflicting ideas, both of which you think are correct but which are mutually exclusive. That can cause a huge amount of stress. We see it a lot in alcoholism. The alcoholic believes, quite rightly, that drink is killing them and they need to stop but seem unable to. At the same time they try to pretend that they can quit at any time but just choose not to because they like a drink. So there's this incredible mental stress of knowing you need to stop and trying to maintain that you can, while at the same time being faced with the reality that you never do. The only resolution is to admit that you're an addict and that you are totally helpless in the face of the addiction, but that takes a lot of courage and has its own consequences. So they try to maintain these two conflicting ideas as long as possible. And it causes so much internal conflict that they need to find some way of medicating the stress."

"So let's have another drink," David suggested.

"Exactly. Then we're back to square one."

"I've seen that a lot with drug addicts. I worked in rehab in Spain for a number of years. They used to describe the sensation as like being in the jaws of a vice – squeezed from both directions and the only way of getting relief is to start using again."

"Yes, some people say it's like being torn apart but it's the same idea. So, Ramon has been a priest. Even though that was a long time ago and he has clearly abandoned his vows and been acting in a way totally contrary to his original calling, you can't shake off a lifetime of values like you take off a coat. So now he has been on a killing spree in some sort of attempt to gain redress for the harm he feels was done to him. He might call it justice but we'd just call it revenge. You hit me so I'm going to hit you back – harder.

In this case it's the church, the community he served, and society in general. So we have these two conflicting pressures: one to adhere to the values that informed his entire training and career, and the other to exact revenge on those he thinks have wronged him. Neither is negotiable but they are completely at odds with each other. A particularly strong case of cognitive dissonance."

"And how in particular does that connect to the game we now seem to be involved in – Ramon's Revenge?"

"Because this way he can set up conditions he can live with that ease the inner conflict," Dr Stokes explained. "Part of him thinks that Andrea, as a representative of the society he served and as someone who specifically testified against him, should be punished. But because of the underlying value base from his earlier life he also believes that he should not kill. However, he's already killed four times, we think. So he's living with a huge amount of guilt that can't be silenced even by his apparent sense of satisfaction in being an agent of justice, as he sees it. So what should he do with Andrea?"

"I think I can see where you're going." David spelled it out. "He thinks she should die but he doesn't want that on his conscience as well. So her life or death has to somehow be dependent on someone else's actions. Or something random, like rolling a dice. He might think, 'She can live if I throw a double six.' Anything else and she dies. Then God or fate decides, not him. If God had wanted her to live he would have controlled the dice and produced the double six. But he didn't, so God has decided she should die and I'm just carrying it out, that's all. It's really not my fault. I'm no longer responsible."

"Exactly. However in this case there's an added twist. As I understand it, from what Alfonso Bances told us, he also has it in for you. You were his hero who had a big influence in leading him into the service of God, then God let him down in the person of the bishop and the lawyer and the church. So he thinks he can kill two birds with one stone – if I can put it that way – by making you culpable for Andrea's death. It's all set up in the form of a game that he invites you to play. There has to be a chance you might win to show that God or fate or whatever could save Andrea's life; otherwise it would just be him responsible for the killing all over again – no transfer of responsibility and no benefit. But since he really does think Andrea should die it has to be very unlikely that you would win. Hence a series of tricky questions with a very tight timescale and the need to produce proof that you have been to where the answer lies. Of course I imagine he would also love the idea of sending you running around the city half mad with worry to get the proof he's demanding – not just pull it off the internet. He might even physically position himself near the location you need to go to just to watch.

"There are three rounds to the game – what he calls 'three levels' – and you only need to get one wrong or fail to provide an answer and he wins and it legitimizes Andrea's death. What would happen if you win all three remains to be seen, because that's going to push him into another crisis. He asked God – in the form of David Hidalgo – whether Andrea should live or die, and God said, 'Live', which is not the outcome he wanted at all. Does that make sense?"

David sat back and breathed out long and slow as if trying to keep his calm.

"Very much so," he said. "Like rolling a die to see if you should ask a girl out, then if you get the wrong answer you go to the best of three. Hell of a responsibility though."

"Indeed."

"And is there any upside to this new role in life?"

"Actually, I think there is," Alison said. "A straight killer – if I can put it that way – a straight killer can kill anywhere, anytime, anyhow. They don't need anyone's permission. Ramon, in an effort to get out of his moral dilemma, has chosen to bind himself by some rules. And to get a legitimate result he really has to abide by his own rules. That means that if you win a level, as you may have done last night, he has to give you the prize for that level – whatever he's decided that's going to be. My hunch is that it might be information of some kind, something he knows you want and value. For him to carry out the killing according to the rules means that he also has to stick to the rules if you win. Now we don't know if that'll go all the way to releasing the girl – I think probably not – however, up to that point he has to play the game as much as you."

"So what you're saying," David tried to clarify, "is that even if we win all three levels – if we solve all three puzzles if that's the form it's going to take – we still may not get the prize. Andrea still may not be safe."

"That's it. We can't be sure what he'll do then, but I think we can say it'll put him into a crisis. Just killing her in cold blood makes him a cheat at his own game. God – through you – determines that she should live, yet he kills her anyway. That's not going to be satisfying or fair, even by his own standards of justice."

"So we have to keep on trying as long as the game lasts?"

"Without a doubt."

"I think we got lucky last night," McIntosh put in. "Gillian got it just before it was too late. That may not happen again, so as well as playing the game as best we can we're throwing everything we have at the investigation. But I think Alison's analysis shows we were right to play. Choosing 'No' would have been tantamount to losing before we started, which would have given Ramon permission to end Andrea's life and claim – to himself at least – that it wasn't his fault. The dice didn't come up in her favour. Curtains."

"It's incredible," David said thoughtfully. "I think what you've said makes perfect sense but I'm going to take some time to process it. Despite being a pastor I'm really not used to playing God."

"Let me get some coffee, then we can talk about how we might respond now we have a better idea of what might be going through his mind."

The coffee when it came was sipped in silence. Once they were refuelled enough to carry on, McIntosh outlined the investigation that was going on in parallel. Searches of abandoned premises, door-to-door inquiries around all the key locations, a blanket media campaign with press conferences and press releases, uniforms and plain clothes out on the street, CCTV checks, posters up in petrol stations, etc.

"An impressive list," David admitted. "Let's hope it turns something up soon. After last night I don't know if my nerves will stand another almost insoluble puzzle."

David's phone buzzed. He flicked it into life.

"Spade," he announced, reading aloud. "Passed level one. Level two puzzle now in. Something else for you to see. Can you come over?" He glanced at his watch.

"Gillian has an important funding meeting she can't miss but should be free after 11."

"Welcome, lady and gentlemen," Spade greeted the group. "Coffee? Tea? Tunnock's Caramel Wafer?"

"Actually yes," Gillian said. "All of the above. Well, maybe just the coffee and the Caramel."

Once food and drink had arrived and they had squeezed into the Bridge, Spade brought his main screen to life and showed them the message. It was the Nintendo castle again but this time the princess was perched precariously on the ledge of her tower. The message on the drawbridge read:

Congratulations, player one. You have passed level one. Here is your reward:

69 72

Click to continue

"That's it?" Gillian asked, incredulous. "Sixty-nine, seventy-two? What's that supposed to mean?"

"Want me to click?" Spade asked.

David nodded. The message on the drawbridge was replaced. They leaned forward to read.

Día dos: nivel dos:

Hay un lugar en Escocia, de cuyo nombre no quiero acordarme donde se encuentra el ingenioso hidalgo. Dame su nombre para salvar a la princesa.

"Translation?" McIntosh asked.

"'Day two, level two'," David read. "'There is a place in Scotland whose name I don't want to remember where the ingenious gentleman is to be found. Give me its name to save the princess.'"

"But the text says '*hidalgo*'," McIntosh queried. "You said 'gentleman'?"

"Yes – I'm sure it's a pun but a *hidalgo* in Spanish is simply the word for a minor nobleman. It's usually translated as 'gentleman'. Anyway, the source of the text is easy enough. It's the opening line of *Don Quixote* by Cervantes – probably the best known line in Spanish literature. Cervantes wanted to locate the story in the contemporary Spain of his time but didn't want to be too specific. So he says, 'in a place in La Mancha whose name I don't want to remember'. The full title is *The Ingenious Gentleman Don Quixote of La Mancha*.

"So a clue and a simultaneous reference at you with the double meaning of *hidalgo*. Neat," McIntosh commented.

"I suppose so."

"So a place in Scotland that would substitute for La Mancha in Spain? Is that it?" Gillian asked. "I suppose somewhere near enough to Edinburgh to make it realistic to take a photo and upload it before midnight. What are the characteristics of La Mancha in Spain then that might connect to somewhere in Scotland?"

"Dry. Windmills. Relatively high up. Quite poor. It's thought the name comes from Arabic *al-mansha*, meaning dry land or wilderness," David replied.

"Well what about the Southern Uplands then? High up, quite dry, and loads of windmills nowadays," McIntosh suggested.

"Might be. But not exactly a wilderness. What's the driest place in Scotland?"

Spade swivelled around to his keyboard, rattled in a query, and said: "Coasts of the East Lothian, Fife, and the Moray Firth."

LES COWAN

"Well, we can rule out the Moray Firth – too far to drive – but East Lothian is pretty local."

"So is there anywhere in East Lothian that has windmills?" Gillian asked.

Spade did another search and read aloud.

"'Aikengall Community Windfarm is located in East Lothian, around 3 km south of the village of Innerwick and 9.5 km south of Dunbar. Aikengall Community Windfarm comprises of sixteen Vestas V90 wind turbines. These turbines have a tip height of 125 metres and a generating rating of 3.0 MW. In total the wind farm has an installed capacity of 48 MW of clean, green electricity.'"

"I'm not convinced," David said slowly. "It would be entirely pot luck choosing one location over another. There must be loads of these locations. And none of them really seems to click with La Mancha. Dry, barren, some sort of wilderness."

"Well what about West Pilton?" McIntosh suggested. "It's not dry or barren but it's certainly an urban wilderness with all the drugs and stuff. Sorry – only joking."

"La Mancha, La Mancha, La Mancha," David repeated. "There has to be something more conclusive."

The group descended into silence trying to conjure something out of nothing but in reality waiting for David, the only one who had ever been in La Mancha and was supposed to be "the ingenious gentleman".

"La Mancha, La Mancha," he kept muttering, alternately staring into space or clenching his eyes tight shut.

Seconds passed to minutes. There wasn't much to say. After their success with level one, the group had started the day quite buoyant, but now a general gloom was descending again. It was horrific to think that Andrea's life or death could be hanging on a moment of inspiration that might not come. They had very nearly missed it last night. McIntosh took the chance to make some calls and keep in touch with his team but as regards the puzzle it was beginning to feel like a dead end.

Spade managed to produce an ancient dog-eared road map,

which McIntosh pored over. David texted a friend in the real La Mancha who had lived in the UK for a bit to see if there was anything they could suggest. Gillian read through the La Mancha Wikipedia entry for inspiration but everything seemed to draw a blank. Was there a Scottish equivalent of Don Quixote and, if so, where did he come from? What about David's birthplace? Actually Simpson Memorial Maternity Hospital in Edinburgh so that didn't help – not much connection with La Mancha there.

"But the clue simply says a place in Scotland where the *hidalgo* is to be found. Why couldn't that be anywhere associated with you?" Gillian asked. "Bruntsfield, Southside Church, your birthplace, where you grew up. Why not?"

"But if that's the case then it could be any one of them. How are we to tell one from the other? Whatever else Ramon is I think he's precise," David responded. "It's got to be something that's clearly the answer, not just a possibility."

From feeling they might be on to something, that dipped everything back into the doldrums again. Spade was happy enough munching in the background, feeling that literary connections weren't really his strong suit, but the others were racking their brains and getting nowhere fast.

"So, is there anything else we can do while we're not getting anywhere on this one?" Gillian finally asked. "What about the numbers – sixty-nine, seventy-two?"

"Take your pick," said McIntosh. "Could be anything. A map reference, a code, a bit of a telephone number, a date, some weird computer thing. Or just something to tease and torment. I wouldn't put it past him."

"No, I think it would have to have some meaning," David said. "Remember what Alison was saying. He has to abide by the rules of his own game. If he promises us a reward if we get the clue, then when we get the clue he has to give us something meaningful. Though as to what it means, I have no more idea than you."

"Well, in that case anything *else* we can do, or shall I at least pop out for some lunch, which would be better than just sitting here banging our heads against the wall?" Gillian suggested.

"Sounds good," Spade put in. "But since we're not doing anything else, there is something I'd like you to see before you go – or listen to, actually."

"Sure. Go ahead," McIntosh nodded.

"Let's just go back to the video of Ramon." He popped up a minimized window and played the video. Nobody needed any reminding of its content.

"Have you noticed something new?" David asked.

"Well, kind of. If you don't mind, I'll take it bit by bit. Anything strike you about the video?"

There weren't any immediate takers.

"Listen again."

They did.

"What do you hear?"

"Ramon," Gillian said.

"And?"

"Nothing."

"No, not nothing," David said. "There are other sounds. Sounds from outside."

"Exactly. What?"

"Traffic," said McIntosh. "Lorries? Cars? Maybe roadworks? I'm not sure."

"Good. Traffic. What else?"

"Is that birdsong?" Gillian asked.

"Yes. Full marks so far. I can't identify the birds but yes – I think we've got some birds in there. What else? No? Ok, listen again. What else is in the background?"

He played the clip again but this time everybody was tuned in not to what Ramon was saying but the background sound.

"Music," David said. "Faint, but definitely music."

"Good," said Spade. "Now we're getting somewhere. I spotted that too. So I thought I'd home in on it a bit and see if we could do anything with it. Just for fun, like." He clicked another application from the taskbar and got a sound editor up with a set of windows with squiggly sound files.

"Listen to this," he said and clicked the first one. It was the entire audio from the video. The second one was just the background, with Ramon's gloating tones now filtered out. There was no doubt about the mix of mechanical noise, natural sounds, and music. The music was much clearer. It sounded maybe like reggae rhythms.

"Better?" Spade asked. Everyone agreed.

"Now this one." He clicked the next file, which played only the music. It wasn't entirely clear but some sort of rhythm and melody could now be picked out.

"And finally – my tour de force." He clicked the lowermost file in the application window with a flourish. Suddenly they were listening to the exact same phrase but this time perfectly clear and distinct. It started with a harmonica, then a drum roll, then bass and a very funky brass section. Finally the vocals.

"Anybody get it?"

"I think I recognize it but I've no idea from where," Gillian put in. "Bob Marley?"

Spade gave a deep groan.

"Ahh. Sometimes I despair, I really do. It's The Specials, 'A Message to You, Rudy'. This is the classic Old Grey Whistle Test live version. I could play you ten different versions but this is my favourite. No?"

David shook his head. "Sorry, I think I was either in Spain then or on the way. I missed thirty years of UK culture."

"Sad," Spade shook his head. "Wonderful ska revival band, 2 Tone Records. Part of the New Wave but political as well as musical. Fantastic."

"I think I do remember them," Gillian said. "It's interesting but I can't see how this actually helps."

"I think I get it," McIntosh came in with a detective's point of view. "Ramon is recording his video and opens the window to make sure he's in silhouette so any detail in the room is lost in the light. But while that obscures the room it also lets in the sounds

LES COWAN

from outside – which might tell us something about his location. From what Spade has played us I think we can say it's an area with some wildlife, quite a lot of traffic, and some source of music. Maybe workmen with a radio on."

"Good. Now we're getting somewhere." Spade was smiling and seemed to be on a roll. "Ladies and gentlemen, one more time." He clicked the version with traffic, birds, and music all together but no voice.

"Applause," David said. "Is there some applause in there?"

"Top of the class," Spade said, only slightly sarcastically. "This is my last version – I promise." He clicked yet another file. This time they listened to everything except voice and music. There was a definite round of applause and maybe what could have been laughter.

"So, we've got the music but couldn't it still be almost anywhere?" Gillian asked. "I mean if it's an old hit anybody could be playing it."

"Maybe," Spade replied. "But not everybody gets applause and laughter. I think it's a busker with a backing track." And with that Spade sat back and folded his arms.

That brightened the mood with a feeling that they had done something worthwhile even if it wasn't the main event. Gillian went off in search of the nearest sandwich shop to get something to sustain them while David took a turn of the map, going over and over the same thoroughly Scottish-sounding place names looking for some pun, anagram, word play, or allusion. Gillian returned with a selection of sandwiches, rolls, drinks, and a couple of cream cookies, hoping to hear some sounds of rejoicing as she came up the stairs but was disappointed. They ate in silence. Gillian didn't have any further classes that day and had explained something of the situation to her departmental head.

"Get out of here and don't come back till the maniac is in jail!" he had said.

Despite his understanding, it was beginning to feel more and more pointless just sitting thinking with no ideas coming. She was on the point of finally suggesting she head off and come back later with a fresher mind when David almost leaped off his seat holding up the map as if it were the Scottish Premier League cup.

"Ha!" he shouted. "You were entirely right, Gillian. I am an idiot. Staring us in the face. Look!"

"What?" Gillian prompted.

He held out the map and pointed.

"La Mancha is Lamancha!"

"What?" McIntosh sounded confused. "La Mancha is indeed La Mancha but how's that the solution?"

"No, sorry, I'm not being very clear. La Mancha – two words – is a province of Spain. Lamancha – one word – is a village in the Borders on the road to Peebles. We were there two weeks ago!"

"I remember," Gillian said, "when we went to Peebles."

"Exactly. We drove south from Edinburgh. You pass a village called Lamancha. It struck me at the time. Not very Scottish but immediately memorable for a Spaniard. Ramon must have come across it somehow and then when he needed a clue it came back to mind. And it was a dig at me too. Sarcastic if you like – if you're so ingenious solve this one!"

"Well, I'm convinced at least," McIntosh offered, looking very relieved. "I was beginning to think it was impossible."

"Ka-ching!" Spade offered with a midair jackpot gesture.

"So we just drive to Lamancha, take a photo of some landmark, upload it, and that's it?" Gillian asked. "And we've got plenty of time. Sounds too easy."

"I'm sure that's it. Maybe Ramon thought we might understand the clue but not know the name of the village. It's very small."

"Excellent. Let's get on to it then," McIntosh concluded. "I've got a police vehicle if that's any help."

They declined the police car and David and Gillian headed straight out in her two seater and drove south through Liberton, over the bypass, and through Leadburn, arriving at Lamancha within the hour. Gillian jumped out and took a couple of photos of the name board on the Lamancha Hub building and anything else that looked official that would identify the place. Another hour and they were back at Spade's and the photo was uploaded.

"Nice," Gillian said as they drove back in the direction of home on the south side of the city. "I wasn't looking forward to it but I think we got it right, I'm sure. Again. Thanks to you this time."

"So 1:1 at half time I think. Not that we're counting."

"So can we now go for a drink and take the rest of the day off?"

"Sorry," David said. "Yes to the drink but there's still one more challenging event today. Charlie Ferguson, *Edinburgh Evening News* crime writer. Remember?"

"Oh no. I'd completely forgotten in the excitement. This article he wants to write on the crime-fighting pastor?"

"Well, I'm hoping we've got a bit beyond that. I think he's going to write more about the needs of the people we've come in contact with. At least that's what I think we said. That's why I agreed anyway."

"Remind me – where and when?"

"My place, 8 p.m. Can you still do it?"

"Sure. I don't think I can risk you doing it on your own. One wrong move and you'll throw him out again!"

Charlie Ferguson turned up on time and was on his best behaviour. He didn't call David "Davey", "Dave", or "Rev" and was friendly and interested but not overfamiliar. His favourite words seemed to be "cool", "awesome", and "totally" but it could have been much worse. He seemed to have done his homework and was informed not only about the problems Edinburgh had but also some of the issues and trends in Europe and worldwide. He knew of course about the drugs scene in the capital, having been reporting on crime related to it for years, but didn't quite get the international commercialization angle. The case of Raúl Alvarez, who had abducted Irene MacInnes's granddaughter, had been widely publicized so he knew the basic facts but more or less begged David to tell him the inside story, promising faithfully not to publish anything that might expose individuals to too much public scrutiny. Raúl's liking for underage entertainment and how that had got Jen MacInnes caught up in the net he swore was completely off the record. On people trafficking and prostitution he was not quite so clued up and needed an explanation. David referred him to Dr James Dalrymple for more background since James had set up "Off the Hook", a charity to help girls caught in the catch-22 of forced prostitution while not having a passport or papers to enable them to escape and stay legally in the country they had been trafficked to. As regards Elvira and Tati, David has already spoken to them and asked if they were willing to be interviewed. The deal seemed to be that the paper wanted to see it as a human interest Edinburgh success story of girls making a go of it in spite of all they had been through. The thought that this might give them a bucketload of free PR wasn't wasted on Tati, who agreed with certain reservations. No salacious sexual details, no accounts of sexual violence, no "John's story" other side of the coin, and no provocative pictures. Ferguson was so keen the get the story he agreed to it all. Finally, he was keen to find out about David's own history and this actually led into quite an interesting discussion – also presumably off the record.

"People my age just don't really have a clue what religion is for," the reporter explained after David had told him something of his history. "I mean, we get radical Islam – we don't like it of course – but I think we understand it gives people in underdeveloped countries some sense of identity in the face of the terrible West and all the nasty things America is supposed to have done. What we don't understand is why people in modern Britain would be religious. I mean, what does it give you? Restrictions on lifestyle, sexuality, obligations we don't want, and a whole story about creation and the virgin birth and all that stuff that we just find laughable – forgive me for putting it that way. I think of it like opera. I hate opera but some intelligent people seem to like it. So I'm sure there must be something good about it but I can't work out what. Does that make sense?"

David began his normal explanation of the difference between religion and relationship with a living, communicating God but Ferguson quickly interrupted him.

"But that's something entirely different you're talking about now," he said. "That's spiritual. Lots of my friends consider themselves spiritual but not religious. Is that what you're saying makes sense of faith? And what's the connection between personal spirituality and religion?"

"Well, as far as faith is concerned," David explained, "it *is* much more an internal thing. But I suppose over the years people have tried to protect it and that means surrounding it with rules and rituals. That's where I see religion coming in. But I think having a spiritual awareness and interest is a pretty good place to start and see where it takes you. I think what you're calling 'religion' is strictly optional. Personally I have very little time for it."

"Well we're agreed on that then," Ferguson said.

"That's where I started," Gillian put in. "I'm still not interested in religion but relationship is much more attractive."

"Awesome," Ferguson agreed. "Now my parents' generation, they made no difference between the two. It was all rubbish. My dad worked at Longannet power station. He was a working bloke. Church had absolutely no part in his life. 'Hatches, matches, and dispatches,' he used to say. You know? But some of my friends do go to church. In fact church, mass, the mosque, an ashram, anything. And they mix it up, without saying they *are* Christian, Catholic, Muslim, Buddhist or anything else. A bit like the world religions buffet table I suppose."

"And how do you feel about that?"

"It's cool. Totally. I'm happy if they get something. And I suppose I'm looking too. Haven't hit the jackpot yet but you never know, I might turn up at Southside some week and surprise you. In fact the editor wants me to so it's actually more than likely. 'Deep background', he calls it."

Hmm, this is turning out to be more interesting than I expected, David thought. *Must remember to thank Gillian for making me do it.*

"Anyway, I better get going shortly," Ferguson announced. "Thursday night. My turn to do the baths and bed. So just one more thing. Have you got any investigation on the go just now and is it in the same sort of field or something else?"

David and Gillian exchanged involuntary glances not lost on Ferguson, who hardly missed a beat, before adding: "I suppose that means 'yes' then."

"Well, it is 'yes'. There is something going on but really I can't talk about it in any detail."

"Wouldn't have anything to do with Ramon, would it?" the reporter asked innocently.

"Who told you that?" David shot back, on the defensive again for the first time that evening.

"Nobody!" Ferguson insisted, holding his hands up. "Just that there are posters up on almost every lamp post. Reporting Scotland are giving it big licks and there's a Police Scotland press conference at 10 a.m. every morning. He's Spanish so I just wondered if you might be on the case somehow."

"How much do you know already?" Gillian asked.

"That he was a paedophile priest, he did time for it, got out, and started bumping off everybody he thought had had something to do with sending him down. As I understand it, four in Spain then he turned up in Edinburgh looking for number five. The girl he was after has been abducted and is currently held by Ramon – as far as anybody knows – though she could be dead already. That's it."

David took off his glasses and rubbed his temples, then brow.

"Well, all of that is true," he said. "Strictly off the record, we had contact with the girl – Andrea – through an English chat group we run. It was in the group that she first thought she might be on Ramon's list. We did what we could to protect her but Ramon got to her anyway. Now we're desperately trying to find him – and her – before it's too late."

"Listen, David. I know you started off thinking I was some kind of pond life. No, I know you did. I hope we've got a bit past that tonight. I have a job to do that does involve intruding into people's lives. But that doesn't mean that crime in the city is just a story. I have a sister Andrea's age. If it was her – sorry, if it *were* her," David smiled in spite of himself, "I'd be going bonkers by now. So anything the paper can do to help… you know."

"Thanks," Gillian said. "I guess we need all the support we can get but I can't see how the paper could help. The problem right now is that we got a video from Ramon with a pretty frightening message on it. We've managed to isolate some of the background sounds to try to get a handle on where it might have been recorded."

"And…?" Ferguson prompted.

"There's traffic noise, some birds singing, and some music. We're racking our brains to think of all the places that might have a combination of these sounds to try to narrow it down a bit."

"And what sort of traffic was it? What sort of music?"

"Oh, just city-centre traffic. I suppose what you would hear next to any set of traffic lights. The expert we're working with thinks the music might be a street entertainer or something. We know what the music track was and there seems to be the sound of applause and some laughter. But nobody has a database of street performers and their background music. So it's another dead end I'm afraid."

"Nobody?" Ferguson asked rather pointedly.

"Well, not as far as I know. I don't think they need a licence any more and the local authority isn't going to have a list of what they do and the music they do it to."

"Our readers know," Ferguson said simply.

"What do you mean?" David asked, suddenly interested again.

"Our readers know everything about Edinburgh. If you want to know who puts their tins in the bottles recycling one of our readers will have seen it happening and remembered. They know everything. It's incredible."

"Hmm. Interesting. So how would we ask them?" David asked, now completely focused again. "If some reader somewhere has seen a busker who used 'A Message to You, Rudy' by The Specials as his backing track, how could we get them to tell us?"

"Easy." Ferguson smiled. "Reader competition." Without changing a gear he slipped into copy mode and started reading the competition headline and instructions that hadn't been written yet.

"Busker Muster: every year Edinburgh is invaded by street performers from all over the country. And every year there are winners and losers. But what about those who work here all year round? We want to hear about your favourite Edinburgh street entertainers who are not just here for the festival. Tell us what they do, why you like them, what music they play (or play to), where they perform, when you heard them, and how much you gave them. We'll sponsor your favourites to play at key venues in the festival and give them a feature promotion free of charge. So get your cameras and phones out and send us a photo or a video and fill in the coupon opposite. And you could win show tickets to a festival event of your choice. Let us know why Edinburgh rocks – all year round!"

David and Gillian sat stunned.

"That's incredible," Gillian finally said. "You just thought that up right now?"

"It's what I do for a living. What do you think?"

"I'm amazed," David admitted. "But the problem is time. We may only have days to play with. How soon could you do something like that?"

"We report on the day's news every evening so we have a very short lead time. You give me the go ahead, I'll make a phone call, and it'll be in tomorrow's paper. Guaranteed."

"I can't believe it," Gillian admitted. "This could be exactly what we need. I can't see any other way to make use of what we know." She looked inquiringly at David.

"Have to admit it sounds promising. And our best chance right now. Let me phone my CID contact and run it by him."

"And I'll speak to my boss as well. Let's see if it's a runner."

Five minutes later the deal was done. McIntosh, who sounded frankly exhausted on the phone, was willing to go with anything and the editor thought it would be a great angle if the paper actually helped catch Ramon.

"And we'll add an extra bonus for internet submissions within twenty-four hours," Ferguson offered as even more icing on the cake. "They know everything, believe me. Let the readership loose then stand well back!"

Chapter 17

ROYAL MILE

Andrea had played the scene in her mind a thousand times. *If he does this, I run. If he does that, I fight.* When the time came she did the only thing she hadn't imagined – nothing. From the moment she saw Silvia in the driver's seat she knew she had no choice. He had outsmarted her again. There could be no fleeing or dodging the bullets when it was somebody else's life. Whatever else he was, he wasn't stupid. So she got into the car in a daze. She felt the blood drain from her face and her brain go into neutral. She couldn't think, couldn't do anything except what she was told. Afterwards, looking back, she couldn't understand why she hadn't just crashed the car. In the tangle of airbags and the shock of an impact she'd have stood as good a chance of getting clear as he would have of shooting her, she was certain. And right now fifty-fifty looked like good enough odds. But in the moment it just didn't occur. Her mind was a blank – she could only do what she was told.

First he ordered her to drive into the park – Holyrood Park, was that it? – under the shadow of Arthur's Chair – no – Arthur's Seat, wasn't it? They drove around the perimeter road, the barrel of his gun pushing painfully into her side. They stopped in a car park in the furthest corner.

"Take off your clothes," he told her.

Here we go, she thought. *This is what I didn't want to happen.*

Then, unexpectedly, he pulled a bag from the back seat and pushed it at her.

"Put all of your clothes in here. Everything."

This was confusing.

"Then put the bag out of the window. I'll be standing outside."

"Do anything I haven't told you to and you'll die here," he said. "This window will be open. I can easily shoot then drag your body out and drive away. Don't even think about it."

So, squirming around in the driver's seat and reaching down past the steering wheel, she managed to get her jeans, socks, shoes, and underwear off, then her top and bra. She sat, desperately trying to cover up, unsure and fearful of what was going to happen next but already feeling the first waves of shock and confusion beginning to pass. She was beginning to think, *At least I'm still alive. He's got something in his head that doesn't involve killing me right away.* She dropped the bag out of the window but Ramon made no effort to pull her out of the car or even look at her. If anything, he seemed almost disconnected. He passed her another bag and said: "Put these on."

The bag had a loose-fitting jogging suit and trainers that didn't fit. There was no underwear. Ramon stood back and while he kept the gun trained on her through the open window, held discreetly, close to his body at waist height, he made no attempt to even watch as she struggled into the new clothing. Then he simply got back into the passenger seat and gave her instructions to start the car and drive over to the waste bin.

"Stop here," he ordered. She did; he lowered his own window and threw the bag containing her old clothes out without a word of explanation. Only later did it occur to her that he might have been protecting against any tracking device concealed in what she was wearing. At the time it was just one more inexplicable event in a nightmare sequence.

"Now get out." She did. With the gun still very obvious he escorted her around to the rear of the vehicle. He lifted the boot lid.

"Inside."

What could she do? She looked desperately around but there wasn't another car in the car park and neither walkers nor joggers to be seen. Again she complied. After that there was only darkness and movement for what seemed like an age but might only have been twenty minutes or so. When they came to a halt in traffic she considered banging on the boot lid and shouting but thought there was a bigger chance of this making things worse. Right now Ramon seemed calm – so calm it was as if he himself was also operating in a dream. It wasn't going to help putting pressure on him that might make him panic and do something desperate when the chances of anyone hearing and trying the boot lid would be so slim. So she tried to calm herself, not think what might happen next, try to breathe normally, and wait. She felt the vehicle bump over a ramp or something then pause and drive on, slowly turning sharply every few seconds and descending. *An underground car park?* she thought. Eventually they came to a complete halt and the engine stopped. A few seconds later the boot lid opened, leaving her blinking in the light.

"Out."

She climbed clumsily out, stumbling slightly in footwear four sizes too big. They headed for a pedestrian exit, climbed six floors – she kept count – and exited the stairwell into a corridor. Several turns, a swing door, then they were in a hall with normal front doors. They stopped at one – 5B, she noticed. Ramon pulled out a set of keys and, with the gun pushed even harder into her back, opened the door and shoved her roughly through the doorway. Inside there were conventional decorations but nothing that looked like a personal possession. *A rented apartment*, she thought. *In Edinburgh, but I have no idea where. Six floors up from the car park underground. From the door number probably the fifth floor.* He directed her into the living room. Conventional furniture, a sofa, an armchair, a coffee table, a dining table in front of a large double window. A couple of bland paintings that looked like they might have been done by a robot. A flimsy desk in one corner with an upright chair. Nothing more.

"Hands out," Ramon ordered. Again she complied and he pulled two pairs of handcuffs out of his pocket. At this point he had to lay the gun down but well out of reach. She knew she stood no chance of grabbing it or running so did what he told her. One set of cuffs on each wrist. The other cuff was locked onto a length of quite light chain so that her hands were locked together, but with about eighteen inches of chain between them. *Enough to eat, use the toilet, shower,* she immediately thought, *but not enough to fight back. So what happens now?* Ramon reached behind the sofa and picked up the loose end of another length of chain. This seemed to be attached to something at its far end though she couldn't see what. The free end he padlocked to the chain between her wrists, then Ramon finally stood back and looked her in the face for what seemed the first time. He made what sounded like a low grunt of satisfaction, then simply turned and left the room.

Well, she thought, *I'm alive when I could have been dead. I haven't been touched when that was what I expected.* For the first time since seeing Silvia in the driver's seat of the limo she thought she might live. Ramon came back in with a sandwich on a plate and a glass of water. He put it on the coffee table without a word then went over to the desk in the opposite corner of the room, pulled out the chair, opened up a laptop, sat down, and started typing. She suddenly realized how dry her mouth was and took a sip of water. The handcuffs and chain made it awkward but nothing more. She put the glass down then realized she was hungry as well so ate the sandwich. Now there was nothing to do except watch Ramon typing and clicking. After about an hour he made her sit with her back to the window while he took a photograph but didn't explain why. Later he took her to a bedroom. *Oh no; this is it,* she thought but he merely padlocked her to another length of chain he already had in place and went back to the living room. She could hear him speaking but couldn't make out the words. She lay on the bed and could just about make out the sound of more keystrokes from the other room. Traffic noises and the sounds of music drifted up from the street. She thought she heard laughter and a round of applause. Then the sounds of the night: the low-frequency diesel throb of black cabs coming and going, the occasional beep of a horn, partygoers laughing and joking. It had been about 3.30 when the car had pulled up alongside her. Ramon had made her drop her watch in the bag, though she was allowed to keep her rings, so she had no idea what time it was now. Maybe ten. It was certainly dark enough. Then, even later – it couldn't have been much off midnight – she was woken by a shout from the other room. It sounded like a cry of rage or frustration. Then nothing more. She drifted into un uneasy sleep.

The next day Ramon brought her another sandwich for breakfast and allowed her use of the toilet. Then it was back to the living room, tethered again and more typing and clicking. Ramon had absolutely no conversation but she noticed he seemed to be constantly muttering and grumbling to himself. Had that been happening yesterday? She wasn't sure. She also noticed a peculiar habit of clearing his throat and shrugging his shoulders as if he had on a shirt that was too tight at the throat. Given Ramon's total preoccupation with the computer and utter lack of conversation, her main emotion was gradually migrating from terror to boredom. There was nothing to do, nothing to see, nothing to listen to except Ramon's mutterings, the rattle of the keyboard, and occasional street sounds drifting up. Then, not long after the lunchtime sandwich, Ramon exploded. He banged the desk, got up, grabbed his laptop, and seemed to be on the point of hurling it at the wall when with difficulty he managed to contain himself. There followed a stream of expletives that shocked her coming from a former priest, though why that should be after all his other conduct she wasn't sure. He had laid the laptop back on the desk but was pacing up and down, increasingly agitated, running his hands through his hair, balling his fists, rubbing his temples, and muttering incomprehensibly but more loudly than before. Even when Andrea could more or less hear what he was saying it made no sense. She wondered if it might be Latin. Then, gradually he regained control and went back to the keyboard. And that was it. Another sandwich at dinnertime and another trip to the toilet but that was the highlight of the day. Ramon ordered her back to the bedroom after dark but this time wouldn't even look at her. It was almost as if somehow she had become dangerous or threatening to him – like he was afraid of her. He snapped the padlock shut and went back to his computer. Was this a man on the edge of madness?

The following morning David got a message to the WhatsApp group Spade had set up for them. "Bingo," it said simply. Then, in a second message, "Here in half an hour?" He typed back "yes", saw Gillian and McIntosh's replies within a few minutes, then went downstairs to wait for Gillian to arrive as they had agreed.

Spade was all smiles as he opened the door. They filed into the Bridge and a tray of tea, coffee, and caramel wafers followed them in a couple of minutes.

"Well done, the Ingenious Gentleman of Lamancha," Spade said, bringing his computer to life.

"By the way, Spade, just before we get started, I forgot to ask," David said once they were seated around the screen. "After all that stuff about IP addresses last time when we were trying to track down Power and Glory's organization in Belarus, how come we can't simply do the same for Ramon?"

"TOR," Spade said simply. "Stands for 'The Onion Router' – what the papers call 'the dark web'. Basically a system that sends data packets bouncing all around the planet, and possibly some other planets as well, before they finally get reunited and appear on your screen – or mine in this case. There may be several thousand links and each packet takes a different route. GCHQ may be able to do something with it but for the rest of us, to all intents and purposes, it would be like looking for a single grain of marked sand on Portobello Beach. No can do. I told you, he's quite a bright boy."

"Is that what they use to sell drugs and things?" Gillian asked.

"Yes, *and things*," Spade replied. "Big market in credit card details, any illegal chemical you care to name, firearms, fake passports, child images, celebrities' email addresses. You name it."

"It's a total nightmare for law enforcement," Stuart McIntosh agreed. "Huge potential for illegal activity. Not just potential in fact; it's like an alternative universe of crime."

"I think of it like the sewers in Gotham City," Spade said brightly. "The Penguin is down there with his hordes of henchmen just ready to break out and take over the city. It's a real possibility, you know. Some very clever people in Russia, China, and Israel who might decide to take over the internet and hold us all to ransom or threaten to wipe the entire data records of a couple of banks unless we play nice. Ramon just wants to conceal his identity, which is what a lot of people use it for but that really is the tip of the iceberg."

"And on that cheery note," David said, "what's the latest from Ramon?"

Spade clicked a minimized window on the taskbar and popped up the now familiar castle, this time with the princess hanging on to her tower by her fingertips.

The message on the drawbridge now read:

Congratulations, player one. You have passed level two. Here is your reward:

49 32

Click to continue

"More gobbledegook!" Gillian sighed. "What on earth are we supposed to make of that?"

"Ah well," Spade interjected. "It's not just the ingenious lady and the gentleman who can solve puzzles."

"You have any idea?" David asked.

"More than just an idea; I think it's ASCII."

"And what might that be when it's at home?" McIntosh asked.

"American Standard Code for Information Interchange. Basically a simple code for every number and character in the alphabet, things like backspace, carriage return, even a beep. It's the standard way of telling a computer to print something to the screen or the printer. Very useful. Pity it's American. Most high-level languages don't really need it for text – you just stick what you want to say in quotes and up it comes so it's the non-printing characters you need it for most. But it still works for everything. Programmers' bread and butter."

"How did you come to that conclusion?" McIntosh asked.

"It was the '32'," Spade shrugged. "It's the code for a space. Use it all the time. The rest could have been anything but the '32' kind of stands out – it just made me think."

"So what do the others mean?" Gillian asked.

"Altogether we've got '69 72 49 32'. That equates to E H 1 Space. It's a postcode, or part of one. He's teasing. Our reward is his whereabouts I suppose – more or less. EH1 is the town centre."

"Spade, you never cease to amaze," Gillian smiled and to give the IT guru his due he did look pleased. "But why would he give away his whereabouts?"

"Cognitive dissonance," David said.

"Cognitive what?"

"Dissonance. We had a lecture from a forensic psychologist the other day. She reckons Ramon has made up this whole game so that we lose and he kills Andrea but then it's not his fault because he gave us a fighting chance. The bargain is that if we do win a level he has to give us something genuinely worthwhile that we want. But that turns out to have been wrapped up in a puzzle as well. However, the man with the brain the size of Hampden Park has solved that as well. So now we know he's in the city centre area. Does that help, Stuart?"

"Excellent. It certainly does – if he's not just sending us misinformation. I think what Alison said the other day makes sense. I'm willing to bet there's something in it. We'll concentrate resources in that area."

"So, what about the final puzzle?" David said.

Spade clicked to continue. The new message now read:

DÍA TRES: NIVEL TRES:

Piedra antigua en entorno moderno.

Asiento de rey y lugar de gobierno.

"It says, 'Day three, level three, ancient stone in a modern place' – could mean surroundings, environment or setting – 'seat of the king and place of government'. Any ideas, since we seem to be on a roll?"

"The Scottish Parliament – Holyrood. That's the seat of power and place of government and it's a very modern setting," McIntosh suggested.

"True but that looks too obvious," David replied cautiously. "And what would be the ancient stone? What about the castle? There you've got the Castle Rock, which is certainly an ancient stone. And it's a symbol of power and I suppose the rulers of Scotland would have been based in the castle if the city was under attack."

"I was thinking of Arthur's Seat," Gillian said. "More of a pun again I suppose but he seems to like those. It's another ancient stone and the park is a modern surrounding. And it's definitely the 'seat of the king' – King Arthur."

"Hmm. From nothing that fitted last time, now we've got three options that could all be right," David said.

"Four," Spade put in. "The Stone of Destiny. An ancient stone that Scottish monarchs sat on during their coronation. Literally 'the seat of kings and place of government'. It's in the castle, which is ancient as well I suppose, but it's all right in the centre of modern Edinburgh."

David let out a groan.

"Any of them could fit. And all in Edinburgh. What do we do now?"

"Take a break," said Spade immediately. "What I always do when I've got a programming problem. And send out for pizza. Pepperoni is good for the brain."

That afternoon the first editions of the paper came out along with the daily internet update. The reader competition was given a high profile and Ferguson, who was watching the web traffic, soon started seeing submissions. Jamie from Stenhouse liked Javier, who played Latin jazz on an alto sax at the top of Cockburn Street. Rosie from Granton proposed Jake, who played

Bob Dylan hits on guitar and harmonica on Princes Street, and Ollie from Causewayside suggested Nate, who had a unicycle act that involved taking a kid from the audience around an obstacle course on his shoulders on the unicycle while playing "Flower of Scotland" on a penny whistle. All good but nothing that suggested "A Message to You, Rudy". Then, about half-past four, Marie from Prestonfield said she had laughed till she was almost sick watching Rude Boy, who juggles sex toys and plastic body parts – also all of the rude variety – while stripping down to his boxers on roller skates. When he wasn't being moved on he had a pitch outside Holy Willie's Bar on the Royal Mile, down from the junction with North Bridge. *Now that looks interesting*, Ferguson thought. *Cool.* He fished out his mobile and clicked on Reverend David Hidalgo.

Back in the Bridge of Spade's flat no further progress was being made. They were rapidly coming to the conclusion that any of the castle, Arthur's Seat, or the Stone of Destiny were equally suitable and there was really no way to choose between them. This made their selection just like closing your eyes and poking to choose the lottery numbers. Totally random. No one was feeling at all comfortable that Andrea's life should hang simply on a random decision, but what choice did they have? Pizza had come and gone along with more coffee, more Tunnock's Caramel Wafers, and finally toast and peanut butter, but none had brought inspiration. Finally Gillian suggested the only thing she could think of.

"While we seem to be completely stuck, why don't we at least get photos of them all? Then when we finally decide we can upload whatever we opt for without having to go out and get the image. I don't mind doing that."

McIntosh looked at his watch.

"Might be cutting it a bit fine for getting into the castle. I'll come with you."

Just as they were heading for the door, David's phone went. It was Ferguson.

"Hang on a minute," he said. "Ferguson from the *Evening News*."

He mainly listened, adding a few oks and yeses, then finished the call.

"Good news?" Gillian asked.

"Could be. They've had an entry proposing a juggler who works on the Royal Mile – which is in EH1 – called Rude Boy. 'A Message to You, Rudy' might fit. Can we investigate?"

"Absolutely," McIntosh confirmed. "I'll get a couple of DCs out there. If he's not there they can speak to the uniforms that work the Mile and see if they know anything."

The Royal Mile is the common name for a succession of streets that run downhill from the Castle Esplanade to Holyrood Palace measuring one Scots mile. On the way it passes more historical sites than most cities have in their entire portfolio and also a plethora of pubs, tartan and giftware shops, and visitor attractions that make it a hub for visitors from all over the world. As a result of all of that it also attracts the buskers and entertainers who feed – almost literally – off the tourists. Rude Boy was a Londoner but previously from Jamaica who had perfected his act in Covent Garden, Trafalgar Square, and outside Kings Cross Station before trying his luck in Edinburgh. So far it had gone pretty well. The Japanese and Koreans were scandalized and stood giggling nervously but watching nevertheless. The less inhibited Europeans seemed to take it more in their stride and went for husbands, wives, and boyfriends to make sure they didn't miss the fun. Local Scots thought it was hilarious and paid up as well. Rude Boy was happy. He slept on the sofa of a friend from Kingstown, did his juggling thing during the day, and smoked ganja at night and talked about going back home. He deliberately travelled light, clothes and personal items fitting in one case and all the other stuff in another. That included his juggling sex toys and plastic body parts and a special velcro suit he was able to rip off while the boobs and vibrators were flying, and finally a small battery amp and his mp3 player. Music definitely helped both his rhythm and the mood of the crowd. He had carefully chosen something that would suit his ethnic origins, get the crowd moving, and suit the theme of his act – "A Message to You, Rudy".

Although the show was a bit on the edge he rarely got much hassle. The local cops seemed to find it as funny as everyone else and the odd straight-faced moralist who came to give him a hard time was generally booed by the crowd and went away without accomplishing much. From time to time he was told to calm things down in a friendly way by the bobbies on the beat, particularly if the crowd was beginning to interfere with traffic, but it was pretty much live and let live, which suited him fine. All that being the case, he was surprised to be approached by two plain-clothes cops that evening as he got his stuff out and started getting set up.

"Excuse me sir," one of them began. "Are you Rude Boy?"

"Yeah, who wants to know?" he answered.

The one who'd spoken to him flashed an ID.

"Police Scotland. CID."

"Hey man. I'm legal. Ain't had no trouble. The cops know me. We get on ok."

"And you're not in any trouble," the other one reassured him. "We just want to check out your act. Totally routine. Can you tell me what you do?"

"Sure. Am a juggler. Wit dat stuff der. You know. Den I do a strip ting wile I juggling. Not de Full Monty, you know. I stop before it get too personal. I don have no trouble."

"And you're not in trouble now," the CID man reassured him again. The idea was to get a completely natural feel for his act without changing anything in terms of volume or routine and check how far the sound carried. So having him tone things down was going to be completely counterproductive.

"Do you have any music while you're doing your act?"

"Sure, but not too loud. Nobody complain."

"Do you always play the same music?"

"Sure – it's ma teem tune. I play 'A Message to You, Rudy'. Cause am de Rude Boy – dat's ma name. By de Specials. They's players from Jamaica and London. It's cool. It gets de crowd goin' you know?"

"Would you mind just playing a snatch of the tune – at the volume you'd normally use?"

"Sure. Jus' lemme get it set up. Ok. It go like dis."

Sure enough Rude Boy's battery amp began pumping out the harmonica, then drums, then horns, then the vocal – exactly as McIntosh had heard it in Spade's Bridge computer room.

"A Message to You, Rudy" – *ah ha!*

McIntosh was standing some fifty yards away to get an idea of how far the sound would travel. *That's it*, he thought. No question. Somewhere up in the cluster of buildings within earshot of the Rude Boy was their quarry. *Now we've got you, Mr Ramon.*

Chapter 18

PRINCES STREET

They used a conference room in St Leonard's later that evening. McIntosh did a quick round of introductions, including David, Gillian, Spade (with his laptop open in front of him), Alison Stokes (the forensic psychologist), and key members of the CID team. Finally a face David didn't recognize.

"Can I also introduce Andy McDonald from Edinburgh City Council Planning Department? Thanks for coming out on a Friday evening at such short notice. Andy will be guiding us through the properties within a hundred metres of the busker's pitch that might be possibilities for Ramon's location. And by the way, we have a community support officer with José, the boyfriend."

The meeting absorbed the information but nobody spoke.

"Ok, we all know why we're here," McIntosh continued, "so this is going to be a very brief resume then we'll move on to what's going to happen tonight.

"Ramon Zapata Murillo is a convicted child abuser. He used to be a parish priest in Seville but took advantage of his position. He was convicted and served seven years of a fourteen-year sentence. He is currently wanted in Spain for questioning in relation to the murder of four citizens from the Seville area: a retired bishop, a lawyer who worked for the church, and two teenagers who gave evidence against him at the trial. We know that he then came to Edinburgh since there was tracking on a vehicle he'd bought; however, we also know that he managed to hack into a laptop I was using to listen to conversations, following which he moved location and disabled the tracker. He was enticed back to Spain under the impression that his mother was ill, an operation of the Seville police, but stopped off at an aunt's on the way, which, unluckily, was where his mother was staying during the supposed illness. We believe that he then came back to Edinburgh. Andrea Suaréz Morán, the girl who alerted us to Ramon's behaviour by believing she might be next on his list, was being sheltered at a hidden location; however, this eventually became too onerous and she opted to return to her normal routine. Not long after that she was abducted.

"It seems that David here and Ramon had some previous dealings many years ago in Spain, and Ramon feels he has some sort of score to settle. So, because of that, he has been communicating with David in a weird sort of computer challenge with daily puzzles to solve. Alison has given us a very plausible psychological explanation of where that comes from, but for now we'll just take that as read. Days one and two of the challenge have been successful. We are now in day three. The implication is that if we don't get the right answer Andrea dies. What happens if we do isn't clear. Finally, by a bit of excellent detective work – not by me – we also now know more or less where he is to within a hundred metres or so. This is what Andy will be guiding us through a bit later.

"So, everybody clear about that? Ok. I'd like to start with the final level of the puzzle. The first two days' questions were tricky but by a bit of inspiration we managed to get them right. Day three is different, not because it's harder but because there are multiple possible solutions that all seem to fit equally. And we have about four hours to get it right and upload the image. David?"

David Hidalgo explained the problem to a mixture of grim smiles and groans around the table.

"We have until midnight to upload our answer," he said. "At least that's what we think. Then we get the response in the morning. We have images of all the options but it's not at all clear which is the right one since they all seem to work. In Spanish the clue reads: '*Piedra antigua en entorno moderno, asiento de rey y lugar de govierno*'. The translation is 'ancient stone in a modern setting, seat of the king and place of government'. We've discarded the Scottish Parliament building as not being an ancient stone or the seat of any kings but that still leaves the castle, Arthur's Seat, and the Stone of Destiny. All of them are ancient stones, all are in modern surroundings one way or another, all could be seen to be the seat of kings – Arthur's Seat in terms of its name, the Stone of Destiny literally as the place Scottish kings sat to be crowned, and the castle as a place kings held court. There are different inclinations among those of us who've been thinking this over since this morning but no consensus. So we're open to persuasion."

"Have you considered that there might not be any right answer?" Alison Stokes spoke up from the far end of the table. "Remember the end game of this is that Ramon feels justified in committing a further murder since we think he's pretending to himself that Alison's fate is now in the hands of the gods – i.e. David Hidalgo and team. But that's not to say he doesn't have a preferred outcome. So if he just sets a series of puzzles and you get them all right, where does that leave him in terms of the grand plan? He should feel morally obliged to let her go but he doesn't want to do that. So how can he absolutely guarantee that you come up with the wrong answer? By giving you a puzzle with no right answer. Maybe he hasn't even decided himself which is the right answer. So whatever you say – he can shift the right answer to one of the other options – and bingo – you were wrong. The victim dies. His big plan is fulfilled and it wasn't even his fault. I know that makes no sense to a rational mind but I think we have to assume that by this stage his thinking is very far from rational."

"So, in effect it makes no difference what we choose?" Gillian asked.

"In effect yes. I don't mean we should be reckless about it. If there is some balance of fit in favour of one option over the others, then we should certainly go for that. But if they all seem more or less equal then maybe that's what Ramon intended, and rather than agonize over it, we just get on with uploading one of them and accept it's going to be wrong and put our major emphasis on the police operation to apprehend him. We have no choice."

"Hmm. Depressing, but that seems to make sense," Gillian replied. "So votes for the castle, the Stone, or Arthur's Seat..."

"It may ultimately be a waste of breath but I would go with Arthur's Seat," David said. "We know he likes puns and wordplay. I think that fits his mindset as well as the facts. Spade?"

"Sticking with the Stone."

"Stuart?"

"I'm going to stick with the castle too. I think it works best as a place of government. But I'm also fairly inclined towards Alison's point. So I'm not going to fight for it. If we can't agree on a first choice – which I think is the case – then I would favour Arthur's Seat as a compromise. Any other views?"

Gillian simply looked bleak and shrugged. "I would have gone with the Stone too but it doesn't really seem to matter."

There were no other takers so David summed up.

"Two for the Stone, two for Arthur's Seat. Casting vote anyone? Nobody?"

After a long pause McIntosh spoke up.

"Ok folks. Reluctantly, because we can't sit here all night, I suggest we go with Arthur's Seat, bearing in mind that if it gets the thumbs down that doesn't mean that one of the others was correct. So no recriminations. Ok? Arthur's Seat it is. Spade?"

Spade tapped and clicked and in a few seconds the deed was done.

"Uploaded," he said.

"Ok, so the die is cast on that one. Now I'll hand over to Andy. I think we've been narrowing down the options here. And again, thanks for coming out at short notice."

"No problem. Glad to help." The planning officer lifted a long tube of plans from the floor and unrolled it on the conference table.

"So I've marked Rude Boy's pitch with the red dot. The green dotted circle is a ring 100 metres from that point. Naturally that takes in both sides of the street, but I imagine what we're looking for is premises that open directly onto the Royal Mile and are available for rent. From the video it looks like standard hotel/

apartment decor. Plain white but clean and fairly freshly painted. Windows in good condition. The chair was indistinct but again could be standard hotel fare. So I don't think we're looking at a storeroom or a depository. Clearly it's not a shop, restaurant, or bar, nor is it a privately owned residence. So that narrows it down quite a lot. Next, I don't think this can be a rent-by-the-night hotel room or there would have been some suspicions raised already what with concierge services and so on. So my hunch is a short- to medium-term let self-contained apartment suite probably with its own kitchen, living room, couple of bedrooms, and a bathroom. All right so far? Ok. I've done a search on that basis and there are two options. Royal Mile Apartments and Capital Apartments. Both would seem to fit the bill. Now I hope nobody minds me jumping ahead of the meeting slightly but I suggested these two options to Stuart, who I think has an update."

McIntosh passed immediately to one of his team.

"Kevin?"

"We've checked them both. Both have had recent lets that would seem to fit the timescale. There are about a dozen choices and four have Spanish names on the lease – none of them Ramon's though, so maybe he's operating with a false passport. Anyway, we've done an initial recce and Ramon's Jag is in the underground parking of Royal Mile Apartments. So we have apartments 3A, 4D, and 5B of Royal Mile Apartments that fit. Looks like he's going to be in one or the other of these."

"That's fantastic!" Gillian said. Even David was looking pleased.

"Unfortunately, it's not just going to be a question of knocking on the door," McIntosh continued. "This is really akin to a hostage rescue. Ramon may feel that his own life is not worth much now since he's bound to know he'll be out of circulation for most of the rest of his life if convicted. He might feel it's worth it not to go quietly and take Andrea with him. So we have to assume a hostile reception; surprise will be of the essence. In terms of the puzzle, we're on day three and so far we've worked on the basis of uploading prior to midnight. We've solved every puzzle Ramon has set. Midnight has always been the deadline. We just have to hope that he's either not watching for updates or is now so wrong-footed that he doesn't know what to do and will wait until the morning. I've informed the company that there will be a police operation tonight with forced entry to up to three of their properties. We have a uniform team that handles the mechanics of the entry. Firearms are being issued since we know from Silvia – the girl he took first to get to Andrea – that he has a weapon. It's not usual practice but I'd like you to accompany the team, David, for the sake of translation. We know he has good English but if he says something in Spanish we'll need to know what it is. Ok with that?"

Gillian groaned and looked down, but David simply nodded.

"I think that's it then. Questions? Ok. So zero one hundred hours outside Royal Mile Apartments. And this time we have a watch on the Jag!"

There were almost four hours to go as the meeting broke up. Andy McDonald went home to wife and children or whatever, Alison Stokes was heading to the airport for a weekend conference in Frankfurt, Spade went back to whatever programmers do in the midnight hour, but David and Gillian were at a loose end.

"Exactly what I thought might happen and didn't want to happen," Gillian said unhappily as they wandered out of the station and headed towards South Clerk Street. "Far too near the business end of guns again."

David was silent.

"I know you've got to go, but what happened to hopes for a quiet life?"

"Life happened," David replied.

"I suppose so. Not in the script and all that. But neither was the last one."

"Nor the one before that, which included you. As I think the Stones put it, 'You can't always get what you want'. I have to say, taken as a whole, I'm happy with what I got."

"I'm glad. Now what do we do with the next three hours?"

They took a taxi to Marchmont, went up to Gillian's flat, and sat holding each other in the dark and listening to "Nights in White Satin".

"Everybody clear?" McIntosh asked at the final briefing in a van outside Royal Mile Apartments. Two police vans and an ambulance were on the street. On a Friday night in the centre of town that didn't attract much attention. In the brief pause for responses David's phone dinged. *Drat that thing*, he thought but checked it anyway. A WhatsApp from Spade. "Wrong answer: the Princess dies," it said simply. He showed it to McIntosh who didn't look surprised but just shrugged.

"No alternative now," he said. "We just need to hope we're in time."

He informed the team but at this stage it made little difference, except perhaps confirming what they had suspected. No surprise there then.

As always David was impressed by the quiet professionalism of the police team. No histrionics, no drama, none of the movie clichés – just quietly getting on with the job. They moved into the apartment building and took the stairs. Two uniformed officers were left to secure the entrance to the building and the ground floor exit to the lift. The rest climbed to the third floor and identified apartment 3A. Just prior to shouting "Police – open up!" and optionally battering in the door, an officer tried the handle and found it unlocked. McIntosh raised his eyebrows. The firearms officers went in first with flashlights. The apartment was a mess. Drug paraphernalia was scattered around on the tables and the floor. Empty pizza boxes littered most other surfaces.

"Over here," an officer called quietly. The figure of a girl was lying face down on the carpet. McIntosh knelt beside her. First he felt for a pulse, then moved the body into the recovery position. Caucasian female, early twenties, but not Andrea.

A uniformed officer spoke quietly into his radio mike.

"Paramedics on the way," he said.

One officer was left in 3A while the others continued up the stairs.

4D wasn't open and one of the forced entry team banged on the door fit to raise the dead while bellowing "Police – open up!" Not surprisingly, at twenty past one in the morning there wasn't a quick response. The battering ram made short work of a flimsy door and again the armed officers were first in. This time there was a groggy response and a nearly naked man came stumbling out of a bedroom. A flashlight was shone in his face while another officer went into the bedroom he'd just left and others fanned out to search the rest of the property. It clearly wasn't Ramon unless he'd put on twenty kilos and thirty years. McIntosh apologized but didn't stop to explain.

That left 5B. The tension was palpable as they climbed one further floor, David bringing up the rear.

"Just go for it," McIntosh whispered to the man with the battering ram and about five seconds later they were in.

McIntosh paused for only a second on the threshold before shouting: "Gas!" and pulled the door immediately shut. There had been just enough time to notice a solitary figure slumped on a chair against the night-time light of the window.

McIntosh quickly gathered his team.

"You – Scottish Gas out of hours service. Report a leak then evacuate the building. You – get paramedics up here pronto. You – open a window then find the source and turn the gas off. You're with me. Take a deep breath – don't breathe in the property. We're going to get the girl out and close the door again."

The door was pushed open and the team went in. McIntosh and his colleague lifted the entire chair to which the slumped figure was tethered and carried it towards the door and out into the corridor. The door was pulled shut as soon as everybody was out.

Andrea was tethered to a dining room chair by silver tape at her ankles and wrists. Her head was hanging limply forward. Froth had gathered at her mouth.

"I think she's breathing," McIntosh muttered. "Right, you and you. Deep breath. Do not breathe in the property. If you run out of breath stick your head out the window or get back out here. Room by room."

The door was pulled open again and two officers entered. David, meanwhile, was wiping Andrea's mouth regardless of whether it would do any good, then pulling at the tape.

"Just leave that to us, sir," a uniformed officer intervened. "Medics should be here any minute."

They were, with about a ton of equipment. A mask was quickly slipped over her face and a drip fed into her arm. A pulse and temperature probe was slipped over one index finger and electrodes attached over her chest. Then she was cut free from the chair and lifted bodily onto a specialist stretcher that could be manoeuvred into lifts or stairs. This time they took the lift and Andrea quickly disappeared, surrounded by a team of quiet professionals who looked as if they would just get on with the job in the face of a kid with his head stuck in the railings or World War Three.

McIntosh reappeared at the door with the two other officers.

"Nobody," he said tersely. "The car's still there but Ramon's done a runner."

Just then one of the uniformed officers put his finger to his earpiece with a look of concentration.

"Say again, over," he said into the radio mike.

"Understood. On our way." The officer took McIntosh to one side and quietly told him.

"I think we know where Ramon might be. There's been a shooting incident on North Bridge and another outside the Balmoral Hotel. Princes Street is being cleared."

The Royal Mile and North Bridge was crawling with uniformed officers, traffic cops and squad cars, vans, and ambulances by the time they got down. Andrea was now being whisked off to the Western General. Just what had happened on the Bridge wasn't immediately clear but the chances of it involving Ramon seemed high so McIntosh took David with him and set off at a run down towards Princes Street looking for the senior officer on site.

"Nutcase with a hand-held firearm," the officer in question explained once they'd found him and McIntosh had identified himself. "Seems to be shooting more or less at random. We think six or seven shots on the Bridge. Nobody hit but lots of people very scared. Then outside the Balmoral he shot an American tourist coming out of the hotel at point-blank range. He may live but it looks pretty serious. Princes Street is on lockdown – nobody in or out and we're processing people as they leave. We have a few good witnesses so we've put them around each of the exit points to identify him if he tries to get past. The idea is to gradually empty the entire street, then we'll go in and see what's what. More firearms officers on their way."

Suddenly a huge explosion behind them rocked the street, shattering windows and flattening anything movable. An enormous fireball lit the night sky, followed by a gigantic plume of smoke. Seconds after, chunks of masonry and charred and burning fragments started raining down. Public and police alike hit the deck immediately, thinking of a terrorist attack. There was a ghastly mix of screaming, the echo of the explosion, the sound of falling debris, sirens, and shouting.

"I guess that's the end of Royal Mile Apartments," David muttered once they'd gathered their wits.

"I imagine you're right. I hope they got everybody out."

David Hidalgo and DI Stuart McIntosh continued down North Bridge towards Princes Street as the cloud of black smoke behind them grew and spread. Now a blanket of dust and soot was falling gently over the street, while the sound of sirens and screaming continued as a soundtrack to the night. At the foot of North Bridge they came to a line of tape guarded by several uniformed officers with firearms and body armour. McIntosh showed his ID and introduced David as his civilian translator. Through the cordon Princes Street looked like the set of a post-apocalyptic movie. It would only need Mad Max in his armoured wagon to come barrelling along, machine gun blazing, to complete the scene. Every exit was cordoned off and uniformed officers with automatic weapons were stationed at every corner. The main focus seemed to be further west towards the middle of the street.

"What's the latest?" McIntosh asked the first officer they came across.

"Intermittent shots, but the street's pretty clear now. I think we're homing in around the Scott Monument."

Over sixty metres high, like a massive steampunk Victorian rocket, the Scott Monument dominates the eastern end of Princes Street on the gardens side just before the Greek Temple architecture of the Royal Scottish Academy. Now it was lit in a lurid fiery glow. Armed officers were stationed around the plinth. The figure of Scott himself inside seemed unimpressed by the action. He was used to drama.

All the way along towards the monument David was preoccupied not only by the utterly surreal situation in which he now found himself but by the man who had brought it all about – and how an Edinburgh pastor had come to be involved. An English chat group in a restaurant. A young Spaniard who decided to bring his flatmate. A news story in the paper. A connection that nobody else seemed to have made. A man bent on senseless revenge who brought his private war to Edinburgh and had that young woman on his list. Efforts to hide and protect her had proved ineffective, and efforts to stop or apprehend her assailant equally so.

So this is where we are now. The girl on a stretcher being pumped full of oxygen on her way to hospital, premises reduced to rubble with who knew how many casualties, and the man at the dark centre of it all shooting randomly as if he had totally lost his grip on reality – which seemed to be a real possibility. What state of mind could lead a man to that sort of behaviour? He had been sane and rational once, then by a series of fatal choices had embraced hate and revenge, plunging him further and further into darkness. Turning towards the darkness, David often reflected, by definition involved turning away from the light. Embracing one meant rejecting the other. And a road that starts in shadow, as it goes deeper into darkness, allows less possibility of finding the way back out. So Ramon had embraced hate and vengeance in some sort of twisted attempt to get even with those he accused of letting him down, or maybe it was with those who had simply exposed his own weaknesses and conflicts. The death of the bishop and the lawyer maybe still had some hint of reason about them, but the children weren't to blame for anything. They hadn't created the systems Ramon had struggled with. They had been exploited by him, not the other way about.

The city around him now seemed to David almost like a physical expression of the conflict in Ramon's head. It was disintegrating in fire. It was empty of normal people going about their normal lives. It was a place of danger and distress, descending into barbarism and death. But what was Ramon thinking now? Were there any coherent thoughts still left in his mind? Was there any way to reach into that chaos and reconnect it to reality? As they pressed on towards the monument, it also struck David that things could so easily have been very different for him too. He had once been disappointed and disillusioned. He had felt wronged and left hung out to dry when all he had trusted in seemed to disintegrate in his hand. But it hadn't happened. Now here he was, wondering if there might be any way to connect with Ramon when, if things had been different, he could have been the one so messed up inside he could have been capable of anything. Why the difference? Destiny, good luck, good choices, or the grace of God? He wasn't sure, but somehow it had happened. The love of a good woman certainly helped, and there had been good choices. But maybe they weren't even his choices, like what Gillian had said about good works prepared in advance, precious stones in his path. He had at least chosen to bend and pick them up rather than on walk on by in a rejection of all that was good. Could Ramon have made different choices, or was it his destiny? David didn't believe in those predestined only for wrath. There had to be a thread that could still reconnect Ramon to reality and love. His behaviour had been heinous but he was still a human being, which meant that there still had to be some fragmented reflection of the maker's image, like a face in a shattered mirror. Simply being human had to mean that he still had some capacity for redemption. That was the bottom line. There had to be a way.

"Sorry, sir. That's as far as you can go," they were told at the foot of the monument.

"What's going on?"

"Shooter's at the top of the tower. An assault team'll be going in shortly. Orders to shoot if there's any doubt. Nobody else allowed near."

David took McIntosh to one side.

"I suppose that means shoot to kill. I'd like to talk to him first," he said.

"Why?"

"I might be able to talk him down. Just shooting the man without even trying to talk to him seems unnecessary. Even after what he's done."

"Nice thought, David," McIntosh replied, "but it's not going to happen. He's live, armed, and dangerous – and quite possibly off his rocker. That doesn't make for a rational conversation and the risks are just too great. Sorry, no chance. He'll be given every opportunity to come down quietly. Then they go in shooting."

David turned away, took a deep breath, and let it slowly out. McIntosh had every bit of logic, caution, and good sense on his side but it still didn't feel right. Practically speaking, Ramon's English might be up to surviving as a stranger in a foreign city while he was still emotionally stable but that was clearly no longer the case. Did that make it ok to shoot him dead without at least one final appeal in his own language?

Just then a shot pinged off the stonework right next to them. It looked like Ramon had changed his vantage point and the entrance to the monument stairway was now in line of sight. McIntosh and the officer on duty immediately took cover around the corner and David saw his chance. Ridiculous, insane, unrealistic to hope it would work, but it still seemed like the right thing to do. He darted into the entrance passage and took the spiral steps two at a time until he was out of breath and had to stop and recover. He thought he heard his name shouted from below but there was no sound of following footsteps.

The monument was officially closed so the power was off. The spiral stone stairway was almost pitch black. He took out his phone and turned the torch on. The light it gave was pitiful but enough for him to at least see a few steps ahead and be able to put one foot after the other. Up, up, and up. His guess was that Ramon wouldn't be on the stairs but would be occupying one of the viewing platforms so he wasn't expecting to bump into him right away. But which level and what height? It was just a matter of time till they came face to face. He continued, not making any particular effort to keep silent as the whole point was to let Ramon know he was there. He stopped at intervals and shouted ahead: "¡Ramon! ¡Soy David! ¡Subo!" Ramon. This is David. I'm coming up.

He reached the first level, breathing hard. It had an internal chamber but it was locked so he made his way slowly around the outer walkway. Every corner might bring him face to face with Ramon – and his gun. But in the end it was empty. So back into the dark and narrow circular staircase. The light of his phone was sufficient only to illuminate a few steps ahead of him. Round and round. Slower now as he tried to pace himself. It was hard to keep listening for any sound of movement ahead when all he could hear was his own breathing and heartbeat hammering in his chest. How much from the exertion and how much from what he knew must lie somewhere ahead, he couldn't say.

Up and up. The faint light of the next level began to soften the darkness slightly. Then, suddenly, he emerged onto the second level. The lights in the street below and around about were just enough to illuminate dark, heavy stone, wrought-iron railings, constricted passageways, and narrow windows. Once again, around the perimeter until this time he hit a dead end. Back to the stairs. At least he and Ramon weren't following each other round and round like in a theatre farce.

Into the spiral staircase again. His breath and heartbeat seemed to have eased a fraction but he felt himself tiring. His legs felt heavy as he went on, plodding now more than racing. Two down, two to go.

"¡Ramon! ¡Soy David! ¡Subo!"

Finally, out onto the third level. Equally dark and now his phone seemed to be losing power, the light dimming. He emerged only to stop, slump against the wall, try to draw breath, and recover, his legs leaden and his muscles trembling. He noticed he was sweating. He slumped against the wall and tried to control his breathing. Once he had calmed, he advanced around the walkway, calling ahead of him. He didn't want Ramon to see a shadow, assume it was the police, and shoot. Right around, eventually back to the spiral stair. Still no Ramon.

So, it's the top, he thought. *At least now we know.* Down below he could hear sirens and see the reflected pulse of blue and orange lights. There was another series of bangs – maybe buildings next to the apartments or something inflammable held in storage. Restaurant kitchens with gas bottles for cooking or a storeroom with petrol for the boss's motorbike. It was all going up now. Someone had gotten hold of a loud hailer and was calling. He could make out only the name Ramon and nothing more – just a series of incomprehensible sounds. How they thought that was going to get through was anybody's guess. Gradually he realized this was merely putting off the inevitable.

"¡Ramon! ¡Soy David! ¡Subo!"

Still no reply but he was there, surely. Now in the narrowest stair of all he began to hear the odd crack like a whip or a dry stick breaking. Yes. He was there. On the top level. Shooting down. Surely not far now. The constantly turning spiral stair was disorientating with no indication of when it might come to an end. Then, again, finally, a slight easing of the darkness.

"¡Ramon! ¡Soy David! ¡Subo!"

Suddenly he was out. The top level. Normally full of tourists from all over the world wanting the best views of Princes Street. But still no Ramon. At least there wasn't any doubt now. It wasn't if, but merely when. He went forward slowly. The same dark stone, narrow archways, wrought iron, and now a series of notices urging visitors to call the Samaritans, talk to someone instead of jumping. Despite it all, David found himself hoping that Ramon would choose to talk – not shoot, not jump. There didn't seem to be any other alternatives.

Finally, he rounded a corner and there he was. Devoid of drama. Down below sirens still wailing and blue lights flashing, but here there was a still centre. Two human beings. Face to face. At last.

Ramon too seemed unnaturally calm. The gun was in his hand but not raised.

"Well, if it's not the Ingenious Hidalgo of Edinburgh! I should congratulate you before I shoot you. I thought you'd never get them. But you did. Well done."

David couldn't think what to say. He stalled for time.

"The third one?" he asked, as if he were merely checking on buses. "We were right, weren't we?"

"Ah, well. That you'll never know. But anyway, *¿Por qué has venido?*" Why have you come?

David matched Ramon's sudden switch to Spanish.

"*Solo para hablar,*" he said. Just to speak.

"Haven't you spoken enough? If you hadn't spoken all these years ago I'd never have been a priest, never made that impossible bargain with God, never failed to keep my vows, never have gone to prison – never killed. Don't you think you've had enough to say?"

"I've tried to think back to that day, Ramon. I think I remember you. Skinny kid with dark hair but your eyes were wide open. You were drinking it all in. I just told my story that day, Ramon. I didn't force you and I didn't try to fool you. Faith is a choice. You made the choice to believe."

"And what good did it do me?"

"If it's true and whether or not it worked out for you are different questions. I just told you what was true for me at that time. We can only tell our own stories."

Ramon paused, lifted his gun lazily, and shot into the stonework, loosing a cloud of dust and fragments of stone. David cringed involuntarily. The sound of the shot echoed around the walls and dust landed on his head and shoulders.

"Power," he said. "That's a different question too. Faith means handing over your choices. Living in a box where you can only go so far in any direction. Whether it's God that draws the boundaries or the church, it amounts to the same thing. You're a prisoner. Do this, don't do that. Obey, trust, believe. Just like being in jail. Power means you make your own choices. You can call the shots. You decide the boundaries of the box."

"Doesn't that mean you just put other people into the same situation you want out of?"

"Of course. But why not? We're all in boxes. Life is competitive. I'd rather make my own box. Isn't it better that the others live in your box than that you live in theirs?"

"You've certainly made your own box, Ramon," David said. "But it's a smaller, poorer, more limiting box than anyone else's. Isn't it a box called hate?"

Ramon snorted.

"You know nothing about my life," he said with contempt. "Nothing. So don't think you can pass judgment so easily. You have no idea how hard I tried. It was an impossible task. The deck was stacked, the dice loaded. I did what I had to do. You'd have done the same. I spent seven years in somebody else's box and I vowed I'd never let it happen again. So I've done what I've done. You don't need to like it. Anyway, enough philosophy. What do you think of the view up here? Magnificent, isn't it?"

David didn't exactly have the time or interest to admire the view but Ramon was right. The castle was lit up to perfection, showing both the rock and the buildings and fortifications piled up as if they were growing out of it. The gardens were in deep shade but falling debris had lit a series of small fires. The shops along Princes Street still had their lights on inside and looked like they were open for business. But nobody was buying. And the buses, taxis, and trams that should normally have been running back and forth even at two o'clock in the morning were absent. The whole buzz that made Edinburgh what it was day or night was silent. Instead, all they could hear were the nightmare sounds of chaos and catastrophe. It was as if Ramon had managed to make the entire city dance to his tune. And the ever-present sirens – were they coming to rescue people trapped in the rubble or were they taking injured and dead to hospital? They were at least probably bringing more police to the town centre to manage the "live shooter situation". And here was David, chatting about the view with the live shooter.

"Andrea?" Ramon suddenly asked

"Alive I think. But what do you care?" David countered.

Ramon shrugged.

"She was the last piece in the puzzle. The last part of the Plan. Then I could have disappeared in peace. You would never have heard of me again."

"But leaving devastation behind you. Andrea herself. Her family. Sevilla as a city. Is that a fair exchange for whatever you wanted to achieve?"

"Ah, we're getting philosophical again, Pastor David," Ramon said with a smile. "You'll be asking about justice in a minute. Don't you ever think about wars and rumours of wars? I'm a very small piece in the puzzle. A minor tragedy and a few casualties. I'm a bit-part player. The generals that command the missiles retire with medals and a pension. And the politicians. What can I say? They become elder statesmen. I go to prison for the rest of my natural life. I can't go back to Morón de la Frontera, Pastor David, whether I deserve to or not."

"So why are you up here? What's the point of this? What are you going to achieve?"

Ramon shrugged again.

"I'm not entirely sure. I like the view. I can take out anyone from up here." Ramon gave a bitter laugh. "I thought I might like one last moment of peace high above the city. High above everything I've done and what has been done to me. Then it would end. I can't go back to Morón."

"I can understand that. But maybe you don't have to – at least not like last time."

"What do you mean?" Ramon asked with his first expression of interest.

"I'm not here to offer you a deal, Ramon. I suppose you will go to court and will go to prison but it doesn't have to be like last time."

"Then what?"

"Look. You're right – I don't know your story. I have no idea about your struggles in the priesthood and I can't imagine what all these years of confinement do to a man. But from what I do know and what I can imagine, the greater prison wasn't the walls round about you. You had imprisoned yourself in hate and the need for revenge."

Ramon smiled.

"Nice try, Pastor David, but it won't wash. A wall is a real thing, not a construction of the mind. Freedom is tangible. Do you know that in Morón you can say what you'll have for breakfast five years in advance?"

David edged slightly closer to Ramon and tried again.

"Well, let me ask you what else you know, Ramon. Do you know that the people who came out of the Gulag or Auschwitz as intact human beings were the ones who did not give in to hate? They were never in prison, despite what the guards did to them. There was a light inside that was brighter than the searchlights."

"Are you suggesting I'm capable of reform? Maybe I could become an inspirational leader for all the gangsters, thugs, and hoodlums in my wing; all the child abusers, murders, rapists, kidnappers – the innocent misunderstood. They'd look to me for inspiration and hope. I don't think you understand, Pastor David. That light went out long ago. It can't be rekindled now."

David took another step forward.

"Are you sure? Whatever you think of the institutions of the church, the bottom line is renovation from the inside out. And you've probably seen it happen. I have. Many times. In fact, I could tell you the second half of my story that you didn't hear twenty years ago because it hadn't happened yet. I could have been you." He paused to let the thought sink in. "Easily. But I managed to find some light somehow. It's not impossible."

David had been slowly inching forward as he spoke.

"Not so close, Pastor," Ramon said, an edge to his voice. "Whatever else I am, I'm not an idiot."

He lifted his gun again and fired, this time into the ground at David's feet. The bullet ricocheted into his calf, knocking David to the ground. He gave an involuntary shout of pain and collapsed on the flagstone floor, gripping his leg. Ramon showed no emotion.

"Your attempts to redeem the irredeemable are very worthy, Pastor David, but it's really not worth it – even if it were possible. And while you're nursing your leg – I do apologize – I should put your question back to you. What are *you* doing up here? Why should you care about what happens to me? Sent by the powers that be or are you a self-employed agent of humanity?"

"Neither," David gasped, gripping his lower leg as the blood began to soak through. "I'm here because I could have been you. But I'm not. So you can become – not me – but a better you. Despite all you've done. That would be better for you and for society than simply locking you away. You can challenge the system in another way. Rise above it."

By now David was hunched over, gripping his leg and trying to staunch the blood. Out of the corner of his eye he thought he could see the reflection of lights coming up the spiral stair.

"There isn't much time. Throw the gun away, or let me have it. Don't give them a reason to shoot you."

Ramon seemed to be pondering. Then suddenly his shoulders seemed to slump.

"I'm tired, Pastor David," he said. "Very tired. Do you know you have to work very hard for the wages of sin? I'd like some peace. I'd like to turn off all the thoughts, the sounds, the voices. Do you know they play in my head every waking moment? I wish it were possible."

The lights were coming closer. Any second David expected to see the barrel of a rifle appearing around the corner.

"Do it, Ramon! Do it now! Throw it away or let me have it!"

"What do you think? Maybe I will let you have it. One last meaningless gesture – because I once admired you…"

He jumped onto the low wall around the flagstone floor and climbed over the railings meant to protect the public.

He lifted the gun into the air and turned half back like a discus thrower. It was pointing just to where David was hunched on the ground. Suddenly there was a sharp crack and a cry. Then all that was left of where Ramon had been were the floodlights on the streets below. And behind David's head, somewhere up on the castle rock behind all the fortifications, all the layers upon layers of stonework, in a small room, lay the Stone of Destiny.

Chapter 19

EDINBURGH

"You are in such serious trouble I can't begin to say," DI Stuart McIntosh said, handing over a copy of *Jazz Monthly*. "Found this in the back seat of the car. Thought it might take your mind off things while you wait to have the riot act read to you."

David was on a treatment bed in casualty at the Western General Hospital about a mile and a half from Princes Street. His trouser leg had been cut off above the knee and the shoe and sock removed. His calf had heavy bandaging, there was a drip in his arm, and he was wired to a monitor that beeped incessantly in the background. He was weak from a mixture of shock, exhaustion, and loss of blood.

"Ramon?" he asked.

"As you'd expect. Bit of a mess. He's in the mortuary – those bits they could put back together again anyway. He bounced off a few of the jaggy rocks on the way down."

"Was it really necessary to shoot him? From where I was it looked like he was about to throw the gun away."

McIntosh shook his head in disbelief.

"And from where I was standing the gun was pointed straight at you and he was shouting something aggressive."

"He could have been about to throw the gun and come down unarmed."

"He could have been about to shoot you, then jump. Or shoot you and not jump. Or let off a few more shots at my team down below while jumping. Or not jumping. Who knows what he might have done? We narrowed his options. I'd do the same again, no question. Despite tonight's performance I would still rather have you alive than Ramon. That clear enough for you?"

David smiled wearily through the painkillers.

"Crystal," he said. "And Andrea?"

"Alive and recovering. She was exposed to high levels of natural gas but for a relatively short period of time. She may have some memory loss – which could be a good thing. I'm told chances of brain damage are low and a full recovery is likely. But half an hour more, as the medics like to say… José is with her now so at least she can speak in Spanish when she comes round."

"And Gillian?"

"On her way. It's four o'clock in the morning remember. It'll take her a few minutes."

When Gillian arrived she swept past the junior doctor on duty and the trauma nurse and grabbed David around the neck.

"I really don't know whether to hug you or kill you myself," she said, backing off. Tears weren't far away. "You're the one that should be in prison, not Ramon. It would be safer. What were you thinking?"

"Thinking I could maybe make a difference, as usual. But it didn't work out that way."

"I'll say. I apologized for calling you an idiot. I take it back."

Gradually she managed to detach herself, then apologized to the staff and grabbed a chair. She was very pale and trembling. "So it wasn't Arthur's Seat then?" she asked.

David gave a laugh partly at the joke and partly in general relief. Andrea was on the mend, he was alive, and Gillian was with him. The riot act from the Chief Constable didn't bother him too much. He figured he was probably still a few points ahead in the game of Ramon's Revenge.

"Apparently not. Or maybe it was. I guess we'll never know. But we saved the princess anyway."

"How is she?"

"Not serious they say but sleeping right now, which is what you should be doing."

"Well, I would if I didn't have to come and collect the 'Crime-Busting Cleric'."

"Is it in the paper?"

"Not yet but Charlie Ferguson has sent us a draft. I want to rewrite it and call you the Reckless Reverend!"

It didn't take long until David was "free to go" but was told to report to his health centre within twenty-four hours to get the dressing changed and the stitches checked. It turned out to be what they called "just a flesh wound", missing arteries and bone but it was really beginning to throb now and would at the very least be highly inconvenient for some weeks to come. They plonked him in a wheelchair with his leg stuck out in front.

"Want the bullet?" the doctor asked but David declined.

The following day was Saturday so nobody had an early start. David had managed a fitful sleep with Gillian lying next to him on top of the downie and bringing him drinks of water and painkillers at regular intervals. She went out early for some papers. *The Scotsman*'s front page was devoted to the "Princes Street Siege" as they were already calling it. There were eyewitness accounts, aerial photographs, background pieces, and a shot of where the Royal Mile Apartments used to be. McIntosh had managed to keep David's part in the proceedings out of the news. Gillian turned on Radio Scotland and got live news coverage, including McIntosh speaking to the reporter. Nice as it would have been to spend the day in bed recovering, there was one appointment that couldn't wait. David was on elbow crutches so Gillian helped him down the stairs, manoeuvred him into the car to an accompanying chorus of yelps – some louder than others – and together they drove back to the Western. Andrea was sitting up but was groggy and a bit befuddled. José was at her side, where he had been since he got the news from the CID team via the community support officer. The doctor on duty was sanguine about her recovery and didn't foresee any issues except a really bad headache that might last a few days.

"Thank you for looking for me," she said quietly.

"I won't say 'any time'," David replied, "but I'm glad it worked out."

"I heard Ramon died."

"That's true. I tried to talk to him to see if there was any way to connect. It's not my ideal outcome but at least it means there's no trial to go through."

"He deserved to die," José said bluntly.

"Well, you may be right," David conceded, "though who deserves what can be difficult to say."

"I think he went mad," Andrea said. "He just sat at his computer all the time muttering to himself. Then there would be some sort of shout, though it was hard to tell if he was happy or angry. José told me about the computer game. Crazy. But I'm glad you got the right answers."

"Not all of them, I'm afraid," Gillian put in. "We got the last one wrong. Or he changed the right answer. Or there was no right answer. We'll never know. I'd like to think we were right and he changed the rules. That would be three out of three."

"I'm sorry the only prize I can give you is to say thank you."

"We got you back. You're well. That's the best prize," Gillian said. José was apparently in agreement.

"What will you do now?" David asked.

Go home for a bit," Andrea said. "I have to see my mum and I just want to be in my own house and sleep in my own bed. José has been in touch with her. She was planning to come to Scotland and see me anyway but when she found out what was happening she wanted to get on the next plane. Martin has said he can keep my job for a month or so."

"So you're coming back then?" Gillian asked.

"For sure," Andrea said, glancing at José, who was looking like he'd won the Christmas Lottery.

The following day David insisted on preaching from a seated position with his leg stuck out in front of him and dosing up to the eyeballs despite Mrs MacInnes's scandalized tutting ("Whatever next") and Juan's concerned whispering before the service and worried looks from the sound desk. The congregation as a whole seemed to take it remarkably in their stride. Having David Hidalgo as their pastor meant they never knew quite what was coming next. To some of the younger ones he seemed to slot in somewhere alongside James Bond, Batman, and his biblical namesake.

The text was the next in his list of parables of the kingdom. Appropriately enough, it was the shepherd who goes looking for the missing sheep – a short parable and more clearly transparent than some. Essentially it taught that every individual is important and that God is interested in individual persons as well as the mass of humanity. His application was that you are special to God. As well as being Scottish, English, British Asian, or whatever, plus male, female, and whatever profession – however you choose to define yourself – God sees you as a unique individual with unique gifts and talents. That means you are valued for what makes you you. So those that think they are ordinary or lacking any ability or unloveable – the ugly ducklings of society – are just plain wrong as far as God is concerned.

"So is that what you were trying to do at the top of the Scott Monument?" Gillian asked innocently as they were preparing lunch. "Rescuing the little lost lamb?"

David grunted from a seated position as he tried to chop vegetables while moving as little as possible.

"I don't know. Maybe you're right to be cynical. I really can't say what I was thinking or what I was hoping for, to be honest. Maybe I was as mad as him to think I could have some influence. Maybe he was so far down the wrong road that he couldn't even distinguish right and wrong any more."

"So why climb up?"

"I suppose I felt he needed one more chance to turn around – or at least someone to speak to him in his own language. I'm not saying I have sympathy for Ramon in terms of what he's done but I just think everyone has to be redeemable or it makes a mockery of grace and mercy."

"And was that worth more than thinking of me if you'd been killed?" Gillian spoke gently enough but she was serious.

David shook his head.

"Absolutely not. I thought I could do it. I was wrong. And I'm sorry." He sat up as straight as he could and turned to her. "You are more important. Have I ever told you – I think you're the very best part of me?"

"That might be the nicest thing anyone has ever said to me. If I understand it... Here – peel these onions before I get weepy. I really thought I might have lost you – when they called me and said you were up there and there had been gunshots. I was anxious but I was partly angry too. I thought you had no right to take such a risk. I thought Ramon didn't deserve another chance – not if it put my future husband at risk. It's a very worthy thought but you've got to ask what you value most. And I have to disagree with you – not everyone is redeemable. Maybe everybody should be but the reality is that some people have just blown their chances. Maybe like calloused skin. It doesn't know how to feel any more. I'm sure there was a time Ramon could have changed – or been changed – but that time had long passed. To what extent it was bad choices, bad genes or bad luck is purely academic. By the time you got to him he was beyond redemption. Literally. In that case you have to protect yourself and not take pointless risks."

"Pearls before swine, eh?"

"Well, Jesus said it, didn't he?"

"He did indeed."

"Do you still think he was about to throw the gun away?"

"Impossible to know. I thought he was at the time. But I admit it seems pretty unlikely looking back. We'll never know for sure."

Just then the doorbell rang.

"Are we expecting visitors?" David asked, surprised.

"Just a couple of random strays I managed to contact, to welcome you back from almost being dead."

It was Tati and Elvira. Tati had brought a pudding and Elvira had brought Michael, her new boyfriend. He was doing his PhD in international human rights law and they had met at an Amnesty International meeting. He had been left in no doubt about the importance of impressing David so had a bottle of Ribera del Duero Gran Reserva and a packet of *jamón* in hand. They were like love birds, completely preoccupied with each other all afternoon, which made Gillian smile whenever she looked at them. Stuart McIntosh arrived on the doorstep at the same time as Andrea and José so they came in together. David had made a point of saying that Stuart's wife, Kirsty was invited too but he had only shrugged and said he would tell her but that they didn't do very much together these days. She would be at her Ramblers Club. Andrea was still obviously weak but otherwise seemed none the worse. She smiled a lot but didn't say much, not only because of the speed of the English zinging around. Ali and Ayeesha arrived with several boxes of Asian sweets, which smelled fantastic even while still in their boxes, and a huge dish of a sweet rice dessert made with pistachios, raisins, and cardamom pods. Juan had declined the invitation as he had to be with Alicia who felt like she was ready to explode and was certainly not fit to climb stairs and party.

Irene MacInnes bustled in with a nice Victoria sponge and a tin of Empire biscuits. Yet again she found herself tutting and puffing at an explanation of what their pastor had been up to. Since he wasn't actually paid, additional danger money wasn't on the table but she did make a mental note to tell him to be more careful in future. Just after her, Sandy and Sonia arrived with the kids. She'd brought a pot of genuine, authentic goulash and he had some of Uncle Giancarlo's Italian pastries. Sonia joked that they'd thought of leaving the kids in the freezer but Gillian had insisted they come. Luca and Mario spent the afternoon trying to get a note out of David's saxophone to his all too obvious consternation.

Even Spade finally made it – two o'clock on a Sunday afternoon was a fairly early start for him. He brought a family-sized tin of Tunnock's Caramel Wafers and somewhat to David's surprise was accompanied by Tina in full goth gear and make-up. She was secretary of the Edinburgh Warhammer Club but when not overseeing mayhem between the orcs and elves apparently also had some facility with baked cheesecake and had brought a sample.

"And why not?" Gillian whispered in David's ear.

Despite David's limited mobility and the whole thing being a total surprise, he took the easy way out and threw together some paella ingredients in twenty minutes or so. It was a bit of a faff preparing everything sitting down but once it was all in his biggest *paellera*, then it was just a case of adding the rice, turmeric (cheaper than saffron and gives a better colour), chicken stock, and a bit of salt, covering it, and turning down the heat. Before the tapas, which Gillian had prepared and brought, they popped a couple of bottles of cava provided by José.

"Nice. Very nice. Thanks for organizing this. I love you," David whispered in Gillian's ear as they toasted Andrea's safe return, David's recovery, and friendship in general.

"My pleasure. I'm glad we've got so much to be happy about," she whispered back and gave him a proper one right on the kisser.

As she was still whizzing around topping everybody up José got to his feet and nervously cleared his throat.

"Just before we start everybody. A little announcement. When Andrea was... em... away... I did a lot of thinking, when I wasn't working – and when I was working..." he flushed red, "I thought if I got her back, I wouldn't take the risk again. So we've decided to make it permanent."

Andrea stood up beside him, all smiles, and showed off the ring she had surreptitiously slipped on – to huge cheering.

"Will you live in Edinburgh?" Ali shouted in among the congratulations.

"We've not quite decided," José answered shyly.

"I vote yes!" Andrea added.

"You'd better. It's the best city in the world!" Mrs MacInnes affirmed, leaving no room for debate.

After complimenting Tina on the cheesecake, David took the chance for a quiet word with Spade.

"I stand amazed at your encyclopaedic knowledge of music as well as your computer skills. Was it just good luck that you recognized the busker's tune?"

Spade shrugged as if it wasn't such a big deal.

"Not really. I've got quite a big music collection. I listen while I'm working."

"But I don't think I've seen a single CD in your flat. It did strike me as a bit weird."

"Ah well, that's because I don't have a single CD. I did some work for Amazon a few years ago – not much, just a few thousand pounds' worth – and I suggested they might like to pay me with access to their music store. Seems they just forgot to turn it off. So I've got a terabyte hard drive more or less full of free downloads – New Wave, Punk, and Prog mainly. So The Specials fall into my area of special interest, you could say."

"Amazing. Well, I forgive you for not being a jazz fan then. More paella?"

Conversation drifted on through the tapas, the paella, the mountain of puddings people had brought, then Ayeesha's fantastic sweets with coffee or sweet Asian tea. Ramon wasn't mentioned. Care was taken to avoid David's awkward bandaged leg but nobody drew attention to how it had happened. In general the mood was one of unspoken relief. Andrea was well, safe, and home against all the odds. She and José were planning a future together which had all come in a bit of a rush but met with universal approval. It had been a successful though incredibly complicated case for Stuart McIntosh in his official role and the others involved less officially. Unfortunately, there had been casualties when Royal Mile Apartments had gone up in a fireball – some critical but none fatal so far. Stuart explained to David in a quiet moment that his team had got everyone out of the building but there hadn't been time to evacuate all the surrounding streets so the explosion had taken its toll. Mostly glass and falling masonry injuries, however, rather than anyone reduced to their constituent molecules, which was a relief.

Finally it was over. Andrea was showing signs of flagging and when she and José left that started the exodus. Eventually only David and Gillian remained. Mrs MacInnes, Ayeesha, and Michael had dealt with the dishes so there wasn't much else to do. Gillian set the living room largely to rights and they sat down on the sofa in peace, with Chet Baker gently caressing every note of "You Go to My Head" in the background.

"So what now, Pastor David?" Gillian asked with a glass of slightly flat cava in her hand. "Once the *Evening News* article comes out you'll have to set up as a consulting detective and get men with bowler hats in states of distress coming to seek your advice."

"Don't know if I can help with bowler hats in distress."

Gillian dug him in the ribs.

"You know what I mean. You'll be able to sit on the chaise longue and say, 'I perceive that you are a modern studies teacher from Dalkeith Academy, that you have recently returned from two weeks in Marbella and that your prize-winning chinchillas have disappeared overnight. You will find them made into moccasins and on sale on Ebay for £14.99."

David laughed out loud.

"That'll be the day."

"Well, that looks like the way it's going. See if I'm not right. I absolutely bet you somebody turns up on the doorstep with a case to solve."

"Does that mean I can play the violin and take cocaine when I don't have a case on?"

"Just you try. More cava?"

"Thank you, madam. I hope you are trying to take advantage of me."

"I would but I don't think you're fit for it. Won't be long now though. Ayeesha and I have the cake sorted. Mrs MacInnes has had the hall booking in her little red jotter for six months and Juan tells me Alicia is shopping for non-maternity wear with a vengeance. So I suppose we'd better get on with it."

"The sooner the better, you know that. Oh, that reminds me. Can you go to my overcoat in the hall? There's an envelope in the inside pocket. Something to show you. Don't look."

"I'm intrigued."

Gillian brought the envelope back, along with another half-full bottle of cava. David took another glug.

"You allowed all of that with the painkillers?" Gillian asked pointedly.

"Doctor's orders," David replied. "On the hour every hour."

He opened the envelope and pulled out a set of A4 stapled pages.

"Mrs MacInnes had a word with me last week. The church are giving us our honeymoon as a gift — flights, accommodation, car hire, even spending money. The whole shebang. And so, I propose a short trip to somewhere nice but not too exotic in August after the event."

"That's incredibly generous. So we can escape the sweltering heat of Edinburgh during the summer?"

"And the festival. So somewhere warm right away, then I'm proposing somewhere else a little later on."

"Wow. Double trouble."

David held out the first page.

"Oh," Gillian said with some surprise. "Nice. Very nice indeed. And not Spain for a change. Are you sure?"

"Definitely. If you're ok with that."

"I am definitely ok. I can learn to scuba dive and look at all the lovely fishes."

"Then," he continued, "I had a word with Fran McGoldrick and she made some suggestions. So in the ridiculous holidays you academics get, I'm proposing another trip. Perhaps involving Christmas on the beach."

He showed her page two. Gillian gasped.

"And the church are going to pay for it all?"

"All of it. I asked Mrs MacInnes what the budget was and she said, 'What budget?' I think she feels guilty that I'm not on the payroll so this is her way of wangling the funds. And if you look here, this is camper van hire, which I gather is all the rage."

"Excellent! I want one of the cool ones with a funky paint job. And we tour from north to south?"

"We do exactly what you want, my love. North to south. East to west. Round and round in circles. I honestly don't care. Or we can spend a month in a car park locked inside getting up to no good. Or you can climb volcanos and bathe in the hot mud pools if you want."

"And you can clean it all off and put my body lotion on."

"Oooh, I love it when you talk like that. Don't let Mrs MacInnes hear."

"Well, for goodness' sake, we've waited long enough."

"You can say that again. I have some sympathy with Ramon and his complaints about clerical celibacy."

"Well. Not long now. But please, let's not speak about Ramon."

"Agreed. One more page to go."

David turned to the final page and held it out. This time Gillian really did give a sharp intake of breath.

"You're joking," she said.

"Not at all. Seems a bit silly to go all that way and not drop in on a Polynesian paradise."

"I have always wanted to visit the South Pacific. Always. How did you know?"

"Well us detectives have our ways and means, you know. For example, I perceive, madam, that you love a slightly crazy pastor who keeps getting into trouble, putting himself at risk for hopeless lost causes, never seems to learn, and whose only redeeming feature is that he's madly in love with you."

"You have a way with words, *caballero*."

"I try. So, you'll come with me, I'll buy you a black pearl, we'll go swimming in the lagoon and eat papaya as the sun goes down and drink that insanely powerful island rum then make love till morning."

"That amount of booze and I challenge you. But in general – yes."

"You are so cute, I could eat you now."

"Save it, sailor. All good things come to those who wait."

"So they say."

"You'll find out, I promise. I've been using my Ann Summers club card."

Chet Baker had moved on to "These Foolish Things". Loving this woman seemed the least foolish thing David Hidalgo had ever done.

Gracias a Dios.

BLOOD BROTHERS

Prologue

LA MEZQUITA

"So, here we are ladies and gentlemen," the guide gestured round, smiling with the air of someone who had just pulled a very large, impressive rabbit out of a deep top hat. "A UNESCO world heritage site, one of the most visited locations in Europe and the jewel in the crown of Al Andalus: the Great Mosque of Córdoba. La Mezquita."

She had probably delivered that opening speech several thousand times before but still tried to make it sound impressive, and mostly succeeded. However, the dozen or so Americans, Australians, and few Brits gathered round weren't really listening. They knew what they had come to see and were ready to be overwhelmed, even without the hard sell. They slowly spread out like snooker balls given a gentle tap, passing awestruck through a forest of delicate rose-marble pillars, which supported arches of alternating pink and white blocks, more like sugar icing than stone. Above the arches, a fairy woodland canopy of ancient beams completed the Hansel and Gretel effect. iPhones and selfie sticks were out in force but conversation was in whispers. They tiptoed up and down the avenues of pillars, craning to see the exquisite carving of the capitals, glancing into side chapels and wondering about the mysterious, exotic Abd al-Rahman I, founder of the Umayyad dynasty and architectural mastermind.

Eventually, the guide called them together and began her description. In comparison with the visual – even spiritual – impact of the mosque, the facts seemed almost commonplace. Started by Abd al-Rahman I, Emir of the Caliphate of Córdoba in 784, the Mezquita had been variously enlarged by his successors until it was finally lost to the Christian *reconquista* of 1236. Thereafter, the central square was summarily flattened to make way for a cathedral. Carlos V, visiting years later commented, "They have taken something unique in all the world, and destroyed it for something commonplace."

The tour continued through the prayer hall towards the cathedral, the guide commenting on interesting features along the way. Two young Asian-looking men in their late teens or twenties brought up the rear.

"So what do you think?" the taller, skinny one whispered, looking around.

"It's incredible!" the shorter, stocky one replied, looking back into the maze of pillars and arches.

"Of course it's incredible. It's Islamic. That's not what I mean. You remember. What we spoke about. What do you think?"

"I don't know. It's been here so long. It's not doing anyone any harm. Can't we just leave it as it is?"

His companion was dismissive. He gave a snort and shook his head.

"You don't get it, little brother, do you?" he said. "It's perfect. Symbolic. It's an image. The heart of Islam defiled by infidels. They knocked down the one of the wonders of the world to put an imposter in its place. Now it's time to reclaim it. To take back what's rightfully ours. It'll mark the beginning of the new age when everything is put right. Our turn to knock something down. The new empire from the ashes of the old. It's exactly what the Prophet we've been following online told us to look for."

His younger brother kept looking round nervously and accidentally caught the eye of a security guard.

"Keep your voice down for goodness sake," he hissed. "They can hear you in Edinburgh."

"I don't care," the older brother laughed. "Let them. We'll be unstoppable."

Then abruptly an idea occurred to him. "We should pray," he said. "Take your shoes off."

"What?"

"You heard me. Take your shoes off. Down on your knees!"

The guard was now watching them closely. As soon as the trainers came off, he was on his radio mike. Burly uniforms rapidly appeared from all directions.

"*No es permitido*," a swarthy man with the build of a boxer said in a tone that didn't invite negotiation. He grabbed the upper arm of the older boy and heaved him to his feet.

"Not permitted," another repeated.

"Get you're hands off me! You've no right."

The tour group twenty yards ahead looked round at the scuffle, but a couple of teenage tourists were no match for a half dozen ex-cops and amateur weightlifters so it didn't last long. Seconds later, they were out on the street. The taller one tried a kick at the one of the guards and ended up on his backside as a result.

"You'll see! You don't know what's coming!" he shouted at the retreating security team who were already backslapping and joking, enjoying a little action for a change.

"You idiot," his brother muttered. "It's you that doesn't know what's coming. You'll get us all killed."